Julian Hawthorne

French, Italian, Spanish, Latin Mystery Stories

࿇ℒeseklassiker࿇

Julian Hawthorne

French, Italian, Spanish, Latin Mystery Stories

ISBN/EAN: 9783955630812

Auflage: 1

Erscheinungsjahr: 2013

Erscheinungsort: Bremen, Deutschland

Leseklassiker

Contents

HENRI RENÉ ALBERT GUY DE MAUPASSANT

The Necklace   1
The Man with the Pale Eyes   11
An Uncomfortable Bed   16
Ghosts   19
Fear   25
The Confession   31
The Horla, or Modern Ghosts   37

PIERRE MILLE

The Miracle of Zobéide   64

VILLIERS DE L'ISLE ADAM

The Torture by Hope   71

ERCKMANN-CHATRIAN

The Owl's Ear   77
The Invisible Eye   88
The Waters of Death   107

HONORÉ DE BALZAC

Melmoth Reconciled   122
The Conscript   172

Introduction to Zadig the Babylonian   189

FRANÇOIS MARIE AROUET DE VOLTAIRE

Zadig the Babylonian   191
    1. THE BLIND OF ONE EYE   191

2. THE NOSE   194

3. THE DOG AND THE HORSE   196

4. THE ENVIOUS MAN   199

5. THE GENEROUS   203

6. THE MINISTER   206

7. THE DISPUTES AND THE AUDIENCES   207

8. JEALOUSY   209

9. THE WOMAN BEATEN   213

10. THE STONE   215

11. THE FUNERAL PILE   217

12. THE SUPPER   219

13. THE ROBBER   220

14. THE FISHERMAN   224

15. THE BASILISK   226

16. THE COMBATS   233

17. THE HERMIT   237

18. THE ENIGMAS   243

PEDRO DE ALARÇON
The Nail   247

LUIGI CAPUANA
The Deposition   271

LUCIUS APULEIUS
The Adventure of the Three Robbers   280

PLINY, THE YOUNGER
Letter to Sura   289

Footnotes   **292**

"Through a Mist in the Depths of the Looking-Glass."

HENRI RENÉ ALBERT GUY DE MAUPASSANT

The Necklace

She was one of those pretty and charming girls who are sometimes, as if by a mistake of destiny, born in a family of clerks. She had no dowry, no expectations, no means of being known, understood, loved, wedded, by any rich and distinguished man; and she let herself be married to a little clerk at the Ministry of Public Instruction.

She dressed plainly because she could not dress well, but she was as unhappy as though she had really fallen from her proper station; since with women there is neither caste nor rank; and beauty, grace, and charm act instead of family and birth. Natural fineness, instinct for what is elegant, suppleness of wit, are the sole hierarchy, and make from women of the people the equals of the very greatest ladies.

She suffered ceaselessly, feeling herself born for all the delicacies and all the luxuries. She suffered from the poverty of her dwelling, from the wretched look of the walls, from the worn-out chairs, from the ugliness of the curtains. All those things, of which another woman of her rank would never even have been conscious, tortured her and made her angry. The sight of the little Breton peasant who did her humble housework aroused in her regrets which were despairing, and distracted dreams. She thought of the silent antechambers hung with Oriental tapestry, lit by tall bronze candelabra, and of the two great footmen in knee breeches who sleep in the big armchairs, made drowsy by the heavy warmth of the hot-air stove. She thought of the long *salons* fatted up with ancient silk, of the delicate furniture carrying priceless curiosities, and of the coquettish perfumed boudoirs made for talks at five o'clock with intimate friends, with men famous and sought after, whom all women envy and whose attention they all desire.

When she sat down to dinner, before the round table covered with a tablecloth three days old, opposite her husband, who uncovered the soup tureen and declared with an enchanted air,

"Ah, the good *pot-au-feu*! I don't know anything better than that," she thought of dainty dinners, of shining silverware, of tapestry which peopled the walls with ancient personages and with strange birds flying in the midst of a fairy forest; and she thought of delicious dishes served on marvelous plates, and of the whispered gallantries which you listen to with a sphinx-like smile, while you are eating the pink flesh of a trout or the wings of a quail.

She had no dresses, no jewels, nothing. And she loved nothing but that; she felt made for that. She would so have liked to please, to be envied, to be charming, to be sought after.

She had a friend, a former schoolmate at the convent, who was rich, and whom she did not like to go and see any more, because she suffered so much when she came back.

But, one evening, her husband returned home with a triumphant air, and holding a large envelope in his hand.

"There," said he, "here is something for you."

She tore the paper sharply, and drew out a printed card which bore these words:

"The Minister of Public Instruction and Mme. Georges Ramponneau request the honor of M. and Mme. Loisel's company at the palace of the Ministry on Monday evening, January 18th."

Instead of being delighted, as her husband hoped, she threw the invitation on the table with disdain, murmuring:

"What do you want me to do with that?"

"But, my dear, I thought you would be glad. You never go out, and this is such a fine opportunity. I had awful trouble to get it. Everyone wants to go; it is very select, and they are not giving many invitations to clerks. The whole official world will be there."

She looked at him with an irritated eye, and she said, impatiently:

"And what do you want me to put on my back?"

2

He had not thought of that; he stammered:

"Why, the dress you go to the theater in. It looks very well, to me."

He stopped, distracted, seeing that his wife was crying. Two great tears descended slowly from the corners of her eyes toward the corners of her mouth. He stuttered:

"What's the matter? What's the matter?"

But, by a violent effort, she had conquered her grief, and she replied, with a calm voice, while she wiped her wet cheeks:

"Nothing. Only I have no dress, and therefore I can't go to this ball. Give your card to some colleague whose wife is better equipped than I."

He was in despair. He resumed:

"Come, let us see, Mathilde. How much would it cost, a suitable dress, which you could use on other occasions, something very simple?"

She reflected several seconds, making her calculations and wondering also what sum she could ask without drawing on herself an immediate refusal and a frightened exclamation from the economical clerk.

Finally, she replied, hesitatingly:

"I don't know exactly, but I think I could manage it with four hundred francs."

He had grown a little pale, because he was laying aside just that amount to buy a gun and treat himself to a little shooting next summer on the plain of Nanterre, with several friends who went to shoot larks down there of a Sunday.

But he said:

"All right. I will give you four hundred francs. And try to have a pretty dress."

The day of the ball drew near, and Mme. Loisel seemed sad, uneasy, anxious. Her dress was ready, however. Her husband said to her one evening:

"What is the matter? Come, you've been so queer these last three days."

And she answered:

"It annoys me not to have a single jewel, not a single stone, nothing to put on. I shall look like distress. I should almost rather not go at all."

He resumed:

"You might wear natural flowers. It's very stylish at this time of the year. For ten francs you can get two or three magnificent roses."

She was not convinced.

"No; there's nothing more humiliating than to look poor among other women who are rich."

But her husband cried:

"How stupid you are! Go look up your friend Mme. Forestier, and ask her to lend you some jewels. You're quite thick enough with her to do that."

She uttered a cry of joy:

"It's true. I never thought of it."

The next day she went to her friend and told of her distress.

Mme. Forestier went to a wardrobe with a glass door, took out a large jewel box, brought it back, opened it, and said to Mme. Loisel:

"Choose, my dear."

She saw first of all some bracelets, then a pearl necklace, then a Venetian cross, gold and precious stones of admirable workmanship. She tried on the ornaments before the glass, hesitated, could not make up her mind to part with them, to give them back. She kept asking:

"Haven't you any more?"

"Why, yes. Look. I don't know what you like."

All of a sudden she discovered, in a black satin box, a superb necklace of diamonds, and her heart began to beat with an immoderate desire. Her hands trembled as she took it. She fastened it around her throat, outside her high-necked dress, and remained lost in ecstasy at the sight of herself.

Then she asked, hesitating, filled with anguish:

"Can you lend me that, only that?"

"Why, yes, certainly."

She sprang upon the neck of her friend, kissed her passionately, then fled with her treasure.

*****

The day of the ball arrived. Mme. Loisel made a great success. She was prettier than them all, elegant, gracious, smiling, and crazy with joy. All the men looked at her, asked her name, endeavored to be introduced. All the attachés of the Cabinet wanted to waltz with her. She was remarked by the minister himself.

She danced with intoxication, with passion, made drunk by pleasure, forgetting all, in the triumph of her beauty, in the glory of her success, in a sort of cloud of happiness composed of all this homage, of all this admiration, of all these awakened desires, and of that sense of complete victory which is so sweet to woman's heart.

She went away about four o'clock in the morning. Her husband had been sleeping since midnight, in a little deserted anteroom, with three other gentlemen whose wives were having a very good time.

He threw over her shoulders the wraps which he had brought, modest wraps of common life, whose poverty contrasted with the elegance of the ball dress. She felt this and wanted to escape so as not to be remarked by the other women, who were enveloping themselves in costly furs.

Loisel held her back.

"Wait a bit. You will catch cold outside. I will go and call a cab."

But she did not listen to him, and rapidly descended the stairs. When they were in the street they did not find a carriage; and they began to look for one, shouting after the cabmen whom they saw passing by at a distance.

They went down toward the Seine, in despair, shivering with cold. At last they found on the quay one of those ancient noctambulent coupés which, exactly as if they were ashamed to show their misery during the day, are never seen round Paris until after nightfall.

It took them to their door in the Rue des Martyrs, and once more, sadly, they climbed up homeward. All was ended for her. And as to him, he reflected that he must be at the Ministry at ten o'clock.

She removed the wraps, which covered her shoulders, before the glass, so as once more to see herself in all her glory. But suddenly she uttered a cry. She had no longer the necklace around her neck!

Her husband, already half undressed, demanded:

"What is the matter with you?"

She turned madly toward him:

"I have — I have — I've lost Mme. Forestier's necklace."

He stood up, distracted.

"What! — how? — Impossible!"

And they looked in the folds of her dress, in the folds of her cloak, in her pockets, everywhere. They did not find it.

He asked:

"You're sure you had it on when you left the ball?"

"Yes, I felt it in the vestibule of the palace."

"But if you had lost it in the street we should have heard it fall. It must be in the cab."

"Yes. Probably. Did you take his number?"

"No. And you, didn't you notice it?"

"No."

They looked, thunderstruck, at one another. At last Loisel put on his clothes.

"I shall go back on foot," said he, "over the whole route which we have taken, to see if I can't find it."

And he went out. She sat waiting on a chair in her ball dress, without strength to go to bed, overwhelmed, without fire, without a thought.

Her husband came back about seven o'clock. He had found nothing.

He went to Police Headquarters, to the newspaper offices, to offer a reward; he went to the cab companies — everywhere, in fact, whither he was urged by the least suspicion of hope.

She waited all day, in the same condition of mad fear before this terrible calamity.

Loisel returned at night with a hollow, pale face; he had discovered nothing.

"You must write to your friend," said he, "that you have broken the clasp of her necklace and that you are having it mended. That will give us time to turn round."

She wrote at his dictation.

At the end of a week they had lost all hope.

And Loisel, who had aged five years, declared:

"We must consider how to replace that ornament."

The next day they took the box which had contained it, and they went to the jeweler whose name was found within. He consulted his books.

"It was not I, madame, who sold that necklace; I must simply have furnished the case."

Then they went from jeweler to jeweler, searching for a necklace like the other, consulting their memories, sick both of them with chagrin and with anguish.

They found, in a shop at the Palais Royal, a string of diamonds which seemed to them exactly like the one they looked for. It was worth forty thousand francs. They could have it for thirty-six.

So they begged the jeweler not to sell it for three days yet. And they made a bargain that he should buy it back for thirty-four thousand francs in case they found the other one before the end of February.

Loisel possessed eighteen thousand francs which his father had left him. He would borrow the rest.

He did borrow, asking a thousand francs of one, five hundred of another, five louis here, three louis there. He gave notes, took up ruinous obligations, dealt with usurers, and all the race of lenders. He compromised all the rest of his life, risked his signature without even knowing if he could meet it; and, frightened by the pains yet to come, by the black misery which was about to fall upon him, by the prospect of all the physical privations and of all the moral tortures which he was to suffer, he went to get the new necklace, putting down upon the merchant's counter thirty-six thousand francs.

When Mme. Loisel took back the necklace, Mme. Forestier said to her, with a chilly manner:

"You should have returned it sooner, I might have needed it."

She did not open the case, as her friend had so much feared. If she had detected the substitution, what would she have thought, what would she have said? Would she not have taken Mme. Loisel for a thief?

Mme. Loisel now knew the horrible existence of the needy. She took her part, moreover, all on a sudden, with heroism. That dreadful debt must be paid. She would pay it. They dismissed their servant; they changed their lodgings; they rented a garret under the roof.

She came to know what heavy housework meant and the odious cares of the kitchen. She washed the dishes, using her rosy nails on the greasy pots and pans. She washed the dirty linen, the shirts, and the dish-cloths, which she dried upon a line; she carried the slops down to the street every morning, and carried up the water, stopping for breath at every landing. And, dressed like a woman of the people, she went to the fruiterer, the grocer, the butcher, her basket on her arm, bargaining, insulted, defending her miserable money sou by sou.

Each month they had to meet some notes, renew others, obtain more time.

Her husband worked in the evening making a fair copy of some tradesman's accounts, and late at night he often copied manuscript for five sous a page.

And this life lasted ten years.

At the end of ten years they had paid everything, everything, with the rates of usury, and the accumulations of the compound interest.

Mme. Loisel looked old now. She had become the woman of impoverished households — strong and hard and rough. With frowsy hair, skirts askew, and red hands, she talked loud while washing the floor with great swishes of water. But sometimes, when her husband was at the office, she sat down near the window, and she thought of that gay evening of long ago, of that ball where she had been so beautiful and so feted.

What would have happened if she had not lost that necklace? Who knows? who knows? How life is strange and changeful! How little a thing is needed for us to be lost or to be saved!

But, one Sunday, having gone to take a walk in the Champs Élysées to refresh herself from the labors of the week, she suddenly perceived a woman who was leading a child. It was Mme. Forestier, still young, still beautiful, still charming.

Mme. Loisel felt moved. Was she going to speak to her? Yes, certainly. And now that she had paid, she was going to tell her all about it. Why not?

She went up.

"Good day, Jeanne."

The other, astonished to be familiarly addressed by this plain good-wife, did not recognize her at all, and stammered:

"But — madame! — I do not know — You must have mistaken."

"No. I am Mathilde Loisel."

Her friend uttered a cry.

"Oh, my poor Mathilde! How you are changed!"

"Yes, I have had days hard enough, since I have seen you, days wretched enough — and that because of you!"

"Of me! How so?"

"Do you remember that diamond necklace which you lent me to wear at the ministerial ball?"

"Yes. Well?"

"Well, I lost it."

"What do you mean? You brought it back."

"I brought you back another just like it. And for this we have been ten years paying. You can understand that it was not easy for us, us who had nothing. At last it is ended, and I am very glad."

Mme. Forestier had stopped.

"You say that you bought a necklace of diamonds to replace mine?"

"Yes. You never noticed it, then! They were very like."

And she smiled with a joy which was proud and naïve at once.

Mme. Forestier, strongly moved, took her two hands.

"Oh, my poor Mathilde! Why, my necklace was paste. It was worth at most five hundred francs!"

The Man with the Pale Eyes

Monsieur Pierre Agénor De Vargnes, the Examining Magistrate, was the exact opposite of a practical joker. He was dignity, staidness, correctness personified. As a sedate man, he was quite incapable of being guilty, even in his dreams, of anything resembling a practical joke, however remotely. I know nobody to whom he could be compared, unless it be the present president of the French Republic. I think it is useless to carry the analogy any further, and having said thus much, it will be easily understood that a cold shiver passed through me when Monsieur Pierre Agénor de Vargnes did me the honor of sending a lady to await on me.

At about eight o'clock, one morning last winter, as he was leaving the house to go to the *Palais de Justice*, his footman handed him a card, on which was printed:

DOCTOR JAMES FERDINAND,
Member of the Academy of Medicine,
Port-au-Prince,
Chevalier of the Legion of Honor.

At the bottom of the card there was written in pencil:

From Lady Frogère.

Monsieur de Vargnes knew the lady very well, who was a very agreeable Creole from Hayti, and whom he had met in many drawing-rooms, and, on the other hand, though the doctor's name did not awaken any recollections in him, his quality and titles alone required that he should grant him an interview, however short it might be. Therefore, although he was in a hurry to get out, Monsieur de Vargnes told the footman to show in his early visitor, but to tell him beforehand that his master was much pressed for time, as he had to go to the Law Courts.

When the doctor came in, in spite of his usual imperturbability, he could not restrain a movement of surprise, for the doctor presented that strange anomaly of being a negro of the purest, blackest type, with the eyes of a white man, of a man from the North, pale, cold, clear, blue eyes, and his surprise increased, when, after a few words of excuse for his untimely visit, he added, with an enigmatical smile:

"My eyes surprise you, do they not? I was sure that they would, and, to tell you the truth, I came here in order that you might look at them well, and never forget them."

His smile, and his words, even more than his smile, seemed to be those of a madman. He spoke very softly, with that childish, lisping voice, which is peculiar to negroes, and his mysterious, almost menacing words, consequently, sounded all the more as if they were uttered at random by a man bereft of his reason. But his looks, the looks of those pale, cold, clear, blue eyes, were certainly not those of a madman. They clearly expressed menace, yes, menace, as well as irony, and, above all, implacable ferocity, and their glance was like a flash of lightning, which one could never forget.

"I have seen," Monsieur de Vargnes used to say, when speaking about it, "the looks of many murderers, but in none of them have I ever observed such a depth of crime, and of impudent security in crime."

And this impression was so strong, that Monsieur de Vargnes thought that he was the sport of some hallucination, especially as when he spoke about his eyes, the doctor continued with a smile, and in his most childish accents: "Of course, Monsieur, you cannot understand what I am saying to you, and I must beg your pardon for it. To-morrow you will receive a letter which will explain it all to you, but, first of all, it was necessary that I should let you have a good, a careful look at my eyes, my eyes, which are myself, my only and true self, as you will see."

With these words, and with a polite bow, the doctor went out, leaving Monsieur de Vargnes extremely surprised, and a prey to this doubt, as he said to himself:

"Is he merely a madman? The fierce expression, and the criminal depths of his looks are perhaps caused merely by the extraordinary contrast between his fierce looks and his pale eyes."

And absorbed in these thoughts, Monsieur de Vargnes unfortunately allowed several minutes to elapse, and then he thought to himself suddenly:

"No, I am not the sport of any hallucination, and this is no case of an optical phenomenon. This man is evidently some terrible criminal, and I have altogether failed in my duty in not arresting him myself at once, illegally, even at the risk of my life."

The judge ran downstairs in pursuit of the doctor, but it was too late; he had disappeared. In the afternoon, he called on Madame Frogère, to ask her whether she could tell him anything about the matter. She, however, did not know the negro doctor in the least, and was even able to assure him that he was a fictitious personage, for, as she was well acquainted with the upper classes in Hayti, she knew that the Academy of Medicine at Port-au-Prince had no doctor of that name among its members. As Monsieur de Vargnes persisted, and gave descriptions of the doctor, especially mentioning his extraordinary eyes, Madame Frogère began to laugh, and said:

"You have certainly had to do with a hoaxer, my dear monsieur. The eyes which you have described are certainly those of a white man, and the individual must have been painted."

On thinking it over, Monsieur de Vargnes remembered that the doctor had nothing of the negro about him, but his black skin, his woolly hair and beard, and his way of speaking, which was easily imitated, but nothing of the negro, not even the characteristic, undulating walk. Perhaps, after all, he was only a practical joker, and during the whole day, Monsieur de Vargnes took refuge in that view, which rather wounded his dignity as a man of consequence, but which appeased his scruples as a magistrate.

The next day, he received the promised letter, which was written, as well as addressed, in letters cut out of the newspapers. It was as follows:

"MONSIEUR: Doctor James Ferdinand does not exist, but the man whose eyes you saw does, and you will certainly recognize his eyes. This man has committed two crimes, for which he does not feel any remorse, but, as he is a psychologist, he is afraid of some day yielding to the irresistible temptation of confessing his crimes. You know better than anyone (and that is your most powerful aid), with what imperious force criminals, especially intellectual ones, feel this temptation. That great Poet, Edgar Poe, has written masterpieces on this subject, which express the truth exactly, but he has omitted to mention the last phenomenon, which I will tell you. Yes, I, a criminal, feel a terrible wish for somebody to know of my crimes, and when this requirement is satisfied, my secret has been revealed to a confidant, I shall be tranquil for the future, and be freed from this demon of perversity, which only tempts us once. Well! Now that is accomplished. You shall have my secret; from the day that you recognize me by my eyes, you will try and find out what I am guilty of, and how I was guilty, and you will discover it, being a master of your profession, which, by the by, has procured you the honor of having been chosen by me to bear the weight of this secret, which now is shared by us, and by us two alone. I say, advisedly, *by us two alone*. You could not, as a matter of fact, prove the reality of this secret to anyone, unless I were to confess it, and I defy you to

14

obtain my public confession, as I have confessed it to you, *and without danger to myself.*"

Three months later, Monsieur de Vargnes met Monsieur X — — at an evening party, and at first sight, and without the slightest hesitation, he recognized in him those very pale, very cold, and very clear blue eyes, eyes which it was impossible to forget.

The man himself remained perfectly impassive, so that Monsieur de Vargnes was forced to say to himself:

"Probably I am the sport of an hallucination at this moment, or else there are two pairs of eyes that are perfectly similar in the world. And what eyes! Can it be possible?"

The magistrate instituted inquiries into his life, and he discovered this, which removed all his doubts.

Five years previously, Monsieur X — — had been a very poor, but very brilliant medical student, who, although he never took his doctor's degree, had already made himself remarkable by his microbiological researches.

A young and very rich widow had fallen in love with him and married him. She had one child by her first marriage, and in the space of six months, first the child and then the mother died of typhoid fever, and thus Monsieur X — — had inherited a large fortune, in due form, and without any possible dispute. Everybody said that he had attended to the two patients with the utmost devotion. Now, were these two deaths the two crimes mentioned in his letter?

But then, Monsieur X — — must have poisoned his two victims with the microbes of typhoid fever, which he had skillfully cultivated in them, so as to make the disease incurable, even by the most devoted care and attention. Why not?

"Do you believe it?" I asked Monsieur de Vargnes.

"Absolutely," he replied. "And the most terrible thing about it is, that the villain is right when he defies me to force him to confess his crime publicly, for I see no means of obtaining a confession, none whatever. For a moment, I thought of magnetism, but who could magnetize that man with those pale, cold, bright eyes? With such eyes, he would force the magnetizer to denounce himself as the culprit."

And then he said, with a deep sigh:

"Ah! Formerly there was something good about justice!"

And when he saw my inquiring looks, he added in a firm and perfectly convinced voice:

"Formerly, justice had torture at its command."

"Upon my word," I replied, with all an author's unconscious and simple egotism, "it is quite certain that without the torture, this strange tale will have no conclusion, and that is very unfortunate, as far as regards the story I intended to make out of it."

An Uncomfortable Bed

One autumn I went to stay for the hunting season with some friends in a chateau in Picardy.

My friends were fond of practical joking, as all my friends are. I do not care to know any other sort of people.

When I arrived, they gave me a princely reception, which at once aroused distrust in my breast. We had some capital shooting. They embraced me, they cajoled me, as if they expected to have great fun at my expense.

I said to myself:

"Look out, old ferret! They have something in preparation for you."

During the dinner, the mirth was excessive, far too great, in fact. I thought: "Here are people who take a double share of amusement, and apparently without reason. They must be looking out in their own minds for some good bit of fun. Assuredly I am to be the victim of the joke. Attention!"

During the entire evening, everyone laughed in an exaggerated fashion. I smelled a practical joke in the air, as a dog smells game. But what was it? I was watchful, restless. I did not let a word or a meaning or a gesture escape me. Everyone seemed to me an object of suspicion, and I even looked distrustfully at the faces of the servants.

The hour rang for going to bed, and the whole household came to escort me to my room. Why? They called to me: "Good night." I entered the apartment, shut the door, and remained standing, without moving a single step, holding the wax candle in my hand.

I heard laughter and whispering in the corridor. Without doubt they were spying on me. I cast a glance around the walls, the furniture, the ceiling, the hangings, the floor. I saw nothing to justify suspicion. I heard persons moving about outside my door. I had no doubt they were looking through the keyhole.

An idea came into my head: "My candle may suddenly go out, and leave me in darkness."

Then I went across to the mantelpiece, and lighted all the wax candles that were on it. After that, I cast another glance around me without discovering anything. I advanced with short steps, carefully examining the apartment. Nothing. I inspected every article one after the other. Still nothing. I went over to the window. The shutters, large wooden shutters, were open. I shut them with great care, and then drew the curtains, enormous velvet curtains, and I placed a chair in front of them, so as to have nothing to fear from without.

Then I cautiously sat down. The armchair was solid. I did not venture to get into the bed. However, time was flying; and I ended by coming to the conclusion that I was ridiculous. If they were spying on me, as I supposed, they must, while waiting for the success of the joke they had been preparing for me, have been laughing enormously at my terror. So I made up my mind to go to bed. But the bed was particularly suspicious-looking. I pulled at the curtains. They seemed to be secure. All the same, there was danger. I was going perhaps to receive a cold shower-bath from overhead, or perhaps, the moment I stretched myself out, to find myself sinking under the floor with my mattress. I searched in my memory for all the practical jokes of which I ever had experience. And I did not want to be caught. Ah! certainly not! certainly not! Then I suddenly bethought myself of a precaution which I consider one of extreme efficacy: I caught hold of the side of the mattress gingerly, and very slowly drew it toward me. It came away, followed by the sheet and the rest of the bedclothes. I dragged all these objects into the very middle of the room, facing the entrance door. I made my bed over again as best I could at some distance from the suspected bedstead and the corner which had filled me with such anxiety. Then, I extinguished all the candles, and, groping my way, I slipped under the bedclothes.

For at least another hour, I remained awake, starting at the slightest sound. Everything seemed quiet in the chateau. I fell asleep.

I must have been in a deep sleep for a long time, but all of a sudden, I was awakened with a start by the fall of a heavy body tumbling right on top of my own body, and, at the same time, I received on my face, on my neck, and on my chest a burning liquid which made me utter a howl of pain. And a dreadful noise, as if a sideboard laden with plates and dishes had fallen down, penetrated my ears.

I felt myself suffocating under the weight that was crushing me and preventing me from moving. I stretched out my hand to find out what was the nature of this object. I felt a face, a nose, and whiskers. Then with all my strength I launched out a blow over this face. But I immediately received a hail of cuffings which made me jump straight out of the soaked sheets, and rush in my nightshirt into the corridor, the door of which I found open.

O stupor! it was broad daylight. The noise brought my friends hurrying into the apartment, and we found, sprawling over my improvised bed, the dismayed valet, who, while bringing me my morning cup of tea, had tripped over this obstacle in the middle of the floor, and fallen on his stomach, spilling, in spite of himself, my breakfast over my face.

The precautions I had taken in closing the shutters and going to sleep in the middle of the room had only brought about the interlude I had been striving to avoid.

Ah! how they all laughed that day!

Ghosts

Just at the time when the *Concordat* was in its most flourishing condition, a young man belonging to a wealthy and highly respected middle-class family went to the office of the head of the police at P — — , and begged for his help and advice, which was immediately promised him.

"My father threatens to disinherit me," the young man then began, "although I have never offended against the laws of the State, of morality or of his paternal authority, merely because I do not share his blind reverence for the Catholic Church and her Ministers. On that account he looks upon me, not merely as Latitudinarian, but as a perfect Atheist, and a faithful old manservant of ours, who is much attached to me, and who accidentally saw my father's will, told me in confidence that he had left all his property to the Jesuits. I think this is highly suspicious, and I fear that the priests have been maligning me to my father. Until less than a year ago, we used to live very quietly and happily together, but ever since he has had so much to do with the clergy, our domestic peace and happiness are at an end."

"What you have told me," the official replied, "is as likely as it is regrettable, but I fail to see how I can interfere in the matter. Your father is in full possession of all his mental faculties, and can dispose of all his property exactly as he pleases. I also think that your protest is premature; you must wait until his will can legally take effect, and then you can invoke the aid of justice; I am sorry to say that I can do nothing for you."

"I think you will be able to," the young man replied; "for I believe that a very clever piece of deceit is being carried on here."

"How? Please explain yourself more clearly."

"When I remonstrated with him, yesterday evening, he referred to my dead mother, and at last assured me, in a voice of the deepest conviction, that she had frequently appeared to him, and had threatened him with all the torments of the damned if he did not disinherit his son, who had fallen away from God, and leave all his property to the Church. Now I do not believe in ghosts."

"Neither do I," the police director replied; "but I cannot well do anything on this dangerous ground if I had nothing but superstitions to go upon. You know how the Church rules all our affairs since the *Concordat* with Rome, and if I investigate this matter, and obtain no results, I am risking my post. It would be very different if you could adduce any proofs for your suspicions. I do not deny that I should like to see the clerical party, which will, I fear, be the ruin of Austria, receive a staggering blow; try, therefore, to get to the bottom of this business, and then we will talk it over again."

About a month passed without the young Latitudinarian being heard of; but then he suddenly came one evening, evidently in a great state of excitement, and told him that he was in a position to expose the priestly deceit which he had mentioned, if the authorities would assist him. The police director asked for further information.

"I have obtained a number of important clews," the young man said. "In the first place, my father confessed to me that my mother did not appear to him in our house, but in the churchyard where she is buried. My mother was consumptive for many years, and a few weeks before her death she went to the village of S — — , where she died and was buried. In addition to this, I found out from our footman that my father has already left the house twice, late at night, in company of X — — , the Jesuit priest, and that on both occasions he did not return till morning. Each time he was remarkably uneasy and low-spirited after his return, and had three masses said for my dead mother. He also told me just now that he has to leave home this evening on business, but immediately he told me that, our footman saw the Jesuit go out of the house. We may, therefore, assume that he intends this evening to consult the spirit of my dead mother again, and this would be an excellent opportunity for getting on the track of the matter, if you do not object to opposing the most powerful force in the Empire, for the sake of such an insignificant individual as myself."

"Every citizen has an equal right to the protection of the State," the police director replied; "and I think that I have shown often enough that I am not wanting in courage to perform my duty, no matter how serious the consequences may be; but only very young men act without any prospects of success, as they are carried away by their feelings. When you came to me the first time, I was obliged to refuse your request for assistance, but to-day your shares have risen in value. It is now eight o'clock, and I shall expect you in two hours' time here in my office. At present, all you have to do is to hold your tongue; everything else is my affair."

As soon as it was dark, four men got into a closed carriage in the yard of the police office, and were driven in the direction of the village of S — — ; their carriage, however, did not enter the village, but stopped at the edge of a small wood in the immediate neighborhood. Here they all four alighted; they were the police director, accompanied by the young Latitudinarian, a police sergeant and an ordinary policeman, who was, however, dressed in plain clothes.

"The first thing for us to do is to examine the locality carefully," the police director said: "it is eleven o'clock and the exercisers of ghosts will not arrive before midnight, so we have time to look round us, and to take our measure."

The four men went to the churchyard, which lay at the end of the village, near the little wood. Everything was as still as death, and not a soul was to be seen. The sexton was evidently sitting in the public house, for they found the door of his cottage locked, as well as the door of the little chapel that stood in the middle of the churchyard.

"Where is your mother's grave?" the police director asked; but as there were only a few stars visible, it was not easy to find it, but at last they managed it, and the police director looked about in the neighborhood of it.

"The position is not a very favorable one for us," he said at last; "there is nothing here, not even a shrub, behind which we could hide."

But just then, the policeman said that he had tried to get into the sexton's hut through the door or the window, and that at last he had succeeded in doing so by breaking open a square in a window, which had been mended with paper, and that he had opened it and obtained posesssion of the key which he brought to the police director.

His plans were very quickly settled. He had the chapel opened and went in with the young Latitudinarian; then he told the police sergeant to lock the door behind him and to put the key back where he had found it, and to shut the window of the sexton's cottage carefully. Lastly, he made arrangements as to what they were to do in case anything unforeseen should occur, whereupon the sergeant and the constable left the churchyard, and lay down in a ditch at some distance from the gate, but opposite to it.

Almost as soon as the clock struck half-past eleven, they heard steps near the chapel, whereupon the police director and the young Latitudinarian went to the window, in order to watch the beginning of the exorcism, and as the chapel was in total darkness, they thought that they should be able to see, without being seen; but matters turned out differently from what they expected.

Suddenly, the key turned in the lock, and they barely had time to conceal themselves behind the altar before two men came in, one of whom was carrying a dark lantern. One was the young man's father, an elderly man of the middle class, who seemed very unhappy and depressed, the other the Jesuit father K — — , a tall, thin, big-boned man, with a thin, bilious face, in which two large gray eyes shone restlessly under their bushy black eyebrows. He lit the tapers, which were standing on the altar, and then began to say a *Requiem Mass;* while the old man knelt on the altar steps and served him.

When it was over, the Jesuit took the book of the Gospels and the holy-water sprinkler, and went slowly out of the chapel, while the old man followed him, with a holy-water basin in one hand and a taper in the other. Then the police director left his hiding place, and stooping down, so as not to be seen, he crept to the chapel window, where he cowered down carefully, and the young man followed his example. They were now looking straight on his mother's grave.

The Jesuit, followed by the superstitious old man, walked three times round the grave, then he remained standing before it, and by the light of the taper he read a few passages from the Gospel; then he dipped the holy-water sprinkler three times into the holy-water basin, and sprinkled the grave three times; then both returned to the chapel, knelt down outside it with their faces toward the grave, and began to pray aloud, until at last the Jesuit sprang up, in a species of wild ecstasy, and cried out three times in a shrill voice:

"Exsurge! Exsurge! Exsurge!" [1]

Scarcely had the last word of the exorcism died away when thick, blue smoke rose out of the grave, which rapidly grew into a cloud, and began to assume the outlines of a human body, until at last a tall, white figure stood behind the grave, and beckoned with its hand.

"Who art thou?" the Jesuit asked solemnly, while the old man began to cry.

"When I was alive, I was called Anna Maria B — — ," the ghost replied in a hollow voice.

"Will you answer all my questions?" the priest continued.

"As far as I can."

"Have you not yet been delivered from purgatory by our prayers, and all the Masses for your soul, which we have said for you?"

23

"Not yet, but soon, soon I shall be."

"When?"

"As soon as that blasphemer, my son, has been punished."

"Has that not already happened? Has not your husband disinherited his lost son, and made the Church his heir, in his place?"

"That is not enough."

"What must he do besides?"

"He must deposit his will with the Judicial Authorities as his last will and testament, and drive the reprobate out of his house."

"Consider well what you are saying; must this really be?"

"It must, or otherwise I shall have to languish in purgatory much longer," the sepulchral voice replied with a deep sigh; but the next moment it yelled out in terror: —

"Oh! Good Lord!" and the ghost began to run away as fast as it could. A shrill whistle was heard, and then another, and the police director laid his hand on the shoulder of the exorciser accompanied with the remark: —

"You are in custody."

Meanwhile, the police sergeant and the policeman, who had come into the churchyard, had caught the ghost, and dragged it forward. It was the sexton, who had put on a flowing, white dress, and who wore a wax mask, which bore striking resemblance to his mother, as the son declared.

When the case was heard, it was proved that the mask had been very skillfully made from a portrait of the deceased woman. The Government gave orders that the matter should be investigated as secretly as possible, and left the punishment of Father K — — to the spiritual authorities, which was a matter of course, at a time when priests were outside the jurisdiction of the Civil Authorities; and it is needless to say that he was very comfortable during his imprisonment, in a monastery in a part of the country which abounded with game and trout.

The only valuable result of the amusing ghost story was that it brought about a reconciliation between father and son, and the former, as a matter of fact, felt such deep respect for priests and their ghosts in consequence of the apparition that a short time after his wife had left purgatory for the last time in order to talk with him — he turned *Protestant*.

Fear

We went up on deck after dinner. Before us the Mediterranean lay without a ripple and shimmering in the moonlight. The great ship glided on, casting upward to the star-studded sky a long serpent of black smoke. Behind us the dazzling white water, stirred by the rapid progress of the heavy bark and beaten by the propeller, foamed, seemed to writhe, gave off so much brilliancy that one could have called it boiling moonlight.

There were six or eight of us silent with admiration and gazing toward far-away Africa whither we were going. The commandant, who was smoking a cigar with us, brusquely resumed the conversation begun at dinner.

"Yes, I was afraid then. My ship remained for six hours on that rock, beaten by the wind and with a great hole in the side. Luckily we were picked up toward evening by an English coaler which sighted us."

Then a tall man of sunburned face and grave demeanor, one of those men who have evidently traveled unknown and far-away lands, whose calm eye seems to preserve in its depths something of the foreign scenes it has observed, a man that you are sure is impregnated with courage, spoke for the first time.

"You say, commandant, that you were afraid. I beg to disagree with you. You are in error as to the meaning of the word and the nature of the sensation that you experienced. An energetic man is never afraid in the presence of urgent danger. He is excited, aroused, full of anxiety, but fear is something quite different."

The commandant laughed and answered: "Bah! I assure you that I was afraid."

Then the man of the tanned countenance addressed us deliberately as follows:

"Permit me to explain. Fear — and the boldest men may feel fear — is something horrible, an atrocious sensation, a sort of decomposition of the soul, a terrible spasm of brain and heart, the very memory of which brings a shudder of anguish, but when one is brave he feels it neither under fire nor in the presence of sure death nor in the face of any well-known danger. It springs up under certain abnormal conditions, under certain mysterious influences in the presence of vague peril. Real fear is a sort of reminiscence of fantastic terror of the past. A man who believes in ghosts and imagines he sees a specter in the darkness must feel fear in all its horror.

"As for me I was overwhelmed with fear in broad daylight about ten years ago and again one December night last winter.

"Nevertheless, I have gone through many dangers, many adventures which seemed to promise death. I have often been in battle. I have been left for dead by thieves. In America I was condemned as an insurgent to be hanged, and off the coast of China have been thrown into the sea from the deck of a ship. Each time I thought I was lost I at once decided upon my course of action without regret or weakness.

"That is not fear.

"I have felt it in Africa, and yet it is a child of the north. The sunlight banishes it like the mist. Consider this fact, gentlemen. Among the Orientals life has no value; resignation is natural. The nights are clear and empty of the somber spirit of unrest which haunts the brain in cooler lands. In the Orient panic is known, but not fear.

"Well, then! Here is the incident that befell me in Africa.

"I was crossing the great sands to the south of Onargla. It is one of the most curious districts in the world. You have seen the solid continuous sand of the endless ocean strands. Well, imagine the ocean itself turned to sand in the midst of a storm. Imagine a silent tempest with motionless billows of yellow dust. They are high as mountains, these uneven, varied surges, rising exactly like unchained billows, but still larger, and stratified like watered silk. On this wild, silent, and motionless sea, the consuming rays of the tropical sun are poured pitilessly and directly. You have to climb these streaks of red-hot ash, descend again on the other side, climb again, climb, climb without halt, without repose, without shade. The horses cough, sink to their knees and slide down the sides of these remarkable hills.

"We were a couple of friends followed by eight spahis and four camels with their drivers. We were no longer talking, overcome by heat, fatigue, and a thirst such as had produced this burning desert. Suddenly one of our men uttered a cry. We all halted, surprised by an unsolved phenomenon known only to travelers in these trackless wastes.

"Somewhere, near us, in an indeterminable direction, a drum was rolling, the mysterious drum of the sands. It was beating distinctly, now with greater resonance and again feebler, ceasing, then resuming its uncanny roll.

"The Arabs, terrified, stared at one another, and one said in his language: 'Death is upon us.' As he spoke, my companion, my friend, almost a brother, dropped from his horse, falling face downward on the sand, overcome by a sunstroke.

"And for two hours, while I tried in vain to save him, this weird drum filled my ears with its monotonous, intermittent and incomprehensible tone, and I felt lay hold of my bones fear, real fear, hideous fear, in the presence of this beloved corpse, in this hole scorched by the sun, surrounded by four mountains of sand, and two hundred leagues from any French settlement, while echo assailed our ears with this furious drum beat.

"On that day I realized what fear was, but since then I have had another, and still more vivid experience — "

The commandant interrupted the speaker:

"I beg your pardon, but what was the drum?"

The traveler replied:

"I cannot say. No one knows. Our officers are often surprised by this singular noise and attribute it generally to the echo produced by a hail of grains of sand blown by the wind against the dry and brittle leaves of weeds, for it has always been noticed that the phenomenon occurs in proximity to little plants burned by the sun and hard as parchment. This sound seems to have been magnified, multiplied, and swelled beyond measure in its progress through the valleys of sand, and the drum therefore might be considered a sort of sound mirage. Nothing more. But I did not know that until later.

"I shall proceed to my second instance.

"It was last winter, in a forest of the Northeast of France. The sky was so overcast that night came two hours earlier than usual. My guide was a peasant who walked beside me along the narrow road, under the vault of fir trees, through which the wind in its fury howled. Between the tree tops, I saw the fleeting clouds, which seemed to hasten as if to escape some object of terror. Sometimes in a fierce gust of wind the whole forest bowed in the same direction with a groan of pain, and a chill laid hold of me, despite my rapid pace and heavy clothing.

"We were to sup and sleep at an old gamekeeper's house not much farther on. I had come out for hunting.

"My guide sometimes raised his eyes and murmured: 'Ugly weather!' Then he told me about the people among whom we were to spend the night. The father had killed a poacher, two years before, and since then had been gloomy and behaved as though haunted by a memory. His two sons were married and lived with him.

"The darkness was profound. I could see nothing before me nor around me and the mass of overhanging interlacing trees rubbed together, filling the night with an incessant whispering. Finally I saw a light and soon my companion was knocking upon a door. Sharp women's voices answered us, then a man's voice, a choking voice, asked, 'Who goes there?' My guide gave his name. We entered and beheld a memorable picture.

"An old man with white hair, wild eyes, and a loaded gun in his hands, stood waiting for us in the middle of the kitchen, while two stalwart youths, armed with axes, guarded the door. In the somber corners I distinguished two women kneeling with faces to the wall.

"Matters were explained, and the old man stood his gun against the wall, at the same time ordering that a room be prepared for me. Then, as the women did not stir: 'Look you, monsieur,' said he, 'two years ago this night I killed a man, and last year he came back to haunt me. I expect him again to-night.'

"Then he added in a tone that made me smile:

"'And so we are somewhat excited.'

"I reassured him as best I could, happy to have arrived on that particular evening and to witness this superstitious terror. I told stories and almost succeeded in calming the whole household.

"Near the fireplace slept an old dog, mustached and almost blind, with his head between his paws, such a dog as reminds you of people you have known.

"Outside, the raging storm was beating against the little house, and suddenly through a small pane of glass, a sort of peep-window placed near the door, I saw in a brilliant flash of lightning a whole mass of trees thrashed by the wind.

"In spite of my efforts, I realized that terror was laying hold of these people, and each time that I ceased to speak, all ears listened for distant sounds. Annoyed at these foolish fears, I was about to retire to my bed, when the old gamekeeper suddenly leaped from his chair, seized his gun and stammered wildly: 'There he is, there he is! I hear him!' The two women again sank upon their knees in the corner and hid their faces, while the sons took up the axes. I was going to try to pacify them once more, when the sleeping dog awakened suddenly and, raising his head and stretching his neck, looked at the fire with his dim eyes and uttered one of those mournful howls which make travelers shudder in the darkness and solitude of the country. All eyes were focused upon him now as he rose on his front feet, as though haunted by a vision, and began to howl at something invisible, unknown, and doubtless horrible, for he was bristling all over. The gamekeeper with livid face cried: 'He scents him! He scents him! He was there when I killed him.' The two women, terrified, began to wail in concert with the dog.

"In spite of myself, cold chills ran down my spine. This vision of the animal at such a time and place, in the midst of these startled people, was something frightful to witness.

"Then for an hour the dog howled without stirring; he howled as though in the anguish of a nightmare; and fear, horrible fear came over me. Fear of what? How can I say? It was fear, and that is all I know.

"We remained motionless and pale, expecting something awful to happen. Our ears were strained and our hearts beat loudly while the slightest noise startled us. Then the beast began to walk around the room, sniffing at the walls and growling constantly. His maneuvers were driving us mad! Then the countryman, who had brought me thither, in a paroxysm of rage, seized the dog, and carrying him to a door, which opened into a small court, thrust him forth.

"The noise was suppressed and we were left plunged in a silence still more terrible. Then suddenly we all started. Some one was gliding along the outside wall toward the forest; then he seemed to be feeling of the door with a trembling hand; then for two minutes nothing was heard and we almost lost our minds. Then he returned, still feeling along the wall, and scratched lightly upon the door as a child might do with his finger nails. Suddenly a face appeared behind the glass of the peep-window, a white face with eyes shining like those of the cat tribe. A sound was heard, an indistinct plaintive murmur.

"Then there was a formidable burst of noise in the kitchen. The old gamekeeper had fired and the two sons at once rushed forward and barricaded the window with the great table, reinforcing it with the buffet.

"I swear to you that at the shock of the gun's discharge, which I did not expect, such an anguish laid hold of my heart, my soul, and my very body that I felt myself about to fall, about to die from fear.

"We remained there until dawn, unable to move, in short, seized by an indescribable numbness of the brain.

"No one dared to remove the barricade until a thin ray of sunlight appeared through a crack in the back room.

"At the base of the wall and under the window, we found the old dog lying dead, his skull shattered by a ball.

"He had escaped from the little court by digging a hole under a fence."

The dark-visaged man became silent, then he added:

"And yet on that night I incurred no danger, but I should rather again pass through all the hours in which I have confronted the most terrible perils than the one minute when that gun was discharged at the bearded head in the window."

The Confession

Marguerite de Thérelles was dying. Although but fifty-six, she seemed like seventy-five at least. She panted, paler than the sheets, shaken by dreadful shiverings, her face convulsed, her eyes haggard, as if she had seen some horrible thing.

Her eldest sister, Suzanne, six years older, sobbed on her knees beside the bed. A little table drawn close to the couch of the dying woman, and covered with a napkin, bore two lighted candles, the priest being momentarily expected to give extreme unction and the communion, which should be the last.

The apartment had that sinister aspect, that air of hopeless farewells, which belongs to the chambers of the dying. Medicine bottles stood about on the furniture, linen lay in the corners, pushed aside by foot or broom. The disordered chairs themselves seemed affrighted, as if they had run, in all the senses of the word. Death, the formidable, was there, hidden, waiting.

The story of the two sisters was very touching. It was quoted far and wide; it had made many eyes to weep.

Suzanne, the elder, had once been madly in love with a young man, who had also been in love with her. They were engaged, and were only waiting the day fixed for the contract, when Henry de Lampierre suddenly died.

The despair of the young girl was dreadful, and she vowed that she would never marry. She kept her word. She put on widow's weeds, which she never took off.

Then her sister, her little sister Marguérite, who was only twelve years old, came one morning to throw herself into the arms of the elder, and said: "Big Sister, I do not want thee to be unhappy. I do not want thee to cry all thy life. I will never leave thee, never, never! I — I, too, shall never marry. I shall stay with thee always, always, always!"

Suzanne, touched by the devotion of the child, kissed her, but did not believe.

Yet the little one, also, kept her word, and despite the entreaties of her parents, despite the supplications of the elder, she never married. She was pretty, very pretty; she refused many a young man who seemed to love her truly; and she never left her sister more.

*****

They lived together all the days of their life, without ever being separated a single time. They went side by side, inseparably united. But Marguérite seemed always sad, oppressed, more melancholy than the elder, as though perhaps her sublime sacrifice had broken her spirit. She aged more quickly, had white hair from the age of thirty, and often suffering, seemed afflicted by some secret, gnawing trouble.

Now she was to be the first to die.

Since yesterday she was no longer able to speak. She had only said, at the first glimmers of day-dawn:

"Go fetch Monsieur le Curé, the moment has come."

And she had remained since then upon her back, shaken with spasms, her lips agitated as though dreadful words were mounting from her heart without power of issue, her look mad with fear, terrible to see.

Her sister, torn by sorrow, wept wildly, her forehead resting on the edge of the bed, and kept repeating:

"Margot, my poor Margot, my little one!"

She had always called her, "Little One," just as the younger had always called her "Big Sister."

Steps were heard on the stairs. The door opened. A choir boy appeared, followed by an old priest in a surplice. As soon as she perceived him, the dying woman, with one shudder, sat up, opened her lips, stammered two or three words, and began to scratch the sheets with her nails as if she had wished to make a hole.

The Abbé Simon approached, took her hand, kissed her brow, and with a soft voice:

"God pardon thee, my child; have courage, the moment is now come, speak."

Then Marguérite, shivering from head to foot, shaking her whole couch with nervous movements, stammered:

"Sit down, Big Sister ... listen."

The priest bent down toward Suzanne, who was still flung upon the bed's foot. He raised her, placed her in an armchair, and taking a hand of each of the sisters in one of his own, he pronounced:

"Lord, my God! Endue them with strength, cast Thy mercy upon them."

And Marguérite began to speak. The words issued from her throat one by one, raucous, with sharp pauses, as though very feeble.

*****

"Pardon, pardon, Big Sister; oh, forgive! If thou knewest how I have had fear of this moment all my life...."

Suzanne stammered through her tears:

"Forgive thee what, Little One? Thou hast given all to me, sacrificed everything; thou art an angel...."

But Marguérite interrupted her:

"Hush, hush! Let me speak ... do not stop me. It is dreadful ... let me tell all ... to the very end, without flinching. Listen. Thou rememberest ... thou rememberest ... Henry...."

Suzanne trembled and looked at her sister. The younger continued:

"Thou must hear all, to understand. I was twelve years old, only twelve years old; thou rememberest well, is it not so? And I was spoiled, I did everything that I liked! Thou rememberest, surely, how they spoiled me? Listen. The first time that he came he had varnished boots. He got down from his horse at the great steps, and he begged pardon for his costume, but he came to bring some news to papa. Thou rememberest, is it not so? Don't speak — listen. When I saw him I was completely carried away, I found him so very beautiful; and I remained standing in a corner of the *salon* all the time that he was talking. Children are strange ... and terrible. Oh yes ... I have dreamed of all that.

"He came back again ... several times ... I looked at him with all my eyes, with all my soul ... I was large of my age ... and very much more knowing than anyone thought. He came back often ... I thought only of him. I said, very low:

"'Henry ... Henry de Lampierre!'"

"Then they said that he was going to marry thee. It was a sorrow; oh, Big Sister, a sorrow ... a sorrow! I cried for three nights without sleeping. He came back every day, in the afternoon, after his lunch ... thou rememberest, is it not so? Say nothing ... listen. Thou madest him cakes which he liked ... with meal, with butter and milk. Oh, I know well how. I could make them yet if it were needed. He ate them at one mouthful, and ... and then he drank a glass of wine, and then he said, 'It is delicious.' Thou rememberest how he would say that?

"I was jealous, jealous! The moment of thy marriage approached. There were only two weeks more. I became crazy. I said to myself: 'He shall not marry Suzanne, no, I will not have it! It is I whom he will marry when I am grown up. I shall never find anyone whom I love so much.' But one night, ten days before the contract, thou tookest a walk with him in front of the chateau by moonlight ... and there ... under the fir, under the great fir ... he kissed thee ... kissed ... holding thee in his two arms ... so long. Thou rememberest, is it not so? It was probably the first time ... yes ... Thou wast so pale when thou earnest back to the *salon*.

"I had seen you two; I was there, in the shrubbery. I was angry! If I could I should have killed you both!

"I said to myself: 'He shall not marry Suzanne, never! He shall marry no one. I should be too unhappy.' And all of a sudden I began to hate him dreadfully.

"Then, dost thou know what I did? Listen. I had seen the gardener making little balls to kill strange dogs. He pounded up a bottle with a stone and put the powdered glass in a little ball of meat.

"I took a little medicine bottle that mamma had; I broke it small with a hammer, and I hid the glass in my pocket. It was a shining powder ... The next day, as soon as you had made the little cakes ... I split them with a knife and I put in the glass ... He ate three of them ... I too, I ate one ... I threw the other six into the pond. The two swans died three days after ... Dost thou remember? Oh, say nothing ... listen, listen. I, I alone did not die ... but I have always been sick. Listen ... He died — thou knowest well ...

listen ... that, that is nothing. It is afterwards, later ... always ... the worst ... listen.

"My life, all my life ... what torture! I said to myself: 'I will never leave my sister. And at the hour of death I will tell her all ...' There! And ever since, I have always thought of that moment when I should tell thee all. Now it is come. It is terrible. Oh ... Big Sister!

"I have always thought, morning and evening, by night and by day, 'Some time I must tell her that ...' I waited ... What agony! ... It is done. Say nothing. Now I am afraid ... am afraid ... oh, I am afraid. If I am going to see him again, soon, when I am dead. See him again ... think of it! The first! Before thou! I shall not dare. I must ... I am going to die ... I want you to forgive me. I want it ... I cannot go off to meet him without that. Oh, tell her to forgive me, Monsieur le Curé, tell her ... I implore you to do it. I cannot die without that...."

*****

She was silent, and remained panting, always scratching the sheet with her withered nails.

Suzanne had hidden her face in her hands, and did not move. She was thinking of him whom she might have loved so long! What a good life they should have lived together! She saw him once again in that vanished bygone time, in that old past which was put out forever. The beloved dead — how they tear your hearts! Oh, that kiss, his only kiss! She had hidden it in her soul. And after it nothing, nothing more her whole life long!

*****

All of a sudden the priest stood straight, and, with a strong vibrant voice, he cried:

"Mademoiselle Suzanne, your sister is dying!"

Then Suzanne, opening her hands, showed her face soaked with tears, and throwing herself upon her sister, she kissed her with all her might, stammering:

"I forgive thee, I forgive thee, Little One."

The Horla, or Modern Ghosts

May 8th. What a lovely day! I have spent all the morning lying in the grass in front of my house, under the enormous plantain tree which covers it, and shades and shelters the whole of it. I like this part of the country and I am fond of living here because I am attached to it by deep roots, profound and delicate roots which attach a man to the soil on which his ancestors were born and died, which attach him to what people think and what they eat, to the usages as well as to the food, local expressions, the peculiar language of the peasants, to the smell of the soil, of the villages and of the atmosphere itself.

I love my house in which I grew up. From my windows I can see the Seine which flows by the side of my garden, on the other side of the road, almost through my grounds, the great and wide Seine, which goes to Rouen and Havre, and which is covered with boats passing to and fro.

On the left, down yonder, lies Rouen, that large town with its blue roofs, under its pointed Gothic towers. They are innumerable, delicate or broad, dominated by the spire of the cathedral, and full of bells which sound through the blue air on fine mornings, sending their sweet and distant iron clang to me; their metallic sound which the breeze wafts in my direction, now stronger and now weaker, according as the wind is stronger or lighter.

What a delicious morning it was!

About eleven o'clock, a long line of boats drawn by a steam tug, as big as a fly, and which scarcely puffed while emitting its thick smoke, passed my gate.

After two English schooners, whose red flag fluttered toward the sky, there came a magnificent Brazilian three-master; it was perfectly white and wonderfully clean and shining. I saluted it, I hardly know why, except that the sight of the vessel gave me great pleasure.

May 12th. I have had a slight feverish attack for the last few days, and I feel ill, or rather I feel low-spirited.

Whence do these mysterious influences come, which change our happiness into discouragement, and our self-confidence into diffidence? One might almost say that the air, the invisible air is full of unknowable Forces, whose mysterious presence we have to endure. I wake up in the best spirits, with an inclination to sing in my throat. Why? I go down by the side of the water, and suddenly, after walking a short distance, I return home wretched, as if some misfortune were awaiting me there. Why? Is it a cold shiver which, passing over my skin, has upset my nerves and given me low spirits? Is it the form of the clouds, or the color of the sky, or the color of the surrounding objects which is so changeable, which have troubled my thoughts as they passed before my eyes? Who can tell? Everything that surrounds us, everything that we see without looking at it, everything that we touch without knowing it, everything that we handle without feeling it, all that we meet without clearly distinguishing it, has a rapid, surprising and inexplicable effect upon us and upon our organs, and through them on our ideas and on our heart itself.

How profound that mystery of the Invisible is! We cannot fathom it with our miserable senses, with our eyes which are unable to perceive what is either too small or too great, too near to, or too far from us; neither the inhabitants of a star nor of a drop of water ... with our ears that deceive us, for they transmit to us the vibrations of the air in sonorous notes. They are fairies who work the miracle of changing that movement into noise, and by that metamorphosis give birth to music, which makes the mute agitation of nature musical ... with our sense of smell which is smaller than that of a dog ... with our sense of taste which can scarcely distinguish the age of a wine!

Oh! If we only had other organs which would work other miracles in our favor, what a number of fresh things we might discover around us!

May 16th. I am ill, decidedly! I was so well last month! I am feverish, horribly feverish, or rather I am in a state of feverish enervation, which makes my mind suffer as much as my body. I have without ceasing that horrible sensation of some danger threatening me, that apprehension of some coming misfortune or of approaching death, that presentiment which is, no doubt, an attack of some illness which is still unknown, which germinates in the flesh and in the blood.

May 18th. I have just come from consulting my medical man, for I could no longer get any sleep. He found that my pulse was high, my eyes dilated, my nerves highly strung, but no alarming symptoms. I must have a course of shower-baths and of bromide of potassium.

May 25th. No change! My state is really very peculiar. As the evening comes on, an incomprehensible feeling of disquietude seizes me, just as if night concealed some terrible menace toward me. I dine quickly, and then try to read, but I do not understand the words, and can scarcely distinguish the letters. Then I walk up and down my drawing-room, oppressed by a feeling of confused and irresistible fear, the fear of sleep and fear of my bed.

About ten o'clock I go up to my room. As soon as I have got in I double lock, and bolt it: I am frightened — of what? Up till the present time I have been frightened of nothing — I open my cupboards, and look under my bed; I listen — I listen — to what? How strange it is that a simple feeling of discomfort, impeded or heightened circulation, perhaps the irritation of a nervous thread, a slight congestion, a small disturbance in the imperfect and delicate functions of our living machinery, can turn the most light-hearted of men into a melancholy one, and make a coward of the bravest! Then, I go to bed, and I wait for sleep as a man might wait for the executioner. I wait for its coming with dread, and my heart beats and my legs tremble, while my whole body shivers beneath the warmth of the bedclothes, until the moment when I suddenly fall asleep, as one would throw oneself into a pool of stagnant water in order to drown oneself. I do not feel coming over me, as I used to do formerly, this perfidious sleep which is close to me and watching me, which is going to seize me by the head, to close my eyes and annihilate me.

I sleep — a long time — two or three hours perhaps — then a dream — no — a nightmare lays hold on me. I feel that I am in bed and asleep — I feel it and I know it — and I feel also that somebody is coming close to me, is looking at me, touching me, is getting on to my bed, is kneeling on my chest, is taking my neck between his hands and squeezing it — squeezing it with all his might in order to strangle me.

I struggle, bound by that terrible powerlessness which paralyzes us in our dreams; I try to cry out — but I cannot; I want to move — I cannot; I try, with the most violent efforts and out of breath, to turn over and throw off this being which is crushing and suffocating me — I cannot!

And then, suddenly, I wake up, shaken and bathed in perspiration; I light a candle and find that I am alone, and after that crisis, which occurs every night, I at length fall asleep and slumber tranquilly till morning.

June 2d. My state has grown worse. What is the matter with me? The bromide does me no good, and the shower-baths have no effect whatever. Sometimes, in order to tire myself out, though I am fatigued enough already, I go for a walk in the forest of Roumare. I used to think at first that the fresh light and soft air, impregnated with the odor of herbs and leaves, would instill new blood into my veins and impart fresh energy to my heart. I turned into a broad ride in the wood, and then I turned toward La Bouille, through a narrow path, between two rows of exceedingly tall trees, which placed a thick, green, almost black roof between the sky and me.

A sudden shiver ran through me, not a cold shiver, but a shiver of agony, and so I hastened my steps, uneasy at being alone in the wood, frightened stupidly and without reason, at the profound solitude. Suddenly it seemed to me as if I were being followed, that somebody was walking at my heels, close, quite close to me, near enough to touch me.

I turned round suddenly, but I was alone. I saw nothing behind me except the straight, broad ride, empty and bordered by high trees, horribly empty; on the other side it also extended until it was lost in the distance, and looked just the same, terrible.

I closed my eyes. Why? And then I began to turn round on one heel very quickly, just like a top. I nearly fell down, and opened my eyes; the trees were dancing round me and the earth heaved; I was obliged to sit down. Then, ah! I no longer remembered how I had come! What a strange idea! What a strange, strange idea! I did not the least know. I started off to the right, and got back into the avenue which had led me into the middle of the forest.

June 3d. I have had a terrible night. I shall go away for a few weeks, for no doubt a journey will set me up again.

July 2d. I have come back, quite cured, and have had a most delightful trip into the bargain. I have been to Mont Saint-Michel, which I had not seen before.

What a sight, when one arrives as I did, at Avranches toward the end of the day! The town stands on a hill, and I was taken into the public garden at the extremity of the town. I uttered a cry of astonishment. An extraordinarily large bay lay extended before me, as far as my eyes could reach, between two hills which were lost to sight in the mist; and in the middle of this immense yellow bay, under a clear, golden sky, a peculiar hill rose up, somber and pointed in the midst of the sand. The sun had just disappeared, and under the still flaming sky the outline of that fantastic rock stood out, which bears on its summit a fantastic monument.

At daybreak I went to it. The tide was low as it had been the night before, and I saw that wonderful abbey rise up before me as I approached it. After several hours' walking, I reached the enormous mass of rocks which supports the little town, dominated by the great church. Having climbed the steep and narrow street, I entered the most wonderful Gothic building that has ever been built to God on earth, as large as a town, full of low rooms which seem buried beneath vaulted roofs, and lofty galleries supported by delicate columns.

I entered this gigantic granite jewel which is as light as a bit of lace, covered with towers, with slender belfries to which spiral staircases ascend, and which raise their strange heads that bristle with chimeras, with devils, with fantastic animals, with monstrous flowers, and which are joined together by finely carved arches, to the blue sky by day, and to the black sky by night.

When I had reached the summit, I said to the monk who accompanied me: "Father, how happy you must be here!" And he replied: "It is very windy, Monsieur;" and so we began to talk while watching the rising tide, which ran over the sand and covered it with a steel cuirass.

And then the monk told me stories, all the old stories belonging to the place, legends, nothing but legends.

One of them struck me forcibly. The country people, those belonging to the Mornet, declare that at night one can hear talking going on in the sand, and then that one hears two goats bleat, one with a strong, the other with a weak voice. Incredulous people declare that it is nothing but the cry of the sea birds, which occasionally resembles bleatings, and occasionally human lamentations; but belated fishermen swear that they have met an old shepherd, whose head, which is covered by his cloak, they can never see, wandering on the downs, between two tides, round the little town placed so far out of the world, and who is guiding and walking before them, a he-goat with a man's face, and a she-goat with a woman's face, and both of them with white hair; and talking incessantly, quarreling in a strange language, and then suddenly ceasing to talk in order to bleat with all their might.

"Do you believe it?" I asked the monk. "I scarcely know," he replied, and I continued: "If there are other beings besides ourselves on this earth, how comes it that we have not known it for so long a time, or why have you not seen them? How is it that I have not seen them?" He replied: "Do we see the hundred thousandth part of what exists? Look here; there is the wind, which is the strongest force in nature, which knocks down men, and blows down buildings, uproots trees, raises the sea into mountains of water, destroys cliffs and casts great ships onto the breakers; the wind which kills, which whistles, which sighs, which roars — have you ever seen it, and can you see it? It exists for all that, however."

I was silent before this simple reasoning. That man was a philosopher, or perhaps a fool; I could not say which exactly, so I held my tongue. What he had said, had often been in my own thoughts.

July 3d. I have slept badly; certainly there is some feverish influence here, for my coachman is suffering in the same way as I am. When I went back home yesterday, I noticed his singular paleness, and I asked him: "What is the matter with you, Jean?" "The matter is that I never get any rest, and my nights devour my days. Since your departure, monsieur, there has been a spell over me."

However, the other servants are all well, but I am very frightened of having another attack, myself.

July 4th. I am decidedly taken again; for my old nightmares have returned. Last night I felt somebody leaning on me who was sucking my life from between my lips with his mouth. Yes, he was sucking it out of my neck, like a leech would have done. Then he got up, satiated, and I woke up, so beaten, crushed and annihilated that I could not move. If this continues for a few days, I shall certainly go away again.

July 5th. Have I lost my reason? What has happened, what I saw last night, is so strange, that my head wanders when I think of it!

As I do now every evening, I had locked my door, and then, being thirsty, I drank half a glass of water, and I accidentally noticed that the water bottle was full up to the cut-glass stopper.

Then I went to bed and fell into one of my terrible sleeps, from which I was aroused in about two hours by a still more terrible shock.

Picture to yourself a sleeping man who is being murdered and who wakes up with a knife in his chest, and who is rattling in

43

his throat, covered with blood, and who can no longer breathe, and is going to die, and does not understand anything at all about it — there it is.

Having recovered my senses, I was thirsty again, so I lit a candle and went to the table on which my water bottle was. I lifted it up and tilted it over my glass, but nothing came out. It was empty! It was completely empty! At first I could not understand it at all, and then suddenly I was seized by such a terrible feeling that I had to sit down, or rather I fell into a chair! Then I sprang up with a bound to look about me, and then I sat down again, overcome by astonishment and fear, in front of the transparent crystal bottle! I looked at it with fixed eyes, trying to conjecture, and my hands trembled! Somebody had drunk the water, but who? I? I without any doubt. It could surely only be I? In that case I was a somnambulist. I lived, without knowing it, that double mysterious life which makes us doubt whether there are not two beings in us, or whether a strange, unknowable and invisible being does not at such moments, when our soul is in a state of torpor, animate our captive body which obeys this other being, as it does us ourselves, and more than it does ourselves.

Oh! Who will understand my horrible agony? Who will understand the emotion of a man who is sound in mind, wide awake, full of sound sense, and who looks in horror at the remains of a little water that has disappeared while he was asleep, through the glass of a water bottle? And I remained there until it was daylight, without venturing to go to bed again.

July 6th. I am going mad. Again all the contents of my water bottle have been drunk during the night — or rather, I have drunk it!

But is it I? Is it I? Who could it be? Who? Oh! God! Am I going mad? Who will save me?

July 10th. I have just been through some surprising ordeals. Decidedly I am mad! And yet! —

On July 6th, before going to bed, I put some wine, milk, water, bread and strawberries on my table. Somebody drank — I drank — all the water and a little of the milk, but neither the wine, bread nor the strawberries were touched.

On the seventh of July I renewed the same experiment, with the same results, and on July 8th, I left out the water and the milk and nothing was touched.

Lastly, on July 9th I put only water and milk on my table, taking care to wrap up the bottles in white muslin and to tie down the stoppers. Then I rubbed my lips, my beard and my hands with pencil lead, and went to bed.

Irresistible sleep seized me, which was soon followed by a terrible awakening. I had not moved, and my sheets were not marked. I rushed to the table. The muslin round the bottles remained intact; I undid the string, trembling with fear. All the water had been drunk, and so had the milk! Ah! Great God! —

I must start for Paris immediately.

July 12th. Paris. I must have lost my head during the last few days! I must be the plaything of my enervated imagination, unless I am really a somnambulist, or that I have been brought under the power of one of those influences which have been proved to exist, but which have hitherto been inexplicable, which are called suggestions. In any case, my mental state bordered on madness, and twenty-four hours of Paris sufficed to restore me to my equilibrium.

Yesterday after doing some business and paying some visits which instilled fresh and invigorating mental air into me, I wound up my evening at the *Théâtre Français*. A play by Alexandre Dumas the Younger was being acted, and his active and powerful mind completed my cure. Certainly solitude is dangerous for active minds. We require men who can think and can talk, around us. When we are alone for a long time we people space with phantoms.

I returned along the boulevards to my hotel in excellent spirits. Amid the jostling of the crowd I thought, not without irony, of my terrors and surmises of the previous week, because I believed, yes, I believed, that an invisible being lived beneath my roof.

How weak our head is, and how quickly it is terrified and goes astray, as soon, as we are struck by a small, incomprehensible fact.

Instead of concluding with these simple words: "I do not understand because the cause escapes me," we immediately imagine terrible mysteries and supernatural powers.

July 14th. Fête of the Republic. I walked through the streets, and the crackers and flags amused me like a child. Still it is very foolish to be merry on a fixed date, by a Government decree. The populace is an imbecile flock of sheep, now steadily patient, and now in ferocious revolt. Say to it: "Amuse yourself," and it amuses itself. Say to it: "Go and fight with your neighbor," and it goes and fights. Say to it: "Vote for the Emperor," and it votes for the Emperor, and then say to it: "Vote for the Republic," and it votes for the Republic.

Those who direct it are also stupid; but instead of obeying men they obey principles, which can only be stupid, sterile, and false, for the very reason that they are principles, that is to say, ideas which are considered as certain and unchangeable, in this world where one is certain of nothing, since light is an illusion and noise is an illusion.

July 16th. I saw some things yesterday that troubled me very much.

I was dining at my cousin's Madame Sablé, whose husband is colonel of the 76th Chasseurs at Limoges. There were two young women there, one of whom had married a medical man, Dr. Parent, who devotes himself a great deal to nervous diseases and the extraordinary manifestations to which at this moment experiments in hypnotism and suggestion give rise.

He related to us at some length, the enormous results obtained by English scientists and the doctors of the medical school at Nancy, and the facts which he adduced appeared to me so strange, that I declared that I was altogether incredulous.

"We are," he declared, "on the point of discovering one of the most important secrets of nature, I mean to say, one of its most important secrets on this earth, for there are certainly some which are of a different kind of importance up in the stars, yonder. Ever since man has thought, since he has been able to express and write down his thoughts, he has felt himself close to a mystery which is impenetrable to his coarse and imperfect senses, and he endeavors to supplement the want of power of his organs by the efforts of his intellect. As long as that intellect still remained in its elementary stage, this intercourse with invisible spirits assumed forms which were commonplace though terrifying. Thence sprang the popular belief in the supernatural, the legends of wandering spirits, of fairies, of gnomes, ghosts, I might even say the legend of God, for our conceptions of the workman-creator, from whatever religion they may have come down to us, are certainly the most mediocre, the stupidest and the most unacceptable inventions that ever sprang from the frightened brain of any human creatures. Nothing is truer than what Voltaire says: 'God made man in His own image, but man has certainly paid Him back again.'

"But for rather more than a century, men seem to have had a presentiment of something new. Mesmer and some others have put us on an unexpected track, and especially within the last two or three years, we have arrived at really surprising results."

My cousin, who is also very incredulous, smiled, and Dr. Parent said to her: "Would you like me to try and send you to sleep, Madame?" "Yes, certainly."

She sat down in an easy-chair, and he began to look at her fixedly, so as to fascinate her. I suddenly felt myself somewhat uncomfortable, with a beating heart and a choking feeling in my throat. I saw that Madame Sablé's eyes were growing heavy, her mouth twitched and her bosom heaved, and at the end of ten minutes she was asleep.

"Stand behind her," the doctor said to me, and so I took a seat behind her. He put a visiting card into her hands, and said to her: "This is a looking-glass; what do you see in it?" And she replied: "I see my cousin." "What is he doing?" "He is twisting his mustache." "And now?" "He is taking a photograph out of his pocket." "Whose photograph is it?" "His own."

That was true, and that photograph had been given me that same evening at the hotel.

"What is his attitude in this portrait?" "He is standing up with his hat in his hand."

So she saw on that card, on that piece of white pasteboard, as if she had seen it in a looking glass.

The young women were frightened, and exclaimed: "That is quite enough! Quite, quite enough!"

But the doctor said to her authoritatively: "You will get up at eight o'clock to-morrow morning; then you will go and call on your cousin at his hotel and ask him to lend you five thousand francs which your husband demands of you, and which he will ask for when he sets out on his coming journey."

Then he woke her up.

On returning to my hotel, I thought over this curious *séance* and I was assailed by doubts, not as to my cousin's absolute and undoubted good faith, for I had known her as well as if she had been my own sister ever since she was a child, but as to a possible trick on the doctor's part. Had not he, perhaps, kept a glass hidden in his hand, which he showed to the young woman in her sleep, at the same time as he did the card? Professional conjurers do things which are just as singular.

So I went home and to bed, and this morning, at about half-past eight, I was awakened by my footman, who said to me: "Madame Sablé has asked to see you immediately, Monsieur," so I dressed hastily and went to her.

She sat down in some agitation, with her eyes on the floor, and without raising her veil she said to me: "My dear cousin, I am going to ask a great favor of you." "What is it, cousin?" "I do not like to tell you, and yet I must. I am in absolute want of five thousand francs." "What, you?" "Yes, I, or rather my husband, who has asked me to procure them for him."

I was so stupefied that I stammered out my answers. I asked myself whether she had not really been making fun of me with Doctor Parent, if it were not merely a very well-acted farce which had been got up beforehand. On looking at her attentively, however, my doubts disappeared. She was trembling with grief, so painful was this step to her, and I was sure that her throat was full of sobs.

I knew that she was very rich and so I continued: "What! Has not your husband five thousand francs at his disposal! Come, think. Are you sure that he commissioned you to ask me for them?"

She hesitated for a few seconds, as if she were making a great effort to search her memory, and then she replied: "Yes ... yes, I am quite sure of it." "He has written to you?"

She hesitated again and reflected, and I guessed the torture of her thoughts. She did not know. She only knew that she was to borrow five thousand francs of me for her husband. So she told a lie. "Yes, he has written to me." "When, pray? You did not mention it to me yesterday." "I received his letter this morning." "Can you show it me?" "No; no ... no ... it contained private matters ... things too personal to ourselves.... I burnt it." "So your husband runs into debt?"

She hesitated again, and then murmured: "I do not know." Thereupon I said bluntly: "I have not five thousand francs at my disposal at this moment, my dear cousin."

She uttered a kind of cry as if she were in pain and said: "Oh! oh! I beseech you, I beseech you to get them for me...."

She got excited and clasped her hands as if she were praying to me! I heard her voice change its tone; she wept and stammered, harassed and dominated by the irresistible order that she had received.

"Oh! oh! I beg you to ... if you knew what I am suffering.... I want them to-day."

I had pity on her: "You shall have them by and by, I swear to you." "Oh! thank you! thank you! How kind you are!"

I continued: "Do you remember what took place at your house last night?" "Yes." "Do you remember that Doctor Parent sent you to sleep?" "Yes." "Oh! Very well then; he ordered you to come to me this morning to borrow five thousand francs, and at this moment you are obeying that suggestion."

She considered for a few moments, and then replied:

"But as it is my husband who wants them...."

For a whole hour I tried to convince her, but could not succeed, and when she had gone I went to the doctor. He was just going out, and he listened to me with a smile, and said: "Do you believe now?" "Yes, I cannot help it." "Let us go to your cousin's."

She was already dozing on a couch, overcome with fatigue. The doctor felt her pulse, looked at her for some time with one hand raised toward her eyes which she closed by degrees under the irresistible power of this magnetic influence, and when she was asleep, he said:

"Your husband does not require the five thousand francs any longer! You must, therefore, forget that you asked your cousin to lend them to you, and, if he speaks to you about it, you will not understand him."

Then he woke her up, and I took out a pocketbook and said: "Here is what you asked me for this morning, my dear cousin." But she was so surprised that I did not venture to persist; nevertheless, I tried to recall the circumstance to her, but she denied it vigorously, thought that I was making fun of her, and in the end very nearly lost her temper.

*****

There! I have just come back, and I have not been able to eat any lunch, for this experiment has altogether upset me.

July 19th. Many people to whom I have told the adventure have laughed at me. I no longer know what to think. The wise man says: Perhaps?

July 21st. I dined at Bougival, and then I spent the evening at a boatmen's ball. Decidedly everything depends on place and surroundings. It would be the height of folly to believe in the supernatural on the *île de la Grenouillière* [2] ... but on the top of Mont Saint-Michel? ... and in India? We are terribly under the influence of our surroundings. I shall return home next week.

July 30th. I came back to my own house yesterday. Everything is going on well.

August 2d. Nothing fresh; it is splendid weather, and I spend my days in watching the Seine flow past.

August 4th. Quarrels among my servants. They declare that the glasses are broken in the cupboards at night. The footman accuses the cook, who accuses the needlewoman, who accuses the other two. Who is the culprit? A clever person, to be able to tell.

August 6th. This time I am not mad. I have seen ... I have seen ... I have seen!... I can doubt no longer ... I have seen it!...

I was walking at two o'clock among my rose trees, in the full sunlight ... in the walk bordered by autumn roses which are beginning to fall. As I stopped to look at a *Géant de Bataille*, which had three splendid blooms, I distinctly saw the stalk of one of the roses bend, close to me, as if an invisible hand had bent it, and then break, as if that hand had picked it! Then the flower raised itself, following the curve which a hand would have described in carrying it toward a mouth, and it remained suspended in the transparent air, all alone and motionless, a terrible red spot, three yards from my eyes. In desperation I rushed at it to take it! I found nothing; it had disappeared. Then I was seized with furious rage against myself, for it is not allowable for a reasonable and serious man to have such hallucinations.

But was it a hallucination? I turned round to look for the stalk, and I found it immediately under the bush, freshly broken, between two other roses which remained on the branch, and I returned home then, with a much disturbed mind; for I am certain now, as certain as I am of the alternation of day and night, that there exists close to me an invisible being that lives on milk and on water, which can touch objects, take them and change their places; which is, consequently, endowed with a material nature, although it is imperceptible to our senses, and which lives as I do, under my roof....

August 7th. I slept tranquilly. He drank the water out of my decanter, but did not disturb my sleep.

I ask myself whether I am mad. As I was walking just now in the sun by the riverside, doubts as to my own sanity arose in me; not vague doubts such as I have had hitherto, but precise and absolute doubts. I have seen mad people, and I have known some who have been quite intelligent, lucid, even clear-sighted in every concern of life, except on one point. They spoke clearly, readily, profoundly on everything, when suddenly their thoughts struck upon the breakers of their madness and broke to pieces there, and were dispersed and foundered in that furious and terrible sea, full of bounding waves, fogs and squalls, which is called *madness*.

I certainly should think that I was mad, absolutely mad, if I were not conscious, did not perfectly know my state, if I did fathom it by analyzing it with the most complete lucidity. I should, in fact, be a reasonable man who was laboring under a hallucination. Some unknown disturbance must have been excited in my brain, one of those disturbances which physiologists of the present day try to note and to fix precisely, and that disturbance must have caused a profound gulf in my mind and in the order and logic of my ideas. Similar phenomena occur in the dreams which lead us through the most unlikely phantasmagoria, without causing us any surprise, because our verifying apparatus and our sense of control has gone to sleep, while our imaginative faculty wakes and works. Is it not possible that one of the imperceptible keys of the cerebral finger-board has been paralyzed in me? Some men lose the recollection of proper names, or of verbs or of numbers or merely of dates, in consequence of an accident. The localization of all the particles of thought has been proved nowadays; what then would there be surprising in the fact that my faculty of controlling the unreality of certain hallucinations should be destroyed for the time being!

I thought of all this as I walked by the side of the water. The sun was shining brightly on the river and made earth delightful, while it filled my looks with love for life, for the swallows, whose agility is always delightful in my eyes, for the plants by the riverside, whose rustling is a pleasure to my ears.

By degrees, however, an inexplicable feeling of discomfort seized me. It seemed to me as if some unknown force were numbing and stopping me, were preventing me from going farther and were calling me back. I felt that painful wish to return which oppresses you when you have left a beloved invalid at home, and when you are seized by a presentiment that he is worse.

I, therefore, returned in spite of myself, feeling certain that I should find some bad news awaiting me, a letter or a telegram. There was nothing, however, and I was more surprised and uneasy than if I had had another fantastic vision.

August 8th. I spent a terrible evening yesterday. He does not show himself any more, but I feel that he is near me, watching me, looking at me, penetrating me, dominating me and more redoubtable when he hides himself thus, than if he were to manifest his constant and invisible presence by supernatural phenomena. However, I slept.

August 9th. Nothing, but I am afraid.

August 10th. Nothing; what will happen to-morrow?

August 11th. Still nothing; I cannot stop at home with this fear hanging over me and these thoughts in my mind; I shall go away.

August 12th. Ten o'clock at night. All day long I have been trying to get away, and have not been able. I wished to accomplish this simple and easy act of liberty — go out — get into my carriage in order to go to Rouen — and I have not been able to do it. What is the reason?

August 13th. When one is attacked by certain maladies, all the springs of our physical being appear to be broken, all our energies destroyed, all our muscles relaxed, our bones to have become as soft as our flesh, and our blood as liquid as water. I am experiencing that in my moral being in a strange and distressing manner. I have no longer any strength, any courage, any self-control, nor even any power to set my own will in motion. I have no power left to *will* anything, but some one does it for me and I obey.

August 14th. I am lost! Somebody possesses my soul and governs it! Somebody orders all my acts, all my movements, all my thoughts. I am no longer anything in myself, nothing except an enslaved and terrified spectator of all the things which I do. I wish to go out; I cannot. He does not wish to, and so I remain, trembling and distracted in the armchair in which he keeps me sitting. I merely wish to get up and to rouse myself, so as to think that I am still master of myself: I cannot! I am riveted to my chair, and my chair adheres to the ground in such a manner that no force could move us.

Then suddenly, I must, I must go to the bottom of my garden to pick some strawberries and eat them, and I go there. I pick the strawberries and I eat them! Oh! my God! my God! Is there a God? If there be one, deliver me! save me! succor me! Pardon! Pity! Mercy! Save me! Oh! what sufferings! what torture! what horror!

August 15th. Certainly this is the way in which my poor cousin was possessed and swayed, when she came to borrow five thousand francs of me. She was under the power of a strange will which had entered into her, like another soul, like another parasitic and ruling soul. Is the world coming to an end?

But who is he, this invisible being that rules me? This unknowable being, this rover of a supernatural race?

Invisible beings exist, then! How is it then that since the beginning of the world they have never manifested themselves in such manner precisely as they do to me? I have never read anything which resembles what goes on in my house. Oh! If I could only leave it, if I could only go away and flee, so as never to return, I should be saved; but I cannot.

August 16th. I managed to escape to-day for two hours, like a prisoner who finds the door of his dungeon accidentally open. I suddenly felt that I was free and that he was far away, and so I gave orders to put the horses in as quickly as possible, and I drove to Rouen. Oh! How delightful to be able to say to a man who obeyed you: "Go to Rouen!"

I made him pull up before the library, and I begged them to lend me Dr. Herrmann Herestauss's treatise on the unknown inhabitants of the ancient and modern world.

Then, as I was getting into my carriage, I intended to say: "To the railway station!" but instead of this I shouted — I did not say, but I shouted — in such a loud voice that all the passers-by turned round: "Home!" and I fell back onto the cushion of my carriage, overcome by mental agony. He had found me out and regained possession of me.

August 17th. Oh! What a night! what a night! And yet it seems to me that I ought to rejoice. I read until one o'clock in the morning! Herestauss, Doctor of Philosophy and Theogony, wrote the history and the manifestation of all those invisible beings which hover around man, or of whom he dreams. He describes their origin, their domains, their power; but none of them resembles the one which haunts me. One might say that man, ever since he has thought, has had a foreboding of, and feared a new being, stronger than himself, his successor in this world, and that, feeling him near, and not being able to foretell the nature of that master, he has, in his terror, created the whole race of hidden beings, of vague phantoms born of fear.

Having, therefore, read until one o'clock in the morning, I went and sat down at the open window, in order to cool my forehead and my thoughts, in the calm night air. It was very pleasant and warm! How I should have enjoyed such a night formerly!

There was no moon, but the stars darted out their rays in the dark heavens. Who inhabits those worlds? What forms, what living beings, what animals are there yonder? What do those who are thinkers in those distant worlds know more than we do? What can they do more than we can? What do they see which we do not know? Will not one of them, some day or other, traversing space, appear on our earth to conquer it, just as the Norsemen formerly crossed the sea in order to subjugate nations more feeble than themselves?

We are so weak, so unarmed, so ignorant, so small, we who live on this particle of mud which turns round in a drop of water.

I fell asleep, dreaming thus in the cool night air, and then, having slept for about three quarters of an hour, I opened my eyes without moving, awakened by I know not what confused and strange sensation. At first I saw nothing, and then suddenly it appeared to me as if a page of a book which had remained open on my table, turned over of its own accord. Not a breath of air had come in at my window, and I was surprised and waited. In about four minutes, I saw, I saw, yes I saw with my own eyes another page lift itself up and fall down on the others, as if a finger had turned it over. My armchair was empty, appeared empty, but I knew that he was there, he, and sitting in my place, and that he was reading. With a furious bound, the bound of an enraged wild beast that wishes to disembowel its tamer, I crossed my room to seize him, to strangle him, to kill him!... But before I could reach it, my chair fell over as if somebody had run away from me ... my table rocked, my lamp fell and went out, and my window closed as if some thief had been surprised and had fled out into the night, shutting it behind him.

So he had run away: he had been afraid; he, afraid of me!

So ... so ... to-morrow ... or later ... some day or other ... I should be able to hold him in my clutches and crush him against the ground! Do not dogs occasionally bite and strangle their masters?

August 18th. I have been thinking the whole day long. Oh! yes, I will obey him, follow his impulses, fulfill all his wishes, show myself humble, submissive, a coward. He is the stronger; but an hour will come....

August 19th. I know, ... I know ... I know all! I have just read the following in the *Revue du Monde Scientifique*: "A curious piece of news comes to us from Rio de Janeiro. Madness, an epidemic of madness, which may be compared to that contagious madness which attacked the people of Europe in the Middle Ages, is at this moment raging in the Province of San-Paulo. The frightened inhabitants are leaving their houses, deserting their villages, abandoning their land, saying that they are pursued, possessed, governed like human cattle by invisible, though tangible beings, a species of vampire, which feed on their life while they are asleep, and who, besides, drink water and milk without appearing to touch any other nourishment.

"Professor Dom Pedro Henriques, accompanied by several medical savants, has gone to the Province of San-Paulo, in order to study the origin and the manifestations of this surprising madness on the spot, and to propose such measures to the Emperor as may appear to him to be most fitted to restore the mad population to reason."

Ah! Ah! I remember now that fine Brazilian three-master which passed in front of my windows as it was going up the Seine, on the 8th of last May! I thought it looked so pretty, so white and bright! That Being was on board of her, coming from there, where its race sprang from. And it saw me! It saw my house which was also white, and it sprang from the ship onto the land. Oh! Good heavens!

Now I know, I can divine. The reign of man is over, and he has come. He whom disquieted priests exorcised, whom sorcerers evoked on dark nights, without yet seeing him appear, to whom the presentiments of the transient masters of the world lent all the monstrous or graceful forms of gnomes, spirits, genii, fairies, and familiar spirits. After the coarse conceptions of primitive fear, more clear-sighted men foresaw it more clearly. Mesmer divined him, and ten years ago physicians accurately discovered the nature of his power, even before he exercised it himself. They played with that weapon of their new Lord, the sway of a mysterious will over the human soul, which had become enslaved. They called it magnetism, hypnotism, suggestion ... what do I know? I have seen them amusing themselves like impudent children with this horrible power! Woe to us! Woe to man! He has come, the ... the ... what does he call himself ... the ... I fancy that he is shouting out his name to me and I do not hear him ... the ... yes ... he is shouting it out ... I am listening ... I cannot ... repeat ... it ... Horla ... I have heard ... the Horla ... it is he ... the Horla ... he has come!...

Ah! the vulture has eaten the pigeon, the wolf has eaten the lamb; the lion has devoured the buffalo with sharp horns; man has killed the lion with an arrow, with a sword, with gunpowder; but the Horla will make of man what we have made of the horse and of the ox: his chattel, his slave and his food, by the mere power of his will. Woe to us!

But, nevertheless, the animal sometimes revolts and kills the man who has subjugated it.... I should also like ... I shall be able to ... but I must know him, touch him, see him! Learned men say that beasts' eyes, as they differ from ours, do not distinguish like ours do ... And my eye cannot distinguish this newcomer who is oppressing me.

Why? Oh! Now I remember the words of the monk at Mont Saint-Michel: "Can we see the hundred-thousandth part of what exists? Look here; there is the wind which is the strongest force in nature, which knocks men, and blows down buildings, uproots trees, raises the sea into mountains of water, destroys cliffs and casts great ships onto the breakers; the wind which kills, which whistles, which sighs, which roars — have you ever seen it, and can you see it? It exists for all that, however!"

And I went on thinking: my eyes are so weak, so imperfect, that they do not even distinguish hard bodies, if they are as transparent as glass!... If a glass without tinfoil behind it were to bar my way, I should run into it, just as a bird which has flown into a room breaks its head against the window panes. A thousand things, moreover, deceive him and lead him astray. How should it then be surprising that he cannot perceive a fresh body which is traversed by the light?

A new being! Why not? It was assuredly bound to come! Why should we be the last? We do not distinguish it, like all the others created before us. The reason is, that its nature is more perfect, its body finer and more finished than ours, that ours is so weak, so awkwardly conceived, encumbered with organs that are always tired, always on the strain like locks that are too complicated, which lives like a plant and like a beast, nourishing itself with difficulty on air, herbs and flesh, an animal machine which is a prey to maladies, to malformations, to decay; broken-winded, badly regulated, simple and eccentric, ingeniously badly made, a coarse and a delicate work, the outline of a being which might become intelligent and grand.

We are only a few, so few in this world, from the oyster up to man. Why should there not be one more, when once that period is accomplished which separates the successive apparitions from all the different species?

Why not one more? Why not, also, other trees with immense, splendid flowers, perfuming whole regions? Why not other elements besides fire, air, earth and water? There are four, only four, those nursing fathers of various beings! What a pity! Why are they not forty, four hundred, four thousand! How poor everything is, how mean and wretched! grudgingly given, dryly invented, clumsily made! Ah! the elephant and the hippopotamus, what grace! And the camel, what elegance!

But, the butterfly you will say, a flying flower! I dream of one that should be as large as a hundred worlds, with wings whose shape, beauty, colors, and motion I cannot even express. But I see it ... it flutters from star to star, refreshing them and perfuming them with the light and harmonious breath of its flight!... And the people up there look at it as it passes in an ecstasy of delight!...

*****

What is the matter with me? It is he, the Horla who haunts me, and who makes me think of these foolish things! He is within me, he is becoming my soul; I shall kill him!

August 19th. I shall kill him. I have seen him! Yesterday I sat down at my table and pretended to write very assiduously. I knew quite well that he would come prowling round me, quite close to me, so close that I might perhaps be able to touch him, to seize him. And then!... then I should have the strength of desperation; I should have my hands, my knees, my chest, my forehead, my teeth to strangle him, to crush him, to bite him, to tear him to pieces. And I watched for him with all my overexcited organs.

I had lighted my two lamps and the eight wax candles on my mantelpiece, as if by this light I could have discovered him.

My bed, my old oak bed with its columns, was opposite to me; on my right was the fireplace; on my left the door which was carefully closed, after I had left it open for some time, in order to attract him; behind me was a very high wardrobe with a looking-glass in it, which served me to make my toilet every day, and in which I was in the habit of looking at myself from head to foot every time I passed it.

So I pretended to be writing in order to deceive him, for he also was watching me, and suddenly I felt, I was certain that he was reading over my shoulder, that he was there, almost touching my ear.

I got up so quickly, with my hands extended, that I almost fell. Eh! well?... It was as bright as at midday, but I did not see myself in the glass!... It was empty, clear, profound, full of light! But my figure was not reflected in it ... and I, I was opposite to it! I saw the large, clear glass from top to bottom, and I looked at it with unsteady eyes; and I did not dare to advance; I did not venture to make a movement, nevertheless, feeling perfectly that he was there, but that he would escape me again, he whose imperceptible body had absorbed my reflection.

How frightened I was! And then suddenly I began to see myself through a mist in the depths of the looking-glass, in a mist as it were through a sheet of water; and it seemed to me as if this water were flowing slowly from left to right, and making my figure clearer every moment. It was like the end of an eclipse. Whatever it was that hid me, did not appear to possess any clearly defined outlines, but a sort of opaque transparency, which gradually grew clearer.

At last I was able to distinguish myself completely, as I do every day when I look at myself.

I had seen it! And the horror of it remained with me and makes me shudder even now.

August 20th. How could I kill it, as I could not get hold of it? Poison? But it would see me mix it with the water; and then, would our poisons have any effect on its impalpable body? No ... no ... no doubt about the matter.... Then?... then?...

August 21st. I sent for a blacksmith from Rouen, and ordered iron shutters of him for my room, such as some private hotels in Paris have on the ground floor, for fear of thieves, and he is going to make me a similar door as well. I have made myself out as a coward, but I do not care about that!...

September 10th. Rouen, Hotel Continental. It is done; ... it is done ... but is he dead? My mind is thoroughly upset by what I have seen.

Well, then, yesterday the locksmith having put on the iron shutters and door, I left everything open until midnight, although it was getting cold.

Suddenly I felt that he was there, and joy, mad joy, took possession of me. I got up softly, and I walked to the right and left for some time, so that he might not guess anything; then I took off my boots and put on my slippers carelessly; then I fastened the iron shutters and going back to the door quickly I double-locked it with a padlock, putting the key into my pocket.

Suddenly I noticed that he was moving restlessly round me, that in his turn he was frightened and was ordering me to let him out. I nearly yielded, though I did not yet, but putting my back to the door I half opened it, just enough to allow me to go out backward, and as I am very tall, my head touched the lintel. I was sure that he had not been able to escape, and I shut him up quite alone, quite alone. What happiness! I had him fast. Then I ran downstairs; in the drawing-room, which was under my bedroom, I took the two lamps and I poured all the oil onto the carpet, the furniture, everywhere; then I set fire to it and made my escape, after having carefully double-locked the door.

I went and hid myself at the bottom of the garden in a clump of laurel bushes. How long it was! how long it was! Everything was dark, silent, motionless, not a breath of air and not a star, but heavy banks of clouds which one could not see, but which weighed, oh! so heavily on my soul.

I looked at my house and waited. How long it was! I already began to think that the fire had gone out of its own accord, or that he had extinguished it, when one of the lower windows gave way under the violence of the flames, and a long, soft, caressing sheet of red flame mounted up the white wall and kissed it as high as the roof. The light fell onto the trees, the branches, and the leaves, and a shiver of fear pervaded them also! The birds awoke; a dog began to howl, and it seemed to me as if the day were breaking! Almost immediately two other windows flew into fragments, and I saw that the whole of the lower part of my house was nothing but a terrible furnace. But a cry, a horrible, shrill, heartrending cry, a woman's cry, sounded through the night, and two garret windows were opened! I had forgotten the servants! I saw the terrorstruck faces, and their frantically waving arms!...

Then, overwhelmed with horror, I set off to run to the village, shouting: "Help! help! fire! fire!" I met some people who were already coming onto the scene, and I went back with them to see!

By this time the house was nothing but a horrible and magnificent funeral pile, a monstrous funeral pile which lit up the whole country, a funeral pile where men were burning, and where he was burning also, He, He, my prisoner, that new Being, the new master, the Horla!

Suddenly the whole roof fell in between the walls, and a volcano of flames darted up to the sky. Through all the windows which opened onto that furnace I saw the flames darting, and I thought that he was there, in that kiln, dead.

Dead? perhaps?... His body? Was not his body, which was transparent, indestructible by such means as would kill ours?

If he was not dead?... Perhaps time alone has power over that Invisible and Redoubtable Being. Why this transparent, unrecognizable body, this body belonging to a spirit, if it also had to fear ills, infirmities and premature destruction?

Premature destruction? All human terror springs from that! After man the Horla. After him who can die every day, at any hour, at any moment, by any accident, he came who was only to die at his own proper hour and minute, because he had touched the limits of his existence!

No ... no ... without any doubt ... he is not dead. Then ... then ... I suppose I must kill myself!

FOOTNOTE. — This story is a tragic experience and prophecy. It was insanity that robbed the world of its most finished short story writer, the author of this tale; and even before his madness became overpowering, de Maupassant complained that he was haunted by his double — by a vision of another Self confronting and threatening him. He had run life at its top speed; this hallucination was the result.

Medical science defines in such cases "an image of memory which differs in intensity from the normal" — that is to say, a fixed idea so persistent and growing that to the thinker it seems utterly real.

— EDITOR.

PIERRE MILLE

The Miracle of Zobéide

Always wise and prudent, Zobéide cautiously put aside the myrtle branches and peeped through to see who were the persons talking by the fountain in the cool shadow of the pink sandstone wall. And when she saw that it was only the Rev. John Feathercock, her lord and master, discoursing as usual with Mohammed-si-Koualdia, she went toward them frankly but slowly.

When she was quite near she stopped, and from the light that played in her deep black eyes you would have thought that surely she was listening with the deepest attention. But the truth is that with all her little brain, with all her mouth, and with all her stomach, she was craving the yellow and odorous pulp of a melon which had been cut open and put on the table near two tall glasses half filled with snowy sherbet. For Zobéide was a turtle of the ordinary kind found in the grass of all the meadows around the city of Damascus.

As she waited, Mohammed continued his story:

"And, as I tell you, O reverend one abounding in virtues, this lion which still lives near Tabariat, was formerly a strong lion, a wonderful lion, a lion among lions! To-day, even, he can strike a camel dead with one blow of his paw, and then, plunging his fangs into the spine of the dead animal, toss it upon his shoulders with a single movement of his neck. But unfortunately, having one day brought down a goat in the chase by simply blowing upon it the breath of his nostrils, the lion was inflated with pride and cried: 'There is no god but God, but I am as strong as God. Let him acknowledge it!' Allah, who heard him, Allah, the All-powerful, said in a loud voice, 'O lion of Tabariat, try now to carry off thy prey!' Then the lion planted his great teeth firmly in the spine of the animal, right under the ears, and attempted to throw it on his back. Onallahi! It was as though he had tried to lift Mount Libanus, and his right leg fell lamed to the ground. And the voice of Allah still held him, declaring: 'Lion, nevermore shalt thou kill a goat!' And it has remained thus to this day: the lion of

Tabariat has still all his old-time power to carry off camels, but he can never do the slightest harm to even a new-born kid. The goats of the flocks dance in front of him at night, deriding him to his face, and always from that moment his right leg has been stiff and lame."

"Mohammed," said the Rev. Mr. Feathercock contemptuously, "these are stories fit only for babies."

"How, then!" replied Mohammed-si-Koualdia. "Do you refuse to believe that God is able to do whatever he may wish, that the world itself is but a perpetual dream of God's and that, in consequence, God may change this dream at will? Are you a Christian if you deny the power of the All-powerful?"

"I am a Christian," replied the clergyman with a trace of embarrassment; "but for a long time we have been obliged to admit, we pastors of the civilized Church of the Occident, that God would not be able, without belying himself, to change the order of things which he established when he created the universe. We consider that faith in miracles is a superstition which we must leave to the monks of the Churches of Rome and of Russia, and also to your Mussulmans who live in ignorance of the truth. And it is in order to teach you this truth that I have come here to your country, and at the same time to fight against the pernicious political influence exerted by these same Romish and Greek monks of whom I have just been speaking."

"By invoking the name of Allah," responded Mohammed with intense solemnity, "and by virtue of the collar-bone of the mighty Solomon, I can perform great miracles. You see this turtle before us? I shall cause it to grow each day the breadth of a finger!"

In saying these words he made a sudden movement of his foot toward Zobéide, and Zobéide promptly drew her head into her shell.

"You claim to be able to work a miracle like that!" said the clergyman scornfully. "You, Mohammed, a man immersed in sin, a Mussulman whom I have seen drunk!"

"I was drunk," replied Mohammed calmly, "but not as drunk as others."

"So you think yourself able to force the power of Allah!" pursued Mr. Feathercock, disdaining the interruption.

"I could do it without a moment's difficulty," said Mohammed.

Taking Zobéide in his hand he lifted her to the table. The frightened turtle had again drawn in her head. Nothing could be seen but the black-encircled golden squares of her shell against a background of juicy melon pulp. Mohammed chanted:

"Thou thyself art a miracle, O turtle! For thy head is the head of a serpent, thy tail the tail of a water rat, thy bones are bird's bones and thy covering is of stone; and yet thou knowest love as it is known by men. And from thy eggs, O turtle of stone, other turtles come forth.

"Thou thyself art a miracle, O turtle! For one would say that thou wert a shell, naught but a shell, and behold! thou art a beast that eats. Eat of this melon, O turtle, and grow this night the length of my nail, if Allah permit!

"And when thou hast grown by the breadth of a finger, O turtle, eat further of this melon, or of its sister, another melon, and grow further by the breadth of a finger until thou hast reached the size of a mosque. Thou thyself art a miracle, O shell endowed with life! Perform still another miracle, if Allah permit, if Allah permit!"

Zobéide, reassured by the monotony of his voice, decided at last to come out of her shell. First she showed the point of her little horny nose, then her black eyes, her flat-pointed tail, and finally her strong little claw-tipped feet. Seeing the melon, she made a gesture of assent, and began to eat.

"Nothing in the world will happen!" remarked the Rev. John Feathercock rather doubtfully.

"Wait and see," answered Mohammed gravely. "I shall come back to-morrow!"

The next morning he returned, measured Zobéide with his fingers and declared:

"She has grown!"

"Do you imagine you can make me believe such a thing?" cried Mr. Feathercock anxiously.

"It is written in the Koran," answered Mohammed: "'I swear by the rosy glow which fills the air when the sun is setting, by the shades of the night, and by the light of the moon, that ye shall all change, in substance and in size!' Allah has manifested himself; the size of this turtle has changed. It will continue to change. Measure it yourself and you will see."

Mr. Feathercock did measure Zobéide, and was forced to admit that she had indeed grown the breadth of a finger. He became thoughtful.

Thus day by day Zobéide grew in size, in vigor and in appetite. At first she had only been as big as a saucer, and took each day but a few ounces of nourishment. Then she reached the size of a dessert plate, then of a soup plate. With her strong beak she could split the rind of a melon at a blow; distinctly could be heard the sound of her heavy jaws as she crunched the sweet pulp of the fruits which she loved, and which she devoured in great quantities. In one week she had grown so tremendously that she was as big as a meat platter. The Rev. Mr. Feathercock no longer dared to go near this monster, from whose eyes seemed to glisten a look of deviltry. And, always and forever, apparently devoured by a perpetual hunger, the monster ate.

The members of Mr. Feathercock's flock came to hear that he was keeping in his house a turtle that had been enchanted in the name of Allah and not by the power of the Occidental Divinity: this proved to be anything but helpful to the evangelical labors of the clergyman. But he himself refused steadily and obstinately to believe in the miracle, although Mohammed-si-Koualdia had never set foot in the house since the day when he had invoked the charm. He remained outside the grounds, seated at the door of a little café, plunged in meditation or in dreams, and consuming hashish in large quantities. At the end of some time Mr. Feathercock succeeded in persuading himself that what he was witnessing was nothing more nor less than a perfectly simple and natural phenomenon, perhaps not well understood hitherto, and due entirely to the extraordinarily favorable action of melon pulp on the physical development of turtles. He decided to cut off Zobé-ide's supply of melons.

Finally there came a day when Mohammed, drunk with hashish, saw Hakem, Mr. Feathercock's valet, returning from market with a large bunch of fresh greens. He rose majestically, though with features distorted by the drug, and followed the boy with hasty steps.

"Miserable one!" cried he to Mr. Feathercock. "Wretched worm, you have tried to break the charm! Rejoice then, for you have succeeded and it is broken. But let despair follow upon the heels of your rapture, for it is broken in a way that you do not dream. Henceforth your turtle shall *dwindle away* day by day!"

The Rev. Mr. Feathercock tried to laugh, but he did not feel entirely happy. On Sundays, at the services, the few faithful souls who remained in his flock looked upon him with suspicion. At the English consulate they spoke very plainly, telling him un-sympathetically that anyone who would make a friend of such a man as Mohammed-si-Koualdia and who would mingle "promis-cuously" with such rabble, need look for nothing but harm from it.

Zobéide, when she was first confronted with the fresh, damp greens, showed the most profound contempt for them. Unques-tionably she preferred melons. Mr. Feathercock applauded his own acumen. "She was eating too much; that was the whole trou-ble," he said to himself. "And that was what made her grow so remarkably. If she eats less she will probably not grow so much. And if she should happen to die, I shall be rid of her. Whatever comes, it will be for the best."

But the next day Zobéide gave up pouting and began very docilely to eat the greens, and when the boy Hakem carried her next bunch to her he said slyly:

"Effendi, she is growing smaller!"

The clergyman attempted to shrug his shoulders, but it was impossible to disguise the fact from himself — Zobéide had certainly shrunk! And within an hour all Damascus knew that Zobéide had shrunk. When Mr. Feathercock went to the barber shop the Greek barber said to him, "Sir, your turtle is no ordinary turtle!" When he went to call on Mrs. Hollingshead, a lady who was always intensely interested in all subjects that she failed to understand and who discussed them with a beautiful freedom, she said to him: "Dear sir, your turtle. How exciting it must be to watch it shrink! I am certainly coming to see it myself." When he went to the Anglican Orphanage, all the little Syrians, all the little Arabs, all the little Armenians, all the little Jews, drew turtles in their copy-books, turtles of every size and every description, the big ones walking behind the little ones, the tail of each in the mouth of another, making an interminable line. And in the street the donkey drivers, the water-carriers, the fishmongers, the venders of broiled meats, of baked breads, of beans, of cream, all cried: "Mister Turtle, Mister Turtle! Try our wares. Buy something for your poor stubborn beast that is pining away!"

And, in truth, the turtle continued to shrink. She became again the size of a soup plate, then of a dessert plate, then of a saucer, till finally one morning there was nothing there but a little round thing, tiny, frail, translucent, a spot about as big as a lady's watch, almost invisible at the base of the fountain. And the next day — ah! the next day there was nothing there, nothing whatever, neither turtle nor the shadow of turtle, or more trace of a turtle than of an elephant in all the grounds!

Mohammed-si-Koualdia had stopped taking hashish, because he was saturated with it. But he remained all day long, huddled in a heap at the door of the little café immediately opposite the clergyman's house, his eyes enlarged out of all proportion, set in a face the color of death, gave him the look of a veritable sorcerer. At this moment the Rev. Mr. Feathercock was returning from a visit to the English consul who had said to him coldly:

"All that I can tell you is that you have made an ass of yourself or, as a Frenchman would say, played the donkey to hear yourself bray. The best thing you can do is to go and hunt up a congregation somewhere else."

The Rev. John Feathercock accepted the advice with deference, and took the train for Bayreuth. That same evening Mohammed-si-Koualdia betook himself to the house of one Antonio, interpreter and public scribe, and ordered him to translate into French the following letter, which he dictated in Arabic. Afterwards he carried this letter to Father Stephen, prior to the monastery of the Greek Hicrosolymites:

"May heaven paint your cheeks with the colors of health, most venerable father, and may happiness reign in your heart! I have the honor to inform you that the Rev. John Feathercock has just left for Bayreuth, but that he has had put upon his trunks the address of a city called Liverpool, which, I am informed, is in the kingdom of England; and also, everything points to the belief that he will never return. Therefore, I dare to hope that you will send me the second part of the reward you agreed upon as well as a generous present for Hakem, Mr. Feathercock's valet, who carried every day a new turtle to the house of the clergyman, and carried away the old one under his cloak.

"I also pray you to tell your friends that I have for sale, at prices exceptionally low, fifty-five turtles, all of different sizes, the last and smallest of which is no larger than the watch of a European *houri*. I have been at infinite pains to find them, and they have served to prove to me with what exquisite care Allah fashions the members of the least of His creatures and ornaments their bodies with the most delicate designs."

VILLIERS DE L'ISLE ADAM

The Torture by Hope

Many years ago, as evening was closing in, the venerable Pedro Arbuez d'Espila, sixth prior of the Dominicans of Segovia, and third Grand Inquisitor of Spain, followed by a *fra redemptor*, and preceded by two familiars of the Holy Office, the latter carrying lanterns, made their way to a subterranean dungeon. The bolt of a massive door creaked, and they entered a mephitic *in-pace*, where the dim light revealed between rings fastened to the wall a bloodstained rack, a brazier, and a jug. On a pile of straw, loaded with fetters and his neck encircled by an iron carcan, sat a haggard man, of uncertain age, clothed in rags.

This prisoner was no other than Rabbi Aser Abarbanel, a Jew of Arragon, who — accused of usury and pitiless scorn for the poor — had been daily subjected to torture for more than a year. Yet "his blindness was as dense as his hide," and he had refused to abjure his faith.

Proud of a filiation dating back thousands of years, proud of his ancestors — for all Jews worthy of the name are vain of their blood — he descended Talmudically from Othoniel and consequently from Ipsiboa, the wife of the last judge of Israel, a circumstance which had sustained his courage amid incessant torture. With tears in his eyes at the thought of this resolute soul rejecting salvation, the venerable Pedro Arbuez d'Espila, approaching the shuddering rabbi, addressed him as follows:

"My son, rejoice: your trials here below are about to end. If in the presence of such obstinacy I was forced to permit, with deep regret, the use of great severity, my task of fraternal correction has its limits. You are the fig tree which, having failed so many times to bear fruit, at last withered, but God alone can judge your soul. Perhaps Infinite Mercy will shine upon you at the last moment! We must hope so. There are examples. So sleep in peace tonight. Tomorrow you will be included in the *auto da fé*: that is, you will be exposed to the *quémadero*, the symbolical flames of the Everlasting Fire: it burns, as you know, only at a distance, my son; and Death is at least two hours (often three) in coming, on account of the wet, iced bandages, with which we protect the heads and hearts of the condemned. There will be forty-three of you. Placed in the last row, you will have time to invoke God and offer to Him this baptism of fire, which is of the Holy Spirit. Hope in the Light, and rest."

With these words, having signed to his companions to unchain the prisoner, the prior tenderly embraced him. Then came the turn of the *fra redemptor*, who, in a low tone, entreated the Jew's forgiveness for what he had made him suffer for the purpose of redeeming him; then the two familiars silently kissed him. This ceremony over, the captive was left, solitary and bewildered, in the darkness.

*****

Rabbi Aser Abarbanel, with parched lips and visage worn by suffering, at first gazed at the closed door with vacant eyes. Closed? The word unconsciously roused a vague fancy in his mind, the fancy that he had seen for an instant the light of the lanterns through a chink between the door and the wall. A morbid idea of hope, due to the weakness of his brain, stirred his whole being. He dragged himself toward the strange *appearance*. Then, very gently and cautiously, slipping one finger into the crevice, he drew the door toward him. Marvelous! By an extraordinary accident the familiar who closed it had turned the huge key an instant before it struck the stone casing, so that the rusty bolt not having entered the hole, the door again rolled on its hinges.

The rabbi ventured to glance outside. By the aid of a sort of luminous dusk he distinguished at first a semicircle of walls indented by winding stairs; and opposite to him, at the top of five or six stone steps, a sort of black portal, opening into an immense corridor, whose first arches only were visible from below.

Stretching himself flat he crept to the threshold. Yes, it was really a corridor, but endless in length. A wan light illuminated it: lamps suspended from the vaulted ceiling lightened at intervals the dull hue of the atmosphere — the distance was veiled in shadow. Not a single door appeared in the whole extent! Only on one side, the left, heavily grated loopholes, sunk in the walls, admitted a light which must be that of evening, for crimson bars at intervals rested on the flags of the pavement. What a terrible silence! Yet, yonder, at the far end of that passage there might be a doorway of escape! The Jew's vacillating hope was tenacious, for it was *the last*.

Without hesitating, he ventured on the flags, keeping close under the loopholes, trying to make himself part of the blackness of the long walls. He advanced slowly, dragging himself along on his breast, forcing back the cry of pain when some raw wound sent a keen pang through his whole body.

Suddenly the sound of a sandaled foot approaching reached his ears. He trembled violently, fear stifled him, his sight grew dim. Well, it was over, no doubt. He pressed himself into a niche and, half lifeless with terror, waited.

It was a familiar hurrying along. He passed swiftly by, holding in his clenched hand an instrument of torture — a frightful figure — and vanished. The suspense which the rabbi had endured seemed to have suspended the functions of life, and he lay nearly an hour unable to move. Fearing an increase of tortures if he were captured, he thought of returning to his dungeon. But the old hope whispered in his soul that divine *perhaps*, which comforts us in our sorest trials. A miracle had happened. He could doubt no longer. He began to crawl toward the chance of escape. Exhausted by suffering and hunger, trembling with pain, he pressed onward. The sepulchral corridor seemed to lengthen mysteriously, while he, still advancing, gazed into the gloom where there *must* be some avenue of escape.

Oh! oh! He again heard footsteps, but this time they were slower, more heavy. The white and black forms of two inquisitors appeared, emerging from the obscurity beyond. They were conversing in low tones, and seemed to be discussing some important subject, for they were gesticulating vehemently.

At this spectacle Rabbi Aser Abarbanel closed his eyes: his heart beat so violently that it almost suffocated him; his rags were damp with the cold sweat of agony; he lay motionless by the wall, his mouth wide open, under the rays of a lamp, praying to the God of David.

Just opposite to him the two inquisitors paused under the light of the lamp — doubtless owing to some accident due to the course of their argument. One, while listening to his companion, gazed at the rabbi! And, beneath the look — whose absence of expression the hapless man did not at first notice — he fancied he again felt the burning pincers scorch his flesh, he was to be once more a living wound. Fainting, breathless, with fluttering eyelids, he shivered at the touch of the monk's floating robe. But — strange yet natural fact — the inquisitor's gaze was evidently that of a man deeply absorbed in his intended reply, engrossed by what he was hearing; his eyes were fixed — and seemed to look at the Jew *without seeing him*.

In fact, after the lapse of a few minutes, the two gloomy figures slowly pursued their way, still conversing in low tones, toward the place whence the prisoner had come; HE HAD NOT BEEN SEEN! Amid the horrible confusion of the rabbi's thoughts, the idea darted through his brain: "Can I be already dead that they did not see me?" A hideous impression roused him from his lethargy: in looking at the wall against which his face was pressed, he imagined he beheld two fierce eyes watching him! He flung his head back in a sudden frenzy of fright, his hair fairly bristling! Yet, no! No. His hand groped over the stones: it was the *reflection* of the inquisitor's eyes, still retained in his own, which had been refracted from two spots on the wall.

Forward! He must hasten toward that goal which he fancied (absurdly, no doubt) to be deliverance, toward the darkness from which he was now barely thirty paces distant. He pressed forward faster on his knees, his hands, at full length, dragging himself painfully along, and soon entered the dark portion of this terrible corridor.

Suddenly the poor wretch felt a gust of cold air on the hands resting upon the flags; it came from under the little door to which the two walls led.

Oh, Heaven, if that door should open outward. Every nerve in the miserable fugitive's body thrilled with hope. He examined it from top to bottom, though scarcely able to distinguish its outlines in the surrounding darkness. He passed his hand over it: no bolt, no lock! A latch! He started up, the latch yielded to the pressure of his thumb: the door silently swung open before him.

"HALLELUIA!" murmured the rabbi in a transport of gratitude as, standing on the threshold, he beheld the scene before him.

The door had opened into the gardens, above which arched a starlit sky, into spring, liberty, life! It revealed the neighboring fields, stretching toward the sierras, whose sinuous blue lines were relieved against the horizon. Yonder lay freedom! Oh, to escape! He would journey all night through the lemon groves, whose fragrance reached him. Once in the mountains and he was safe! He inhaled the delicious air; the breeze revived him, his lungs expanded! He felt in his swelling heart the *Veni foràs* of Lazarus! And to thank once more the God who had bestowed this mercy upon him, he extended his arms, raising his eyes toward Heaven. It was an ecstasy of joy!

Then he fancied he saw the shadow of his arms approach him — fancied that he felt these shadowy arms inclose, embrace him — and that he was pressed tenderly to some one's breast. A tall figure actually did stand directly before him. He lowered his eyes — and remained motionless, gasping for breath, dazed, with fixed eyes, fairly driveling with terror.

Horror! He was in the clasp of the Grand Inquisitor himself, the venerable Pedro Arbuez d'Espila, who gazed at him with tearful eyes, like a good shepherd who had found his stray lamb.

The dark-robed priest pressed the hapless Jew to his heart with so fervent an outburst of love, that the edges of the monochal haircloth rubbed the Dominican's breast. And while Aser

Abarbanel with protruding eyes gasped in agony in the ascetic's embrace, vaguely comprehending that *all the phases of this fatal evening were only a prearranged torture, that of* HOPE, the Grand Inquisitor, with an accent of touching reproach and a look of consternation, murmured in his ear, his breath parched and burning from long fasting:

"What, my son! On the eve, perchance, of salvation — you wished to leave us?"

ERCKMANN-CHATRIAN

The Owl's Ear

On the 29th of July, 1835, Kasper Boeck, a shepherd of the little village of Hirschwiller, with his large felt hat tipped back, his wallet of stringy sackcloth hanging at his hip, and his great tawny dog at his heels, presented himself at about nine o'clock in the evening at the house of the burgomaster, Petrus Mauerer, who had just finished supper and was taking a little glass of kirchwasser to facilitate digestion.

This burgomaster was a tall, thin man, and wore a bushy gray mustache. He had seen service in the armies of the Archduke Charles. He had a jovial disposition, and ruled the village, it is said, with his finger and with the rod.

"Mr. Burgomaster," cried the shepherd in evident excitement.

But Petrus Mauerer, without awaiting the end of his speech, frowned and said:

"Kasper Boeck, begin by taking off your hat, put your dog out of the room, and then speak distinctly, intelligibly, without stammering, so that I may understand you."

Hereupon the burgomaster, standing near the table, tranquilly emptied his little glass and wiped his great gray mustachios indifferently.

Kasper put his dog out, and came back with his hat off.

"Well!" said Petrus, seeing that he was silent, "what has happened?"

"It happens that the *spirit* has appeared again in the ruins of Geierstein!"

"Ha! I doubt it. You've seen it yourself?"

"Very clearly, Mr. Burgomaster."

"Without closing your eyes?"

"Yes, Mr. Burgomaster — my eyes were wide open. There was plenty of moonlight."

"What form did it have?"

"The form of a small man."

"Good!"

And turning toward a glass door at the left:

"Katel!" cried the burgomaster.

An old serving woman opened the door.

"Sir?"

"I am going out for a walk — on the hillside — sit up for me until ten o'clock. Here's the key."

"Yes, sir."

Then the old soldier took down his gun from the hook over the door, examined the priming, and slung it over his shoulder; then he addressed Kasper Boeck:

"Go and tell the rural guard to meet me in the holly path, and tell him behind the mill. Your *spirit* must be some marauder. But if it's a fox, I'll make a fine hood of it, with long earlaps."

Master Petrus Mauerer and humble Kasper then went out. The weather was superb, the stars innumerable. While the shepherd went to knock at the rural guard's door, the burgomaster plunged among the elder bushes, in a little lane that wound around behind the old church.

Two minutes later Kasper and Hans Goerner, whinger at his side, by running overtook Master Petrus in the holly path.

All three made their way together toward the ruins of Geierstein.

These ruins, which are twenty minutes' walk from the village, seem to be insignificant enough; they consist of the ridges of a few decrepit walls, from four to six feet high, which extend among the brier bushes. Archaeologists call them the aqueducts of Seranus, the Roman camp of Holderlock, or vestiges of Theodoric, according to their fantasy. The only thing about these ruins which could be considered remarkable is a stairway to a cistern cut in the rock. Inside of this spiral staircase, instead of concentric circles which twist around with each complete turn, the involutions become wider as they proceed, in such a way that the bottom of the pit is three times as large as the opening. Is it an architectural freak, or did some reasonable cause determine such an odd construction? It matters little to us. The result was to cause in the cistern that vague reverberation which anyone may hear upon placing a shell at his ear, and to make you aware of steps on the gravel path, murmurs of the air, rustling of the leaves, and even distant words spoken by people passing the foot of the hill.

Our three personages then followed the pathway between the vineyards and gardens of Hirschwiller.

"I see nothing," the burgomaster would say, turning up his nose derisively.

"Nor I either," the rural guard would repeat, imitating the other's tone.

"It's down in the hole," muttered the shepherd.

"We shall see, we shall see," returned the burgomaster.

It was in this fashion, after a quarter of an hour, that they came upon the opening of the cistern. As I have said, the night was clear, limpid, and perfectly still.

The moon portrayed, as far as the eye could reach, one of those nocturnal landscapes in bluish lines, studded with slim trees, the shadows of which seemed to have been drawn with a black crayon. The blooming brier and broom perfumed the air with a rather sharp odor, and the frogs of a neighboring swamp sang their oily anthem, interspersed with silences. But all these details escaped the notice of our good rustics; they thought of nothing but laying hands on the *spirit*.

When they had reached the stairway, all three stopped and listened, then gazed into the dark shadows. Nothing appeared — nothing stirred.

"The devil!" said the burgomaster, "we forgot to bring a bit of candle. Descend, Kasper, you know the way better than I — I'll follow you."

At this proposition the shepherd recoiled promptly. If he had consulted his inclinations the poor man would have taken to flight; his pitiful expression made the burgomaster burst out laughing.

"Well, Hans, since he doesn't want to go down, show me the way," he said to the game warden.

"But, Mr. Burgomaster," said the latter, "you know very well that steps are missing; we should risk breaking our necks."

"Then what's to be done?"

"Yes, what's to be done?"

"Send your dog," replied Petrus.

The shepherd whistled to his dog, showed him the stairway, urged him — but he did not wish to take the chances any more than the others.

At this moment, a bright idea struck the rural guardsman.

"Ha! Mr. Burgomaster," said he, "if you should fire your gun inside."

"Faith," cried the other, "you're right, we shall catch a glimpse at least."

And without hesitating the worthy man approached the stairway and leveled his gun.

But, by the acoustic effect which I have already pointed out, the *spirit*, the marauder, the individual who chanced to be actually in the cistern, had heard everything. The idea of stopping a gunshot did not strike him as amusing, for in a shrill, piercing voice he cried:

"Stop! Don't fire — I'm coming."

Then the three functionaries looked at each other and laughed softly, and the burgomaster, leaning over the opening again, cried rudely:

"Be quick about it, you varlet, or I'll shoot! Be quick about it!"

He cocked his gun, and the click seemed to hasten the ascent of the mysterious person; they heard him rolling down some stones. Nevertheless it still took him another minute before he appeared, the cistern being at a depth of sixty feet.

What was this man doing in such deep darkness? He must be some great criminal! So at least thought Petrus Mauerer and his acolytes.

At last a vague form could be discerned in the dark, then slowly, by degrees, a little man, four and a half feet high at the most, frail, ragged, his face withered and yellow, his eye gleaming like a magpie's, and his hair tangled, came out shouting:

"By what right do you come to disturb my studies, wretched creatures?"

This grandiose apostrophe was scarcely in accord with his costume and physiognomy. Accordingly the burgomaster indignantly replied:

"Try to show that you're honest, you knave, or I'll begin by administering a correction."

"A correction!" said the little man, leaping with anger, and drawing himself up under the nose of the burgomaster.

"Yes," replied the other, who, nevertheless, did not fail to admire the pygmy's courage; "if you do not answer the questions satisfactorily I am going to put to you. I am the burgomaster of Hirschwiller; here are the rural guard, the shepherd and his dog. We are stronger than you — be wise and tell me peaceably who you are, what you are doing here, and why you do not dare to appear in broad daylight. Then we shall see what's to be done with you."

"All that's none of your business," replied the little man in his cracked voice. "I shall not answer."

"In that case, forward, march," ordered the burgomaster, who grasped him firmly by the nape of the neck; "you are going to sleep in prison."

The little man writhed like a weasel; he even tried to bite, and the dog was sniffing at the calves of his legs, when, quite exhausted, he said, not without a certain dignity:

"Let go, sir, I surrender to superior force — I'm yours!"

The burgomaster, who was not entirely lacking in good breeding, became calmer.

"Do you promise?" said he.

"I promise!"

"Very well — walk in front."

And that is how, on the night of the 29th of July, 1835, the burgomaster took captive a little red-haired man, issuing from the cavern of Geierstein.

Upon arriving at Hirschwiller the rural guard ran to find the key of the prison and the vagabond was locked in and double-locked, not to forget the outside bolt and padlock.

Everyone then could repose after his fatigues, and Petrus Mauerer went to bed and dreamed till midnight of this singular adventure.

On the morrow, toward nine o'clock, Hans Goerner, the rural guard, having been ordered to bring the prisoner to the town house for another examination, repaired to the cooler with four husky daredevils. They opened the door, all of them curious to look upon the Will-o'-the-wisp. But imagine their astonishment upon seeing him hanging from the bars of the window by his necktie! Some said that he was still writhing; others that he was already stiff. However that may be, they ran to Petrus Mauerer's house to inform him of the fact, and what is certain is that upon the latter's arrival the little man had breathed his last.

The justice of the peace and the doctor of Hirschwiller drew up a formal statement of the catastrophe; then they buried the unknown in a field of meadow grass and it was all over!

Now about three weeks after these occurrences, I went to see my cousin, Petrus Mauerer, whose nearest relative I was, and consequently his heir. This circumstance sustained an intimate acquaintance between us. We were at dinner, talking on indifferent matters, when the burgomaster recounted the foregoing little story, as I have just reported it.

"'Tis strange, cousin," said I, "truly strange. And you have no other information concerning the unknown?"

"None."

"And you have found nothing which could give you a clew as to his purpose?"

"Absolutely nothing, Christian."

"But, as a matter of fact, what could he have been doing in the cistern? On what did he live?"

The burgomaster shrugged his shoulders, refilled our glasses, and replied with:

"To your health, cousin."

"To yours."

We remained silent a few minutes. It was impossible for me to accept the abrupt conclusion of the adventure, and, in spite of myself, I mused with some melancholy on the sad fate of certain men who appear and disappear in this world like the grass of the field, without leaving the least memory or the least regret.

"Cousin," I resumed, "how far may it be from here to the ruins of Geierstein?"

"Twenty minutes' walk at the most. Why?"

"Because I should like to see them."

"You know that we have a meeting of the municipal council, and that I can't accompany you."

"Oh! I can find them by myself."

"No, the rural guard will show you the way; he has nothing better to do."

And my worthy cousin, having rapped on his glass, called his servant:

"Katel, go and find Hans Goerner — let him hurry, and get here by two o'clock. I must be going."

The servant went out and the rural guard was not tardy in coming.

He was directed to take me to the ruins.

While the burgomaster proceeded gravely toward the hall of the municipal council, we were already climbing the hill. Hans Goerner, with a wave of the hand, indicated the remains of the aqueduct. At the same moment the rocky ribs of the plateau, the blue distances of Hundsrück, the sad crumbling walls covered with somber ivy, the tolling of the Hirschwiller bell summoning the notables to the council, the rural guardsman panting and catching at the brambles — assumed in my eyes a sad and severe tinge, for which I could not account: it was the story of the hanged man which took the color out of the prospect.

The cistern staircase struck me as being exceedingly curious, with its elegant spiral. The bushes bristling in the fissures at every step, the deserted aspect of its surroundings, all harmonized with my sadness. We descended, and soon the luminous point of the opening, which seemed to contract more and more, and to take the shape of a star with curved rays, alone sent us its pale light. When we attained the very bottom of the cistern, we found a superb sight was to be had of all those steps, lighted from above and cutting off their shadows with marvelous precision. I then heard the hum of which I have already spoken: the immense granite conch had as many echoes as stones!

"Has nobody been down here since the little man?" I asked the rural guardsman.

"No, sir. The peasants are afraid. They imagine that the hanged man will return."

"And you?"

"I — oh, I'm not curious."

"But the justice of the peace? His duty was to — "

"Ha! What could he have come to the *Owl's Ear* for?"

"They call this the *Owl's Ear*?"

"Yes."

"That's pretty near it," said I, raising my eyes. "This reversed vault forms the *pavilion* well enough; the under side of the steps makes the covering of the *tympanum*, and the winding of the staircase the *cochlea*, the *labyrinth*, and *vestibule* of the ear. That is the cause of the murmur which we hear: we are at the back of a colossal ear."

"It's very likely," said Hans Goerner, who did not seem to have understood my observations.

We started up again, and I had ascended the first steps when I felt something crush under my foot; I stopped to see what it could be, and at that moment perceived a white object before me. It was a torn sheet of paper. As for the hard object, which I had felt grinding up, I recognized it as a sort of glazed earthenware jug.

"Aha!" I said to myself; "this may clear up the burgomaster's story."

I rejoined Hans Goerner, who was now waiting for me at the edge of the pit.

"Now, sir," cried he, "where would you like to go?"

"First, let's sit down for a while. We shall see presently."

I sat down on a large stone, while the rural guard cast his falcon eyes over the village to see if there chanced to be any trespassers in the gardens. I carefully examined the glazed vase, of which nothing but splinters remained. These fragments presented the appearance of a funnel, lined with wool. It was impossible for me to perceive its purpose. I then read the piece of a letter, written in an easy running and firm hand. I transcribe it here below, word for word. It seems to follow the other half of the sheet, for which I looked vainly all about the ruins:

"My *micracoustic* ear trumpet thus has the double advantage of infinitely multiplying the intensity of sounds, and of introducing them into the ear without causing the observer the least discomfort. You would never have imagined, dear master, the charm which one feels in perceiving these thousands of imperceptible sounds which are confounded, on a fine summer day, in an immense murmuring. The bumble-bee has his song as well as the nightingale, the honey-bee is the warbler of the mosses, the cricket is the lark of the tall grass, the maggot is the wren — it has only a sigh, but the sigh is melodious!

"This discovery, from the point of view of sentiment, which makes us live in the universal life, surpasses in its importance all that I could say on the matter.

"After so much suffering, privations, and weariness, how happy it makes one to reap the rewards of all his labors! How the soul soars toward the divine Author of all these microscopic worlds, the magnificence of which is revealed to us! Where now are the long hours of anguish, hunger, contempt, which overwhelmed us before? Gone, sir, gone! Tears of gratitude moisten our eyes. One is proud to have achieved, through suffering, new joys for humanity and to have contributed to its mental development. But howsoever vast, howsoever admirable may be the first fruits of my *micracoustic* ear trumpet, these do not delimit its advantages. There are more positive ones, more material, and ones which may be expressed in figures.

"Just as the telescope brought the discovery of myriads of worlds performing their harmonious revolutions in infinite space — so also will my *micracoustic* ear trumpet extend the sense of the unbearable beyond all possible bounds. Thus, sir, the circulation of the blood and the fluids of the body will not give me pause; you shall hear them flow with the impetuosity of cataracts; you shall perceive them so distinctly as to startle you; the slightest irregularity of the pulse, the least obstacle, is striking, and produces the same effect as a rock against which the waves of a torrent are dashing!

"It is doubtless an immense conquest in the development of our knowledge of physiology and pathology, but this is not the point on which I would emphasize. Upon applying your ear to the ground, sir, you may hear the mineral waters springing up at immeasurable depths; you may judge of their volume, their currents, and the obstacles which they meet!

"Do you wish to go further? Enter a subterranean vault which is so constructed as to gather a quantity of loud sounds; then at night when the world sleeps, when nothing will be confused with the interior noises of our globe — listen!

"Sir, all that it is possible for me to tell you at the present moment — for in the midst of my profound misery, of my privations, and often of my despair, I am left only a few lucid instants to pursue my geological observations — all that I can affirm is that the seething of glow worms, the explosions of boiling fluids, is something terrifying and sublime, which can only be compared to the impression of the astronomer whose glass fathoms depths of limitless extent.

"Nevertheless, I must avow that these impressions should be studied further and classified in a methodical manner, in order that definite conclusions may be derived therefrom. Likewise, as soon as you shall have deigned, dear and noble master, to transmit the little sum for use at Neustadt as I asked, to supply my first needs, we shall see our way to an understanding in regard to the establishment of three great subterranean observatories, one in the valley of Catania, another in Iceland, then a third in Capac-Uren, Songay, or Cayembé-Uren, the deepest of the Cordilleras, and consequently — "

Here the letter stopped.

I let my hands fall in stupefaction. Had I read the conceptions of an idiot — or the inspirations of a genius which had been realized? What am I to say? to think? So this man, this miserable creature, living at the bottom of a burrow like a fox, dying of hunger, had had perhaps one of those inspirations which the Supreme Being sends on earth to enlighten future generations!

And this man had hanged himself in disgust, despair! No one had answered his prayer, though he asked only for a crust of bread in exchange for his discovery. It was horrible. Long, long I sat there dreaming, thanking Heaven for having limited my intelligence to the needs of ordinary life — for not having desired to make me a superior man in the community of martyrs. At length the rural guardsman, seeing me with fixed gaze and mouth agape, made so bold as to touch me on the shoulder.

"Mr. Christian," said he, "see — it's getting late — the burgomaster must have come back from the council."

"Ha! That's a fact," cried I, crumpling up the paper, "come on."

We descended the hill.

My worthy cousin met me, with a smiling face, at the threshold of his house.

"Well! well! Christian, so you've found no trace of the imbecile who hanged himself?"

"No."

"I thought as much. He was some lunatic who escaped from Stefansfeld or somewhere — Faith, he did well to hang himself. When one is good for nothing, that's the simplest way for it."

The following day I left Hirschwiller. I shall never return.

The Invisible Eye

About this time (said Christian), poor as a church mouse, I took refuge in the roof of an old house in Minnesänger Street, Nuremberg, and made my nest in the corner of the garret.

I was compelled to work over my straw bed to reach the window, but this window was in the gable end, and the view from it was magnificent, both town and country being spread out before me.

I could see the cats walking gravely in the gutters; the storks, their beaks filled with frogs, carrying nourishment to their ravenous brood; the pigeons, springing from their cotes, their tails spread like fans, hovering over the streets.

In the evening, when the bells called the world to the Angelus, with my elbows upon the edge of the roof, I listened to their melancholy chimes; I watched the windows as, one by one, they were lighted up; the good burghers smoking their pipes on the sidewalks; the young girls in their red skirts, with their pitchers under their arms, laughing and chatting around the fountain "Saint Sebalt." Insensibly all this faded away, the bats commenced their rapid course, and I retired to my mattress in sweet peace and tranquillity.

The old curiosity seller, Toubac, knew the way to my little lodging as well as I did, and was not afraid to climb the ladder. Every week his ugly head, adorned with a reddish cap, raised the trapdoor, his fingers grasped the ledge, and he cried out in a nasal tone:

"Well, well, Master Christian, have you anything?"

To which I replied:

"Come in. Why in the devil don't you come in? I am just finishing a little landscape, and you must tell me what you think of it."

Then his great back, seeming to elongate, grew up, even to the roof, and the good man laughed silently.

I must do justice to Toubac: he never haggled with me about prices; he bought all my paintings at fifteen florins, one with the other, and sold them again for forty each. "This was an honest Jew!"

I began to grow fond of this mode of existence, and to find new charms in it day by day.

Just at this time the city of Nuremberg was agitated by a strange and mysterious event. Not far from my dormer window, a little to the left, stood the Inn Boeuf-Gras, an old *auberge* much patronized throughout the country. Three or four wagons, filled with sacks or casks, were always drawn up before the door, where the rustic drivers were in the habit of stopping, on their way to the market, to take their morning draught of wine.

The gable end of the inn was distinguished by its peculiar form. It was very narrow, pointed, and, on two sides, cut-in teeth, like a saw. The carvings were strangely grotesque, interwoven and ornamenting the cornices and surrounding the windows; but the most remarkable fact was that the house opposite reproduced exactly the same sculptures, the same ornaments; even the sign-board, with its post and spiral of iron, was exactly copied.

One might have thought that these two ancient houses reflected each other. Behind the inn, however, was a grand old oak, whose somber leaves darkened the stones of the roof, while the other house stood out in bold relief against the sky. To complete the description, this old building was as silent and dreary as the Inn Boeuf-Gras was noisy and animated.

On one side, a crowd of merry drinkers were continually entering in and going out, singing, tripping, cracking their whips; on the other, profound silence reigned.

Perhaps, once or twice during the day, the heavy door seemed to open of itself, to allow a little old woman to go out, with her back almost in a semicircle, her dress fitting tight about her hips, an enormous basket on her arm, and her hand contracted against her breast.

It seemed to me that I saw at a glance, as I looked upon her, a whole existence of good works and pious meditations.

The physiognomy of this old woman had struck me more than once: her little green eyes, long, thin nose, the immense bouquets of flowers on her shawl, which must have been at least a hundred years old, the withered smile which puckered her cheeks into a cockade, the lace of her bonnet falling down to her eyebrows — all this was fantastic, and interested me much. Why did this old woman live in this great deserted house? I wished to explore the mystery.

One day as I paused in the street and followed her with my eyes, she turned suddenly and gave me a look, the horrible expression of which I know not how to paint; made three or four hideous grimaces, and then, letting her palsied head fall upon her breast, drew her great shawl closely around her, and advanced slowly to the heavy door, behind which I saw her disappear.

"She's an old fool!" I said to myself, in a sort of stupor. My faith, it was the height of folly in me to be interested in her!

However, I would like to see her grimace again; old Toubac would willingly give me fifteen florins if I could paint it for him.

I must confess that these pleasantries of mine did not entirely reassure me.

The hideous glance which the old shrew had given me pursued me everywhere. More than once, while climbing the almost perpendicular ladder to my loft, feeling my clothing caught on some point, I trembled from head to foot, imagining that the old wretch was hanging to the tails of my coat in order to destroy me.

Toubac, to whom I related this adventure, was far from laughing at it; indeed, he assumed a grave and solemn air.

"Master Christian," said he, "if the old woman wants you, take care! Her teeth are small, pointed, and of marvelous whiteness, and that is not natural at her age. She has an 'evil eye.' Children flee from her, and the people of Nuremberg call her 'Fledermausse.'"

I admired the clear, sagacious intellect of the Jew, and his words gave me cause for reflection.

Several weeks passed away, during which I often encountered Fledermausse without any alarming consequences. My fears were dissipated, and I thought of her no more.

But an evening came, during which, while sleeping very soundly, I was awakened by a strange harmony. It was a kind of vibration, so sweet, so melodious, that the whispering of the breeze among the leaves can give but a faint idea of its charm.

For a long time I listened intently, with my eyes wide open, and holding my breath, so as not to lose a note. At last I looked toward the window, and saw two wings fluttering against the glass. I thought, at first, that it was a bat, caught in my room; but, the moon rising at that instant, I saw the wings of a magnificent butterfly of the night delineated upon her shining disk. Their vibrations were often so rapid that they could not be distinguished; then they reposed, extended upon the glass, and their frail fibers were again brought to view.

This misty apparition, coming in the midst of the universal silence, opened my heart to all sweet emotions. It seemed to me that an airy sylph, touched with a sense of my solitude, had come to visit me, and this idea melted me almost to tears.

"Be tranquil, sweet captive, be tranquil," said I; "your confidence shall not be abused. I will not keep you against your will. Return to heaven and to liberty." I then opened my little window. The night was calm, and millions of stars were glittering in the sky. For a moment I contemplated this sublime spectacle, and words of prayer and praise came naturally to my lips; but, judge of my amazement, when, lowering my eyes, I saw a man hanging from the crossbeam of the sign of the Boeuf-Gras, the hair disheveled, the arms stiff, the legs elongated to a point, and casting their gigantic shadows down to the street!

The immobility of this figure under the moon's rays was terrible. I felt my tongue freezing, my teeth clinched. I was about to cry out in terror when, by some incomprehensible mysterious attraction, my glance fell below, and I distinguished, confusedly, the old woman crouched at her window in the midst of dark shadows, and contemplating the dead man with an air of diabolic satisfaction.

Then I had a vertigo of terror. All my strength abandoned me, and, retreating to the wall of my loft, I sank down and became insensible.

I do not know how long this sleep of death continued. When restored to consciousness, I saw that it was broad day. The mists of the night had penetrated to my garret, and deposited their fresh dew upon my hair, and the confused murmurs of the street ascended to my little lodging. I looked without. The burgomaster and his secretary were stationed at the door of the inn, and remained there a long time; crowds of people came and went, and paused to look in; then recommenced their course. The good women of the neighborhood, who were sweeping before their doors, looked on from afar, and talked gravely with each other.

At last a litter, and upon this litter a body, covered with a linen cloth, issued from the inn, carried by two men. They descended to the street, and the children, on their way to school, ran behind them.

All the people drew back as they advanced.

The window opposite was still open; the end of a rope floated from the crossbeam.

I had not dreamed. I had, indeed, seen the butterfly of the night; I had seen the man hanging, and I had seen Fledermausse.

That day Toubac made me a visit, and, as his great nose appeared on a level with the floor, he exclaimed:

"Master Christian, have you nothing to sell?"

I did not hear him. I was seated upon my one chair, my hands clasped upon my knees, and my eyes fixed before me.

Toubac, surprised at my inattention, repeated in a louder voice:

"Master Christian, Master Christian!" Then, striding over the sill, he advanced and struck me on the shoulder.

"Well, well, what is the matter now?"

"Ah, is that you, Toubac?"

"Eh, *parbleu*! I rather think so; are you ill?"

"No, I am only thinking."

"What in the devil are you thinking about?"

"Of the man who was hanged."

"Oh, oh!" cried the curiosity vender. "You have seen him, then? The poor boy! What a singular history! The third in the same place."

"How — the third?"

"Ah, yes! I ought to have warned you; but it is not too late. There will certainly be a fourth, who will follow the example of the others. *Il n'y à que le premier pas qui coûte.*"

Saying this, Toubac took a seat on the corner of my trunk, struck his match-box, lighted his pipe, and blew three or four powerful whiffs of smoke with a meditative air.

"My faith," said he, "I am not fearful; but, if I had full permission to pass the night in that chamber, I should much prefer to sleep elsewhere.

"Listen, Master Christian. Nine or ten months ago a good man of Tübingen, wholesale dealer in furs, dismounted at the Inn Boeuf-Gras. He called for supper; he ate well; he drank well; and was finally conducted to that room in the third story — it is called the Green Room. Well, the next morning he was found hanging to the crossbeam of the signboard.

"Well, that might do *for once*; nothing could be said.

"Every proper investigation was made, and the stranger was buried at the bottom of the garden. But, look you, about six months afterwards a brave soldier from Neustadt arrived; he had received his final discharge, and was rejoicing in the thought of returning to his native village. During the whole evening, while emptying his wine cups, he spoke fondly of his little cousin who was waiting to marry him. At last this big monsieur was conducted to his room — the Green Room — and, the same night, the watchman, passing down the street Minnesänger, perceived something hanging to the crossbeam; he raised his lantern, and lo! it was the soldier, with his final discharge in a bow on his left hip, and his hands gathered up to the seam of his pantaloons, as if on parade.

"'Truth to say, this is extraordinary!' cried the burgomaster; 'the devil's to pay.' Well, the chamber was much visited; the walls were replastered, and the dead man was sent to Neustadt.

"The registrar wrote this marginal note:

"'Died of apoplexy.'

"All Nuremberg was enraged against the innkeeper. There were many, indeed, who wished to force him to take down his iron crossbeam, under the pretext that it inspired people with dangerous ideas; but you may well believe that old Michael Schmidt would not lend his ear to this proposition.

"'This crossbeam,' said he, 'was placed here by my grandfather; it has borne the sign of Boeuf-Gras for one hundred and fifty years, from father to son; it harms no one, not even the hay wagons which pass beneath, for it is thirty feet above them. Those who don't like it can turn their heads aside, and not see it.'

"Well, gradually the town calmed down, and, during several months, no new event agitated it. Unhappily, a student of Heidelberg, returning to the university, stopped, day before yesterday, at the Inn Boeuf-Gras, and asked for lodging. He was the son of a minister of the gospel.

"How could anyone suppose that the son of a pastor could conceive the idea of hanging himself on the crossbeam of a signboard, because a big monsieur and an old soldier had done so? We must admit, Master Christian, that the thing was not probable; these reasons would not have seemed sufficient to myself or to you."

"Enough, enough!" I exclaimed; "this is too horrible! I see a frightful mystery involved in all this. It is not the crossbeam; it is not the room — "

"What! Do you suspect the innkeeper, the most honest man in the world, and belonging to one of the oldest families in Nuremberg?"

"No, no; may God preserve me from indulging in unjust suspicions! but there is an abyss before me, into which I scarcely dare glance."

"You are right," said Toubac, astonished at the violence of my excitement. "We will speak of other things. Apropos, Master Christian, where is our landscape of 'Saint Odille'?"

This question brought me back to the world of realities. I showed the old man the painting I had just completed. The affair was soon concluded, and Toubac, well satisfied, descended the ladder, entreating me to think no more of the student of Heidelberg.

I would gladly have followed my good friend's counsel; but, when the devil once mixes himself up in our concerns, it is not easy to disembarrass ourselves of him.

In my solitary hours all these events were reproduced with frightful distinctness in my mind.

"This old wretch," I said to myself, "is the cause of it all; she alone has conceived these crimes, and has consummated them. But by what means? Has she had recourse to cunning alone, or has she obtained the intervention of invisible powers?" I walked to and fro in my retreat. An inward voice cried out: "It is not in vain that Providence permitted you to see Fledermausse contemplating the agonies of her victim. It is not in vain that the soul of the poor young man came in the form of a butterfly of the night to awake you. No, no; all this was not accidental, Christian. The heavens impose upon you a terrible mission. If you do not accomplish it, tremble lest you fall yourself into the hands of the old murderess! Perhaps, at this moment, she is preparing her snares in the darkness."

During several days these hideous images followed me without intermission. I lost my sleep; it was impossible for me to do anything; my brush fell from my hand; and, horrible to confess, I found myself sometimes gazing at the crossbeam with a sort of complacency. At last I could endure it no longer, and one evening I descended the ladder and hid myself behind the door of Fledermausse, hoping to surprise her fatal secret.

From that time no day passed in which I was not *en route*, following the old wretch, watching, spying, never losing sight of her; but she was so cunning, had a scent so subtle that, without even turning her head, she knew I was behind her.

However, she feigned not to perceive this; she went to the market, to the butcher's, like any good, simple woman, only hastening her steps and murmuring confused words.

At the close of the month I saw that it was impossible for me to attain my object in this way, and this conviction made me inexpressibly sad.

"What can I do?" I said to myself. "The old woman divines my plans; she is on her guard; every hope abandons me. Ah! old hag, you think you already see me at the end of your rope." I was continually asking myself this question: "What can I do? what can I do?" At last a luminous idea struck me. My chamber overlooked the house of Fledermausse; but there was no window on this side. I adroitly raised a slate, and no pen could paint my joy when the whole ancient building was thus exposed to me. "At last, I have you!" I exclaimed; "you cannot escape me now; from here I can see all that passes — your goings, your comings, your arts and snares. You will not suspect this invisible eye — this watchful eye, which will surprise crime at the moment it blooms. Oh, Justice, Justice! She marches slowly; but she arrives."

Nothing could be more sinister than the den now spread out before me — a great courtyard, the large slabs of which were covered with moss; in one corner, a well, whose stagnant waters you shuddered to look upon; a stairway covered with old shells; at the farther end a gallery, with wooden balustrade, and hanging upon it some old linen and the tick of an old straw mattress; on the first floor, to the left, the stone covering of a common sewer indicated the kitchen; to the right the lofty windows of the building looked out upon the street; then a few pots of dried, withered flowers — all was cracked, somber, moist. Only one or two hours during the day could the sun penetrate this loathsome spot; after that, the shadows took possession; then the sunshine fell upon the crazy walls, the worm-eaten balcony, the dull and tarnished glass, and upon the whirlwind of atoms floating in its golden rays, disturbed by no breath of air.

I had scarcely finished these observations and reflections, when the old woman entered, having just returned from market. I heard the grating of her heavy door. Then she appeared with her basket. She seemed fatigued — almost out of breath. The lace of her bonnet fell to her nose. With one hand she grasped the banister and ascended the stairs.

The heat was intolerable, suffocating; it was precisely one of those days in which all insects — crickets, spiders, mosquitoes, etc. — make old ruins resound with their strange sounds.

Fledermausse crossed the gallery slowly, like an old ferret who feels at home. She remained more than a quarter of an hour in the kitchen, then returned, spread out her linen, took the broom, and brushed away some blades of straw on the floor. At last she raised her head, and turned her little green eyes in every direction, searching, investigating carefully.

Could she, by some strange intuition, suspect anything? I do not know; but I gently lowered the slate, and gave up my watch for the day.

In the morning Fledermausse appeared reassured. One angle of light fell upon the gallery. In passing, she caught a fly on the wing, and presented it delicately to a spider established in a corner of the roof. This spider was so bloated that, notwithstanding the distance, I saw it descend from round to round, then glide along a fine web, like a drop of venom, seize its prey from the hands of the old shrew, and remount rapidly. Fledermausse looked at it very attentively, with her eyes half closed; then sneezed, and said to herself, in a jeering tone, "God bless you, beautiful one; God bless you!"

I watched during six weeks, and could discover nothing concerning the power of Fledermausse. Sometimes, seated upon a stool, she peeled her potatoes, then hung out her linen upon the balustrade.

Sometimes I saw her spinning; but she never sang, as good, kind old women are accustomed to do, their trembling voices mingling well with the humming of the wheel.

Profound silence always reigned around her; she had no cat — that cherished society of old women — not even a sparrow came to rest under her roof. It seemed as if all animated nature shrank from her glance. The bloated spider alone took delight in her society.

I cannot now conceive how my patience could endure those long hours of observation: nothing escaped me; nothing was matter of indifference. At the slightest sound I raised my slate; my curiosity was without limit, insatiable.

Toubac complained greatly.

"Master Christian," said he, "how in the devil do you pass your time? Formerly you painted something for me every week; now you do not finish a piece once a month. Oh, you painters! 'Lazy as a painter' is a good, wise proverb. As soon as you have a few kreutzers in possession, you put your hands in your pockets and go to sleep!"

I confess that I began to lose courage — I had watched, spied, and discovered nothing. I said to myself that the old woman could not be so dangerous as I had supposed; that I had perhaps done her injustice by my suspicions; in short, I began to make excuses for her. One lovely afternoon, with my eye fixed at my post of observation, I abandoned myself to these benevolent reflections, when suddenly the scene changed: Fledermausse passed through the gallery with the rapidity of lightning. She was no longer the same person; she was erect, her jaws were clinched, her glance fixed, her neck extended; she walked with grand strides, her gray locks floating behind her.

"Oh, at last," I said to myself, "something is coming, attention!" But, alas! the shadows of evening descended upon the old building, the noises of the city expired, and silence prevailed.

Fatigued and disappointed, I lay down upon my bed, when, casting my eyes toward my dormer window, I saw the room opposite illuminated. So! a traveler occupied the Green Room — fatal to strangers.

Now, all my fears were reawakened; the agitation of Fledermausse was explained — she scented a new victim.

No sleep for me that night; the rustling of the straw, the nibbling of the mice under the floor, gave me nervous chills.

I rose and leaned out of my window; I listened. The light in the room opposite was extinguished. In one of those moments of poignant anxiety, I cannot say if it was illusion or reality, I thought I saw the old wretch also watching and listening.

The night passed, and the gray dawn came to my windows; by degrees the noise and movements in the street ascended to my loft. Harassed by fatigue and emotion I fell asleep, but my slumber was short, and by eight o'clock I had resumed my post of observation.

It seemed as if the night had been as disturbed and tempestuous to Fledermausse as to myself. When she opened the door of the gallery, I saw that a livid pallor covered her cheeks and thin throat; she had on only her chemise and a woolen skirt; a few locks of reddish gray hair fell on her shoulders. She looked toward my hiding place with a dreamy, abstracted air, but she saw nothing; she was thinking of other things.

Suddenly she descended, leaving her old shoes at the bottom of the steps. "Without doubt," thought I, "she is going to see if the door below is well fastened."

I saw her remount hastily, springing up three or four steps at a time — it was terrible.

She rushed into the neighboring chamber, and I heard something like the falling of the top of a great chest; then Fledermausse appeared in the gallery, dragging a manikin after her, and this manikin was clothed like the Heidelberg student.

With surprising dexterity the old woman suspended this hideous object to a beam of the shed, then descended rapidly to the courtyard to contemplate it. A burst of sardonic laughter escaped from her lips; she remounted, then descended again like a maniac, and each time uttered new cries and new bursts of laughter.

A noise was heard near the door, and the old woman bounded forward, unhooked the manikin and carried it off; then, leaning over the balustrade with her throat elongated, her eyes flashing, she listened earnestly. The noise was lost in the distance, the muscles of her face relaxed, and she drew long breaths. It was only a carriage which had passed.

The old wretch had been frightened.

She now returned to the room, and I heard the chest close. This strange scene confounded all my ideas. What did this manikin signify? I became more than ever attentive.

Fledermausse now left the house with her basket on her arm. I followed her with my eyes till she turned the corner of the street. She had reassumed the air of a trembling old woman, took short steps, and from time to time turned her head partly around, to peer behind from the corner of her eye.

Fledermausse was absent fully five hours. For myself, I went, I came, I meditated. The time seemed insupportable. The sun heated the slate of the roof, and scorched my brain.

Now I saw, at the window, the good man who occupied the fatal Green Chamber; he was a brave peasant of Nassau, with a large three-cornered hat, a scarlet vest, and a laughing face; he smoked his pipe of Ulm tranquillity, and seemed to fear no evil.

I felt a strong desire to cry out to him: "Good man, be on your guard! Do not allow yourself to be entrapped by the old wretch; distrust yourself!" but he would not have comprehended me. Toward two o'clock Fledermausse returned. The noise of her door resounded through the vestibule. Then alone, all alone, she entered the yard, and seated herself on the interior step of the stairway; she put down her basket before her, and drew out first some packets of herbs, then vegetables, then a red vest, then a three-cornered hat, a coat of brown velvet, pants of plush, and coarse woolen hose — the complete costume of the peasant from Nassau.

For a moment I felt stunned; then flames passed before my eyes.

I recollected those precipices which entice with an irresistible power; those wells or pits, which the police have been compelled to close, because men threw themselves into them; those trees which had been cut down because they inspired men with the idea of hanging themselves; that contagion of suicides, of robberies, of murders, at certain epochs, by desperate means; that strange and subtile enticement of example, which makes you yawn because another yawns, suffer because you see another suffer, kill yourself because you see others kill themselves — and my hair stood up with horror.

How could this Fledermausse, this base, sordid creature, have derived so profound a law of human nature? how had she found the means to use this law to the profit or indulgence of her sanguinary instincts? This I could not comprehend; it surpassed my wildest imaginations.

But reflecting longer upon this inexplicable mystery, I resolved to turn the fatal law against her, and to draw the old murderess into her own net.

So many innocent victims called out for vengeance!

I felt myself to be on the right path.

I went to all the old-clothes sellers in Nuremberg, and returned in the afternoon to the Inn Boeuf-Gras, with an enormous packet under my arm.

Nichel Schmidt had known me for a long time; his wife was fat and good-looking; I had painted her portrait.

"Ah, Master Christian," said he, squeezing my hand, "what happy circumstance brings you here? What procures me the pleasure of seeing you?"

"My dear Monsieur Schmidt, I feel a vehement, insatiable desire to sleep in the Green Room."

We were standing on the threshold of the inn, and I pointed to the room. The good man looked at me distrustfully.

"Fear nothing," I said; "I have no desire to hang myself.".

"*À la bonne heure! à la bonne heure!* For frankly that would give me pain; an artist of such merit! When do you wish the room, Master Christian?"

"This evening."

"Impossible! it is occupied!"

"Monsieur can enter immediately," said a voice just behind me, "I will not be in the way."

We turned around in great surprise; the peasant of Nassau stood before us, with his three-cornered hat, and his packet at the end of his walking stick. He had just learned the history of his three predecessors in the Green Room, and was trembling with rage.

"Rooms like yours!" cried he, stuttering; "but it is murderous to put people there — it is assassination! You deserve to be sent to the galleys immediately!"

"Go — go — calm yourself," said the innkeeper; "that did not prevent you from sleeping well."

"Happily, I said my prayers at night," said the peasant; "without that, where would I be?" and he withdrew, with his hands raised to heaven.

"Well," said Nichel Schmidt, stupefied, "the room is vacant, but I entreat you, do not serve me a bad trick."

"It would be a worse trick for myself than for you, monsieur."

I gave my packet to the servants, and installed myself for the time with the drinkers. For a long time I had not felt so calm and happy. After so many doubts and disquietudes, I touched the goal. The horizon seemed to clear up, and it appeared that some invisible power gave me the hand. I lighted my pipe, placed my elbow on the table, my wine before me, and listened to the chorus in "Freischütz," played by a troupe of gypsies from the Black Forest. The trumpets, the hue and cry of the chase, the hautboys, plunged me into a vague reverie, and, at times rousing up to look at the hour, I asked myself gravely, if all which *had* happened to me was not a dream. But the watchman came to ask us to leave the *salle*, and soon other and more solemn thoughts were surging in my soul, and in deep meditation I followed little Charlotte, who preceded me with a candle to my room.

We mounted the stairs to the third story. Charlotte gave me the candle and pointed to the door.

"There," said she, and descended rapidly.

I opened the door. The Green Room was like any other inn room. The ceiling was very low, the bed very high. With one glance I explored the interior, and then glided to the window.

Nothing was to be seen in the house of Fledermausse; only, in some distant room, an obscure light was burning. Some one was on the watch. "That is well," said I, closing the curtain. "I have all necessary time."

I opened my packet, I put on a woman's bonnet with hanging lace; then, placing myself before a mirror, I took a brush and painted wrinkles in my face. This took me nearly an hour. Then I put on the dress and a large shawl, and I was actually afraid of myself. Fledermausse seemed to me to look at me from the mirror.

At this moment the watchman cried out, "Eleven o'clock!" I seized the manikin which I had brought in my packet, and muffled it in a costume precisely similar to that worn by the old wretch. I then opened the curtain.

Certainly, after all that I had seen of the Fledermausse, of her infernal cunning, her prudence, her adroitness, she could not in any way surprise me; and yet I was afraid. The light which I had remarked in the chamber was still immovable, and now cast its yellow rays on the manikin of the peasant of Nassau, which was crouched on the corner of the bed, with the head hanging on the breast, the three-cornered hat pulled down over the face, the arms suspended, and the whole aspect that of absolute despair.

The shadows, managed with diabolical art, allowed nothing to be seen but the general effect of the face. The red vest, and six round buttons alone, seemed top shine out in the darkness. But the silence of the night, the complete immobility of the figure, the exhausted, mournful air, were well calculated to take possession of a spectator with a strange power. For myself, although fore-warned, I was chilled even to my bones.

How would it, then, have fared with the poor, simple peasant, if he had been surprised unawares? He would have been utterly cast down. Despairing, he would have lost all power of self-control, and the spirit of imitation would have done the rest.

Scarcely had I moved the curtain, when I saw Fledermausse on the watch behind her window. She could not see me. I opened my window softly; the window opposite was opened! Then her manikin appeared to rise slowly and advance before me. I, also, advanced my manikin, and seizing my torch with one hand, with the other I quickly opened the shutters. And now the old woman and myself were face to face. Struck with sudden terror, she had let her manikin fall!

We gazed at each other with almost equal horror. *She* extended her finger — I advanced *mine*. *She* moved her lips — I agitated *mine*. She breathed a profound sigh, and leaned upon her elbow. I imitated her.

To describe all the terrors of this scene would be impossible. It bordered upon confusion, madness, delirium. It was a death struggle between two wills; between two intelligences; between two souls — each one wishing to destroy the other; and, in this struggle, I had the advantage — her victims struggled with me.

After having imitated for some seconds every movement of Fledermausse, I pulled a rope from under my skirt, and attached it to the crossbeam.

The old woman gazed at me with gaping mouth. I passed the rope around my neck; her pupils expanded, lightened; her face was convulsed.

"No, no!" said she, in a whistling voice.

I pursued her with the impassability of an executioner.

Then rage seemed to take possession of her.

"Old fool!" she exclaimed, straightening herself up, and her hands contracted on the crossbeam. "Old fool!" I gave her no time to go on blowing out my lamp. I stooped, like a man going to make a vigorous spring, and, seizing my manikin, I passed the rope around its neck, and precipitated it below.

A terrible cry resounded through the street, and then silence, which I seemed to feel. Perspiration bathed my forehead. I listened a long time. At the end of a quarter of an hour I heard, far away, very far away, the voice of the watchman, crying, "Inhabitants of Nuremberg, midnight, midnight sounds!"

"Now justice is satisfied!" I cried, "and three victims are avenged. Pardon me, O Lord!"

About five minutes after the cry of the watchman, I saw Fledermausse attracted, allured by my manikin (her exact image), spring from the window, with a rope around her neck, and rest suspended from the crossbeam.

I saw the shadow of death undulating through her body, while the moon, calm, silent, majestic, inundated the summit of the roof, and her cold, pale rays reposed upon the old, disheveled, hideous head.

Just as I had seen the poor young student of Heidelberg, just so did I now see Fledermausse.

In the morning, all Nuremberg learned that the old wretch had hanged herself, and this was the last event of that kind in the Street Minnesänger.

The Waters of Death

The warm mineral waters of Spinbronn, situated in the Hundsrück, several leagues from Pirmesens, formerly enjoyed a magnificent reputation. All who were afflicted with gout or gravel in Germany repaired thither; the savage aspect of the country did not deter them. They lodged in pretty cottages at the head of the defile; they bathed in the cascade, which fell in large sheets of foam from the summit of the rocks; they drank one or two decanters of mineral water daily, and the doctor of the place, Daniel Hâselnoss, who distributed his prescriptions clad in a great wig and chestnut coat, had an excellent practice.

To-day the waters of Spinbronn figure no longer in the "Codex"; [3] in this poor village one no longer sees anyone but a few miserable woodcutters, and, sad to say, Dr. Hâselnoss has left!

All this resulted from a series of very strange catastrophes which lawyer Brêmer of Pirmesens told me about the other day.

You should know, Master Frantz (said he), that the spring of Spinbronn issues from a sort of cavern, about five feet high and twelve or fifteen feet wide; the water has a warmth of sixty-seven degrees Centigrade; it is salt. As for the cavern, entirely covered without with moss, ivy, and brushwood, its depth is unknown because the hot exhalations prevent all entrance.

Nevertheless, strangely enough, it was noticed early in the last century that birds of the neighborhood — thrushes, doves, hawks — were engulfed in it in full flight, and it was never known to what mysterious influence to attribute this particular.

In 1801, at the height of the season, owing to some circumstance which is still unexplained, the spring became more abundant, and the bathers, walking below on the greensward, saw a human skeleton as white as snow fall from the cascade.

You may judge, Master Frantz, of the general fright; it was thought naturally that a murder had been committed at Spinbronn in a recent year, and that the body of the victim had been thrown in the spring. But the skeleton weighed no more than a dozen francs, and Hâselnoss concluded that it must have sojourned more than three centuries in the sand to have become reduced to such a state of desiccation.

This very plausible reasoning did not prevent a crowd of patrons, wild at the idea of having drunk the saline water, from leaving before the end of the day; those worst afflicted with gout and gravel consoled themselves. But the overflow continuing, all the rubbish, slime, and detritus which the cavern contained was disgorged on the following days; a veritable bone-yard came down from the mountain: skeletons of animals of every kind — of quadrupeds, birds, and reptiles — in short, all that one could conceive as most horrible.

Hâselnoss issued a pamphlet demonstrating that all these bones were derived from an antediluvian world: that they were fossil bones, accumulated there in a sort of funnel during the universal flood — that is to say, four thousand years before Christ, and that, consequently, one might consider them as nothing but stones, and that it was needless to be disgusted. But his work had scarcely reassured the gouty when, one fine morning, the corpse of a fox, then that of a hawk with all its feathers, fell from the cascade.

It was impossible to establish that these remains antedated the Flood. Anyway, the disgust was so great that everybody tied up his bundle and went to take the waters elsewhere.

"How infamous!" cried the beautiful ladies — "how horrible! So that's what the virtue of these mineral waters came from! Oh, 'twere better to die of gravel than continue such a remedy!"

At the end of a week there remained at Spinbronn only a big Englishman who had gout in his hands as well as in his feet, who had himself addressed as Sir Thomas Hawerburch, Commodore; and he brought a large retinue, according to the usage of a British subject in a foreign land.

This personage, big and fat, with a florid complexion, but with hands simply knotted with gout, would have drunk skeleton soup if it would have cured his infirmity. He laughed heartily over the desertion of the other sufferers, and installed himself in the prettiest *châlet* at half price, announcing his design to pass the winter at Spinbronn.

*****

(Here lawyer Brêmer slowly absorbed an ample pinch of snuff as if to quicken his reminiscences; he shook his laced ruff with his finger tips and continued:)

*****

Five or six years before the Revolution of 1789, a young doctor of Pirmesens, named Christian Weber, had gone out to San Domingo in the hope of making his fortune. He had actually amassed some hundred thousand francs m the exercise of his profession when the negro revolt broke out.

I need not recall to you the barbarous treatment to which our unfortunate fellow countrymen were subjected at Haiti. Dr. Weber had the good luck to escape the massacre and to save part of his fortune. Then he traveled in South America, and especially in French Guiana. In 1801 he returned to Pirmesens, and established himself at Spinbronn, where Dr. Hâselnoss made over his house and defunct practice.

Christian Weber brought with him an old negress called Agatha: a frightful creature, with a flat nose and lips as large as your fist, and her head tied up in three bandanas of razor-edged colors. This poor old woman adored red; she had earrings which hung down to her shoulders, and the mountaineers of Hundsrück came from six leagues around to stare at her.

As for Dr. Weber, he was a tall, lean man, invariably dressed in a sky-blue coat with codfish tails and deerskin breeches. He wore a hat of flexible straw and boots with bright yellow tops, on the front of which hung two silver tassels. He talked little; his laugh was like a nervous attack, and his gray eyes, usually calm and meditative, shone with singular brilliance at the least sign of contradiction. Every morning he fetched a turn round about the mountain, letting his horse ramble at a venture, whistling forever the same tune, some negro melody or other. Lastly, this rum chap had brought from Haiti a lot of bandboxes filled with queer insects — some black and reddish brown, big as eggs; others little and shimmering like sparks. He seemed to set greater store by them than by his patients, and, from time to time, on coming back from his rides, he brought a quantity of butterflies pinned to his hat brim.

Scarcely was he settled in Hâselnoss's vast house when he peopled the back yard with outlandish birds — Barbary geese with scarlet cheeks, Guinea hens, and a white peacock, which perched habitually on the garden wall, and which divided with the negress the admiration of the mountaineers.

If I enter into these details, Master Frantz, it's because they recall my early youth; Dr. Christian found himself to be at the same time my cousin and my tutor, and as early as on his return to Germany he had come to take me and install me in his house at Spinbronn. The black Agatha at first sight inspired me with some fright, and I only got seasoned to that fantastic visage with considerable difficulty; but she was such a good woman — she knew so well how to make spiced patties, she hummed such strange songs in a guttural voice, snapping her fingers and keeping time with a heavy shuffle, that I ended by taking her in fast friendship.

Dr. Weber was naturally thick with Sir Thomas Hawerburch, as representing the only one of his clientele then in evidence, and I was not slow in perceiving that these two eccentrics held long conventicles together. They conversed on mysterious matters, on the transmission of fluids, and indulged in certain odd signs which one or the other had picked up in his voyages — Sir Thomas in the Orient, and my tutor in America. This puzzled me greatly. As children will, I was always lying in wait for what they seemed to want to conceal from me; but despairing in the end of discovering anything, I took the course of questioning Agatha, and the poor old woman, after making me promise to say nothing about it, admitted that my tutor was a sorcerer.

For the rest, Dr. Weber exercised a singular influence over the mind of this negress, and this woman, habitually so gay and forever ready to be amused by nothing, trembled like a leaf when her master's gray eyes chanced to alight on her.

All this, Master Frantz, seems to have no bearing on the springs of Spinbronn. But wait, wait — you shall see by what a singular concourse of circumstances my story is connected with it.

I told you that birds darted into the cavern, and even other and larger creatures. After the final departure of the patrons, some of the old inhabitants of the village recalled that a young girl named Louise Müller, who lived with her infirm old grandmother in a cottage on the pitch of the slope, had suddenly disappeared half a hundred years before. She had gone out to look for herbs in the forest, and there had never been any more news of her afterwards, except that, three or four days later, some woodcutters who were descending the mountain had found her sickle and her apron a few steps from the cavern.

From that moment it was evident to everyone that the skeleton which had fallen from the cascade, on the subject of which Hâselnoss had turned such fine phrases, was no other than that of Louise Müller. The poor girl had doubtless been drawn into the gulf by the mysterious influence which almost daily overcame weaker beings!

What could this influence be? None knew. But the inhabitants of Spinbronn, superstitious like all mountaineers, maintained that the devil lived in the cavern, and terror spread in the whole region.

*****

Now one afternoon in the middle of the month of July, 1802, my cousin undertook a new classification of the insects in his bandboxes. He had secured several rather curious ones the preceding afternoon. I was with him, holding the lighted candle with one hand and with the other a needle which I heated red-hot.

Sir Thomas, seated, his chair tipped back against the sill of a window, his feet on a stool, watched us work, and smoked his cigar with a dreamy air.

I stood in with Sir Thomas Hawerburch, and I accompanied him every day to the woods in his carriage. He enjoyed hearing me chatter in English, and wished to make of me, as he said, a thorough gentleman.

The butterflies labeled, Dr. Weber at last opened the box of the largest insects, and said:

"Yesterday I secured a magnificent horn beetle, the great *Lucanus cervus* of the oaks of the Hartz. It has this peculiarity — the right claw divides in five branches. It's a rare specimen."

At the same time I offered him the needle, and as he pierced the insect before fixing it on the cork, Sir Thomas, until then impassive, got up, and, drawing near a bandbox, he began to examine the spider crab of Guiana with a feeling of horror which was strikingly portrayed on his fat vermilion face.

"That is certainly," he cried, "the most frightful work of the creation. The mere sight of it — it makes me shudder!"

In truth, a sudden pallor overspread his face.

"Bah!" said my tutor, "all that is only a prejudice from childhood — one hears his nurse cry out — one is afraid — and the impression sticks. But if you should consider the spider with a strong microscope, you would be astonished at the finish of his members, at their admirable arrangement, and even at their elegance."

"It disgusts me," interrupted the commodore brusquely. "Pouah!"

It had turned over in his fingers.

"Oh! I don't know why," he declared, "spiders have always frozen my blood!"

Dr. Weber began to laugh, and I, who shared the feelings of Sir Thomas, exclaimed:

"Yes, cousin, you ought to take this villainous beast out of the box — it is disgusting — it spoils all the rest."

"Little chump," he said, his eyes sparkling, "what makes you look at it? If you don't like it, go take yourself off somewhere."

Evidently he had taken offense; and Sir Thomas, who was then before the window contemplating the mountain, turned suddenly, took me by the hand, and said to me in a manner full of good will:

"Your tutor, Frantz, sets great store by his spider; we like the trees better — the verdure. Come, let's go for a walk."

"Yes, go," cried the doctor, "and come back for supper at six o'clock."

Then raising his voice:

"No hard feelings, Sir Hawerburch."

The commodore replied laughingly, and we got into the carriage, which was always waiting in front of the door of the house.

Sir Thomas wanted to drive himself and dismissed his servant. He made me sit beside him on the same seat and we started off for Rothalps.

While the carriage was slowly ascending the sandy path, an invincible sadness possessed itself of my spirit. Sir Thomas, on his part, was grave. He perceived my sadness and said:

"You don't like spiders, Frantz, nor do I either. But thank Heaven, there aren't any dangerous ones in this country. The spider crab which your tutor has in his box comes from French Guiana. It inhabits the great, swampy forests filled with warm vapors, with scalding exhalations; this temperature is necessary to its life. Its web, or rather its vast snare, envelops an entire thicket. In it it takes birds as our spiders take flies. But drive these disgusting images from your mind, and drink a swallow of my old Burgundy."

Then turning, he raised the cover of the rear seat, and drew from the straw a sort of gourd from which he poured me a full bumper in a leather goblet.

When I had drunk all my good humor returned and I began to laugh at my fright.

The carriage was drawn by a little Ardennes horse, thin and nervous as a goat, which clambered up the nearly perpendicular path. Thousands of insects hummed in the bushes. At our right, at a hundred paces or more, the somber outskirts of the Rothalp forests extended below us, the profound shades of which, choked with briers and foul brush, showed here and there an opening filled with light. On our left tumbled the stream of Spinbronn, and the more we climbed the more did its silvered sheets, floating in the abyss, grow tinged with azure and redouble their sound of cymbals.

I was captivated by this spectacle. Sir Thomas, leaning back in the seat, his knees as high as his chin, abandoned himself to his habitual reveries, while the horse, laboring with his feet and hanging his head on his chest as a counter-weight to the carriage, held on as if suspended on the flank of the rock. Soon, however, we reached a pitch less steep: the haunt of the roebuck, surrounded by tremulous shadows. I always lost my head, and my eyes too, in an immense perspective. At the apparition of the shadows I turned my head and saw the cavern of Spinbronn close at hand. The encompassing mists were a magnificent green, and the stream which, before falling, extends over a bed of black sand and pebbles, was so clear that one would have thought it frozen if pale vapors did not follow its surface.

The horse had just stopped of his own accord to breathe; Sir Thomas, rising, cast his eye over the countryside.

"How calm everything is!" said he.

Then, after an instant of silence:

"If you weren't here, Frantz, I should certainly bathe in the basin."

"But, Commodore," said I, "why not bathe? I would do well to stroll around in the neighborhood. On the next hill is a great glade filled with wild strawberries. I'll go and pick some. I'll be back in an hour."

"Ha! I should like to, Frantz; it's a good idea. Dr. Weber contends that I drink too much Burgundy. It's necessary to offset wine with mineral water. This little bed of sand pleases me."

Then, having set both feet on the ground, he hitched the horse to the trunk of a little birch and waved his hand as if to say:

"You may go."

I saw him sit down on the moss and draw off his boots. As I moved away he turned and called out:

"In an hour, Frantz."

They were his last words.

An hour later I returned to the spring. The horse, the carriage, and the clothes of Sir Thomas alone met my eyes. The sun was setting. The shadows were getting long. Not a bird's song under the foliage, not the hum of an insect in the tall grass. A silence like death looked down on this solitude! The silence frightened me. I climbed up on the rock which overlooks the cavern; I looked to the right and to the left. Nobody! I called. No answer! The sound of my voice, repeated by the echoes, filled me with fear. Night settled down slowly. A vague sense of horror oppressed me. Suddenly the story of the young girl who had disappeared occurred to me; and I began to descend on the run; but, arriving before the cavern, I stopped, seized with unaccountable terror: in casting a glance in the deep shadows of the spring I had caught sight of two motionless red points. Then I saw long lines wavering in a strange manner in the midst of the darkness, and that at a depth where no human eye had ever penetrated. Fear lent my sight, and all my senses, an unheard-of subtlety of perception. For several seconds I heard very distinctly the evening plaint of a cricket down at the edge of the wood, a dog barking far away, very far in the valley. Then my heart, compressed for an instant by emotion, began to beat furiously and I no longer heard anything!

Then uttering a horrible cry, I fled, abandoning the horse, the carriage. In less than twenty minutes, bounding over the rocks and brush, I reached the threshold of our house, and cried in a stifled voice:

"Run! Run! Sir Hawerburch is dead! Sir Hawerburch is in the cavern — !"

After these words, spoken in the presence of my tutor, of the old woman Agatha, and of two or three people invited in that evening by the doctor, I fainted. I have learned since that during a whole hour I raved deliriously.

The whole village had gone in search of the commodore. Christian Weber hurried them off. At ten o'clock in the evening all the crowd came back, bringing the carriage, and in the carriage the clothes of Sir Hawerburch. They had discovered nothing. It was impossible to take ten steps in the cavern without being suffocated.

During their absence Agatha and I waited, sitting in the chimney corner. I, howling incoherent words of terror; she, with hands crossed on her knees, eyes wide open, going from time to time to the window to see what was taking place, for from the foot of the mountain one could see torches flitting in the woods. One could hear hoarse voices, in the distance, calling to each other in the night.

At the approach of her master, Agatha began to tremble. The doctor entered brusquely, pale, his lips compressed, despair written on his face. A score of woodcutters followed him tumultuously, in great felt hats with wide brims — swarthy visaged — shaking the ash from their torches. Scarcely was he in the hall when my tutor's glittering eyes seemed to look for something. He caught sight of the negress, and without a word having passed between them, the poor woman began to cry:

"No! no! I don't want to!"

"And I wish it," replied the doctor in a hard tone.

One would have said that the negress had been seized by an invincible power. She shuddered from head to foot, and Christian Weber showing her a bench, she sat down with a corpse-like stiffness.

All the bystanders, witnesses of this shocking spectacle, good folk with primitive and crude manners, but full of pious sentiments, made the sign of the cross, and I who knew not then, even by name, of the terrible magnetic power of the will, began to tremble, believing that Agatha was dead.

Christian Weber approached the negress, and making a rapid pass over her forehead:

"Are you there?" said he.

"Yes, master."

"Sir Thomas Hawerburch?"

At these words she shuddered again.

"Do you see him?"

"Yes — yes," she gasped in a strangling voice, "I see him."

"Where is he?"

"Up there — in the back of the cavern — dead!"

"Dead!" said the doctor, "how?"

"The spider — Oh! the spider crab — Oh! — "

"Control your agitation," said the doctor, who was quite pale, "tell us plainly — "

"The spider crab holds him by the throat — he is there — at the back — under the rock — wound round by webs — Ah!"

117

Christian Weber cast a cold glance toward his assistants, who, crowding around, with their eyes sticking out of their heads, were listening intently, and I heard him murmur:

"It's horrible! horrible!"

Then he resumed:

"You see him?"

"I see him — "

"And the spider — is it big?"

"Oh, master, never — never have I seen such a large one — not even on the banks of the Mocaris — nor in the lowlands of Konanama. It is as large as my head — !"

There was a long silence. All the assistants looked at each other, their faces livid, their hair standing up. Christian Weber alone seemed calm; having passed his hand several times over the negress's forehead, he continued:

"Agatha, tell us how death befell Sir Hawerburch."

"He was bathing in the basin of the spring — the spider saw him from behind, with his bare back. It was hungry, it had fasted for a long time; it saw him with his arms on the water. Suddenly it came out like a flash and placed its fangs around the commodore's neck, and he cried out: 'Oh! oh! my God!' It stung and fled. Sir Hawerburch sank down in the water and died. Then the spider returned and surrounded him with its web, and he floated gently, gently, to the back of the cavern. It drew in on the web. Now he is all black."

The doctor, turning to me, who no longer felt the shock, asked:

"Is it true, Frantz, that the commodore went in bathing?"

"Yes, Cousin Christian."

"At what time?"

"At four o'clock."

"At four o'clock — it was very warm, wasn't it?"

"Oh, yes!"

"It's certainly so," said he, striking his forehead. "The monster could come out without fear — "

He pronounced a few unintelligible words, and then, looking toward the mountaineers:

"My friends," he cried, "that is where this mass of débris came from — of skeletons — which spread terror among the bathers. That is what has ruined you all — it is the spider crab! It is there — hidden in its web — awaiting its prey in the back of the cavern! Who can tell the number of its victims?"

And full of fury, he led the way, shouting:

"Fagots! Fagots!"

The woodcutters followed him, vociferating.

Ten minutes later two large wagons laden with fagots were slowly mounting the slope. A long file of woodcutters, their backs bent double, followed, enveloped in the somber night. My tutor and I walked ahead, leading the horses by their bridles, and the melancholy moon vaguely lighted this funereal march. From time to time the wheels grated. Then the carts, raised by the irregularities of the rocky road, fell again in the track with a heavy jolt.

As we drew near the cavern, on the playground of the roebucks, our cortége halted. The torches were lit, and the crowd advanced toward the gulf. The limpid water, running over the sand, reflected the bluish flame of the resinous torches, the rays of which revealed the tops of the black firs leaning over the rock.

"This is the place to unload," the doctor then said. "It's necessary to block up the mouth of the cavern."

And it was not without a feeling of terror that each undertook the duty of executing his orders. The fagots fell from the top of the loads. A few stakes driven down before the opening of the spring prevented the water from carrying them away.

Toward midnight the mouth of the cavern was completely closed. The water running over spread to both sides on the moss. The top fagots were perfectly dry; then Dr. Weber, supplying himself with a torch, himself lit the fire. The flames ran from twig to twig with an angry crackling, and soon leaped toward the sky, chasing clouds of smoke before them.

It was a strange and savage spectacle, the great pile with trembling shadows lit up in this way.

This cavern poured forth black smoke, unceasingly renewed and disgorged. All around stood the woodcutters, somber, motionless, expectant, their eyes fixed on the opening; and I, although trembling from head to foot in fear, could not tear away my gaze.

It was a good quarter of an hour that we waited, and Dr. Weber was beginning to grow impatient, when a black object, with long hooked claws, appeared suddenly in the shadow and precipitated itself toward the opening.

A cry resounded about the pyre.

The spider, driven back by the live coals, reëntered its cave. Then, smothered doubtless by the smoke, it returned to the charge and leaped out into the midst of the flames. Its long legs curled up. It was as large as my head, and of a violet red.

One of the woodcutters, fearing lest it leap clear of the fire, threw his hatchet at it, and with such good aim that on the instant the fire around it was covered with blood. But soon the flames burst out more vigorously over it and consumed the horrible destroyer.

*****

Such, Master Frantz, was the strange event which destroyed the fine reputation which the waters of Spinbronn formerly enjoyed. I can certify the scrupulous precision of my account. But as for giving you an explanation, that would be impossible for me to do. At the same time, allow me to tell you that it does not seem to me absurd to admit that a spider, under the influence of a temperature raised by thermal waters, which affords the same conditions of life and development as the scorching climates of Africa and South America, should attain a fabulous size. It was this same extreme heat which explains the prodigious exuberance of the antediluvian creation!

However that may be, my tutor, judging that it would be impossible after this event to reestablish the waters of Spinbronn, sold the house back to Hâselnoss, in order to return to America with his negress and collections. I was sent to board in Strasbourg, where I remained until 1809.

The great political events of the epoch then absorbing the attention of Germany and France explain why the affair I have just told you about passed completely unobserved.

HONORÉ DE BALZAC

Melmoth Reconciled [4]

To Monsieur le Général Baron de Pommereul, a token of the friendship between our fathers, which survives in their sons.

DE BALZAC.

There is a special variety of human nature obtained in the Social Kingdom by a process analogous to that of the gardener's craft in the Vegetable Kingdom, to wit, by the forcing-house — a species of hybrid which can be raised neither from seed nor from slips. This product is known as the Cashier, an anthropomorphous growth, watered by religious doctrine, trained up in fear of the guillotine, pruned by vice, to flourish on a third floor with an estimable wife by his side and an uninteresting family. The number of cashiers in Paris must always be a problem for the physiologist. Has anyone as yet been able to state correctly the terms of the proportion sum wherein the cashier figures as the unknown x? Where will you find the man who shall live with wealth, like a cat with a caged mouse? This man, for further qualification, shall be capable of sitting boxed in behind an iron grating for seven or eight hours a day during seven-eighths of the year, perched upon a cane-seated chair in a space as narrow as a lieutenant's cabin on board a man-of-war. Such a man must be able to defy anchylosis of the knee and thigh joints; he must have a soul above meanness, in order to live meanly; must lose all relish for money by dint of handling it. Demand this peculiar specimen of any creed, educational system, school, or institution you please, and select Paris, that city of fiery ordeals and branch establishment of hell, as the soil in which to plant the said cashier. So be it. Creeds, schools, institutions, and moral systems, all human rules and regulations, great and small, will, one after another, present much the same face that an intimate friend turns upon you when you ask him to lend you a thousand francs. With a dolorous dropping of the jaw, they indicate the guillotine, much as your friend aforesaid will furnish you with the address of the money lender, pointing you to one of the hundred gates by which a man comes to the last refuge of the destitute.

Yet Nature has her freaks in the making of a man's mind; she indulges herself and makes a few honest folk now and again, and now and then a cashier.

Wherefore, that race of corsairs whom we dignify with the title of bankers, the gentry who take out a license for which they pay a thousand crowns, as the privateer takes out his letters of marque, hold these rare products of the incubations of virtue in such esteem that they confine them in cages in their counting-houses, much as governments procure and maintain specimens of strange beasts at their own charges.

If the cashier is possessed of an imagination or of a fervid temperament; if, as will sometimes happen to the most complete cashier, he loves his wife, and that wife grows tired of her lot, has ambitions, or merely some vanity in her composition, the cashier is undone. Search the chronicles of the counting-house. You will not find a single instance of a cashier attaining *a position*, as it is called. They are sent to the hulks; they go to foreign parts; they vegetate on a second floor in the Rue Saint-Louis among the market gardens of the Marais. Some day, when the cashiers of Paris come to a sense of their real value, a cashier will be hardly obtainable for money. Still, certain it is that there are people who are fit for nothing but to be cashiers, just as the bent of a certain order of mind inevitably makes for rascality. But, oh marvel of our civilization! Society rewards virtue with an income of a hundred louis in old age, a dwelling on a second floor, bread sufficient, occasional new bandana handkerchiefs, an elderly wife and her offspring.

So much for virtue. But for the opposite course, a little boldness, a faculty for keeping on the windward side of the law, as Turenne outflanked Montecuculli, and Society will sanction the theft of millions, shower ribbons upon the thief, cram him with honors, and smother him with consideration.

Government, moreover, works harmoniously with this profoundly illogical reasoner — Society. Government levies a conscription on the young intelligence of the kingdom at the age of seventeen or eighteen, a conscription of precocious power. Great ability is prematurely exhausted by excessive brain work before it is sent up to be submitted to a process of selection. Nurserymen sort and select seeds in much the same way. To this process the Government brings professional appraisers of talent, men who can assay brains as experts assay gold at the Mint. Five hundred such heads, set afire with hope, are sent up annually by the most progressive portion of the population; and of these the Government takes one third, puts them in sacks called the Écoles, and shakes them up together for three years. Though every one of these young plants represents vast productive power, they are made, as one may say, into cashiers. They receive appointments; the rank and file of engineers is made up of them; they are employed as captains of artillery; there is no (subaltern) grade to which they may not aspire. Finally, when these men, the pick of the youth of the nation, fattened on mathematics and stuffed with knowledge, have attained the age of fifty years, they have their reward, and receive as the price of their services the third-floor lodging, the wife and family, and all the comforts that sweeten life for mediocrity. If from among this race of dupes there should escape some five or six men of genius who climb the highest heights, is it not miraculous?

This is an exact statement of the relations between Talent and Probity on the one hand, and Government and Society on the other, in an age that considers itself to be progressive. Without this prefatory explanation a recent occurrence in Paris would seem improbable; but preceded by this summing up of the situation, it will perhaps receive some thoughtful attention from minds capable of recognizing the real plague spots of our civilization, a civilization which since 1815 has been moved by the spirit of gain rather than by principles of honor.

*****

About five o'clock, on a dull autumn afternoon, the cashier of one of the largest banks in Paris was still at his desk, working by the light of a lamp that had been lit for some time. In accordance with the use and wont of commerce, the counting-house was in the darkest corner of the low-ceiled and far from spacious mezzanine floor, and at the very end of a passage lighted only by borrowed lights. The office doors along this corridor, each with its label, gave the place the look of a bath-house. At four o'clock the stolid porter had proclaimed, according to his orders, "The bank is closed." And by this time the departments were deserted, the letters dispatched, the clerks had taken their leave. The wives of the partners in the firm were expecting their lovers; the two bankers dining with their mistresses. Everything was in order.

The place where the strong boxes had been bedded in sheet iron was just behind the little sanctum, where the cashier was busy. Doubtless he was balancing his books. The open front gave a glimpse of a safe of hammered iron, so enormously heavy (thanks to the science of the modern inventor) that burglars could not carry it away. The door only opened at the pleasure of those who knew its password. The letter-lock was a warden who kept its own secret and could not be bribed; the mysterious word was an ingenious realization of the "Open sesame!" in the *Arabian Nights*. But even this was as nothing. A man might discover the password; but unless he knew the lock's final secret, the *ultima ratio* of this gold-guarding dragon of mechanical science, it discharged a blunderbuss at his head.

The door of the room, the walls of the room, the shutters of the windows in the room, the whole place, in fact, was lined with sheet iron a third of an inch in thickness, concealed behind the thin wooden paneling. The shutters had been closed, the door had been shut. If ever man could feel confident that he was absolutely alone, and that there was no remote possibility of being watched by prying eyes, that man was the cashier of the house of Nucingen and Company in the Rue Saint-Lazare.

Accordingly the deepest silence prevailed in that iron cave. The fire had died out in the stove, but the room was full of that tepid warmth which produces the dull heavy-headedness and nauseous queasiness of a morning after an orgy. The stove is a mesmerist that plays no small part in the reduction of bank clerks and porters to a state of idiocy.

A room with a stove in it is a retort in which the power of strong men is evaporated, where their vitality is exhausted, and their wills enfeebled. Government offices are part of a great scheme for the manufacture of the mediocrity necessary for the maintenance of a Feudal System on a pecuniary basis — and money is the foundation of the Social Contract. (See *Les Employés*.) The mephitic vapors in the atmosphere of a crowded room contribute in no small degree to bring about a gradual deterioration of intelligences, the brain that gives off the largest quantity of nitrogen asphyxiates the others, in the long run.

The cashier was a man of five and forty or thereabouts. As he sat at the table, the light from a moderator lamp shining full on his bald head and glistening fringe of iron-gray hair that surrounded it — this baldness and the round outlines of his face made his head look very like a ball. His complexion was brick-red, a few wrinkles had gathered about his eyes, but he had the smooth, plump hands of a stout man. His blue cloth coat, a little rubbed and worn, and the creases and shininess of his trousers, traces of hard wear that the clothes-brush fails to remove, would impress a superficial observer with the idea that here was a thrifty and upright human being, sufficient of the philosopher or of the aristocrat to wear shabby clothes. But, unluckily, it is easy to find penny-wise people who will prove weak, wasteful, or incompetent in the capital things of life.

The cashier wore the ribbon of the Legion of Honor at his buttonhole, for he had been a major of dragoons in the time of the Emperor. M. de Nucingen, who had been a contractor before he became a banker, had had reason in those days to know the honorable disposition of his cashier, who then occupied a high position. Reverses of fortune had befallen the major, and the banker out of regard for him paid him five hundred francs a month. The soldier had become a cashier in the year 1813, after his recovery from a wound received at Studzianka during the Retreat from Moscow, followed by six months of enforced idleness at Strasbourg, whither several officers had been transported by order of the Emperor, that they might receive skilled attention. This particular officer, Castanier by name, retired with the honorary grade of colonel, and a pension of two thousand four hundred francs.

In ten years' time the cashier had completely effaced the soldier, and Castanier inspired the banker with such trust in him, that he was associated in the transactions that went on in the private office behind his little counting-house. The baron himself had access to it by means of a secret staircase. There, matters of business were decided. It was the bolting room where proposals were sifted; the privy council chamber where the reports of the money market were analyzed; circular notes issued thence; and finally, the private ledger and the journal which summarized the work of all the departments were kept there.

Castanier had gone himself to shut the door which opened on to a staircase that led to the parlor occupied by the two bankers on the first floor of their hotel. This done, he had sat down at his desk again, and for a moment he gazed at a little collection of letters of credit drawn on the firm of Watschildine of London. Then he had taken up the pen and imitated the banker's signature upon each. *Nucingen* he wrote, and eyed the forged signatures critically to see which seemed the most perfect copy.

Suddenly he looked up as if a needle had pricked him. "You are not alone!" a boding voice seemed to cry in his heart; and indeed the forger saw a man standing at the little grated window of the counting-house, a man whose breathing was so noiseless that he did not seem to breathe at all. Castanier looked, and saw that the door at the end of the passage was wide open; the stranger must have entered by that way.

For the first time in his life the old soldier felt a sensation of dread that made him stare open-mouthed and wide-eyed at the man before him; and for that matter, the appearance of the apparition was sufficiently alarming even if unaccompanied by the mysterious circumstances of so sudden an entry. The rounded forehead, the harsh coloring of the long oval face, indicated quite as plainly as the cut of his clothes that the man was an Englishman, reeking of his native isles. You had only to look at the collar of his overcoat, at the voluminous cravat which smothered the crushed frills of a shirt front so white that it brought out the changeless leaden hue of an impassive face, and the thin red line of the lips that seemed made to suck the blood of corpses; and you could guess at once at the black gaiters buttoned up to the knee, and the half-puritanical costume of a wealthy Englishman dressed for a walking excursion. The intolerable glitter of the stranger's eyes produced a vivid and unpleasant impression, which was only deepened by the rigid outlines of his features. The dried-up, emaciated creature seemed to carry within him some gnawing thought that consumed him and could not be appeased.

He must have digested his food so rapidly that he could doubtless eat continually without bringing any trace of color into his face or features. A tun of Tokay *vin de succession* would not have caused any faltering in that piercing glance that read men's inmost thoughts, nor dethroned the merciless reasoning faculty that always seemed to go to the bottom of things. There was something of the fell and tranquil majesty of a tiger about him.

"I have come to cash this bill of exchange, sir," he said. Castanier felt the tones of his voice thrill through every nerve with a violent shock similar to that given by a discharge of electricity.

"The safe is closed," said Castanier.

"It is open," said the Englishman, looking round the counting-house. "To-morrow is Sunday, and I cannot wait. The amount is for five hundred thousand francs. You have the money there, and I must have it."

"But how did you come in, sir?"

The Englishman smiled. That smile frightened Castanier. No words could have replied more fully nor more peremptorily than that scornful and imperial curl of the stranger's lips. Castanier turned away, took up fifty packets, each containing ten thousand francs in bank notes, and held them out to the stranger, receiving in exchange for them a bill accepted by the Baron de Nucingen. A sort of convulsive tremor ran through him as he saw a red gleam in the stranger's eyes when they fell on the forged signature on the letter of credit.

"It ... it wants your signature ..." stammered Castanier, handing back the bill.

"Hand me your pen," answered the Englishman.

Castanier handed him the pen with which he had just committed forgery. The stranger wrote *John Melmoth*, then he returned the slip of paper and the pen to the cashier. Castanier looked at the handwriting, noticing that it sloped from right to left in the Eastern fashion, and Melmoth disappeared so noiselessly that when Castanier looked up again an exclamation broke from him, partly because the man was no longer there, partly because he felt a strange painful sensation such as our imagination might take for an effect of poison.

The pen that Melmoth had handled sent the same sickening heat through him that an emetic produces. But it seemed impossible to Castanier that the Englishman should have guessed his crime. His inward qualms he attributed to the palpitation of the heart that, according to received ideas, was sure to follow at once on such a "turn" as the stranger had given him.

"The devil take it; I am very stupid. Providence is watching over me; for if that brute had come round to see my gentlemen tomorrow, my goose would have been cooked!" said Castanier, and he burned the unsuccessful attempts at forgery in the stove.

He put the bill that he meant to take with him in an envelope, and helped himself to five hundred thousand francs in French and English bank notes from the safe, which he locked. Then he put everything in order, lit a candle, blew out the lamp, took up his hat and umbrella, and went out sedately, as usual, to leave one of the two keys of the strong room with Madame de Nucingen, in the absence of her husband the baron.

"You are in luck, M. Castanier," said the banker's wife as he entered her room; "we have a holiday on Monday; you can go into the country, or to Soizy."

"Madame, will you be so good as to tell your husband that the bill of exchange on Watschildine, which was behind time, has just been presented? The five hundred thousand francs have been paid; so I shall not come back till noon on Tuesday."

"Good-by, monsieur; I hope you will have a pleasant time."

"The same to you, madame," replied the old dragoon as he went out. He glanced as he spoke at a young man well known in fashionable society at that time, a M. de Rastignac, who was regarded as Madame de Nucingen's lover.

"Madame," remarked this latter, "the old boy looks to me as if he meant to play you some ill turn."

"Pshaw! impossible; he is too stupid."

"Piquoizeau," said the cashier, walking into the porter's room, "what made you let anybody come up after four o'clock?"

"I have been smoking a pipe here in the doorway ever since four o'clock," said the man, "and nobody has gone into the bank. Nobody has come out either except the gentlemen — "

"Are you quite sure?"

"Yes, upon my word and honor. Stay, though, at four o'clock M. Werbrust's friend came, a young fellow from Messrs. du Tillet & Co., in the Rue Joubert."

"All right," said Castanier, and he hurried away.

The sickening sensation of heat that he had felt when he took back the pen returned in greater intensity. *Mille diables!* thought he, as he threaded his way along the Boulevard de Gand, "haven't I taken proper precautions? Let me think! Two clear days, Sunday and Monday, then a day of uncertainty before they begin to look for me; altogether, three days and four nights' respite. I have a couple of passports and two different disguises; is not that enough to throw the cleverest detective off the scent? On Tuesday morning I shall draw a million francs in London before the slightest suspicion has been aroused. My debts I am leaving behind for the benefit of my creditors, who will put a 'P' [5] on the bills, and I shall live comfortably in Italy for the rest of my days as the Conte Ferraro. I was alone with him when he died, poor fellow, in the marsh of Zembin, and I shall slip into his skin.... *Mille diables!* the woman who is to follow after me might give them a clew! Think of an old campaigner like me infatuated enough to tie myself to a petticoat tail!... Why take her? I must leave her behind. Yes, I could make up my mind to it; but — I know myself — I should be ass enough to go back for her. Still, nobody knows Aquilina. Shall I take her or leave her?"

"You will not take her!" cried a voice that filled Castanier with sickening dread. He turned sharply, and saw the Englishman.

"The devil is in it!" cried the cashier aloud.

Melmoth had passed his victim by this time; and if Castanier's first impulse had been to fasten a quarrel on a man who read his own thoughts, he was so much torn by opposing feelings that the immediate result was a temporary paralysis. When he resumed his walk he fell once more into that fever of irresolution which besets those who are so carried away by passion that they are ready to commit a crime, but have not sufficient strength of character to keep it to themselves without suffering terribly in the process. So, although Castanier had made up his mind to reap the fruits of a crime which was already half executed, he hesitated to carry out his designs. For him, as for many men of mixed character in whom weakness and strength are equally blended, the least trifling consideration determines whether they shall continue to lead blameless lives or become actively criminal. In the vast masses of men enrolled in Napoleon's armies there were many who, like Castanier, possessed the purely physical courage demanded on the battlefield, yet lacked the moral courage which makes a man as great in crime as he could have been in virtue.

The letter of credit was drafted in such terms that immediately on his arrival he might draw twenty-five thousand pounds on the firm of Watschildine, the London correspondents of the house of Nucingen. The London house had been already advised of the draft about to be made upon them; he had written to them himself. He had instructed an agent (chosen at random) to take his passage in a vessel which was to leave Portsmouth with a wealthy English family on board, who were going to Italy, and the passage money had been paid in the name of the Conte Ferraro. The smallest details of the scheme had been thought out. He had arranged matters so as to divert the search that would be made for him into Belgium and Switzerland, while he himself was at sea in the English vessel. Then, by the time that Nucingen might flatter himself that he was on the track of his late cashier, the said cashier, as the Conte Ferraro, hoped to be safe in Naples. He had determined to disfigure his face in order to disguise himself the more completely, and by means of an acid to imitate the scars of smallpox. Yet, in spite of all these precautions, which surely seemed as if they must secure him complete immunity, his conscience tormented him; he was afraid. The even and peaceful life that he had led for so long had modified the morality of the camp. His life was stainless as yet; he could not sully it without a pang. So for the last time he abandoned himself to all the influences of the better self that strenuously resisted.

"Pshaw!" he said at last, at the corner of the Boulevard and the Rue Montmartre, "I will take a cab after the play this evening and go out to Versailles. A post-chaise will be ready for me at my old quartermaster's place. He would keep my secret even if a dozen men were standing ready to shoot him down. The chances are all in my favor, so far as I see; so I shall take my little Naqui with me, and I will go."

"You will not go!" exclaimed the Englishman, and the strange tones of his voice drove all the cashier's blood back to his heart.

Melmoth stepped into a tilbury which was waiting for him, and was whirled away so quickly, that when Castanier looked up he saw his foe some hundred paces away from him, and before it even crossed his mind to cut off the man's retreat the tilbury was far on its way up the Boulevard Montmartre.

"Well, upon my word, there is something supernatural about this!" said he to himself. "If I were fool enough to believe in God, I should think that He had set Saint Michael on my tracks. Suppose that the devil and the police should let me go on as I please, so as to nab me in the nick of time? Did anyone ever see the like! But there, this is folly...."

Castanier went along the Rue du Faubourg-Montmartre, slackening his pace as he neared the Rue Richer. There, on the second floor of a block of buildings which looked out upon some gardens, lived the unconscious cause of Castanier's crime — a young woman known in the quarter as Mme. de la Garde. A concise history of certain events in the cashier's past life must be given in order to explain these facts, and to give a complete presentment of the crisis when he yielded to temptation.

Mme. de la Garde said that she was a Piedmontese. No one, not even Castanier, knew her real name. She was one of those young girls who are driven by dire misery, by inability to earn a living, or by fear of starvation, to have recourse to a trade which most of them loathe, many regard with indifference, and some few follow in obedience to the laws of their constitution. But on the brink of the gulf of prostitution in Paris, the young girl of sixteen, beautiful and pure as the Madonna, had met with Castanier. The old dragoon was too rough and homely to make his way in society, and he was tired of tramping the boulevard at night and of the kind of conquests made there by gold. For some time past he had desired to bring a certain regularity into an irregular life. He was struck by the beauty of the poor child who had drifted by chance into his arms, and his determination to rescue her from the life of the streets was half benevolent, half selfish, as some of the thoughts of the best of men are apt to be. Social conditions mingle elements of evil with the promptings of natural goodness of heart, and the mixture of motives underlying a man's intentions should be leniently judged. Castanier had just cleverness enough to be very shrewd where his own interests were concerned. So he concluded to be a philanthropist on either count, and at first made her his mistress.

"Hey! hey!" he said to himself, in his soldierly fashion, "I am an old wolf, and a sheep shall not make a fool of me. Castanier, old man, before you set up housekeeping, reconnoiter the girl's character for a bit, and see if she is a steady sort."

This irregular union gave the Piedmontese a status the most nearly approaching respectability among those which the world declines to recognize. During the first year she took the *nom de guerre* of Aquilina, one of the characters in *Venice Preserved* which she had chanced to read. She fancied that she resembled the courtesan in face and general appearance, and in a certain precocity of heart and brain of which she was conscious. When Castanier found that her life was as well regulated and virtuous as was possible for a social outlaw, he manifested a desire that they should live as husband and wife. So she took the name of Mme. de la Garde, in order to approach, as closely as Parisian usages permit, the conditions of a real marriage. As a matter of fact, many of these unfortunate girls have one fixed idea, to be looked upon as respectable middle-class women, who lead humdrum lives of faithfulness to their husbands; women who would make excellent mothers, keepers of household accounts, and menders of household linen. This longing springs from a sentiment so laudable that society should take it into consideration. But society, incorrigible as ever, will assuredly persist in regarding the married woman as a corvette duly authorized by her flag and papers to go on her own course, while the woman who is a wife in all but name is a pirate and an outlaw for lack of a document. A day came when Mme. de la Garde would fain have signed herself "Mme. Castanier." The cashier was put out by this.

"So you do not love me well enough to marry me?" she said.

Castanier did not answer; he was absorbed by his thoughts. The poor girl resigned herself to her fate. The ex-dragoon was in despair. Naqui's heart softened toward him at the sight of his trouble; she tried to soothe him, but what could she do when she did not know what ailed him? When Naqui made up her mind to know the secret, although she never asked him a question, the cashier dolefully confessed to the existence of a Mme. Castanier. This lawful wife, a thousand times accursed, was living in a humble way in Strasbourg on a small property there; he wrote to her twice a year, and kept the secret of her existence so well, that no one suspected that he was married. The reason of this reticence? If it is familiar to many military men who may chance to be in a like predicament, it is perhaps worth while to give the story.

Your genuine trooper (if it is allowable here to employ the word which in the army signifies a man who is destined to die as a captain) is a sort of serf, a part and parcel of his regiment, an essentially simple creature, and Castanier was marked out by nature as a victim to the wiles of mothers with grown-up daughters left too long on their hands. It was at Nancy, during one of those brief intervals of repose when the Imperial armies were not on active service abroad, that Castanier was so unlucky as to pay some attention to a young lady with whom he danced at a *ridotto*, the provincial name for the entertainments often given by the military to the townsfolk, or *vice versâ*, in garrison towns. A scheme for inveigling the gallant captain into matrimony was immediately set on foot, one of those schemes by which mothers secure accomplices in a human heart by touching all its motive springs, while they convert all their friends into fellow-conspirators. Like all people possessed by one idea, these ladies press everything into the service of their great project, slowly elaborating their toils, much as the ant-lion excavates its funnel in the sand and lies in wait at the bottom for its victim. Suppose that no one strays, after all, into that carefully constructed labyrinth? Suppose that the ant-lion dies of hunger and thirst in her pit? Such things may be, but if any heedless creature once enters in, it never comes out. All the wires which could be pulled to induce action on the captain's part were tried; appeals were made to the secret interested motives that always come into play in such cases; they worked on Castanier's hopes and on the weaknesses and vanity of human nature. Unluckily, he had praised the daughter to her mother when he brought her back after a waltz, a little chat followed, and then an invitation in the most natural way in the world. Once introduced into the house, the dragoon was dazzled by the hospitality of a family who appeared to conceal their real wealth beneath a show of careful economy. He was skillfully flattered on all sides, and everyone extolled for his benefit the various treasures there displayed. A neatly timed dinner, served on plate lent by an uncle, the attention shown to him by the only daughter of the house, the gossip of the town, a well-to-do sub-lieutenant who seemed likely to cut the ground from under his feet — all the innumerable snares, in short, of the provincial ant-lion were set for him, and to such good purpose, that Castanier said five years later, "To this day I do not know how it came about!"

The dragoon received fifteen thousand francs with the lady, who, after two years of marriage, became the ugliest and consequently the most peevish woman on earth. Luckily they had no children. The fair complexion (maintained by a Spartan regimen), the fresh, bright color in her face, which spoke of an engaging modesty, became overspread with blotches and pimples; her figure, which had seemed so straight, grew crooked, the angel became a suspicious and shrewish creature who drove Castanier frantic. Then the fortune took to itself wings. At length the dragoon, no longer recognizing the woman whom he had wedded, left her to live on a little property at Strasbourg, until the time when it should please God to remove her to adorn Paradise. She was one of those virtuous women who, for want of other occupation, would weary the life out of an angel with complainings, who pray till (if their prayers are heard in heaven) they must exhaust the patience of the Almighty, and say everything that is bad of their husbands in dove-like murmurs over a game of boston with their neighbors. When Aquilina learned all these troubles she clung still more affectionately to Castanier, and made him so happy, varying with woman's ingenuity the pleasures with which she filled his life, that all unwittingly she was the cause of the cashier's downfall.

Like many women who seem by nature destined to sound all the depths of love, Mme. de la Garde was disinterested. She asked neither for gold nor for jewelry, gave no thought to the future, lived entirely for the present and for the pleasures of the present. She accepted expensive ornaments and dresses, the carriage so eagerly coveted by women of her class, as one harmony the more in the picture of life. There was absolutely no vanity in her desire not to appear at a better advantage but to look the fairer, and, moreover, no woman could live without luxuries more cheerfully. When a man of generous nature (and military men are mostly of this stamp) meets with such a woman, he feels a sort of exasperation at finding himself her debtor in generosity. He feels that he could stop a mail coach to obtain money for her if he has not sufficient for her whims. He will commit a crime if so he may be great and noble in the eyes of some woman or of his special public; such is the nature of the man. Such a lover is like a gambler who would be dishonored in his own eyes if he did not repay the sum he borrowed from a waiter in a gaming house; but will shrink from no crime, will leave his wife and children without a penny, and rob and murder, if so he may come to the gaming table with a full purse, and his honor remain untarnished among the frequenters of that fatal abode. So it was with Castanier.

He had begun by installing Aquilina in a modest fourth-floor dwelling, the furniture being of the simplest kind. But when he saw the girl's beauty and great qualities, when he had known inexpressible and unlooked-for happiness with her, he began to dote upon her, and longed to adorn his idol. Then Aquilina's toilet was so comically out of keeping with her poor abode, that for both their sakes it was clearly incumbent on him to move. The change swallowed up almost all Castanier's savings, for he furnished his domestic paradise with all the prodigality that is lavished on a kept mistress. A pretty woman must have everything pretty about her; the unity of charm in the woman and her surroundings singles her out from among her sex. This sentiment of homogeneity indeed, though it has frequently escaped the attention of observers, is instinctive in human nature; and the same prompting leads elderly spinsters to surround themselves with dreary relies of the past. But the lovely Piedmontese must have the newest and latest fashions, and all that was daintiest and prettiest in stuffs for hangings, in silks or jewelry, in fine china and other brittle and fragile wares. She asked for nothing; but when she was called upon to make a choice, when Castanier asked her, "Which do you like?" she would answer, "Why, this is the nicest!" Love never counts the cost, and Castanier therefore always took the "nicest."

When once the standard had been set up, there was nothing for it but everything in the household must be in conformity, from the linen, plate, and crystal through a thousand and one items of expenditure down to the pots and pans in the kitchen. Castanier had meant to "do things simply," as the saying goes, but he gradually found himself more and more in debt. One expense entailed another. The clock called for candle sconces. Fires must be lighted in the ornamental grates, but the curtains and hangings were too fresh and delicate to be soiled by smuts, so they must be replaced by patent and elaborate fireplaces, warranted to give out no smoke, recent inventions of the people who are clever at drawing up a prospectus. Then Aquilina found it so nice to run about barefooted on the carpet in her room that Castanier must have soft carpets laid everywhere for the pleasure of playing with Naqui. A bathroom, too, was built for her, everything to the end that she might be more comfortable.

Shopkeepers, workmen, and manufacturers in Paris have a mysterious knack of enlarging a hole in a man's purse. They cannot give the price of anything upon inquiry; and as the paroxysm of longing cannot abide delay, orders are given by the feeble light of an approximate estimate of cost. The same people never send in the bills at once, but ply the purchaser with furniture till his head spins. Everything is so pretty, so charming; and everyone is satisfied.

A few months later the obliging furniture dealers are metamorphosed, and reappear in the shape of alarming totals on invoices that fill the soul with their horrid clamor; they are in urgent want of the money; they are, as you may say, on the brink of bankruptcy, their tears flow, it is heartrending to hear them! And then — the gulf yawns and gives up serried columns of figures marching four deep; when as a matter of fact they should have issued innocently three by three.

Before Castanier had any idea of how much he had spent, he had arranged for Aquilina to have a carriage from a livery stable when she went out, instead of a cab. Castanier was a gourmand; he engaged an excellent cook; and Aquilina, to please him, had herself made the purchases of early fruit and vegetables, rare delicacies, and exquisite wines. But, as Aquilina had nothing of her own, these gifts of hers, so precious by reason of the thought and tact and graciousness that prompted them, were no less a drain upon Castanier's purse; he did not like his Naqui to be without money, and Naqui could not keep money in her pocket. So the table was a heavy item of expenditure for a man with Castanier's income. The ex-dragoon was compelled to resort to various shifts for obtaining money, for he could not bring himself to renounce this delightful life. He loved the woman too well to cross the freaks of the mistress. He was one of those men who, through self-love or through weakness of character, can refuse nothing to a woman; false shame overpowers them, and they rather face ruin than make the admissions: "I cannot — " "My means will not permit — " "I cannot afford — "

When, therefore, Castanier saw that if he meant to emerge from the abyss of debt into which he had plunged, he must part with Aquilina and live upon bread and water, he was so unable to do without her or to change his habits of life, that daily he put off his plans of reform until the morrow. The debts were pressing, and he began by borrowing money. His position and previous character inspired confidence, and of this he took advantage to devise a system of borrowing money as he required it. Then, as the total amount of debt rapidly increased, he had recourse to those commercial inventions known as *accommodation bills*. This form of bill does not represent goods or other value received, and the first indorser pays the amount named for the obliging person who accepts it. This species of fraud is tolerated because it is impossible to detect it, and, moreover, it is an imaginary fraud which only becomes real if payment is ultimately refused.

When at length it was evidently impossible to borrow any longer, whether because the amount of the debt was now so greatly increased, or because Castanier was unable to pay the large amount of interest on the aforesaid sums of money, the cashier saw bankruptcy before him. On making this discovery, he decided for a fraudulent bankruptcy rather than an ordinary failure, and preferred a crime to a misdemeanor. He determined, after the fashion of the celebrated cashier of the Royal Treasury, to abuse the trust deservedly won, and to increase the number of his creditors by making a final loan of the sum sufficient to keep him in comfort in a foreign country for the rest of his days. All this, as has been seen, he had prepared to do.

Aquilina knew nothing of the irksome cares of this life; she enjoyed her existence, as many a woman does, making no inquiry as to where the money came from, even as sundry other folk will eat their buttered rolls untroubled by any restless spirit of curiosity as to the culture and growth of wheat; but as the labor and miscalculations of agriculture lie on the other side of the baker's oven, so, beneath the unappreciated luxury of many a Parisian household lie intolerable anxieties and exorbitant toil.

While Castanier was enduring the torture of the strain, and his thoughts were full of the deed that should change his whole life, Aquilina was lying luxuriously back in a great armchair by the fireside, beguiling the time by chatting with her waiting-maid. As frequently happens in such cases, the maid had become the mistress's confidante, Jenny having first assured herself that her mistress's ascendancy over Castanier was complete.

What are we to do this evening? Léon seems determined to come," Mme. de la Garde was saying, as she read a passionate epistle indicted upon a faint gray note paper.

"Here is the master!" said Jenny.

Castanier came in. Aquilina, nowise disconcerted, crumpled up the letter, took it with the tongs, and held it in the flames.

"So that is what you do with your love letters, is it?" asked Castanier.

"Oh, goodness, yes," said Aquilina; "is it not the best way of keeping them safe? Besides, fire should go to the fire, as water makes for the river."

"You are talking as if it were a real love letter, Naqui — "

"Well, am I not handsome enough to receive them?" she said, holding up her forehead for a kiss. There was a carelessness in her manner that would have told any man less blind than Castanier that it was only a piece of conjugal duty, as it were, to give this joy to the cashier; but use and wont had brought Castanier to the point where clear-sightedness is no longer possible for love.

"I have taken a box at the Gymnase this evening," he said; "let us have dinner early, and then we need not dine in a hurry."

"Go and take Jenny. I am tired of plays. I do not know what is the matter with me this evening; I would rather stay here by the fire."

"Come, all the same though, Naqui; I shall not be here to bore you much longer. Yes, Quiqui, I am going to start to-night, and it will be some time before I come back again. I am leaving everything in your charge. Will you keep your heart for me too?"

"Neither my heart nor anything else," she said; "but when you come back again, Naqui will still be Naqui for you."

"Well, this is frankness. So you would not follow me?"

"No."

"Why not?"

"Eh! why, how can I leave the lover who writes me such sweet little notes?" she asked, pointing to the blackened scrap of paper with a mocking smile.

"Is there any truth in it?" asked Castanier. "Have you really a lover?"

"Really!" cried Aquilina; "and have you never given it a serious thought, dear? To begin with, you are fifty years old. Then you have just the sort of face to put on a fruit stall; if the woman tried to sell you for a pumpkin, no one would contradict her. You puff and blow like a seal when you come upstairs; your paunch rises and falls like the diamond on a woman's forehead! It is pretty plain that you served in the dragoons; you are a very ugly-looking old man. Fiddle-de-dee. If you have any mind to keep my respect, I recommend you not to add imbecility to these qualities by imagining that such a girl as I am will be content with your asthmatic love, and not look for youth and good looks and pleasure by way of variety — "

"Aquilina! you are laughing, of course?"

"Oh, very well; and are you not laughing too? Do you take me for a fool, telling me that you are going away? 'I am going to start to-night!'" she said, mimicking his tones. "Stuff and nonsense! Would you talk like that if you were really going away from your Naqui? You would cry, like the booby that you are!"

"After all, if I go, will you follow?" he asked.

"Tell me first whether this journey of yours is a bad joke or not."

"Yes, seriously, I am going."

"Well, then, seriously, I shall stay. A pleasant journey to you, my boy! I will wait till you come back. I would sooner take leave of life than take leave of my dear, cozy Paris — "

"Will you not come to Italy, to Naples, and lead a pleasant life there — a delicious, luxurious life, with this stout old fogey of yours, who puffs and blows like a seal?"

"No."

"Ungrateful girl!"

"Ungrateful?" she cried, rising to her feet. "I might leave this house this moment and take nothing out of it but myself. I shall have given you all the treasures a young girl can give, and something that not every drop in your veins and mine can ever give me back. If, by any means whatever, by selling my hopes of eternity, for instance, I could recover my past self, body as soul (for I have, perhaps, redeemed my soul), and be pure as a lily for my lover I would not hesitate a moment! What sort of devotion has rewarded mine? You have housed and fed me, just as you give a dog food and a kennel because he is a protection to the house, and he may take kicks when we are out of humor, and lick our hands as soon as we are pleased to call to him. And which of us two will have been the more generous?"

"Oh! dear child, do you not see that I am joking?" returned Castanier. "I am going on a short journey; I shall not be away for very long. But come with me to the Gymnase; I shall start just before midnight, after I have had time to say good-by to you."

"Poor pet! so you are really going, are you?" she said. She put her arms round his neck, and drew down his head against her bodice.

"You are smothering me!" cried Castanier, with his face buried in Aquilina's breast. That damsel turned to say in Jenny's ear, "Go to Léon, and tell him not to come till one o'clock. If you do not find him, and he comes here during the leave-taking, keep him in your room. — Well," she went on, setting free Castanier, and giving a tweak to the tip of his nose, "never mind, handsomest of seals that you are. I will go to the theater with you this evening. But all in good time; let us have dinner! There is a nice little dinner for you — just what you like."

"It is very hard to part from such a woman as you!" exclaimed Castanier.

"Very well then, why do you go?" asked she.

"Ah! why? why? If I were to begin to explain the reasons why, I must tell you things that would prove to you that I love you almost to madness. Ah! if you have sacrificed your honor for me, I have sold mine for you; we are quits. Is that love?"

"What is all this about?" said she. "Come, now, promise me that if I had a lover you would still love me as a father; that would be love! Come, now, promise it at once, and give us your fist upon it."

"I should kill you," and Castanier smiled as he spoke.

They sat down to the dinner table, and went thence to the Gymnase. When the first part of the performance was over, it occurred to Castanier to show himself to some of his acquaintances in the house, so as to turn away any suspicion of his departure. He left Mme. de la Garde in the corner box where she was seated, according to her modest wont, and went to walk up and down in the lobby. He had not gone many paces before he saw the Englishman, and with a sudden return of the sickening sensation of heat that once before had vibrated through him, and of the terror that he had felt already, he stood face to face with Melmoth.

"Forger!"

At the word, Castanier glanced round at the people who were moving about them. He fancied that he could see astonishment and curiosity in their eyes, and wishing to be rid of this Englishman at once, he raised his hand to strike him — and felt his arm paralyzed by some invisible power that sapped his strength and nailed him to the spot. He allowed the stranger to take him by the arm, and they walked together to the greenroom like two friends.

"Who is strong enough to resist me?" said the Englishman, addressing him. "Do you not know that everything here on earth must obey me, that it is in my power to do everything? I read men's thoughts, I see the future, and I know the past. I am here, and I can be elsewhere also. Time and space and distance are nothing to me. The whole world is at my beck and call. I have the power of continual enjoyment and of giving joy. I can see through walls, discover hidden treasures, and fill my hands with them. Palaces arise at my nod, and my architect makes no mistakes. I can make all lands break forth into blossom, heap up their gold and precious stones, and surround myself with fair women and ever new faces; everything is yielded up to my will. I could gamble on the Stock Exchange, and my speculations would be infallible; but a man who can find the hoards that misers have hidden in the earth need not trouble himself about stocks. Feel the strength of the hand that grasps you; poor wretch, doomed to shame! Try to bend the arm of iron! try to soften the adamantine heart! Fly from me if you dare! You would hear my voice in the depths of the caves that lie under the Seine; you might hide in the Catacombs, but would you not see me there? My voice could be heard through the sound of the thunder, my eyes shine as brightly as the sun, for I am the peer of Lucifer!"

Castanier heard the terrible words, and felt no protest nor contradiction within himself. He walked side by side with the Englishman, and had no power to leave him.

"You are mine; you have just committed a crime. I have found at last the mate whom I have sought. Have you a mind to learn your destiny? Aha! you came here to see a play, and you shall see a play — nay, two. Come. Present me to Mme. de la Garde as one of your best friends. Am I not your last hope of escape?"

Castanier, followed by the stranger, returned to his box; and in accordance with the order he had just received, he hastened to introduce Melmoth to Mme. de la Garde. Aquilina seemed to be not in the least surprised. The Englishman declined to take a seat in front, and Castanier was once more beside his mistress; the man's slightest wish must be obeyed. The last piece was about to begin, for, at that time, small theaters only gave three pieces. One of the actors had made the Gymnase the fashion, and that evening Perlet (the actor in question) was to play in a vaudeville called *Le Comédien d'Étampes*, in which he filled four different parts.

When the curtain rose, the stranger stretched out his hand over the crowded house. Castanier's cry of terror died away, for the walls of his throat seemed glued together as Melmoth pointed to the stage, and the cashier knew that the play had been changed at the Englishman's desire.

He saw the strong room at the bank; he saw the Baron de Nucingen in conference with a police officer from the prefecture, who was informing him of Castanier's conduct, explaining that the cashier had absconded with money taken from the safe, giving the history of the forged signature. The information was put in writing; the document signed and duly dispatched to the public prosecutor.

"Are we in time, do you think?" asked Nucingen.

"Yes," said the agent of police; "he is at the Gymnase, and has no suspicion of anything."

Castanier fidgeted on his chair, and made as if he would leave the theater, but Melmoth's hand lay on his shoulder, and he was obliged to sit and watch; the hideous power of the man produced an effect like that of nightmare, and he could not move a limb. Nay, the man himself was the nightmare; his presence weighed heavily on his victim like a poisoned atmosphere. When the wretched cashier turned to implore the Englishman's mercy, he met those blazing eyes that discharged electric currents, which pierced through him and transfixed him like darts of steel.

"What have I done to you?" he said, in his prostrate helplessness, and he breathed hard like a stag at the water's edge. "What do you want of me?"

"Look!" cried Melmoth.

Castanier looked at the stage. The scene had been changed. The play seemed to be over, and Castanier beheld himself stepping from the carriage with Aquilina; but as he entered the courtyard of the house in the Rue Richer, the scene again was suddenly changed, and he saw his own house. Jenny was chatting by the fire in her mistress's room with a subaltern officer of a line regiment then stationed at Paris.

"He is going, is he?" said the sergeant, who seemed to belong to a family in easy circumstances; "I can be happy at my ease! I love Aquilina too well to allow her to belong to that old toad! I, myself, am going to marry Mme. de la Garde!" cried the sergeant.

"Old toad!" Castanier murmured piteously.

"Here come the master and mistress; hide yourself! Stay, get in here, Monsieur Léon," said Jenny. "The master won't stay here for very long."

Castanier watched the sergeant hide himself among Aquilina's gowns in her dressing room. Almost immediately he himself appeared upon the scene, and took leave of his mistress, who made fun of him in "asides" to Jenny, while she uttered the sweetest and tenderest words in his ears. She wept with one side of her face, and laughed with the other. The audience called for an encore.

"Accursed creature!" cried Castanier from his box.

Aquilina was laughing till the tears came into her eyes.

"Goodness!" she cried, "how funny Perlet is as the English-woman!... Why don't you laugh? Everyone else in the house is laughing. Laugh, dear!" she said to Castanier.

Melmoth burst out laughing, and the unhappy cashier shuddered. The Englishman's laughter wrung his heart and tortured his brain; it was as if a surgeon had bored his skull with a red-hot iron.

"Laughing! are they laughing?" stammered Castanier.

He did not see the prim English lady whom Perlet was acting with such ludicrous effect, nor hear the English-French that had filled the house with roars of laughter; instead of all this, he beheld himself hurrying from the Rue Richer, hailing a cab on the Boulevard, bargaining with the man to take him to Versailles. Then once more the scene changed. He recognized the sorry inn at the corner of the Rue de l'Orangerie and the Rue des Récollets, which was kept by his old quartermaster. It was two o'clock in the morning, the most perfect stillness prevailed, no one was there to watch his movements. The post-horses were put into the carriage (it came from a house in the Avenue de Paris in which an Englishman lived, and had been ordered in the foreigner's name to avoid raising suspicion). Castanier saw that he had his bills and his passports, stepped into the carriage, and set out. But at the barrier he saw two gendarmes lying in wait for the carriage. A cry of horror burst from him, but Melmoth gave him a glance, and again the sound died in his throat.

"Keep your eyes on the stage, and be quiet!" said the Englishman.

In another moment Castanier saw himself flung into prison at the Conciergerie; and in the fifth act of the drama, entitled *The Cashier*, he saw himself, in three months' time, condemned to twenty years of penal servitude. Again a cry broke from him. He was exposed upon the Place du Palais-de-Justice, and the executioner branded him with a red-hot iron. Then came the last scene

147

of all; among some sixty convicts in the prison yard of the Bicêtre, he was awaiting his turn to have the irons riveted on his limbs.

"Dear me! I cannot laugh any more!..." said Aquilina. "You are very solemn, dear boy; what can be the matter? The gentleman has gone."

"A word with you, Castanier," said Melmoth when the piece was at an end, and the attendant was fastening Mme. de la Garde's cloak.

The corridor was crowded, and escape impossible.

"Very well, what is it?"

"No human power can hinder you from taking Aquilina home, and going next to Versailles, there to be arrested."

"How so?"

"Because you are in a hand that will never relax its grasp," returned the Englishman.

Castanier longed for the power to utter some word that should blot him out from among living men and hide him in the lowest depths of hell.

"Suppose that the devil were to make a bid for your soul, would you not give it to him now in exchange for the power of God? One single word, and those five hundred thousand francs shall be back in the Baron de Nucingen's safe; then you can tear up your letter of credit, and all traces of your crime will be obliterated. Moreover, you would have gold in torrents. You hardly believe in anything perhaps? Well, if all this comes to pass, you will believe at least in the devil."

"If it were only possible!" said Castanier joyfully.

"The man who can do it all gives you his word that it is possible," answered the Englishman.

Melmoth, Castanier, and Mme. de la Garde were standing out in the Boulevard when Melmoth raised his arm. A drizzling rain was falling, the streets were muddy, the air was close, there was thick darkness overhead; but in a moment, as the arm was outstretched, Paris was filled with sunlight; it was high noon on a bright July day. The trees were covered with leaves; a double stream of joyous holiday makers strolled beneath them. Sellers of licorice water shouted their cool drinks. Splendid carriages rolled past along the streets. A cry of terror broke from the cashier, and at that cry rain and darkness once more settled down upon the Boulevard.

Mme. de la Garde had stepped into the carriage. "Do be quick, dear!" she cried; "either come in or stay out. Really, you are as dull as ditch-water this evening — "

"What must I do?" Castanier asked of Melmoth.

"Would you like to take my place?" inquired the Englishman.

"Yes."

"Very well, then; I will be at your house in a few moments."

"By the bye, Castanier, you are rather off your balance," Aquilina remarked. "There is some mischief brewing; you were quite melancholy and thoughtful all through the play. Do you want anything that I can give you, dear? Tell me."

"I am waiting till we are at home to know whether you love me."

"You need not wait till then," she said, throwing her arms round his neck. "There!" she said, as she embraced him, passionately to all appearance, and plied him with the coaxing caresses that are part of the business of such a life as hers, like stage action for an actress.

"Where is the music?" asked Castanier.

"What next? Only think of your hearing music now!"

"Heavenly music!" he went on. "The sounds seem to come from above."

"What? You have always refused to give me a box at the Italiens because you could not abide music, and are you turning music-mad at this time of day? Mad — that you are! The music is inside your own noddle, old addle-pate!" she went on, as she took his head in her hands and rocked it to and fro on her shoulder. "Tell me now, old man; isn't it the creaking of the wheels that sings in your ears?"

"Just listen, Naqui! If the angels make music for God Almighty, it must be such music as this that I am drinking in at every pore, rather than hearing. I do not know how to tell you about it; it is as sweet as honey water!"

"Why, of course, they have music in heaven, for the angels in all the pictures have harps in their hands. He is mad, upon my word!" she said to herself, as she saw Castanier's attitude; he looked like an opium eater in a blissful trance.

They reached the house. Castanier, absorbed by the thought of all that he had just heard and seen, knew not whether to believe it or no; he was like a drunken man, and utterly unable to think connectedly. He came to himself in Aquilina's room, whither he had been supported by the united efforts of his mistress, the porter, and Jenny; for he had fainted as he stepped from the carriage.

"*He* will be here directly! Oh, my friends, my friends!" he cried, and he flung himself despairingly into the depths of a low chair beside the fire.

Jenny heard the bell as he spoke, and admitted the Englishman. She announced that "a gentleman had come who had made an appointment with the master," when Melmoth suddenly appeared, and deep silence followed. He looked at the porter — the porter went; he looked at Jenny — and Jenny went likewise.

"Madame," said Melmoth, turning to Aquilina, "with your permission, we will conclude a piece of urgent business."

He took Castanier's hand, and Castanier rose, and the two men went into the drawing-room. There was no light in the room, but Melmoth's eyes lit up the thickest darkness. The gaze of those strange eyes had left Aquilina like one spellbound; she was helpless, unable to take any thought for her lover; moreover, she believed him to be safe in Jenny's room, whereas their early return had taken the waiting woman by surprise, and she had hidden the officer in the dressing room. It had all happened exactly as in the drama that Melmoth had displayed for his victim. Presently the house door was slammed violently, and Castanier reappeared.

"What ails you?" cried the horror-struck Aquilina.

There was a change in the cashier's appearance. A strange pallor overspread his once rubicund countenance; it wore the peculiarly sinister and stony look of the mysterious visitor. The sullen glare of his eyes was intolerable, the fierce light in them seemed to scorch. The man who had looked so good-humored and good-natured had suddenly grown tyrannical and proud. The courtesan thought that Castanier had grown thinner; there was a terrible majesty in his brow; it was as if a dragon breathed forth a malignant influence that weighed upon the others like a close, heavy atmosphere. For a moment Aquilina knew not what to do.

"What passed between you and that diabolical-looking man in those few minutes?" she asked at length.

"I have sold my soul to him. I feel it; I am no longer the same. He has taken my *self*, and given me his soul in exchange."

"What?"

"You would not understand it at all.... Ah! he was right," Castanier went on, "the fiend was right! I see everything and know all things. — You have been deceiving me!"

Aquilina turned cold with terror. Castanier lighted a candle and went into the dressing room. The unhappy girl followed him in dazed bewilderment, and great was her astonishment when Castanier drew the dresses that hung there aside and disclosed the sergeant.

"Come out, my boy," said the cashier; and, taking Léon by a button of his overcoat, he drew the officer into his room.

The Piedmontese, haggard and desperate, had flung herself into her easy chair. Castanier seated himself on a sofa by the fire, and left Aquilina's lover in a standing position.

"You have been in the army," said Léon; "I am ready to give you satisfaction."

"You are a fool," said Castanier dryly. "I have no occasion to fight. I could kill you by a look if I had any mind to do it. I will tell you what it is, youngster; why should I kill you? I can see a red line round your neck — the guillotine is waiting for you. Yes, you will end in the Place de Grève. You are the headsman's property! there is no escape for you. You belong to a *vendita* of the Carbonari. You are plotting against the Government."

"You did not tell me that," cried the Piedmontese, turning to Léon.

"So you do not know that the Minister decided this morning to put down your Society?" the cashier continued. "The Procureur-Général has a list of your names. You have been betrayed. They are busy drawing up the indictment at this moment."

"Then was it you who betrayed him?" cried Aquilina, and with a hoarse sound in her throat like the growl of a tigress she rose to her feet; she seemed as if she would tear Castanier in pieces.

"You know me too well to believe it," Castanier retorted. Aquilina was benumbed by his coolness.

"Then how did you know it?" she murmured.

"I did not know it until I went into the drawing-room; now I know it — now I see and know all things, and can do all things."

The sergeant was overcome with amazement.

"Very well then, save him, save him, dear!" cried the girl, flinging herself at Castanier's feet. "If nothing is impossible to you, save him! I will love you, I will adore you, I will be your slave and not your mistress. I will obey your wildest whims; you shall do as you will with me. Yes, yes, I will give you more than love; you shall have a daughter's devotion as well as ... Rodolphe! why will you not understand! After all, however violent my passions may be, I shall be yours forever! What should I say to persuade you? I will invent pleasures ... I ... Great heavens! one moment! whatever you shall ask of me — to fling myself from the window, for instance — you will need to say but one word, 'Léon!' and I will plunge down into hell. I would bear any torture, any pain of body or soul, anything you might inflict upon me!"

Castanier heard her with indifference. For all answer, he indicated Léon to her with a fiendish laugh.

"The guillotine is waiting for him," he repeated.

"No, no, no! He shall not leave this house. I will save him!" she cried. "Yes; I will kill anyone who lays a finger upon him! Why will you not save him?" she shrieked aloud; her eyes were blazing, her hair unbound. "Can you save him?"

"I can do everything."

"Why do you not save him?"

"Why?" shouted Castanier, and his voice made the ceiling ring. — "Eh! it is my revenge! Doing evil is my trade!"

"Die?" said Aquilina; "must he die, my lover? Is it possible?"

She sprang up and snatched a stiletto from a basket that stood on the chest of drawers and went to Castanier, who began to laugh.

"You know very well that steel cannot hurt me now — "

Aquilina's arm suddenly dropped like a snapped harp string.

"Out with you, my good friend," said the cashier, turning to the sergeant, "and go about your business."

He held out his hand; the other felt Castanier's superior power, and could not choose but obey.

"This house is mine; I could send for the commissary of police if I chose, and give you up as a man who has hidden himself on my premises, but I would rather let you go; I am a fiend, I am not a spy."

"I shall follow him!" said Aquilina.

"Then follow him," returned Castanier. — "Here, Jenny — "

Jenny appeared.

"Tell the porter to hail a cab for them. — Here, Naqui," said Castanier, drawing a bundle of banknotes from his pocket; "you shall not go away like a pauper from a man who loves you still."

He held out three hundred thousand francs. Aquilina took the notes, flung them on the floor, spat on them, and trampled upon them in a frenzy of despair.

"We will leave this house on foot," she cried, "without a farthing of your money. — Jenny, stay where you are."

"Good evening!" answered the cashier, as he gathered up the notes again. "I have come back from my journey. — Jenny," he added, looking at the bewildered waiting maid, "you seem to me to be a good sort of girl. You have no mistress now. Come here. This evening you shall have a master."

Aquilina, who felt safe nowhere, went at once with the sergeant to the house of one of her friends. But all Léon's movements were suspiciously watched by the police, and after a time he and three of his friends were arrested. The whole story may be found in the newspapers of that day.

*****

Castanier felt that he had undergone a mental as well as a physical transformation. The Castanier of old no longer existed — the boy, the young Lothario, the soldier who had proved his courage, who had been tricked into a marriage and disillusioned, the cashier, the passionate lover who had committed a crime for Aquilina's sake. His inmost nature had suddenly asserted itself. His brain had expanded, his senses had developed. His thoughts comprehended the whole world; he saw all the things of earth as if he had been raised to some high pinnacle above the world.

Until that evening at the play he had loved Aquilina to distraction. Rather than give her up he would have shut his eyes to her infidelities; and now all that blind passion had passed away as a cloud vanishes in the sunlight.

Jenny was delighted to succeed to her mistress's position and fortune, and did the cashier's will in all things; but Castanier, who could read the inmost thoughts of the soul, discovered the real motive underlying this purely physical devotion. He amused himself with her, however, like a mischievous child who greedily sucks the juice of the cherry and flings away the stone. The next morning at breakfast time, when she was fully convinced that she was a lady and the mistress of the house, Castanier uttered one by one the thoughts that filled her mind as she drank her coffee.

"Do you know what you are thinking, child?" he said, smiling. "I will tell you: 'So all that lovely rosewood furniture that I coveted so much, and the pretty dresses that I used to try on, are mine now! All on easy terms that madame refused, I do not know why. My word! if I might drive about in a carriage, have jewels and pretty things, a box at the theater, and put something by! with me he should lead a life of pleasure fit to kill him if he were not as strong as a Turk! I never saw such a man!' — Was not that just what you were thinking?" he went on, and something in his voice made Jenny turn pale. "Well, yes, child; you could not stand it, and I am sending you away for your own good; you would perish in the attempt. Come, let us part good friends," and he coolly dismissed her with a very small sum of money.

The first use that Castanier had promised himself that he would make of the terrible power bought at the price of his eternal happiness, was the full and complete indulgence of all his tastes.

He first put his affairs in order, readily settled his account with M. de Nucingen, who found a worthy German to succeed him, and then determined on a carouse worthy of the palmiest days of the Roman Empire. He plunged into dissipation as recklessly as Belshazzar of old went to that last feast in Babylon. Like Belshazzar, he saw clearly through his revels a gleaming hand that traced his doom in letters of flame, not on the narrow walls of the banqueting chamber, but over the vast spaces of heaven that the rainbow spans. His feast was not, indeed, an orgy confined within the limits of a banquet, for he squandered all the powers of soul and body in exhausting all the pleasures of earth. The table was in some sort earth itself, the earth that trembled beneath his feet. He was the last festival of the reckless spendthrift who has thrown all prudence to the winds. The devil had given him the key of the storehouse of human pleasures; he had filled and refilled his hands, and he was fast nearing the bottom. In a moment he had felt all that that enormous power could accomplish; in a moment he had exercised it, proved it, wearied of it. What had hitherto been the sum of human desires became as nothing. So often it happens that with possession the vast poetry of desire must end, and the thing possessed is seldom the thing that we dreamed of.

Beneath Melmoth's omnipotence lurked this tragical anticlimax of so many a passion, and now the inanity of human nature was revealed to his successor, to whom infinite power brought Nothingness as a dowry.

To come to a clear understanding of Castanier's strange position, it must be borne in mind how suddenly these revolutions of thought and feeling had been wrought; how quickly they had succeeded each other; and of these things it is hard to give any idea to those who have never broken the prison bonds of time, and space, and distance. His relation to the world without had been entirely changed with the expansion of his faculties.

Like Melmoth himself, Castanier could travel in a few moments over the fertile plains of India, could soar on the wings of demons above African desert spaces, or skim the surface of the seas. The same insight that could read the inmost thoughts of others, could apprehend at a glance the nature of any material object, just as he caught as it were all flavors at once upon his tongue. He took his pleasure like a despot; a blow of the ax felled the tree that he might eat its fruits. The transitions, the alternations that measure joy and pain, and diversify human happiness, no longer existed for him. He had so completely glutted his appetites that pleasure must overpass the limits of pleasure to tickle a palate cloyed with satiety, and suddenly grown fastidious beyond all measure, so that ordinary pleasures became distasteful. Conscious that at will he was the master of all the women that he could desire, knowing that his power was irresistible, he did not care to exercise it; they were pliant to his unexpressed wishes, to his most extravagant caprices, until he felt a horrible thirst for love, and would have love beyond their power to give.

The world refused him nothing save faith and prayer, the soothing and consoling love that is not of this world. He was obeyed — it was a horrible position.

The torrents of pain, and pleasure, and thought that shook his soul and his bodily frame would have overwhelmed the strongest human being; but in him there was a power of vitality proportioned to the power of the sensations that assailed him. He felt within him a vague immensity of longing that earth could not satisfy. He spent his days on outspread wings, longing to traverse the luminous fields of space to other spheres that he knew afar by intuitive perception, a clear and hopeless knowledge. His soul dried up within him, for he hungered and thirsted after things that can neither be drunk nor eaten, but for which he could not choose but crave. His lips, like Melmoth's, burned with desire; he panted for the unknown, for he knew all things.

The mechanism and the scheme of the world was apparent to him, and its working interested him no longer; he did not long disguise the profound scorn that makes of a man of extraordinary powers a sphinx who knows everything and says nothing, and sees all things with an unmoved countenance. He felt not the slightest wish to communicate his knowledge to other men. He was rich with all the wealth of the world, with one effort he could make the circle of the globe, and riches and power were meaningless for him. He felt the awful melancholy of omnipotence, a melancholy which Satan and God relieve by the exercise of infinite power in mysterious ways known to them alone. Castanier had not, like his Master, the inextinguishable energy of hate and malice; he felt that he was a devil, but a devil whose time was not yet come, while Satan is a devil through all eternity, and being damned beyond redemption, delights to stir up the world, like a dungheap, with his triple fork and to thwart therein the designs of God. But Castanier, for his misfortune, had one hope left.

If in a moment he could move from one pole to the other as a bird springs restlessly from side to side in its cage, when, like the bird, he had crossed his prison, he saw the vast immensity of space beyond it. That vision of the Infinite left him forever unable to see humanity and its affairs as other men saw them. The insensate fools who long for the power of the Devil gauge its desirability from a human standpoint; they do not see that with the Devil's power they will likewise assume his thoughts, and that they will be doomed to remain as men among creatures who will no longer understand them. The Nero unknown to history who dreams of setting Paris on fire for his private entertainment, like an exhibition of a burning house on the boards of a theater, does not suspect that if he had that power, Paris would become for him as little interesting as an ant heap by the roadside to a hurrying passer-by. The circle of the sciences was for Castanier something like a logogriph for a man who does not know the key to it. Kings and Governments were despicable in his eyes. His great debauch had been in some sort a deplorable farewell to his life as a man. The earth had grown too narrow for him, for the infernal gifts laid bare for him the secrets of creation — he saw the cause and foresaw its end. He was shut out from all that men call "heaven" in all languages under the sun; he could no longer think of heaven.

Then he came to understand the look on his predecessor's face and the drying up of the life within; then he knew all that was meant by the baffled hope that gleamed in Melmoth's eyes; he, too, knew the thirst that burned those red lips, and the agony of a continual struggle between two natures grown to giant size. Even yet he might be an angel, and he knew himself to be a fiend. His was the fate of a sweet and gentle creature that a wizard's malice has imprisoned in a misshapen form, entrapping it by a pact, so that another's will must set it free from its detested envelope.

As a deception only increases the ardor with which a man of really great nature explores the infinite of sentiment in a woman's heart, so Castanier awoke to find that one idea lay like a weight upon his soul, an idea which was perhaps the key to loftier spheres. The very fact that he had bartered away his eternal happiness led him to dwell in thought upon the future of those who pray and believe. On the morrow of his debauch, when he entered into the sober possession of his power, this idea made him feel himself a prisoner; he knew the burden of the woe that poets, and prophets, and great oracles of faith have set forth for us in such mighty words; he felt the point of the Flaming Sword plunged into his side, and hurried in search of Melmoth. What had become of his predecessor?

The Englishman was living in a mansion in the Rue Férou, near Saint-Sulpice — a gloomy, dark, damp, and cold abode. The Rue Férou itself is one of the most dismal streets in Paris; it has a north aspect like all the streets that lie at right angles to the left bank of the Seine, and the houses are in keeping with the site. As Castanier stood on the threshold he found that the door itself, like the vaulted roof, was hung with black; rows of lighted tapers shone brilliantly as though some king were lying in state; and a priest stood on either side of a catafalque that had been raised there.

"There is no need to ask why you have come, sir," the old hall porter said to Castanier; "you are so like our poor dear master that is gone. But if you are his brother, you have come too late to bid him good-by. The good gentleman died the night before last."

"How did he die?" Castanier asked of one of the priests.

"Set your mind at rest," said an old priest; he partly raised as he spoke the black pall that covered the catafalque.

Castanier, looking at him, saw one of those faces that faith has made sublime; the soul seemed to shine forth from every line of it, bringing light and warmth for other men, kindled by the unfailing charity within. This was Sir John Melmoth's confessor.

"Your brother made an end that men may envy, and that must rejoice the angels. Do you know what joy there is in heaven over a sinner that repents? His tears of penitence, excited by grace, flowed without ceasing; death alone checked them. The Holy Spirit dwelt in him. His burning words, full of lively faith, were worthy of the Prophet-King. If, in the course of my life, I have never heard a more dreadful confession than from the lips of this Irish gentleman, I have likewise never heard such fervent and passionate prayers. However great the measures of his sins may have been, his repentance has filled the abyss to overflowing. The hand of God was visibly stretched out above him, for he was completely changed, there was such heavenly beauty in his face. The hard eyes were softened by tears; the resonant voice that struck terror into those who heard it took the tender and compassionate tones of those who themselves have passed through deep humiliation. He so edified those who heard his words that some who had felt drawn to see the spectacle of a Christian's death fell on their knees as he spoke of heavenly things, and of the infinite glory of God, and gave thanks and praise to Him. If he is leaving no worldly wealth to his family, no family can possess a greater blessing than this that he surely gained for them, a soul among the blessed, who will watch over you all and direct you in the path to heaven."

These words made such a vivid impression upon Castanier that he instantly hurried from the house to the Church of Saint-Sulpice, obeying what might be called a decree of fate. Melmoth's repentance had stupefied him.

At that time, on certain mornings in the week, a preacher, famed for his eloquence, was wont to hold conferences, in the course of which he demonstrated the truths of the Catholic faith for the youth of a generation proclaimed to be indifferent in matters of belief by another voice no less eloquent than his own. The conference had been put off to a later hour on account of Melmoth's funeral, so Castanier arrived just as the great preacher was epitomizing the proofs of a future existence of happiness with all the charm of eloquence and force of expression which have made him famous. The seeds of divine doctrine fell into a soil prepared for them in the old dragoon, into whom the Devil had glided. Indeed, if there is a phenomenon well attested by experience, is it not the spiritual phenomenon commonly called "the faith of the peasant"? The strength of belief varies inversely with the amount of use that a man has made of his reasoning faculties. Simple people and soldiers belong to the unreasoning class. Those who have marched through life beneath the banner of instinct are far more ready to receive the light than minds and hearts overwearied with the world's sophistries.

Castanier had the southern temperament; he had joined the army as a lad of sixteen, and had followed the French flag till he was nearly forty years old. As a common trooper, he had fought day and night, and day after day, and, as in duty bound, had thought of his horse first, and of himself afterwards. While he served his military apprenticeship, therefore, he had but little leisure in which to reflect on the destiny of man, and when he became an officer he had his men to think of. He had been swept from battlefield to battlefield, but he had never thought of what comes after death. A soldier's life does not demand much thinking. Those who cannot understand the lofty political ends involved and the interests of nation and nation; who cannot grasp political schemes as well as plans of campaign and combine the science of the tactician with that of the administrator, are bound to live in a state of ignorance; the most boorish peasant in the most backward district in France is scarcely in a worse case. Such men as these bear the brunt of war, yield passive obedience to the brain that directs them, and strike down the men opposed to them as the woodcutter fells timber in the forest. Violent physical exertion is succeeded by times of inertia, when they repair the waste. They fight and drink, fight and eat, fight and sleep, that they may the better deal hard blows; the powers of the mind are not greatly exercised in this turbulent round of existence, and the character is as simple as heretofore.

When the men who have shown such energy on the battlefield return to ordinary civilization, most of those who have not risen to high rank seem to have acquired no ideas, and to have no aptitude, no capacity, for grasping new ideas. To the utter amazement of a younger generation, those who made our armies so glorious and so terrible are as simple as children, and as slow-witted as a clerk at his worst, and the captain of a thundering squadron is scarcely fit to keep a merchant's day-book. Old soldiers of this stamp, therefore, being innocent of any attempt to use their reasoning faculties, act upon their strongest impulses. Castanier's crime was one of those matters that raise so many questions, that, in order to debate about it, a moralist might call for its "discussion by clauses," to make use of a parliamentary expression.

Passion had counseled the crime; the cruelly irresistible power of feminine witchery had driven him to commit it; no man can say of himself, "I will never do that," when a siren joins in the combat and throws her spells over him.

So the word of life fell upon a conscience newly awakened to the truths of religion which the French Revolution and a soldier's career had forced Castanier to neglect. The solemn words, "You will be happy or miserable for all eternity!" made but the more terrible impression upon him, because he had exhausted earth and shaken it like a barren tree; because his desires could effect all things, so that it was enough that any spot in earth or heaven should be forbidden him, and he forthwith thought of nothing else. If it were allowable to compare such great things with social follies, Castanier's position was not unlike that of a banker who, finding that his all-powerful millions cannot obtain for him an entrance into the society of the noblesse, must set his heart upon entering that circle, and all the social privileges that he has already acquired are as nothing in his eyes from the moment when he discovers that a single one is lacking.

Here was a man more powerful than all the kings on earth put together; a man who, like Satan, could wrestle with God Himself; leaning against one of the pillars in the Church of Saint-Sulpice, weighed down by the feelings and thoughts that oppressed him, and absorbed in the thought of a Future, the same thought that had engulfed Melmoth.

"He was very happy, was Melmoth!" cried Castanier. "He died in the certain knowledge that he would go to heaven."

In a moment the greatest possible change had been wrought in the cashier's ideas. For several days he had been a devil, now he was nothing but a man; an image of the fallen Adam, of the sacred tradition embodied in all cosmogonies. But while he had thus shrunk to manhood, he retained a germ of greatness, he had been steeped in the Infinite. The power of hell had revealed the divine power. He thirsted for heaven as he had never thirsted after the pleasures of earth, that are so soon exhausted. The enjoyments which the fiend promises are but the enjoyments of earth on a larger scale, but to the joys of heaven there is no limit. He believed in God, and the spell that gave him the treasures of the world was as nothing to him now; the treasures themselves seemed to him as contemptible as pebbles to an admirer of diamonds; they were but gewgaws compared with the eternal glories of the other life. A curse lay, he thought, on all things that came to him from this source. He sounded dark depths of painful thought as he listened to the service performed for Melmoth. The *Dies iræ* filled him with awe; he felt all the grandeur of that cry of a repentant soul trembling before the Throne of God. The Holy Spirit, like a devouring flame, passed through him as fire consumes straw.

The tears were falling from his eyes when — "Are you a relation of the dead?" the beadle asked him.

"I am his heir," Castanier answered.

"Give something for the expenses of the services!" cried the man.

"No," said the cashier. (The Devil's money should not go to the Church.)

"For the poor!"

"No."

"For repairing the Church!"

"No."

"The Lady Chapel!"

"No."

"For the schools!"

"No."

Castanier went, not caring to expose himself to the sour looks that the irritated functionaries gave him.

Outside, in the street, he looked up at the Church of Saint-Sulpice. "What made people build the giant cathedrals I have seen in every country?" he asked himself. "The feeling shared so widely throughout all time must surely be based upon something."

"Something! Do you call God *something*?" cried his conscience. "God! God! God!..."

The word was echoed and reëchoed by an inner voice, till it overwhelmed him; but his feeling of terror subsided as he heard sweet distant sounds of music that he had caught faintly before. They were singing in the church, he thought, and his eyes scanned the great doorway. But as he listened more closely, the sounds poured upon him from all sides; he looked round the square, but there was no sign of any musicians. The melody brought visions of a distant heaven and far-off gleams of hope; but it also quickened the remorse that had set the lost soul in a ferment. He went on his way through Paris, walking as men walk who are crushed beneath the burden of their sorrow, seeing everything with unseeing eyes, loitering like an idler, stopping without cause, muttering to himself, careless of the traffic, making no effort to avoid a blow from a plank of timber.

Imperceptibly repentance brought him under the influence of the divine grace that soothes while it bruises the heart so terribly. His face came to wear a look of Melmoth, something great, with a trace of madness in the greatness. A look of dull and hopeless distress, mingled with the excited eagerness of hope, and, beneath it all, a gnawing sense of loathing for all that the world can give. The humblest of prayers lurked in the eyes that saw with such dreadful clearness. His power was the measure of his anguish. His body was bowed down by the fearful storm that shook his soul, as the tall pines bend before the blast. Like his predecessor, he could not refuse to bear the burden of life; he was afraid to die while he bore the yoke of hell. The torment grew intolerable.

At last, one morning, he bethought himself how that Melmoth (now among the blessed) had made the proposal of an exchange, and how that he had accepted it; others, doubtless, would follow his example; for in an age proclaimed, by the inheritors of the eloquence of the Fathers of the Church, to be fatally indifferent to religion, it should be easy to find a man who would accept the conditions of the contract in order to prove its advantages.

"There is one place where you can learn what kings will fetch in the market; where nations are weighed in the balance and systems appraised; where the value of a government is stated in terms of the five-franc piece; where ideas and beliefs have their price, and everything is discounted; where God Himself, in a manner, borrows on the security of His revenue of souls, for the Pope has a running account there. Is it not there that I should go to traffic in souls?"

Castanier went quite joyously on 'Change, thinking that it would be as easy to buy a soul as to invest money in the Funds. Any ordinary person would have feared ridicule, but Castanier knew by experience that a desperate man takes everything seriously. A prisoner lying under sentence of death would listen to the madman who should tell him that by pronouncing some gibberish he could escape through the keyhole; for suffering is credulous, and clings to an idea until it fails, as the swimmer borne along by the current clings to the branch that snaps in his hand.

Toward four o'clock that afternoon Castanier appeared among the little knots of men who were transacting private business after 'Change. He was personally known to some of the brokers; and while affecting to be in search of an acquaintance, he managed to pick up the current gossip and rumors of failure.

"Catch me negotiating bills for Claparon & Co., my boy. The bank collector went round to return their acceptances to them this morning," said a fat banker in his outspoken way. "If you have any of their paper, look out."

Claparon was in the building, in deep consultation with a man well known for the ruinous rate at which he lent money. Castanier went forthwith in search of the said Claparon, a merchant who had a reputation for taking heavy risks that meant wealth or utter ruin. The money lender walked away as Castanier came up. A gesture betrayed the speculator's despair.

"Well, Claparon, the bank wants a hundred thousand francs of you, and it is four o'clock; the thing is known, and it is too late to arrange your little failure comfortably," said Castanier.

"Sir!"

"Speak lower," the cashier went on. "How if I were to propose a piece of business that would bring you in as much money as you require?"

"It would not discharge my liabilities; every business that I ever heard of wants a little time to simmer in."

"I know of something that will set you straight in a moment," answered Castanier; "but first you would have to — "

"Do what?"

"Sell your share of Paradise. It is a matter of business like anything else, isn't it? We all hold shares in the great Speculation of Eternity."

"I tell you this," said Claparon angrily, "that I am just the man to lend you a slap in the face. When a man is in trouble, it is no time to play silly jokes on him."

"I am talking seriously," said Castanier, and he drew a bundle of notes from his pocket.

"In the first place," said Claparon, "I am not going to sell my soul to the Devil for a trifle. I want five hundred thousand francs before I strike — "

"Who talks of stinting you?" asked Castanier, cutting him short. "You should have more gold than you could stow in the cellars of the Bank of France."

He held out a handful of notes. That decided Claparon.

"Done," he cried; "but how is the bargain to be made?"

"Let us go over yonder, no one is standing there," said Castanier, pointing to a corner of the court.

Claparon and his tempter exchanged a few words, with their faces turned to the wall. None of the onlookers guessed the nature of this by-play, though their curiosity was keenly excited by the strange gestures of the two contracting parties. When Castanier returned, there was a sudden outburst of amazed exclamation. As in the Assembly where the least event immediately attracts attention, all faces were turned to the two men who had caused the sensation, and a shiver passed through all beholders at the change that had taken place in them.

The men who form the moving crowd that fills the Stock Exchange are soon known to each other by sight. They watch each other like players round a card table. Some shrewd observers can tell how a man will play and the condition of his exchequer from a survey of his face; and the Stock Exchange is simply a vast card table. Everyone, therefore, had noticed Claparon and Castanier. The latter (like the Irishman before him [6]) had been muscular and powerful, his eyes were full of light, his color high. The dignity and power in his face had struck awe into them all; they wondered how old Castanier had come by it; and now they beheld Castanier divested of his power, shrunken, wrinkled, aged, and feeble. He had drawn Claparon out of the crowd with the energy of a sick man in a fever fit; he had looked like an opium eater during the brief period of excitement that the drug can give; now, on his return, he seemed to be in the condition of utter exhaustion in which the patient dies after the fever departs, or to be suffering from the horrible prostration that follows on excessive indulgence in the delights of narcotics. The infernal power that had upheld him through his debauches had left him, and the body was left unaided and alone to endure the agony of remorse and the heavy burden of sincere repentance. Claparon's troubles everyone could guess; but Claparon reappeared, on the other hand, with sparkling eyes, holding his head high with the pride of Lucifer. The crisis had passed from the one man to the other.

"Now you can drop off with an easy mind, old man," said Claparon to Castanier.

"For pity's sake, send for a cab and for a priest; send for the curate of Saint-Sulpice!" answered the old dragoon, sinking down upon the curbstone.

The words "a priest" reached the ears of several people, and produced uproarious jeering among the stockbrokers, for faith with these gentlemen means a belief that a scrap of paper called a mortgage represents an estate, and the List of Fundholders is their Bible.

"Shall I have time to repent?" said Castanier to himself, in a piteous voice, that impressed Claparon.

A cab carried away the dying man; the speculator went to the bank at once to meet his bills; and the momentary sensation produced upon the throng of business men by the sudden change on the two faces, vanished like the furrow cut by a ship's keel in the sea. News of the greatest importance kept the attention of the world of commerce on the alert; and when commercial interests are at stake, Moses might appear with his two luminous horns, and his coming would scarcely receive the honors of a pun; the gentlemen whose business it is to write the Market Reports would ignore his existence.

When Claparon had made his payments, fear seized upon him. There was no mistake about his power. He went on 'Change again, and offered his bargain to other men in embarrassed cir- cumstances. The Devil's bond, "together with the rights, ease- ments, and privileges appertaining thereunto," — to use the ex- pression of the notary who succeeded Claparon, changed hands for the sum of seven hundred thousand francs. The notary in his turn parted with the agreement with the Devil for five hundred thousand francs to a building contractor in difficulties, who likewise was rid of it to an iron merchant in consideration of a hundred thousand crowns. In fact, by five o'clock people had ceased to believe in the strange contract, and purchasers were lacking for want of confidence.

At half-past five the holder of the bond was a house painter, who was lounging by the door of the building in the Rue Feydeau, where at that time stockbrokers temporarily congregated. The house painter, simple fellow, could not think what was the matter with him. He "felt all anyhow"; so he told his wife when he went home.

The Rue Feydeau, as idlers about town are aware, is a place of pilgrimage for youths who for lack of a mistress bestow their ardent affection upon the whole sex. On the first floor of the most rigidly respectable domicile therein dwelt one of those exquisite creatures whom it has pleased heaven to endow with the rarest and most surpassing beauty. As it is impossible that they should all be duchesses or queens (since there are many more pretty women in the world than titles and thrones for them to adorn), they are content to make a stockbroker or a banker happy at a fixed price. To this good-natured beauty, Euphrasia by name, an unbounded ambition had led a notary's clerk to aspire. In short, the second clerk in the office of Maître Crottat, notary, had fallen in love with her, as youth at two and twenty can fall in love. The scrivener would have murdered the Pope and run amuck through the whole sacred college to procure the miserable sum of a hundred louis to pay for a shawl which had turned Euphrasia's head, at which price her waiting woman had promised that Euphrasia should be his. The infatuated youth walked to and fro under Madame Euphrasia's windows, like the polar bears in their cage at the Jardin des Plantes, with his right hand thrust beneath his waistcoat in the region of the heart, which he was fit to tear from his bosom, but as yet he had only wrenched at the elastic of his braces.

"What can one do to raise ten thousand francs?" he asked himself. "Shall I make off with the money that I must pay on the registration of that conveyance? Good heavens! my loan would not ruin the purchaser, a man with seven millions! And then next day I would fling myself at his feet and say, 'I have taken ten thousand francs belonging to you, sir; I am twenty-two years of age, and I am in love with Euphrasia — that is my story. My father is rich, he will pay you back; do not ruin me! Have not you yourself been twenty-two years old and madly in love?' But these beggarly landowners have no souls! He would be quite likely to give me up to the public prosecutor, instead of taking pity upon me. Good God! if it were only possible to sell your soul to the Devil! But there is neither a God nor a Devil; it is all nonsense out of nursery tales and old wives' talk. What shall I do?"

"If you have a mind to sell your soul to the Devil, sir," said the house painter, who had overheard something that the clerk let fall, "you can have the ten thousand francs."

"And Euphrasia!" cried the clerk, as he struck a bargain with the devil that inhabited the house painter.

The pact concluded, the frantic clerk went to find the shawl, and mounted Madame Euphrasia's staircase; and as (literally) the devil was in him, he did not come down for twelve days, drowning the thought of hell and of his privileges in twelve days of love and riot and forgetfulness, for which he had bartered away all his hopes of a paradise to come.

And in this way the secret of the vast power discovered and acquired by the Irishman, the offspring of Maturin's brain, was lost to mankind; and the various Orientalists, Mystics, and Archaeologists who take an interest in these matters were unable to hand down to posterity the proper method of invoking the Devil, for the following sufficient reasons: —

On the thirteenth day after these frenzied nuptials the wretched clerk lay on a pallet bed in a garret in his master's house in the Rue Saint-Honoré. Shame, the stupid goddess who dares not behold herself, had taken possession of the young man. He had fallen ill; he would nurse himself; misjudged the quantity of a remedy devised by the skill of a practitioner well known on the walls of Paris, and succumbed to the effects of an overdose of mercury. His corpse was as black as a mole's back. A devil had left unmistakable traces of its passage there; could it have been Ashtaroth?

*****

"The estimable youth to whom you refer has been carried away to the planet Mercury," said the head clerk to a German demonologist who came to investigate the matter at first hand.

"I am quite prepared to believe it," answered the Teuton.

"Oh!"

"Yes, sir," returned the other. "The opinion you advance coincides with the very words of Jacob Boehme. In the forty-eighth proposition of *The Threefold Life of Man* he says that 'if God hath brought all things to pass with a LET THERE BE, the FIAT is the secret matrix which comprehends and apprehends the nature which is formed by the spirit born of Mercury and of God.'"

"What do you say, sir?"

The German delivered his quotation afresh.

"We do not know it," said the clerks.

"*Fiat?...*" said a clerk. "*Fiat lux!*"

"You can verify the citation for yourselves," said the German. "You will find the passage in the *Treatise of the Threefold Life of Man*, page 75; the edition was published by M. Migneret in 1809. It was translated into French by a philosopher who had a great admiration for the famous shoemaker."

"Oh! he was a shoemaker, was he?" said the head clerk.

"In Prussia," said the German.

"Did he work for the King of Prussia?" inquired a Boeotian of a second clerk.

"He must have vamped up his prose," said a third.

"That man is colossal!" cried the fourth, pointing to the Teuton.

171

That gentleman, though a demonologist of the first rank, did not know the amount of devilry to be found in a notary's clerk. He went away without the least idea that they were making game of him, and fully under the impression that the young fellows regarded Boehme as a colossal genius.

"Education is making strides in France," said he to himself.

The Conscript

[The inner self] ... by a phenomenon of vision or of locomotion has been known at times to abolish Space in its two modes of Time and Distance — the one intellectual, the other physical.

— HISTORY OF LOUIS LAMBERT.

On a November evening in the year 1793 the principal citizens of Carentan were assembled in Mme. de Dey's drawing-room. Mme. de Dey held this *reception* every night of the week, but an unwonted interest attached to this evening's gathering, owing to certain circumstances which would have passed altogether unnoticed in a great city, though in a small country town they excited the greatest curiosity. For two days before Mme. de Dey had not been at home to her visitors, and on the previous evening her door had been shut, on the ground of indisposition. Two such events at any ordinary time would have produced in Carentan the same sensation that Paris knows on nights when there is no performance at the theaters — existence is in some sort incomplete; but in those times when the least indiscretion on the part of an aristocrat might be a matter of life and death, this conduct of Mme. de Dey's was likely to bring about the most disastrous consequences for her. Her position in Carentan ought to be made clear, if the reader is to appreciate the expression of keen curiosity and cunning fanaticism on the countenances of these Norman citizens, and, what is of most importance, the part that the lady played among them. Many a one during the days of the Revolution has doubtless passed through a crisis as difficult as hers at that moment, and the sympathies of more than one reader will fill in all the coloring of the picture.

Mme. de Dey was the widow of a Lieutenant-General, a Knight of the Orders of Saint Michael and of the Holy Ghost. She had left the Court when the Emigration began, and taken refuge in the neighborhood of Carentan, where she had large estates, hoping that the influence of the Reign of Terror would be but little felt there. Her calculations, based on a thorough knowledge of the district, proved correct. The Revolution made little disturbance in Lower Normandy. Formerly, when Mme. de Dey had spent any time in the country, her circle of acquaintance had been confined to the noble families of the district; but now, from politic motives, she opened her house to the principal citizens and to the Revolutionary authorities of the town, endeavoring to touch and gratify their social pride without arousing either hatred or jealousy. Gracious and kindly, possessed of the indescribable charm that wins good will without loss of dignity or effort to pay court to any, she had succeeded in gaining universal esteem; the discreet warnings of exquisite tact enabled her to steer a difficult course among the exacting claims of this mixed society, without wounding the overweening self-love of parvenus on the one hand, or the susceptibilities of her old friends on the other.

She was about thirty-eight years of age, and still preserved, not the fresh, high-colored beauty of the Basse-Normandes, but a fragile loveliness of what may be called an aristocratic type. Her figure was lissome and slender, her features delicate and clearly cut; the pale face seemed to light up and live when she spoke; but there was a quiet and devout look in the great dark eyes, for all their graciousness of expression — a look that seemed to say that the springs of her life lay without her own existence.

In her early girlhood she had been married to an elderly and jealous soldier. Her false position in the midst of a gay Court had doubtless done something to bring a veil of sadness over a face that must once have been bright with the charms of quick-pulsed life and love. She had been compelled to set constant restraint upon her frank impulses and emotions at an age when a woman feels rather than thinks, and the depths of passion in her heart had never been stirred. In this lay the secret of her greatest charm, a youthfulness of the inmost soul, betrayed at times by her face, and a certain tinge of innocent wistfulness in her ideas. She was reserved in her demeanor, but in her bearing and in the tones of her voice there was still something that told of girlish longings directed toward a vague future. Before very long the least susceptible fell in love with her, and yet stood somewhat in awe of her dignity and high-bred manner. Her great soul, strengthened by the cruel ordeals through which she had passed, seemed to set her too far above the ordinary level, and these men weighed themselves, and instinctively felt that they were found wanting. Such a nature demanded an exalted passion.

Moreover, Mme. de Dey's affections were concentrated in one sentiment — a mother's love for her son. All the happiness and joy that she had not known as a wife, she had found later in her boundless love for him. The coquetry of a mistress, the jealousy of a wife mingled with the pure and deep affection of a mother. She was miserable when they were apart, and nervous about him while he was away; she could never see enough of him, and lived through and for him alone. Some idea of the strength of this tie may be conveyed to the masculine understanding by adding that this was not only Mme. de Dey's only son, but all she had of kith or kin in the world, the one human being on earth bound to her by all the fears and hopes and joys of her life.

The late Comte de Dey was the last of his race, and she, his wife, was the sole heiress and descendant of her house. So worldly ambitions and family considerations, as well as the noblest cravings of the soul, combined to heighten in the Countess a sentiment that is strong in every woman's heart. The child was all the dearer, because only with infinite care had she succeeded in rearing him to man's estate; medical science had predicted his death a score of times, but she had held fast to her presentiments and her hopes, and had known the inexpressible joy of watching him pass safely through the perils of infancy, of seeing his constitution strengthen in spite of the decrees of the Faculty.

Thanks to her constant care, the boy had grown up and developed so favorably, that at twenty years of age he was regarded as one of the most accomplished gentlemen at the Court of Versailles. One final happiness that does not always crown a mother's efforts was hers — her son worshiped her; and between these two there was the deep sympathy of kindred souls. If they had not been bound to each other already by a natural and sacred tie, they would instinctively have felt for each other a friendship that is rarely met with between two men.

At the age of eighteen, the young Count had received an appointment as sub-lieutenant in a regiment of dragoons, and had made it a point of honor to follow the emigrant Princes into exile.

Then Mme. de Dey faced the dangers of her cruel position. She was rich, noble, and the mother of an Emigrant. With the one desire to look after her son's great fortune, she had denied herself the happiness of being with him; and when she read the rigorous laws in virtue of which the Republic was daily confiscating the property of Emigrants at Carentan, she congratulated herself on the courageous course that she had taken. Was she not keeping watch over the wealth of her son at the risk of her life? Later, when news came of the horrible executions ordered by the Convention, she slept, happy in the knowledge that her own treasure was in safety, out of reach of peril, far from the scaffolds of the Revolution. She loved to think that she had followed the best course, that she had saved her darling and her darling's fortunes; and to this secret thought she made such concessions as the misfortunes of the times demanded, without compromising her dignity or her aristocratic tenets, and enveloped her sorrows in reserve and mystery. She had foreseen the difficulties that would beset her at Carentan. Did she not tempt the scaffold by the very fact of going thither to take a prominent place? Yet, sustained by a mother's courage, she succeeded in winning the affection of the poor, ministering without distinction to everyone in trouble; and made herself necessary to the well-to-do, by providing amusements for them.

The procureur of the commune might be seen at her house, the mayor, the president of the "district," and the public prosecutor, and even the judges of the Revolutionary tribunals went there. The four first-named gentlemen were none of them married, and each paid court to her, in the hope that Mme. de Dey would take him for her husband, either from fear of making an enemy or from a desire to find a protector.

The public prosecutor, once an attorney at Caen, and the Countess's man of business, did what he could to inspire love by a system of devotion and generosity, a dangerous game of cunning! He was the most formidable of all her suitors. He alone knew the amount of the large fortune of his sometime client, and his fervor was inevitably increased by the cupidity of greed, and by the consciousness that he wielded an enormous power, the power of life and death in the district. He was still a young man, and, owing to the generosity of his behavior, Mme. de Dey was unable as yet to estimate him truly. But, in despite of the danger of matching herself against Norman cunning, she used all the craft and inventiveness that Nature has bestowed on women to play off the rival suitors one against another. She hoped, by gaining time, to emerge safe and sound from her difficulties at last; for at that time Royalists in the provinces flattered themselves with a hope, daily renewed, that the morrow would see the end of the Revolution — a conviction that proved fatal to many of them.

In spite of difficulties, the Countess had maintained her independence with considerable skill until the day when, by an inexplicable want of prudence, she took occasion to close her salon. So deep and sincere was the interest that she inspired, that those who usually filled her drawing-room felt a lively anxiety when the news was spread; then, with the frank curiosity characteristic of provincial manners, they went to inquire into the misfortune, grief, or illness that had befallen Mme. de Dey.

To all these questions, Brigitte, the housekeeper, answered with the same formula: her mistress was keeping her room, and would see no one, not even her own servants. The almost claustral lives of dwellers in small towns fosters a habit of analysis and conjectural explanation of the business of everybody else; so strong is it, that when everyone had exclaimed over poor Mme.

de Dey (without knowing whether the lady was overcome by joy or sorrow), each one began to inquire into the causes of her sudden seclusion.

"If she were ill, she would have sent for the doctor," said gossip number one; "now the doctor has been playing chess in my house all day. He said to me, laughing, that in these days there is only one disease, and that, unluckily, it is incurable."

The joke was hazarded discreetly. Women and men, elderly folk and young girls, forthwith betook themselves to the vast fields of conjecture. Everyone imagined that there was some secret in it, and every head was busy with the secret. Next day the suspicions became malignant. Everyone lives in public in a small town, and the women-kind were the first to find out that Brigitte had laid in an extra stock of provisions. The thing could not be disputed. Brigitte had been seen in the market-place betimes that morning, and, wonderful to relate, she had bought the one hare to be had. The whole town knew that Mme. de Dey did not care for game. The hare became a starting point for endless conjectures.

Elderly gentlemen, taking their constitutional, noticed a sort of suppressed bustle in the Countess's house; the symptoms were the more apparent because the servants were at evident pains to conceal them. The man-servant was beating a carpet in the garden. Only yesterday no one would have remarked the fact, but today everybody began to build romances upon that harmless piece of household stuff. Everyone had a version.

On the following day, that on which Mme. de Dey gave out that she was not well, the magnates of Carentan went to spend the evening at the mayor's brother's house. He was a retired merchant, a married man, a strictly honorable soul; everyone respected him, and the Countess held him in high regard. There all the rich widows' suitors were fain to invent more or less probable fictions, each one thinking the while how to turn to his own advantage the secret that compelled her to compromise herself in such a manner.

The public prosecutor spun out a whole drama to bring Mme. de Dey's son to her house of a night. The mayor had a belief in a priest who had refused the oath, a refugee from La Vendée; but this left him not a little embarrassed how to account for the purchase of a hare on a Friday. The president of the district had strong leanings toward a Chouan chief, or a Vendean leader hotly pursued. Others voted for a noble escaped from the prisons of Paris. In short, one and all suspected that the Countess had been guilty of some piece of generosity that the law of those days defined as a crime, an offense that was like to bring her to the scaffold. The public prosecutor, moreover, said, in a low voice, that they must hush the matter up, and try to save the unfortunate lady from the abyss toward which she was hastening.

"If you spread reports about," he added, "I shall be obliged to take cognizance of the matter, and to search the house, and then!..."

He said no more, but everyone understood what was left unsaid.

The Countess's real friends were so much alarmed for her, that on the morning of the third day the *Procureur Syndic* of the commune made his wife write a few lines to persuade Mme. de Dey to hold her reception as usual that evening. The old merchant took a bolder step. He called that morning upon the lady. Strong in the thought of the service he meant to do her, he insisted that he must see Mme. de Dey, and was amazed beyond expression to find her out in the garden, busy gathering the last autumn flowers in her borders to fill the vases.

"She has given refuge to her lover, no doubt," thought the old man, struck with pity for the charming woman before him.

The Countess's face wore a strange look, that confirmed his suspicions. Deeply moved by the devotion so natural to women, but that always touches us, because all men are flattered by the sacrifices that any woman makes for any one of them, the merchant told the Countess of the gossip that was circulating in the town, and showed her the danger that she was running. He wound up at last with saying that "if there are some of our public functionaries who are sufficiently ready to pardon a piece of heroism on your part so long as it is a priest that you wish to save, no one will show you any mercy if it is discovered that you are sacrificing yourself to the dictates of your heart."

At these words Mme. de Dey gazed at her visitor with a wild excitement in her manner that made him tremble, old though he was.

"Come in," she said, taking him by the hand to bring him to her room, and as soon as she had assured herself that they were alone, she drew a soiled, torn letter from her bodice. — "Read it!" she cried, with a violent effort to pronounce the words.

She dropped as if exhausted into her armchair. While the old merchant looked for his spectacles and wiped them, she raised her eyes, and for the first time looked at him with curiosity; then, in an uncertain voice, "I trust in you," she said softly.

"Why did I come but to share in your crime?" the old merchant said simply.

She trembled. For the first time since she had come to the little town her soul found sympathy in another soul. A sudden light dawned meantime on the old merchant; he understood the Countess's joy and her prostration.

Her son had taken part in the Granville expedition; he wrote to his mother from his prison, and the letter brought her a sad, sweet hope. Feeling no doubts as to his means of escape, he wrote that within three days he was sure to reach her, disguised. The same letter that brought these weighty tidings was full of heart-rending farewells in case the writer should not be in Carentan by the evening of the third day, and he implored his mother to send a considerable sum of money by the bearer, who had gone through dangers innumerable to deliver it. The paper shook in the old man's hands.

"And to-day is the third day!" cried Mme. de Dey. She sprang to her feet, took back the letter, and walked up and down.

"You have set to work imprudently," the merchant remarked, addressing her. "Why did you buy provisions?"

"Why, he may come in dying of hunger, worn out with fatigue, and — " She broke off.

"I am sure of my brother," the old merchant went on; "I will engage him in your interests."

The merchant in this crisis recovered his old business shrewdness, and the advice that he gave Mme. de Dey was full of prudence and wisdom. After the two had agreed together as to what they were to do and say, the old merchant went on various ingenious pretexts to pay visits to the principal houses of Carentan, announcing wherever he went that he had just been to see Mme. de Dey, and that, in spite of her indisposition, she would receive that evening. Matching his shrewdness against Norman wits in the cross-examination he underwent in every family as to the Countess's complaint, he succeeded in putting almost everyone who took an interest in the mysterious affair upon the wrong scent.

His very first call worked wonders. He told, in the hearing of a gouty old lady, how that Mme. de Dey had all but died of an attack of gout in the stomach; how that the illustrious Tronchin had recommended her in such a case to put the skin from a live hare on her chest, to stop in bed, and keep perfectly still. The Countess, he said, had lain in danger of her life for the past two days; but after carefully following out Tronchin's singular prescription, she was now sufficiently recovered to receive visitors that evening.

This tale had an immense success in Carentan. The local doctor, a Royalist *in petto*, added to its effect by gravely discussing the specific. Suspicion, nevertheless, had taken too deep root in a few perverse or philosophical minds to be entirely dissipated; so it fell out that those who had the right of entry into Mme. de Dey's drawing-room hurried thither at an early hour, some to watch her face, some out of friendship, but the more part attracted by the fame of the marvelous cure.

They found the Countess seated in a corner of the great chimney-piece in her room, which was almost as modestly furnished as similar apartments in Carentan; for she had given up the enjoyment of luxuries to which she had formerly been accustomed, for fear of offending the narrow prejudices of her guests, and she had made no changes in her house. The floor was not even polished. She had left the old somber hangings on the walls, had kept the old-fashioned country furniture, burned tallow candles, had fallen in with the ways of the place and adopted provincial life without flinching before its cast-iron narrowness, its most disagreeable hardships; but knowing that her guests would forgive her for any prodigality that conduced to their comfort, she left nothing undone where their personal enjoyment was concerned; her dinners, for instance, were excellent. She even went so far as to affect avarice to recommend herself to these sordid natures; and had the ingenuity to make it appear that certain concessions to luxury had been made at the instance of others, to whom she had graciously yielded.

Toward seven o'clock that evening, therefore, the nearest approach to polite society that Carentan could boast was assembled in Mme. de Dey's drawing-room, in a wide circle, about the fire. The old merchant's sympathetic glances sustained the mistress of the house through this ordeal; with wonderful strength of mind, she underwent the curious scrutiny of her guests, and bore with their trivial prosings. Every time there was a knock at the door, at every sound of footsteps in the street, she hid her agitation by raising questions of absorbing interest to the countryside. She led the conversation on to the burning topic of the quality of various ciders, and was so well seconded by her friend who shared her secret, that her guests almost forgot to watch her, and her face wore its wonted look; her self-possession was unshaken. The public prosecutor and one of the judges of the Revolutionary Tribunal kept silence, however; noting the slightest change that flickered over her features, listening through the noisy talk to every sound in the house. Several times they put awkward questions, which the Countess answered with wonderful presence of mind. So brave is a mother's heart!

Mme. de Dey had drawn her visitors into little groups, had made parties of whist, boston, or reversis, and sat talking with some of the young people; she seemed to be living completely in the present moment, and played her part like a consummate actress. She elicited a suggestion of loto, and saying that no one else knew where to find the game, she left the room.

"My good Brigitte, I cannot breathe down there!" she cried, brushing away the tears that sprang to her eyes that glittered with fever, sorrow, and impatience. — She had gone up to her son's room, and was looking round it. "He does not come," she said. "Here I can breathe and live. A few minutes more, and he will be here, for he is alive, I am sure that he is alive! my heart tells me so. Do you hear nothing, Brigitte? Oh! I would give the rest of my life to know whether he is still in prison or tramping across the country. I would rather not think."

Once more she looked to see that everything was in order. A bright fire blazed on the hearth, the shutters were carefully closed, the furniture shone with cleanliness, the bed had been made after a fashion that showed that Brigitte and the Countess had given their minds to every trifling detail. It was impossible not to read her hopes in the dainty and thoughtful preparations about the room; love and a mother's tenderest caresses seemed to pervade the air in the scent of flowers. None but a mother could have foreseen the requirements of a soldier and arranged so completely for their satisfaction. A dainty meal, the best of wine, clean linen, slippers — no necessary, no comfort, was lacking for the weary traveler, and all the delights of home heaped upon him should reveal his mother's love.

"Oh, Brigitte!..." cried the Countess, with a heart-rending inflection in her voice. She drew a chair to the table as if to strengthen her illusions and realize her longings.

"Ah! madame, he is coming. He is not far off.... I haven't a doubt that he is living and on his way," Brigitte answered. "I put a key in the Bible and held it on my fingers while Cottin read the Gospel of St. John, and the key did not turn, madame."

"Is that a certain sign?" the Countess asked.

"Why, yes, madame! everybody knows that. He is still alive; I would stake my salvation on it; God cannot be mistaken."

"If only I could see him here in the house, in spite of the danger."

"Poor Monsieur Auguste!" cried Brigitte; "I expect he is tramping along the lanes!"

"And that is eight o'clock striking now!" cried the Countess in terror.

She was afraid that she had been too long in the room where she felt sure that her son was alive; all those preparations made for him meant that he was alive. She went down, but she lingered a moment in the peristyle for any sound that might waken the sleeping echoes of the town. She smiled at Brigitte's husband, who was standing there on guard; the man's eyes looked stupid with the strain of listening to the faint sounds of the night. She stared into the darkness, seeing her son in every shadow everywhere; but it was only for a moment. Then she went back to the drawing-room with an assumption of high spirits, and began to play at loto with the little girls. But from time to time she complained of feeling unwell, and went to sit in her great chair by the fireside. So things went in Mme. de Dey's house and in the minds of those beneath her roof.

Meanwhile, on the road from Paris to Cherbourg, a young man, dressed in the inevitable brown *carmagnole* of those days, was plodding his way toward Carentan. When the first levies were made, there was little or no discipline kept up. The exigencies of the moment scarcely admitted of soldiers being equipped at once, and it was no uncommon thing to see the roads thronged with conscripts in their ordinary clothes. The young fellows went ahead of their company to the next halting place, or lagged behind it; it depended upon their fitness to bear the fatigues of a long march. This particular wayfarer was some considerable way in advance of a company of conscripts on the way to Cherbourg, whom the mayor was expecting to arrive every hour, for it was his duty to distribute their billets. The young man's footsteps were still firm as he trudged along, and his bearing seemed to indicate that he was no stranger to the rough life of a soldier. The moon shone on the pasture land about Carentan, but he had noticed great masses of white cloud that were about to scatter showers of snow over the country, and doubtless the fear of being overtaken by a storm had quickened his pace in spite of his weariness.

The wallet on his back was almost empty, and he carried a stick in his hand, cut from one of the high, thick box hedges that surround most of the farms in Lower Normandy. As the solitary wayfarer came into Carentan, the gleaming moonlit outlines of its towers stood out for a moment with ghostly effect against the sky. He met no one in the silent streets that rang with the echoes of his own footsteps, and was obliged to ask the way to the mayor's house of a weaver who was working late. The magistrate was not far to seek, and in a few minutes the conscript was sitting on a stone bench in the mayor's porch waiting for his billet. He was sent for, however, and confronted with that functionary, who scrutinized him closely. The foot soldier was a good-looking young man, who appeared to be of gentle birth. There was something aristocratic in his bearing, and signs in his face of intelligence developed by a good education.

"What is your name?" asked the mayor, eying him shrewdly.

"Julien Jussieu," answered the conscript.

"From — ?" queried the official, and an incredulous smile stole over his features.

"From Paris."

"Your comrades must be a good way behind?" remarked the Norman in sarcastic tones.

"I am three leagues ahead of the battalion."

"Some sentiment attracts you to Carentan, of course, citizen-conscript," said the mayor astutely. "All right, all right!" he added, with a wave of the hand, seeing that the young man was about to speak. "We know where to send you. There, off with you, *Citizen Jussieu*," and he handed over the billet.

There was a tinge of irony in the stress the magistrate laid on the two last words while he held out a billet on Mme. de Dey. The conscript read the direction curiously.

"He knows quite well that he has not far to go, and when he gets outside he will very soon cross the marketplace," said the mayor to himself, as the other went out. "He is uncommonly bold! God guide him!... He has an answer ready for everything. Yes, but if somebody else had asked to see his papers it would have been all up with him!"

The clocks in Carentan struck half-past nine as he spoke. Lanterns were being lit in Mme. de Dey's antechamber, servants were helping their masters and mistresses into sabots, greatcoats, and calashes. The card players settled their accounts, and everybody went out together, after the fashion of all little country towns.

"It looks as if the prosecutor meant to stop," said a lady, who noticed that that important personage was not in the group in the market-place, where they all took leave of one another before going their separate ways home. And, as a matter of fact, that redoubtable functionary was alone with the Countess, who waited trembling till he should go. There was something appalling in their long silence.

"Citoyenne," said he at last, "I am here to see that the laws of the Republic are carried out — "

Mme. de Dey shuddered.

"Have you nothing to tell me?"

"Nothing!" she answered, in amazement.

"Ah! madame," cried the prosecutor, sitting down beside her and changing his tone. "At this moment, for lack of a word, one of us — you or I — may carry our heads to the scaffold. I have watched your character, your soul, your manner, too closely to share the error into which you have managed to lead your visitors to-night. You are expecting your son, I could not doubt it."

The Countess made an involuntary sign of denial, but her face had grown white and drawn with the struggle to maintain the composure that she did not feel, and no tremor was lost on the merciless prosecutor.

"Very well," the Revolutionary official went on, "receive him; but do not let him stay under your roof after seven o'clock to-morrow morning; for to-morrow, as soon as it is light, I shall come with a denunciation that I will have made out, and — "

She looked at him, and the dull misery in her eyes would have softened a tiger.

"I will make it clear that the denunciation was false by making a thorough search," he went on in a gentle voice; "my report shall be such that you will be safe from any subsequent suspicion. I shall make mention of your patriotic gifts, your civism, and *all* of us will be safe."

Mme. de Dey, fearful of a trap, sat motionless, her face afire, her tongue frozen. A knock at the door rang through the house.

"Oh!..." cried the terrified mother, falling upon her knees; "save him! save him!"

"Yes, let us save him!" returned the public prosecutor, and his eyes grew bright as he looked at her, "if it costs *us* our lives!"

"Lost!" she wailed. The prosecutor raised her politely.

"Madame," said he with a flourish of eloquence, "to your own free will alone would I owe — "

"Madame, he is — " cried Brigitte, thinking that her mistress was alone. At the sight of the public prosecutor, the old servant's joy-flushed countenance became haggard and impassive.

"Who is it, Brigitte?" the prosecutor asked kindly, as if he too were in the secret of the household.

"A conscript that the mayor has sent here for a night's lodging," the woman replied, holding out the billet.

"So it is," said the prosecutor, when he had read the slip of paper. "A battalion is coming here to-night."

And he went.

The Countess's need to believe in the faith of her sometime attorney was so great, that she dared not entertain any suspicion of him. She fled upstairs; she felt scarcely strength enough to stand; she opened the door, and sprang, half dead with fear, into her son's arms.

"Oh! my child! my child!" she sobbed, covering him with almost frenzied kisses.

"Madame!..." said a stranger's voice.

"Oh! it is not he!" she cried, shrinking away in terror, and she stood face to face with the conscript, gazing at him with haggard eyes.

"*O saint bon Dieu!* how like he is!" cried Brigitte.

There was silence for a moment; even the stranger trembled at the sight of Mme. de Dey's face.

"Ah! monsieur," she said, leaning on the arm of Brigitte's husband, feeling for the first time the full extent of a sorrow that had all but killed her at its first threatening; "ah! monsieur, I cannot stay to see you any longer ... permit my servants to supply my place, and to see that you have all that you want."

She went down to her own room, Brigitte and the old serving-man half carrying her between them. The housekeeper set her mistress in a chair, and broke out:

"What, madame! is that man to sleep in Monsieur Auguste's bed, and wear Monsieur Auguste's slippers, and eat the pasty that I made for Monsieur Auguste? Why, if they were to guillotine me for it, I — "

"Brigitte!" cried Mme. de Dey.

Brigitte said no more.

"Hold your tongue, chatterbox," said her husband, in a low voice; "do you want to kill madame?"

A sound came from the conscript's room as he drew his chair to the table.

"I shall not stay here," cried Mme. de Dey; "I shall go into the conservatory; I shall hear better there if anyone passes in the night."

She still wavered between the fear that she had lost her son and the hope of seeing him once more. That night was hideously silent. Once, for the Countess, there was an awful interval, when the battalion of conscripts entered the town, and the men went by, one by one, to their lodgings. Every footfall, every sound in the street, raised hopes to be disappointed; but it was not for long, the dreadful quiet succeeded again. Toward morning the Countess was forced to return to her room. Brigitte, ever keeping watch over her mistress's movements, did not see her come out again; and when she went, she found the Countess lying there dead.

"I expect she heard that conscript," cried Brigitte, "walking about Monsieur Auguste's room, whistling that accursed *Marseillaise* of theirs while he dressed, as if he had been in a stable! That must have killed her."

But it was a deeper and a more solemn emotion, and doubtless some dreadful vision, that had caused Mme. de Dey's death; for at the very hour when she died at Carentan, her son was shot in le Morbihan.

*****

This tragical story may be added to all the instances on record of the workings of sympathies uncontrolled by the laws of time and space. These observations, collected with scientific curiosity by a few isolated individuals, will one day serve as documents on which to base the foundations of a new science which hitherto has lacked its man of genius.

Introduction to Zadig the Babylonian

A work (says the author) which performs more than it promises.

Voltaire never heard of a "detective story"; and yet he wrote the first in modern literature, so clever as to be a model for all the others that followed.

He describes his hero Zadig thus: "His chief talent consisted in discovering the truth," — in making swift, yet marvelous deductions, worthy of Sherlock Holmes or any other of the ingenious modern "thinking machines."

But no one would be more surprised than Voltaire to behold the part that Zadig now "performs." The amusing Babylonian, now regarded as the aristocratic ancestor of modern story-detectives, was created as a chief mocker in a satire on eighteenth-century manners, morals, and metaphysics.

Voltaire breathed his dazzling brilliance into "Zadig" as he did into a hundred other characters — for a political purpose. Their veiled and bitter satire was to make Europe think — to sting reason into action — to ridicule out of existence a humbugging System of special privileges. It did, *via* the French Revolution and the resulting upheavals. His prose romances are the most perfect of Voltaire's manifold expressions to this end, which mark him the most powerful literary man of the century.

But the arch-wit of his age outdid his brilliant self in "Zadig." So surpassingly sharp and quick was this finished sleuth that his methods far outlived his satirical mission. His razor-mind was reincarnated a century later as the fascinator of nations — M. Dupin. And from Poe's wizard up to Sherlock Holmes, no one of the thousand "detectives," drawn in a myriad scenes that thrill the world of readers, but owes his outlines, at least, to "Zadig."

"Don't use your reason — act like your friends — respect conventionalities — otherwise the world will absolutely refuse to let you be happy." This sums up the theory of life that Zadig satires. His comical troubles proceed entirely from his use of independent reason as opposed to the customs of his times.

The satire fitted ancient Babylonia — it fitted eighteenth-century France — and perhaps the reader of these volumes can find some points of contact with his own surroundings.

It is still piquant, however, to remember Zadig's original *raison d'être*. He happened to be cast in the part of what we now know as "a detective," merely because Voltaire had been reading stories in the "Arabian Nights" whose heroes get out of scrapes by marvelous deductions from simple signs. (See Vol. VI.)

Voltaire must have grinned at the delicious human interest, the subtle irony to pierce complacent humbugs, that lurked behind these Oriental situations. He made the most of his chance for a quaint parable, applicable to the courts, the church and science of Europe. As the story runs on, midst many and sudden adventures, the Babylonian reads causes from events in guileless fashion, enthusiastic as Sherlock Holmes, and no less efficient — and all the while, behind this innocent mask, Voltaire is insinuating a comparison between the practical results of Zadig's common sense and the futile mental cobwebs spun by the alleged thought of the time.

Especially did "Zadig" caricature orthodox science, and the metaphysicians, whose solemn searches after final causes, after the reality behind the appearance of things, mostly wandered into hopeless tangles, and thus formed a great weapon of political oppression, by postponing the age of reason and independent thought. Zadig "did not employ himself in calculating how many inches of water flow in a second of time under the arches of a bridge, or whether there fell a cube line of rain in the month of the Mouse more than in the month of the Sheep. He never dreamed of making silk of cobwebs, or porcelain of broken bottles; but he chiefly studied the properties of plants and animals; and soon acquired a sagacity that made him *discover a thousand differences where other men see nothing but uniformity*."

FRANÇOIS MARIE AROUET DE VOLTAIRE

Zadig the Babylonian

1. THE BLIND OF ONE EYE

There lived at Babylon, in the reign of King Moabdar, a young man named Zadig, of a good natural disposition, strengthened and improved by education. Though rich and young, he had learned to moderate his passions; he had nothing stiff or affected in his behavior, he did not pretend to examine every action by the strict rules of reason, but was always ready to make proper allowances for the weakness of mankind.

It was matter of surprise that, notwithstanding his sprightly wit, he never exposed by his raillery those vague, incoherent, and noisy discourses, those rash censures, ignorant decisions, coarse jests, and all that empty jingle of words which at Babylon went by the name of conversation. He had learned, in the first book of Zoroaster, that self love is a football swelled with wind, from which, when pierced, the most terrible tempests issue forth.

Above all, Zadig never boasted of his conquests among the women, nor affected to entertain a contemptible opinion of the fair sex. He was generous, and was never afraid of obliging the ungrateful; remembering the grand precept of Zoroaster, "When thou eatest, give to the dogs, should they even bite thee." He was as wise as it is possible for man to be, for he sought to live with the wise.

Instructed in the sciences of the ancient Chaldeans, he understood the principles of natural philosophy, such as they were then supposed to be; and knew as much of metaphysics as hath ever been known in any age, that is, little or nothing at all. He was firmly persuaded, notwithstanding the new philosophy of the times, that the year consisted of three hundred and sixty-five days and six hours, and that the sun was in the center of the world. But when the principal magi told him, with a haughty and contemptuous air, that his sentiments were of a dangerous tendency, and that it was to be an enemy to the state to believe that the sun revolved round its own axis, and that the year had twelve months, he held his tongue with great modesty and meekness.

Possessed as he was of great riches, and consequently of many friends, blessed with a good constitution, a handsome figure, a mind just and moderate, and a heart noble and sincere, he fondly imagined that he might easily be happy. He was going to be married to Semira, who, in point of beauty, birth, and fortune, was the first match in Babylon. He had a real and virtuous affection for this lady, and she loved him with the most passionate fondness.

The happy moment was almost arrived that was to unite them forever in the bands of wedlock, when happening to take a walk together toward one of the gates of Babylon, under the palm trees that adorn the banks of the Euphrates, they saw some men approaching, armed with sabers and arrows. These were the attendants of young Orcan, the minister's nephew, whom his uncle's creatures had flattered into an opinion that he might do everything with impunity. He had none of the graces nor virtues of Zadig; but thinking himself a much more accomplished man, he was enraged to find that the other was preferred before him. This jealousy, which was merely the effect of his vanity, made him imagine that he was desperately in love with Semira; and accordingly he resolved to carry her off. The ravishers seized her; in the violence of the outrage they wounded her, and made the blood flow from a person, the sight of which would have softened the tigers of Mount Imaus. She pierced the heavens with her complaints. She cried out, "My dear husband! they tear me from the man I adore." Regardless of her own danger, she was only concerned for the fate of her dear Zadig, who, in the meantime, defended himself with all the strength that courage and love could inspire. Assisted only by two slaves, he put the ravishers to flight and carried home Semira, insensible and bloody as she was.

On opening her eyes and beholding her deliverer, "O Zadig!" said she, "I loved thee formerly as my intended husband; I now love thee as the preserver of my honor and my life." Never was heart more deeply affected than that of Semira. Never did a more charming mouth express more moving sentiments, in those glowing words inspired by a sense of the greatest of all favors, and by the most tender transports of a lawful passion.

Her wound was slight and was soon cured. Zadig was more dangerously wounded; an arrow had pierced him near his eye, and penetrated to a considerable depth. Semira wearied Heaven with her prayers for the recovery of her lover. Her eyes were constantly bathed in tears; she anxiously waited the happy moment when those of Zadig should be able to meet hers; but an abscess growing on the wounded eye gave everything to fear. A messenger was immediately dispatched to Memphis for the great physician Hermes, who came with a numerous retinue. He visited the patient and declared that he would lose his eye. He even foretold the day and hour when this fatal event would happen. "Had it been the right eye," said he, "I could easily have cured it; but the wounds of the left eye are incurable." All Babylon lamented the fate of Zadig, and admired the profound knowledge of Hermes.

In two days the abscess broke of its own accord and Zadig was perfectly cured. Hermes wrote a book to prove that it ought not to have been cured. Zadig did not read it; but, as soon as he was able to go abroad, he went to pay a visit to her in whom all his hopes of happiness were centered, and for whose sake alone he wished to have eyes. Semira had been in the country for three days past. He learned on the road that that fine lady, having openly declared that she had an unconquerable aversion to one-eyed men, had the night before given her hand to Orcan. At this news he fell speechless to the ground. His sorrow brought him almost to the brink of the grave. He was long indisposed; but reason at last got the better of his affliction, and the severity of his fate served to console him.

"Since," said he, "I have suffered so much from the cruel caprice of a woman educated at court, I must now think of marrying the daughter of a citizen." He pitched upon Azora, a lady of the greatest prudence, and of the best family in town. He married her and lived with her for three months in all the delights of the most tender union. He only observed that she had a little levity; and was too apt to find that those young men who had the most handsome persons were likewise possessed of most wit and virtue.

2. THE NOSE

One morning Azora returned from a walk in a terrible passion, and uttering the most violent exclamations. "What aileth thee," said he, "my dear spouse? What is it that can thus have discomposed thee?"

"Alas," said she, "thou wouldst be as much enraged as I am hadst thou seen what I have just beheld. I have been to comfort the young widow Cosrou, who, within these two days, hath raised a tomb to her young husband, near the rivulet that washes the skirts of this meadow. She vowed to heaven, in the bitterness of her grief, to remain at this tomb while the water of the rivulet should continue to run near it."

"Well," said Zadig, "she is an excellent woman, and loved her husband with the most sincere affection."

"Ah," replied Azora, "didst thou but know in what she was employed when I went to wait upon her!"

"In what, pray, beautiful Azora? Was she turning the course of the rivulet?"

Azora broke out into such long invectives and loaded the young widow with such bitter reproaches, that Zadig was far from being pleased with this ostentation of virtue.

Zadig had a friend named Cador, one of those young men in whom his wife discovered more probity and merit than in others. He made him his confidant, and secured his fidelity as much as possible by a considerable present. Azora, having passed two days with a friend in the country, returned home on the third. The servants told her, with tears in their eyes, that her husband died suddenly the night before; that they were afraid to send her an account of this mournful event; and that they had just been depositing his corpse in the tomb of his ancestors, at the end of the garden. She wept, she tore her hair, and swore she would follow him to the grave.

In the evening Cador begged leave to wait upon her, and joined his tears with hers. Next day they wept less, and dined together. Cador told her that his friend had left him the greatest part of his estate; and that he should think himself extremely happy in sharing his fortune with her. The lady wept, fell into a passion, and at last became more mild and gentle. They sat longer at supper than at dinner. They now talked with greater confidence. Azora praised the deceased; but owned that he had many failings from which Cador was free.

During supper Cador complained of a violent pain in his side. The lady, greatly concerned, and eager to serve him, caused all kinds of essences to be brought, with which she anointed him, to try if some of them might not possibly ease him of his pain. She lamented that the great Hermes was not still in Babylon. She even condescended to touch the side in which Cador felt such exquisite pain.

"Art thou subject to this cruel disorder?" said she to him with a compassionate air.

"It sometimes brings me," replied Cador, "to the brink of the grave; and there is but one remedy that can give me relief, and that is to apply to my side the nose of a man who is lately dead."

"A strange remedy, indeed!" said Azora.

"Not more strange," replied he, "than the sachels of Arnon against the apoplexy." This reason, added to the great merit of the young man, at last determined the lady.

"After all," says she, "when my husband shall cross the bridge Tchinavar, in his journey to the other world, the angel Asrael will not refuse him a passage because his nose is a little shorter in the second life than it was in the first." She then took a razor, went to her husband's tomb, bedewed it with her tears, and drew near to cut off the nose of Zadig, whom she found extended at full length in the tomb. Zadig arose, holding his nose with one hand, and, putting back the razor with the other, "Madam," said he, "don't exclaim so violently against young Cosrou; the project of cutting off my nose is equal to that of turning the course of a rivulet."

3. THE DOG AND THE HORSE

Zadig found by experience that the first month of marriage, as it is written in the book of Zend, is the moon of honey, and that the second is the moon of wormwood. He was some time after obliged to repudiate Azora, who became too difficult to be pleased; and he then sought for happiness in the study of nature. "No man," said he, "can be happier than a philosopher who reads in this great book which God hath placed before our eyes. The truths he discovers are his own, he nourishes and exalts his soul; he lives in peace; he fears nothing from men; and his tender spouse will not come to cut off his nose."

Possessed of these ideas he retired to a country house on the banks of the Euphrates. There he did not employ himself in calculating how many inches of water flow in a second of time under the arches of a bridge, or whether there fell a cube line of rain in the month of the Mouse more than in the month of the Sheep. He never dreamed of making silk of cobwebs, or porcelain of broken bottles; but he chiefly studied the properties of plants and animals; and soon acquired a sagacity that made him discover a thousand differences where other men see nothing but uniformity.

One day, as he was walking near a little wood, he saw one of the queen's eunuchs running toward him, followed by several officers, who appeared to be in great perplexity, and who ran to and fro like men distracted, eagerly searching for something they had lost of great value. "Young man," said the first eunuch, "hast thou seen the queen's dog?" "It is a female," replied Zadig. "Thou art in the right," returned the first eunuch. "It is a very small she spaniel," added Zadig; "she has lately whelped; she limps on the left forefoot, and has very long ears." "Thou hast seen her," said the first eunuch, quite out of breath. "No," replied Zadig, "I have not seen her, nor did I so much as know that the queen had a dog."

Exactly at the same time, by one of the common freaks of fortune, the finest horse in the king's stable had escaped from the jockey in the plains of Babylon. The principal huntsman and all the other officers ran after him with as much eagerness and anxiety as the first eunuch had done after the spaniel. The principal huntsman addressed himself to Zadig, and asked him if he had not seen the king's horse passing by. "He is the fleetest horse in the king's stable," replied Zadig; "he is five feet high, with very small hoofs, and a tail three feet and a half in length; the studs on his bit are gold of twenty-three carats, and his shoes are silver of eleven pennyweights." "What way did he take? where is he?" demanded the chief huntsman. "I have not seen him," replied Zadig, "and never heard talk of him before."

The principal huntsman and the first eunuch never doubted but that Zadig had stolen the king's horse and the queen's spaniel. They therefore had him conducted before the assembly of the grand desterham, who condemned him to the knout, and to spend the rest of his days in Siberia. Hardly was the sentence passed when the horse and the spaniel were both found. The judges were reduced to the disagreeable necessity of reversing their sentence; but they condemned Zadig to pay four hundred ounces of gold for having said that he had not seen what he had seen. This fine he was obliged to pay; after which he was permitted to plead his cause before the counsel of the grand desterham, when he spoke to the following effect:

"Ye stars of justice, abyss of sciences, mirrors of truth, who have the weight of lead, the hardness of iron, the splendor of the diamond, and many properties of gold: Since I am permitted to speak before this august assembly, I swear to you by Oramades that I have never seen the queen's respectable spaniel, nor the sacred horse of the king of kings. The truth of the matter was as follows: I was walking toward the little wood, where I afterwards met the venerable eunuch, and the most illustrious chief huntsman. I observed on the sand the traces of an animal, and could easily perceive them to be those of a little dog. The light and long furrows impressed on little eminences of sand between the marks of the paws plainly discovered that it was a female, whose dugs were hanging down, and that therefore she must have whelped a few days before. Other traces of a different kind, that always appeared to have gently brushed the surface of the sand near the marks of the forefeet, showed me that she had very long ears; and as I remarked that there was always a slighter impression made on the sand by one foot than the other three, I found that the spaniel of our august queen was a little lame, if I may be allowed the expression.

"With regard to the horse of the king of kings, you will be pleased to know that, walking in the lanes of this wood, I observed the marks of a horse's shoes, all at equal distances. This must be a horse, said I to myself, that gallops excellently. The dust on the trees in the road that was but seven feet wide was a little brushed off, at the distance of three feet and a half from the middle of the road. This horse, said I, has a tail three feet and a half long, which being whisked to the right and left, has swept away the dust. I observed under the trees that formed an arbor five feet in height, that the leaves of the branches were newly fallen; from whence I inferred that the horse had touched them, and that he must therefore be five feet high. As to his bit, it must be gold of twenty-three carats, for he had rubbed its bosses against a stone which I knew to be a touchstone, and which I have tried. In a word, from the marks made by his shoes on flints of another kind, I concluded that he was shod with silver eleven deniers fine."

All the judges admired Zadig for his acute and profound discernment. The news of this speech was carried even to the king and queen. Nothing was talked of but Zadig in the antechambers, the chambers, and the cabinet; and though many of the magi were of opinion that he ought to be burned as a sorcerer, the king ordered his officers to restore him the four hundred ounces of gold which he had been obliged to pay. The register, the attorneys, and bailiffs, went to his house with great formality, to carry him back his four hundred ounces. They only retained three hundred and ninety-eight of them to defray the expenses of justice; and their servants demanded their fees.

Zadig saw how extremely dangerous it sometimes is to appear too knowing, and therefore resolved that on the next occasion of the like nature he would not tell what he had seen.

Such an opportunity soon offered. A prisoner of state made his escape, and passed under the window of Zadig's house. Zadig was examined and made no answer. But it was proved that he had looked at the prisoner from this window. For this crime he was condemned to pay five hundred ounces of gold; and, according to the polite custom of Babylon, he thanked his judges for their indulgence.

"Great God!" said he to himself, "what a misfortune it is to walk in a wood through which the queen's spaniel or the king's horse has passed! how dangerous to look out at a window! and how difficult to be happy in this life!"

4. THE ENVIOUS MAN

Zadig resolved to comfort himself by philosophy and friendship for the evils he had suffered from fortune. He had in the suburbs of Babylon a house elegantly furnished, in which he assembled all the arts and all the pleasures worthy the pursuit of a gentleman. In the morning his library was open to the learned. In the evening his table was surrounded by good company. But he soon found what very dangerous guests these men of letters are. A warm dispute arose on one of Zoroaster's laws, which forbids the eating of a griffin. "Why," said some of them, "prohibit the eating of a griffin, if there is no such an animal in nature?" "There must necessarily be such an animal," said the others, "since Zoroaster forbids us to eat it." Zadig would fain have reconciled them by saying, "If there are no griffins, we cannot possibly eat them; and thus either way we shall obey Zoroaster."

A learned man who had composed thirteen volumes on the properties of the griffin, and was besides the chief theurgite, hastened away to accuse Zadig before one of the principal magi, named Yebor, the greatest blockhead and therefore the greatest fanatic among the Chaldeans. This man would have impaled Zadig to do honors to the sun, and would then have recited the breviary of Zoroaster with greater satisfaction. The friend Cador (a friend is better than a hundred priests) went to Yebor, and said to him, "Long live the sun and the griffins; beware of punishing Zadig; he is a saint; he has griffins in his inner court and does not eat them; and his accuser is an heretic, who dares to maintain that rabbits have cloven feet and are not unclean."

"Well," said Yebor, shaking his bald pate, "we must impale Zadig for having thought contemptuously of griffins, and the other for having spoken disrespectfully of rabbits." Cador hushed up the affair by means of a maid of honor with whom he had a love affair, and who had great interest in the College of the Magi. Nobody was impaled.

This levity occasioned a great murmuring among some of the doctors, who from thence predicted the fall of Babylon. "Upon what does happiness depend?" said Zadig. "I am persecuted by everything in the world, even on account of beings that have no existence." He cursed those men of learning, and resolved for the future to live with none but good company.

He assembled at his house the most worthy men and the most beautiful ladies of Babylon. He gave them delicious suppers, often preceded by concerts of music, and always animated by polite conversation, from which he knew how to banish that affectation of wit which is the surest method of preventing it entirely, and of spoiling the pleasure of the most agreeable society. Neither the choice of his friends, nor that of the dishes was made by vanity; for in everything he preferred the substance to the shadow; and by these means he procured that real respect to which he did not aspire.

Opposite to his house lived one Arimazes, a man whose deformed countenance was but a faint picture of his still more deformed mind. His heart was a mixture of malice, pride, and envy. Having never been able to succeed in any of his undertakings, he revenged himself on all around him by loading them with the blackest calumnies. Rich as he was, he found it difficult to procure a set of flatterers. The rattling of the chariots that entered Zadig's court in the evening filled him with uneasiness; the sound of his praises enraged him still more. He sometimes went to Zadig's house, and sat down at table without being desired; where he spoiled all the pleasure of the company, as the harpies are said to infect the viands they touch. It happened that one day he took it in his head to give an entertainment to a lady, who, instead of accepting it, went to sup with Zadig. At another time, as he was talking with Zadig at court, a minister of state came up to them, and invited Zadig to supper without inviting Arimazes. The most implacable hatred has seldom a more solid foundation. This man, who in Babylon was called the Envious, resolved to ruin Zadig because he was called the Happy. "The opportunity of doing mischief occurs a hundred times in a day, and that of doing good but once a year," as sayeth the wise Zoroaster.

The envious man went to see Zadig, who was walking in his garden with two friends and a lady, to whom he said many gallant things, without any other intention than that of saying them. The conversation turned upon a war which the king had just brought to a happy conclusion against the prince of Hircania, his vassal. Zadig, who had signalized his courage in this short war, bestowed great praises on the king, but greater still on the lady. He took out his pocketbook, and wrote four lines extempore, which he gave to this amiable person to read. His friends begged they might see them; but modesty, or rather a well-regulated self love, would not allow him to grant their request. He knew that extemporary verses are never approved of by any but by the person in whose honor they are written. He therefore tore in two the leaf on which he had wrote them, and threw both the pieces into a thicket of rosebushes, where the rest of the company sought for them in vain. A slight shower falling soon after obliged them to return to the house. The envious man, who stayed in the garden, continued the search till at last he found a piece of the leaf. It had been torn in such a manner that each half of a line formed a complete sense, and even a verse of a shorter measure; but what was still more surprising, these short verses were found to contain the most injurious reflections on the king. They ran thus:

To flagrant crimes.
His crown he owes.
To peaceful times.
The worst of foes.

The envious man was now happy for the first time of his life. He had it in his power to ruin a person of virtue and merit. Filled with this fiendlike joy, he found means to convey to the king the satire written by the hand of Zadig, who, together with the lady and his two friends, was thrown into prison.

His trial was soon finished, without his being permitted to speak for himself. As he was going to receive his sentence, the envious man threw himself in his way and told him with a loud voice that his verses were good for nothing. Zadig did not value himself on being a good poet; but it filled him with inexpressible concern to find that he was condemned for high treason; and that the fair lady and his two friends were confined in prison for a crime of which they were not guilty. He was not allowed to speak because his writing spoke for him. Such was the law of Babylon. Accordingly he was conducted to the place of execution, through an immense crowd of spectators, who durst not venture to express their pity for him, but who carefully examined his countenance to see if he died with a good grace. His relations alone were inconsolable, for they could not succeed to his estate. Three fourths of his wealth were confiscated into the king's treasury, and the other fourth was given to the envious man.

Just as he was preparing for death the king's parrot flew from its cage and alighted on a rosebush in Zadig's garden. A peach had been driven thither by the wind from a neighboring tree, and had fallen on a piece of the written leaf of the pocketbook to which it stuck. The bird carried off the peach and the paper and laid them on the king's knee. The king took up the paper with great eagerness and read the words, which formed no sense, and seemed to be the endings of verses. He loved poetry; and there is always some mercy to be expected from a prince of that disposition. The adventure of the parrot set him a-thinking.

The queen, who remembered what had been written on the piece of Zadig's pocketbook, caused it to be brought. They compared the two pieces together and found them to tally exactly; they then read the verses as Zadig had wrote them.

TYRANTS ARE PRONE TO FLAGRANT CRIMES.

TO CLEMENCY HIS CROWN HE OWES.

TO CONCORD AND TO PEACEFUL TIMES.

LOVE ONLY IS THE WORST OF FOES.

The king gave immediate orders that Zadig should be brought before him, and that his two friends and the lady should be set at liberty. Zadig fell prostrate on the ground before the king and queen; humbly begged their pardon for having made such bad verses and spoke with so much propriety, wit, and good sense, that their majesties desired they might see him again. He did himself that honor, and insinuated himself still farther into their good graces. They gave him all the wealth of the envious man; but Zadig restored him back the whole of it. And this instance of generosity gave no other pleasure to the envious man than that of having preserved his estate.

The king's esteem for Zadig increased every day. He admitted him into all his parties of pleasure, and consulted him in all affairs of state. From that time the queen began to regard him with an eye of tenderness that might one day prove dangerous to herself, to the king, her august comfort, to Zadig, and to the kingdom in general. Zadig now began to think that happiness was not so unattainable as he had formerly imagined.

5. THE GENEROUS

The time now arrived for celebrating a grand festival, which returned every five years. It was a custom in Babylon solemnly to declare at the end of every five years which of the citizens had performed the most generous action. The grandees and the magi were the judges. The first satrap, who was charged with the government of the city, published the most noble actions that had passed under his administration. The competition was decided by votes; and the king pronounced the sentence. People came to this solemnity from the extremities of the earth. The conqueror received from the monarch's hand a golden cup adorned with precious stones, his majesty at the same time making him this compliment:

"Receive this reward of thy generosity, and may the gods grant me many subjects like to thee."

This memorable day being come, the king appeared on his throne, surrounded by the grandees, the magi, and the deputies of all nations that came to these games, where glory was acquired not by the swiftness of horses, nor by strength of body, but by virtue. The first satrap recited, with an audible voice, such actions as might entitle the authors of them to this invaluable prize. He did not mention the greatness of soul with which Zadig had restored the envious man his fortune, because it was not judged to be an action worthy of disputing the prize.

He first presented a judge who, having made a citizen lose a considerable cause by a mistake, for which, after all, he was not accountable, had given him the whole of his own estate, which was just equal to what the other had lost.

He next produced a young man who, being desperately in love with a lady whom he was going to marry, had yielded her up to his friend, whose passion for her had almost brought him to the brink of the grave, and at the same time had given him the lady's fortune.

He afterwards produced a soldier who, in the wars of Hircania, had given a still more noble instance of generosity. A party of the enemy having seized his mistress, he fought in her defense with great intrepidity. At that very instant he was informed that another party, at the distance of a few paces, were carrying off his mother; he therefore left his mistress with tears in his eyes and flew to the assistance of his mother. At last he returned to the dear object of his love and found her expiring. He was just going to plunge his sword in his own bosom; but his mother remonstrating against such a desperate deed, and telling him that he was the only support of her life, he had the courage to endure to live.

The judges were inclined to give the prize to the soldier. But the king took up the discourse and said: "The action of the soldier, and those of the other two, are doubtless very great, but they have nothing in them surprising. Yesterday Zadig performed an action that filled me with wonder. I had a few days before disgraced Coreb, my minister and favorite. I complained of him in the most violent and bitter terms; all my courtiers assured me that I was too gentle and seemed to vie with each other in speaking ill of Coreb. I asked Zadig what he thought of him, and he had the courage to commend him. I have read in our histories of many people who have atoned for an error by the surrender of their fortune; who have resigned a mistress; or preferred a mother to the object of their affection; but never before did I hear of a courtier who spoke favorably of a disgraced minister that labored under the displeasure of his sovereign. I give to each of those whose generous actions have been now recited twenty thousand pieces of gold; but the cup I give to Zadig."

"May it please your majesty," said Zadig, "thyself alone deservest the cup; thou hast performed an action of all others the most uncommon and meritorious, since, notwithstanding thy being a powerful king, thou wast not offended at thy slave when he presumed to oppose thy passion." The king and Zadig were equally the object of admiration. The judge, who had given his estate to his client; the lover, who had resigned his mistress to a friend; and the soldier, who had preferred the safety of his mother to that of his mistress, received the king's presents and saw their names enrolled in the catalogue of generous men. Zadig had the cup, and the king acquired the reputation of a good prince, which he did not long enjoy. The day was celebrated by feasts that lasted longer than the law enjoined; and the memory of it is still preserved in Asia. Zadig said, "Now I am happy at last"; but he found himself fatally deceived.

6. THE MINISTER

The king had lost his first minister and chose Zadig to supply his place. All the ladies in Babylon applauded the choice; for since the foundation of the empire there had never been such a young minister. But all the courtiers were filled with jealousy and vexation. The envious man in particular was troubled with a spitting of blood and a prodigious inflammation in his nose. Zadig, having thanked the king and queen for their goodness, went likewise to thank the parrot. "Beautiful bird," said he, "'tis thou that hast saved my life and made me first minister. The queen's spaniel and the king's horse did me a great deal of mischief; but thou hast done me much good. Upon such slender threads as these do the fates of mortals hang! But," added he, "this happiness perhaps will vanish very soon."

"Soon," replied the parrot.

Zadig was somewhat startled at this word. But as he was a good natural philosopher and did not believe parrots to be prophets, he quickly recovered his spirits and resolved to execute his duty to the best of his power.

He made everyone feel the sacred authority of the laws, but no one felt the weight of his dignity. He never checked the deliberation of the diran; and every vizier might give his opinion without the fear of incurring the minister's displeasure. When he gave judgment, it was not he that gave it, it was the law; the rigor of which, however, whenever it was too severe, he always took care to soften; and when laws were wanting, the equity of his decisions was such as might easily have made them pass for those of Zoroaster. It is to him that the nations are indebted for this grand principle, to wit, that it is better to run the risk of sparing the guilty than to condemn the innocent. He imagined that laws were made as well to secure the people from the suffering of injuries as to restrain them from the commission of crimes. His chief talent consisted in discovering the truth, which all men seek to obscure.

This great talent he put in practice from the very beginning of his administration. A famous merchant of Babylon, who died in the Indies, divided his estate equally between his two sons, after having disposed of their sister in marriage, and left a present of thirty thousand pieces of gold to that son who should be found to have loved him best. The eldest raised a tomb to his memory; the youngest increased his sister's portion, by giving her part of his inheritance. Everyone said that the eldest son loved his father best, and the youngest his sister; and that the thirty thousand pieces belonged to the eldest.

Zadig sent for both of them, the one after the other. To the eldest he said: "Thy father is not dead; he is recovered of his last illness, and is returning to Babylon." "God be praised," replied the young man; "but his tomb cost me a considerable sum." Zadig afterwards said the same to the youngest. "God be praised," said he, "I will go and restore to my father all that I have; but I could wish that he would leave my sister what I have given her." "Thou shalt restore nothing," replied Zadig, "and thou shalt have the thirty thousand pieces, for thou art the son who loves his father best."

7. THE DISPUTES AND THE AUDIENCES

In this manner he daily discovered the subtilty of his genius and the goodness of his heart. The people at once admired and loved him. He passed for the happiest man in the world. The whole empire resounded with his name. All the ladies ogled him. All the men praised him for his justice. The learned regarded him as an oracle; and even the priests confessed that he knew more than the old arch-magi Yebor. They were now so far from prosecuting him on account of the griffin, that they believed nothing but what he thought credible.

There had reigned in Babylon, for the space of fifteen hundred years, a violent contest that had divided the empire into two sects. The one pretended that they ought to enter the temple of Mitra with the left foot foremost; the other held this custom in detestation and always entered with the right foot first. The people waited with great impatience for the day on which the solemn feast of the sacred fire was to be celebrated, to see which sect Zadig would favor. All the world had their eyes fixed on his two feet, and the whole city was in the utmost suspense and perturbation. Zadig jumped into the temple with his feet joined together, and afterwards proved, in an eloquent discourse, that the Sovereign of heaven and earth, who accepted not the persons of men, makes no distinction between the right and left foot. The envious man and his wife alleged that his discourse was not figurative enough, and that he did not make the rocks and mountains to dance with sufficient agility.

"He is dry," said they, "and void of genius; he does not make the flea to fly, and stars to fall, nor the sun to melt wax; he has not the true Oriental style." Zadig contented himself with having the style of reason. All the world favored him, not because he was in the right road or followed the dictates of reason, or was a man of real merit, but because he was prime vizier.

He terminated with the same happy address the grand difference between the white and the black magi. The former maintained that it was the height of impiety to pray to God with the face turned toward the east in winter; the latter asserted that God abhorred the prayers of those who turned toward the west in summer. Zadig decreed that every man should be allowed to turn as he pleased.

Thus he found out the happy secret of finishing all affairs, whether of a private or public nature, in the morning. The rest of the day he employed in superintending and promoting the embellishments of Babylon. He exhibited tragedies that drew tears from the eyes of the spectators, and comedies that shook their sides with laughter; a custom which had long been disused, and which his good taste now induced him to revive. He never affected to be more knowing in the polite arts than the artists themselves; he encouraged them by rewards and honors, and was never jealous of their talents. In the evening the king was highly entertained with his conversation, and the queen still more. "Great minister!" said the king. "Amiable minister!" said the queen; and both of them added, "It would have been a great loss to the state had such a man been hanged."

Never was man in power obliged to give so many audiences to the ladies. Most of them came to consult him about no business at all, that so they might have some business with him. But none of them won his attention.

Meanwhile Zadig perceived that his thoughts were always distracted, as well when he gave audience as when he sat in judgment. He did not know to what to attribute this absence of mind; and that was his only sorrow.

He had a dream in which he imagined that he laid himself down upon a heap of dry herbs, among which there were many prickly ones that gave him great uneasiness, and that he afterwards reposed himself on a soft bed of roses from which there sprung a serpent that wounded him to the heart with its sharp and venomed tongue. "Alas," said he, "I have long lain on these dry and prickly herbs, I am now on the bed of roses; but what shall be the serpent?"

8. JEALOUSY

Zadig's calamities sprung even from his happiness and especially from his merit. He every day conversed with the king and Astarte, his august comfort. The charms of his conversation were greatly heightened by that desire of pleasing, which is to the mind what dress is to beauty. His youth and graceful appearance insensibly made an impression on Astarte, which she did not at first perceive. Her passion grew and flourished in the bosom of innocence. Without fear or scruple, she indulged the pleasing satisfaction of seeing and hearing a man who was so dear to her husband and to the empire in general. She was continually praising him to the king. She talked of him to her women, who were always sure to improve on her praises. And thus everything contributed to pierce her heart with a dart, of which she did not seem to be sensible. She made several presents to Zadig, which discovered a greater spirit of gallantry than she imagined. She intended to speak to him only as a queen satisfied with his services and her expressions were sometimes those of a woman in love.

Astarte was much more beautiful than that Semira who had such a strong aversion to one-eyed men, or that other woman who had resolved to cut off her husband's nose. Her unreserved familiarity, her tender expressions, at which she began to blush; and her eyes, which, though she endeavored to divert them to other objects, were always fixed upon his, inspired Zadig with a passion that filled him with astonishment. He struggled hard to get the better of it. He called to his aid the precepts of philosophy, which had always stood him in stead; but from thence, though he could derive the light of knowledge, he could procure no remedy to cure the disorders of his lovesick heart. Duty, gratitude, and violated majesty presented themselves to his mind as so many avenging gods. He struggled; he conquered; but this victory, which he was obliged to purchase afresh every moment, cost him many sighs and tears. He no longer dared to speak to the queen with that sweet and charming familiarity which had been so agreeable to them both. His countenance was covered with a cloud. His conversation was constrained and incoherent. His eyes were fixed on the ground; and when, in spite of all his endeavors to the contrary, they encountered those of the queen, they found them bathed in tears and darting arrows of flame. They seemed to say, We adore each other and yet are afraid to love; we both burn with a fire which we both condemn.

Zadig left the royal presence full of perplexity and despair, and having his heart oppressed with a burden which he was no longer able to bear. In the violence of his perturbation he involuntarily betrayed the secret to his friend Cador, in the same manner as a man who, having long supported the fits of a cruel disease, discovered his pain by a cry extorted from him by a more severe fit and by the cold sweat that covers his brow.

"I have already discovered," said Cador, "the sentiments which thou wouldst fain conceal from thyself. The symptoms by which the passions show themselves are certain and infallible. Judge, my dear Zadig, since I have read thy heart, whether the king will not discover something in it that may give him offense.

He has no other fault but that of being the most jealous man in the world. Thou canst resist the violence of thy passion with greater fortitude than the queen because thou art a philosopher, and because thou art Zadig. Astarte is a woman: she suffers her eyes to speak with so much the more imprudence, as she does not as yet think herself guilty. Conscious of her innocence she unhappily neglects those external appearances which are so necessary. I shall tremble for her so long as she has nothing wherewithal to reproach herself. Were ye both of one mind, ye might easily deceive the whole world. A growing passion, which we endeavor to suppress, discovers itself in spite of all our efforts to the contrary; but love, when gratified, is easily concealed."

Zadig trembled at the proposal of betraying the king, his benefactor; and never was he more faithful to his prince than when guilty of an involuntary crime against him.

Meanwhile the queen mentioned the name of Zadig so frequently and with such a blushing and downcast look; she was sometimes so lively and sometimes so perplexed when she spoke to him in the king's presence, and was seized with such deep thoughtfulness at his going away, that the king began to be troubled. He believed all that he saw and imagined all that he did not see. He particularly remarked that his wife's shoes were blue and that Zadig's shoes were blue; that his wife's ribbons were yellow and that Zadig's bonnet was yellow; and these were terrible symptoms to a prince of so much delicacy. In his jealous mind suspicions were turned into certainty.

All the slaves of kings and queens are so many spies over their hearts. They soon observed that Astarte was tender and that Moabdar was jealous. The envious man brought false report to the king. The monarch now thought of nothing but in what manner he might best execute his vengeance. He one night resolved to poison the queen and in the morning to put Zadig to death by the bowstring. The orders were given to a merciless eunuch, who commonly executed his acts of vengeance. There happened at that time to be in the king's chamber a little dwarf, who, though dumb, was not deaf. He was allowed, on account of his insignificance, to go wherever he pleased, and as a domestic animal, was a witness of what passed in the most profound secrecy. This little mute was strongly attached to the queen and Zadig. With equal horror and surprise he heard the cruel orders given. But how to prevent the fatal sentence that in a few hours was to be carried into execution! He could not write, but he could paint; and excelled particularly in drawing a striking resemblance. He employed a part of the night in sketching out with his pencil what he meant to impart to the queen. The piece represented the king in one corner, boiling with rage, and giving orders to the eunuch; a bowstring, and a bowl on a table; the queen in the middle of the picture, expiring in the arms of her woman, and Zadig strangled at her feet. The horizon represented a rising sun, to express that this shocking execution was to be performed in the morning. As soon as he had finished the picture he ran to one of Astarte's women, awakened her, and made her understand that she must immediately carry it to the queen.

At midnight a messenger knocks at Zadig's door, awakes him, and gives him a note from the queen. He doubts whether it is a dream; and opens the letter with a trembling hand. But how great was his surprise! and who can express the consternation and despair into which he was thrown upon reading these words: "Fly this instant, or thou art a dead man. Fly, Zadig, I conjure thee by our mutual love and my yellow ribbons. I have not been guilty, but I find I must die like a criminal."

Zadig was hardly able to speak. He sent for Cador, and, without uttering a word, gave him the note. Cador forced him to obey, and forthwith to take the road to Memphis. "Shouldst thou dare," said he, "to go in search of the queen, thou wilt hasten her death. Shouldst thou speak to the king, thou wilt infallibly ruin her. I will take upon me the charge of her destiny; follow thy own. I will spread a report that thou hast taken the road to India. I will soon follow thee, and inform thee of all that shall have passed in Babylon." At that instant, Cador caused two of the swiftest dromedaries to be brought to a private gate of the palace. Upon one of these he mounted Zadig, whom he was obliged to carry to the door, and who was ready to expire with grief. He was accompanied by a single domestic; and Cador, plunged in sorrow and astonishment, soon lost sight of his friend.

This illustrious fugitive arriving on the side of a hill, from whence he could take a view of Babylon, turned his eyes toward the queen's palace, and fainted away at the sight; nor did he recover his senses but to shed a torrent of tears and to wish for death. At length, after his thoughts had been long engrossed in lamenting the unhappy fate of the loveliest woman and the greatest queen in the world, he for a moment turned his views on himself and cried: "What then is human life? O virtue, how hast thou served me! Two women have basely deceived me, and now a third, who is innocent, and more beautiful than both the others, is going to be put to death! Whatever good I have done hath been to me a continual source of calamity and affliction; and I have only been raised to the height of grandeur, to be tumbled down the most horrid precipice of misfortune." Filled with these gloomy reflections, his eyes overspread with the veil of grief, his countenance covered with the paleness of death, and his soul plunged in an abyss of the blackest despair, he continued his journey toward Egypt.

9. THE WOMAN BEATEN

Zadig directed his course by the stars. The constellation of Orion and the splendid Dog Star guided his steps toward the pole of Cassiopæa. He admired those vast globes of light, which appear to our eyes but as so many little sparks, while the earth, which in reality is only an imperceptible point in nature, appears to our fond imaginations as something so grand and noble.

He then represented to himself the human species as it really is, as a parcel of insects devouring one another on a little atom of clay. This true image seemed to annihilate his misfortunes, by making him sensible of the nothingness of his own being, and of that of Babylon. His soul launched out into infinity, and, detached from the senses, contemplated the immutable order of the universe. But when afterwards, returning to himself, and entering into his own heart, he considered that Astarte had perhaps died for him, the universe vanished from his sight, and he beheld nothing in the whole compass of nature but Astarte expiring and Zadig unhappy. While he thus alternately gave up his mind to this flux and reflux of sublime philosophy and intolerable grief, he advanced toward the frontiers of Egypt; and his faithful domestic was already in the first village, in search of a lodging.

Upon reaching the village Zadig generously took the part of a woman attacked by her jealous lover. The combat grew so fierce that Zadig slew the lover. The Egyptians were then just and humane. The people conducted Zadig to the town house. They first of all ordered his wound to be dressed, and then examined him and his servant apart, in order to discover the truth. They found that Zadig was not an assassin; but as he was guilty of having killed a man, the law condemned him to be a slave. His two camels were sold for the benefit of the town; all the gold he had brought with him was distributed among the inhabitants; and his person, as well as that of the companion of his journey, was exposed to sale in the marketplace.

An Arabian merchant, named Setoc, made the purchase; but as the servant was fitter for labor than the master, he was sold at a higher price. There was no comparison between the two men. Thus Zadig became a slave subordinate to his own servant. They were linked together by a chain fastened to their feet, and in this condition they followed the Arabian merchant to his house.

By the way Zadig comforted his servant, and exhorted him to patience; but he could not help making, according to his usual custom, some reflections on human life. "I see," said he, "that the unhappiness of my fate hath an influence on thine. Hitherto everything has turned out to me in a most unaccountable manner. I have been condemned to pay a fine for having seen the marks of a spaniel's feet. I thought that I should once have been impaled on account of a griffin. I have been sent to execution for having made some verses in praise of the king. I have been upon the point of being strangled because the queen had yellow ribbons; and now I am a slave with thee, because a brutal wretch beat his mistress. Come, let us keep a good heart; all this perhaps will have an end. The Arabian merchants must necessarily have slaves; and why not me as well as another, since, as well as another, I am a man? This merchant will not be cruel; he must treat his slaves well, if he expects any advantage from them." But while he spoke thus, his heart was entirely engrossed by the fate of the Queen of Babylon.

Two days after, the merchant Setoc set out for Arabia Deserta, with his slaves and his camels. His tribe dwelt near the Desert of Oreb. The journey was long and painful. Setoc set a much greater value on the servant than the master, because the former was more expert in loading the camels; and all the little marks of distinction were shown to him. A camel having died within two days' journey of Oreb, his burden was divided and laid on the backs of the servants; and Zadig had his share among the rest.

Setoc laughed to see all his slaves walking with their bodies inclined. Zadig took the liberty to explain to him the cause, and inform him of the laws of the balance. The merchant was astonished, and began to regard him with other eyes. Zadig, finding he had raised his curiosity, increased it still further by acquainting him with many things that related to commerce, the specific gravity of metals, and commodities under an equal bulk; the properties of several useful animals; and the means of rendering those useful that are not naturally so. At last Setoc began to consider Zadig as a sage, and preferred him to his companion, whom he had formerly so much esteemed. He treated him well and had no cause to repent of his kindness.

10. THE STONE

As soon as Setoc arrived among his own tribe he demanded the payment of five hundred ounces of silver, which he had lent to a Jew in presence of two witnesses; but as the witnesses were dead, and the debt could not be proved, the Hebrew appropriated the merchant's money to himself, and piously thanked God for putting it in his power to cheat an Arabian. Setoc imparted this troublesome affair to Zadig, who was now become his counsel.

215

"In what place," said Zadig, "didst thou lend the five hundred ounces to this infidel?"

"Upon a large stone," replied the merchant, "that lies near Mount Oreb."

"What is the character of thy debtor?" said Zadig.

"That of a knave," returned Setoc.

"But I ask thee whether he is lively or phlegmatic, cautious or imprudent?"

"He is, of all bad payers," said Setoc, "the most lively fellow I ever knew."

"Well," resumed Zadig, "allow me to plead thy cause." In effect Zadig, having summoned the Jew to the tribunal, addressed the judge in the following terms: "Pillow of the throne of equity, I come to demand of this man, in the name of my master, five hundred ounces of silver, which he refuses to pay."

"Hast thou any witnesses?" said the judge.

"No, they are dead; but there remains a large stone upon which the money was counted; and if it please thy grandeur to order the stone to be sought for, I hope that it will bear witness. The Hebrew and I will tarry here till the stone arrives; I will send for it at my master's expense."

"With all my heart," replied the judge, and immediately applied himself to the discussion of other affairs.

When the court was going to break up, the judge said to Zadig, "Well, friend, is not thy stone come yet?"

The Hebrew replied with a smile, "Thy grandeur may stay here till the morrow, and after all not see the stone. It is more than six miles from hence; and it would require fifteen men to move it."

"Well," cried Zadig, "did not I say that the stone would bear witness? Since this man knows where it is, he thereby confesses that it was upon it that the money was counted." The Hebrew was disconcerted, and was soon after obliged to confess the truth. The judge ordered him to be fastened to the stone, without meat or drink, till he should restore the five hundred ounces, which were soon after paid.

The slave Zadig and the stone were held in great repute in Arabia.

11. THE FUNERAL PILE

Setoc, charmed with the happy issue of this affair, made his slave his intimate friend. He had now conceived as great esteem for him as ever the King of Babylon had done; and Zadig was glad that Setoc had no wife. He discovered in his master a good natural disposition, much probity of heart, and a great share of good sense; but he was sorry to see that, according to the ancient custom of Arabia, he adored the host of heaven; that is, the sun, moon, and stars. He sometimes spoke to him on this subject with great prudence and discretion. At last he told him that these bodies were like all other bodies in the universe, and no more deserving of our homage than a tree or a rock.

"But," said Setoc, "they are eternal beings; and it is from them we derive all we enjoy. They animate nature; they regulate the seasons; and, besides, are removed at such an immense distance from us that we cannot help revering them."

"Thou receivest more advantage," replied Zadig, "from the waters of the Red Sea, which carry thy merchandise to the Indies. Why may not it be as ancient as the stars? and if thou adorest what is placed at a distance from thee, thou oughtest to adore the land of the Gangarides, which lies at the extremity of the earth."

"No," said Setoc, "the brightness of the stars command my adoration."

At night Zadig lighted up a great number of candles in the tent where he was to sup with Setoc; and the moment his patron appeared, he fell on his knees before these lighted tapers, and said, "Eternal and shining luminaries! be ye always propitious to me." Having thus said, he sat down at table, without taking the least notice of Setoc.

"What art thou doing?" said Setoc to him in amaze.

"I act like thee," replied Zadig, "I adore these candles, and neglect their master and mine." Setoc comprehended the profound sense of this apologue. The wisdom of his slave sunk deep into his soul; he no longer offered incense to the creatures, but adored the eternal Being who made them.

There prevailed at that time in Arabia a shocking custom, sprung originally from Scythia, and which, being established in the Indies by the credit of the Brahmans, threatened to overrun all the East. When a married man died, and his beloved wife aspired to the character of a saint, she burned herself publicly on the body of her husband. This was a solemn feast and was called the Funeral Pile of Widowhood, and that tribe in which most women had been burned was the most respected.

An Arabian of Setoc's tribe being dead, his widow, whose name was Almona, and who was very devout, published the day and hour when she intended to throw herself into the fire, amidst the sound of drums and trumpets. Zadig remonstrated against this horrible custom; he showed Setoc how inconsistent it was with the happiness of mankind to suffer young widows to burn themselves every other day, widows who were capable of giving children to the state, or at least of educating those they already had; and he convinced him that it was his duty to do all that lay in his power to abolish such a barbarous practice.

"The women," said Setoc, "have possessed the right of burning themselves for more than a thousand years; and who shall dare to abrogate a law which time hath rendered sacred? Is there anything more respectable than ancient abuses?"

"Reason is more ancient," replied Zadig; "meanwhile, speak thou to the chiefs of the tribes and I will go to wait on the young widow."

Accordingly he was introduced to her; and, after having insinuated himself into her good graces by some compliments on her beauty and told her what a pity it was to commit so many charms to the flames, he at last praised her for her constancy and courage. "Thou must surely have loved thy husband," said he to her, "with the most passionate fondness."

"Who, I?" replied the lady. "I loved him not at all. He was a brutal, jealous, insupportable wretch; but I am firmly resolved to throw myself on his funeral pile."

"It would appear then," said Zadig, "that there must be a very delicious pleasure in being burned alive."

"Oh! it makes nature shudder," replied the lady, "but that must be overlooked. I am a devotee, and I should lose my reputation and all the world would despise me if I did not burn myself." Zadig having made her acknowledge that she burned herself to gain the good opinion of others and to gratify her own vanity, entertained her with a long discourse, calculated to make her a little in love with life, and even went so far as to inspire her with some degree of good will for the person who spoke to her.

"Alas!" said the lady, "I believe I should desire thee to marry me."

Zadig's mind was too much engrossed with the idea of Astarte not to elude this declaration; but he instantly went to the chiefs of the tribes, told them what had passed, and advised them to make a law, by which a widow should not be permitted to burn herself till she had conversed privately with a young man for the space of an hour. Since that time not a single woman hath burned herself in Arabia. They were indebted to Zadig alone for destroying in one day a cruel custom that had lasted for so many ages and thus he became the benefactor of Arabia.

12. THE SUPPER

Setoc, who could not separate himself from this man, in whom dwelt wisdom, carried him to the great fair of Balzora, whither the richest merchants in the earth resorted. Zadig was highly pleased to see so many men of different countries united in the same place. He considered the whole universe as one large family assembled at Balzora.

Setoc, after having sold his commodities at a very high price, returned to his own tribe with his friend Zadig; who learned, upon his arrival, that he had been tried in his absence, and was now going to be burned by a slow fire. Only the friendship of Almona saved his life. Like so many pretty women, she possessed great influence with the priesthood. Zadig thought it best to leave Arabia.

Setoc was so charmed with the ingenuity and address of Almona that he made her his wife. Zadig departed, after having thrown himself at the feet of his fair deliverer. Setoc and he took leave of each other with tears in their eyes, swearing an eternal friendship, and promising that the first of them that should acquire a large fortune should share it with the other.

Zadig directed his course along the frontiers of Assyria, still musing on the unhappy Astarte, and reflecting on the severity of fortune which seemed determined to make him the sport of her cruelty and the object of her persecution. "What," said he to himself, "four hundred ounces of gold for having seen a spaniel! condemned to lose my head for four bad verses in praise of the king! ready to be strangled because the queen had shoes of the color of my bonnet! reduced to slavery for having succored a woman who was beat! and on the point of being burned for having saved the lives of all the young widows of Arabia!"

13. THE ROBBER

Arriving on the frontiers which divide Arabia Petræa from Syria, he passed by a pretty strong castle, from which a party of armed Arabians sallied forth. They instantly surrounded him and cried, "All thou hast belongs to us, and thy person is the property of our master." Zadig replied by drawing his sword; his servant, who was a man of courage, did the same. They killed the first Arabians that presumed to lay hands on them; and, though the number was redoubled, they were not dismayed, but resolved to perish in the conflict. Two men defended themselves against a multitude; and such a combat could not last long.

The master of the castle, whose name was Arbogad, having observed from a window the prodigies of valor performed by Zadig, conceived a high esteem for this heroic stranger. He descended in haste and went in person to call off his men and deliver the two travelers.

"All that passes over my lands," said he, "belongs to me, as well as what I find upon the lands of others; but thou seemest to be a man of such undaunted courage that I will exempt thee from the common law." He then conducted him to his castle, ordering his men to treat him well; and in the evening Arbogad supped with Zadig.

The lord of the castle was one of those Arabians who are commonly called robbers; but he now and then performed some good actions amid a multitude of bad ones. He robbed with a furious rapacity, and granted favors with great generosity; he was intrepid in action; affable in company; a debauchee at table, but gay in debauchery; and particularly remarkable for his frank and open behavior. He was highly pleased with Zadig, whose lively conversation lengthened the repast.

At last Arbogad said to him: "I advise thee to enroll thy name in my catalogue; thou canst not do better; this is not a bad trade; and thou mayest one day become what I am at present."

"May I take the liberty of asking thee," said Zadig, "how long thou hast followed this noble profession?"

"From my most tender youth," replied the lord. "I was a servant to a pretty good-natured Arabian, but could not endure the hardships of my situation. I was vexed to find that fate had given me no share of the earth, which equally belongs to all men. I imparted the cause of my uneasiness to an old Arabian, who said to me: 'My son, do not despair; there was once a grain of sand that lamented that it was no more than a neglected atom in the deserts; at the end of a few years it became a diamond; and is now the brightest ornament in the crown of the king of the Indies.'

This discourse made a deep impression on my mind. I was the grain of sand, and I resolved to become the diamond. I began by stealing two horses; I soon got a party of companions; I put myself in a condition to rob small caravans; and thus, by degrees, I destroyed the difference which had formerly subsisted between me and other men. I had my share of the good things of this world; and was even recompensed with usury for the hardships I had suffered. I was greatly respected, and became the captain of a band of robbers. I seized this castle by force. The Satrap of Syria had a mind to dispossess me of it; but I was too rich to have anything to fear. I gave the satrap a handsome present, by which means I preserved my castle and increased my possessions. He even appointed me treasurer of the tributes which Arabia Petræa pays to the king of kings. I perform my office of receiver with great punctuality; but take the freedom to dispense with that of paymaster.

"The grand Desterham of Babylon sent hither a pretty satrap in the name of King Moabdar, to have me strangled. This man arrived with his orders: I was apprised of all; I caused to be strangled in his presence the four persons he had brought with him to draw the noose; after which I asked him how much his commission of strangling me might be worth. He replied, that his fees would amount to above three hundred pieces of gold. I then convinced him that he might gain more by staying with me. I made him an inferior robber; and he is now one of my best and richest officers. If thou wilt take my advice thy success may be equal to his; never was there a better season for plunder, since King Moabdar is killed, and all Babylon thrown into confusion."

"Moabdar killed!" said Zadig, "and what is become of Queen Astarte?"

"I know not," replied Arbogad. "All I know is, that Moabdar lost his senses and was killed; that Babylon is a scene of disorder and bloodshed; that all the empire is desolated; that there are some fine strokes to be struck yet; and that, for my own part, I have struck some that are admirable."

"But the queen," said Zadig; "for heaven's sake, knowest thou nothing of the queen's fate?"

"Yes," replied he, "I have heard something of a prince of Hircania; if she was not killed in the tumult, she is probably one of his concubines; but I am much fonder of booty than news. I have taken several women in my excursions; but I keep none of them. I sell them at a high price, when they are beautiful, without inquiring who they are. In commodities of this kind rank makes no difference, and a queen that is ugly will never find a merchant. Perhaps I may have sold Queen Astarte; perhaps she is dead; but, be it as it will, it is of little consequence to me, and I should imagine of as little to thee." So saying he drank a large draught which threw all his ideas into such confusion that Zadig could obtain no further information.

Zadig remained for some time without speech, sense, or motion. Arbogad continued drinking; told stories; constantly repeated that he was the happiest man in the world; and exhorted Zadig to put himself in the same condition. At last the soporiferous fumes of the wine lulled him into a gentle repose.

Zadig passed the night in the most violent perturbation. "What," said he, "did the king lose his senses? and is he killed? I cannot help lamenting his fate. The empire is rent in pieces; and this robber is happy. O fortune! O destiny! A robber is happy, and the most beautiful of nature's works hath perhaps perished in a barbarous manner or lives in a state worse than death. O Astarte! what is become of thee?"

At daybreak he questioned all those he met in the castle; but they were all busy, and he received no answer. During the night they had made a new capture, and they were now employed in dividing the spoils. All he could obtain in this hurry and confusion was an opportunity of departing, which he immediately embraced, plunged deeper than ever in the most gloomy and mournful reflections.

Zadig proceeded on his journey with a mind full of disquiet and perplexity, and wholly employed on the unhappy Astarte, on the King of Babylon, on his faithful friend Cador, on the happy robber Arbogad; in a word, on all the misfortunes and disappointments he had hitherto suffered.

14. THE FISHERMAN

At a few leagues' distance from Arbogad's castle he came to the banks of a small river, still deploring his fate, and considering himself as the most wretched of mankind. He saw a fisherman lying on the brink of the river, scarcely holding, in his weak and feeble hand, a net which he seemed ready to drop, and lifting up his eyes to Heaven.

"I am certainly," said the fisherman, "the most unhappy man in the world. I was universally allowed to be the most famous dealer in cream cheese in Babylon, and yet I am ruined. I had the most handsome wife that any man in my station could have; and by her I have been betrayed. I had still left a paltry house, and that I have seen pillaged and destroyed. At last I took refuge in this cottage, where I have no other resource than fishing, and yet I cannot catch a single fish. Oh, my net! no more will I throw thee into the water; I will throw myself in thy place." So saying, he arose and advanced forward in the attitude of a man ready to throw himself into the river, and thus to finish his life.

"What!" said Zadig to himself, "are there men as wretched as I?" His eagerness to save the fisherman's life was as this reflection. He ran to him, stopped him, and spoke to him with a tender and compassionate air. It is commonly supposed that we are less miserable when we have companions in our misery. This, according to Zoroaster, does not proceed from malice, but necessity. We feel ourselves insensibly drawn to an unhappy person as to one like ourselves. The joy of the happy would be an insult; but two men in distress are like two slender trees, which, mutually supporting each other, fortify themselves against the storm.

"Why," said Zadig to the fisherman, "dost thou sink under thy misfortunes?"

"Because," replied he, "I see no means of relief. I was the most considerable man in the village of Derlback, near Babylon, and with the assistance of my wife I made the best cream cheese in the empire. Queen Astarte and the famous minister Zadig were extremely fond of them."

Zadig, transported, said, "What, knowest thou nothing of the queen's fate?"

"No, my lord," replied the fisherman; "but I know that neither the queen nor Zadig has paid me for my cream cheeses; that I have lost my wife, and am now reduced to despair."

"I flatter myself," said Zadig, "that thou wilt not lose all thy money. I have heard of this Zadig; he is an honest man; and if he returns to Babylon, as he expects, he will give thee more than he owes thee. Believe me, go to Babylon. I shall be there before thee, because I am on horseback, and thou art on foot. Apply to the illustrious Cador; tell him thou hast met his friend; wait for me at his house; go, perhaps thou wilt not always be unhappy."

"O powerful Oromazes!" continued he, "thou employest me to comfort this man; whom wilt thou employ to give me consolation?" So saying, he gave the fisherman half the money he had brought from Arabia. The fisherman, struck with surprise and ravished with joy, kissed the feet of the friend of Cador, and said, "Thou are surely an angel sent from Heaven to save me!"

Meanwhile, Zadig continued to make fresh inquiries, and to shed tears. "What, my lord!" cried the fisherman, "art thou then so unhappy, thou who bestowest favors?"

"An hundred times more unhappy than thou art," replied Zadig.

"But how is it possible," said the good man, "that the giver can be more wretched than the receiver?"

"Because," replied Zadig, "thy greatest misery arose from poverty, and mine is seated in the heart."

"Did Orcan take thy wife from thee?" said the fisherman.

This word recalled to Zadig's mind the whole of his adventures. He repeated the catalogue of his misfortunes, beginning with the queen's spaniel, and ending with his arrival at the castle of the robber Arbogad. "Ah!" said he to the fisherman, "Orcan deserves to be punished; but it is commonly such men as those that are the favorites of fortune. However, go thou to the house of Lord Cador, and there wait my arrival." They then parted, the fisherman walked, thanking Heaven for the happiness of his condition; and Zadig rode, accusing fortune for the hardness of his lot.

15. THE BASILISK

Arriving in a beautiful meadow, he there saw several women, who were searching for something with great application. He took the liberty to approach one of them, and to ask if he might have the honor to assist them in their search. "Take care that thou dost not," replied the Syrian; "what we are searching for can be touched only by women."

"Strange," said Zadig, "may I presume to ask thee what it is that women only are permitted to touch?"

"It is a basilisk," said she.

"A basilisk, madam! and for what purpose, pray, dost thou seek for a basilisk?"

"It is for our lord and master Ogul, whose cattle thou seest on the bank of that river at the end of the meadow. We are his most humble slaves. The lord Ogul is sick. His physician hath ordered him to eat a basilisk, stewed in rose water; and as it is a very rare animal, and can only be taken by women, the lord Ogul hath promised to choose for his well-beloved wife the woman that shall bring him a basilisk; let me go on in my search; for thou seest what I shall lose if I am prevented by my companions."

Zadig left her and the other Assyrians to search for their basilisk, and continued to walk in the meadow; when coming to the brink of a small rivulet, he found another lady lying on the grass, and who was not searching for anything. Her person seemed to be majestic; but her face was covered with a veil. She was inclined toward the rivulet, and profound sighs proceeded from her mouth. In her hand she held a small rod with which she was tracing characters on the fine sand that lay between the turf and the brook. Zadig had the curiosity to examine what this woman was writing. He drew near; he saw the letter Z, then an A; he was astonished; then appeared a D; he started. But never was surprise equal to his when he saw the two last letters of his name.

He stood for some time immovable. At last, breaking silence with a faltering voice: "O generous lady! pardon a stranger, an unfortunate man, for presuming to ask thee by what surprising adventure I here find the name of Zadig traced out by thy divine hand!"

At this voice, and these words, the lady lifted up the veil with a trembling hand, looked at Zadig, sent forth a cry of tenderness, surprise and joy, and sinking under the various emotions which at once assaulted her soul, fell speechless into his arms. It was Astarte herself; it was the Queen of Babylon; it was she whom Zadig adored, and whom he had reproached himself for adoring; it was she whose misfortunes he had so deeply lamented, and for whose fate he had been so anxiously concerned.

He was for a moment deprived of the use of his senses, when he had fixed his eyes on those of Astarte, which now began to open again with a languor mixed with confusion and tenderness: "O ye immortal powers!" cried he, "who preside over the fates of weak mortals, do ye indeed restore Astarte to me! at what a time, in what a place, and in what a condition do I again behold her!" He fell on his knees before Astarte, and laid his face in the dust at her feet. The Queen of Babylon raised him up, and made him sit by her side on the brink of the rivulet. She frequently wiped her eyes, from which the tears continued to flow afresh. She twenty times resumed her discourse, which her sighs as often interrupted; she asked by what strange accident they were brought together, and suddenly prevented his answers by other questions; she waived the account of her own misfortunes, and desired to be informed of those of Zadig.

At last, both of them having a little composed the tumult of their souls, Zadig acquainted her in a few words by what adventure he was brought into that meadow. "But, O unhappy and respectable queen! by what means do I find thee in this lonely place, clothed in the habit of a slave, and accompanied by other female slaves, who are searching for a basilisk, which, by order of the physician, is to be stewed in rose water?"

"While they are searching for their basilisk," said the fair Astarte, "I will inform thee of all I have suffered, for which Heaven has sufficiently recompensed me by restoring thee to my sight. Thou knowest that the king, my husband, was vexed to see thee the most amiable of mankind; and that for this reason he one night resolved to strangle thee and poison me. Thou knowest how Heaven permitted my little mute to inform me of the orders of his sublime majesty. Hardly had the faithful Cador advised thee to depart, in obedience to my command, when he ventured to enter my apartment at midnight by a secret passage. He carried me off and conducted me to the temple of Oromazes, where the magi his brother shut me up in that huge statue whose base reaches to the foundation of the temple and whose top rises to the summit of the dome. I was there buried in a manner; but was saved by the magi; and supplied with all the necessaries of life. At break of day his majesty's apothecary entered my chamber with a potion composed of a mixture of henbane, opium, hemlock, black hellebore, and aconite; and another officer went to thine with a bowstring of blue silk. Neither of us was to be found. Cador, the better to deceive the king, pretended to come and accuse us both. He said that thou hadst taken the road to the Indies, and I that to Memphis, on which the king's guards were immediately dispatched in pursuit of us both.

"The couriers who pursued me did not know me. I had hardly ever shown my face to any but thee, and to thee only in the presence and by the order of my husband. They conducted themselves in the pursuit by the description that had been given them of my person. On the frontiers of Egypt they met with a woman of the same stature with me, and possessed perhaps of greater charms. She was weeping and wandering. They made no doubt but that this woman was the Queen of Babylon and accordingly brought her to Moabdar. Their mistake at first threw the king into a violent passion; but having viewed this woman more attentively, he found her extremely handsome and was comforted. She was called Missouf. I have since been informed that this name in the Egyptian language signifies the capricious fair one. She was so in reality; but she had as much cunning as caprice. She pleased Moabdar and gained such an ascendancy over him as to make him choose her for his wife. Her character then began to appear in its true colors. She gave herself up, without scruple, to all the freaks of a wanton imagination. She would have obliged the chief of the magi, who was old and gouty, to dance before her; and on his refusal, she persecuted him with the most unrelenting cruelty. She ordered her master of the horse to make her a pie of sweetmeats. In vain did he represent that he was not a pastry-cook; he was obliged to make it, and lost his place, because it was baked a little too hard. The post of master of the horse she gave to her dwarf, and that of chancellor to her page. In this manner did she govern Babylon. Everybody regretted the loss of me. The king, who till the moment of his resolving to poison me and strangle thee, had been a tolerably good kind of man, seemed now to have drowned all his virtues in his immoderate fondness for this capricious fair one. He came to the temple on the great day of the feast held in honor of the sacred fire. I saw him implore the gods in behalf of Missouf, at the feet of the statue in which I was inclosed. I raised my voice, I cried out, 'The gods reject the prayers of a king who is now become a tyrant, and who attempted to murder a reasonable wife, in order to marry a woman remarkable for nothing but her folly and extravagance.' At these words Moabdar was confounded and his head became disordered. The oracle I had pronounced, and the tyranny of Missouf, conspired to deprive him of his judgment, and in a few days his reason entirely forsook him.

"Moabdar's madness, which seemed to be the judgment of Heaven, was the signal to a revolt. The people rose and ran to arms; and Babylon, which had been so long immersed in idleness and effeminacy, became the theater of a bloody civil war. I was taken from the heart of my statue and placed at the head of a party. Cador flew to Memphis to bring thee back to Babylon. The Prince of Hircania, informed of these fatal events, returned with his army and made a third party in Chaldea. He attacked the king, who fled before him with his capricious Egyptian. Moabdar died pierced with wounds. I myself had the misfortune to be taken by a party of Hircanians, who conducted me to their prince's tent, at the very moment that Missouf was brought before him. Thou wilt doubtless be pleased to hear that the prince thought me beautiful; but thou wilt be sorry to be informed that he designed me for his seraglio. He told me, with a blunt and resolute air, that as soon as he had finished a military expedition, which he was just going to undertake, he would come to me. Judge how great must have been my grief. My ties with Moabdar were already dissolved; I might have been the wife of Zadig; and I was fallen into the hands of a barbarian. I answered him with all the pride which my high rank and noble sentiment could inspire. I had always heard it affirmed that Heaven stamped on persons of my condition a mark of grandeur, which, with a single word or glance, could reduce to the lawliness of the most profound respect those rash and forward persons who presume to deviate from the rules of politeness. I spoke like a queen, but was treated like a maidservant. The Hircanian, without even deigning to speak to me, told his black eunuch that I was impertinent, but that he thought me handsome. He ordered him to take care of me, and to put me under the regimen of favorites, that so my complexion being improved, I might be the more worthy of his favors when he should be at leisure to honor me with them. I told him that rather than submit to his desires I would put an end to my life. He replied, with a smile, that women, he believed, were not so bloodthirsty, and that he was accustomed to such violent expressions; and then left me with the air of a man who had just put another parrot into his aviary. What a state for the first queen of the universe, and, what is more, for a heart devoted to Zadig!"

At these words Zadig threw himself at her feet and bathed them with his tears. Astarte raised him with great tenderness and thus continued her story: "I now saw myself in the power of a barbarian and rival to the foolish woman with whom I was confined. She gave me an account of her adventures in Egypt. From the description she gave me of your person, from the time, from the dromedary on which you were mounted, and from every other circumstance, I inferred that Zadig was the man who had fought for her. I doubted not but that you were at Memphis, and, therefore, resolved to repair thither. Beautiful Missouf, said I, thou art more handsome than I, and will please the Prince of Hircania much better. Assist me in contriving the means of my escape; thou wilt then reign alone; thou wilt at once make me happy and rid thyself of a rival. Missouf concerted with me the means of my flight; and I departed secretly with a female Egyptian slave.

"As I approached the frontiers of Arabia, a famous robber, named Arbogad, seized me and sold me to some merchants, who brought me to this castle, where Lord Ogul resides. He bought me without knowing who I was. He is a voluptuary, ambitious of nothing but good living, and thinks that God sent him into the world for no other purpose than to sit at table. He is so extremely corpulent that he is always in danger of suffocation. His physician, who has but little credit with him when he has a good digestion, governs him with a despotic sway when he has ate too much. He has persuaded him that a basilisk stewed in rose water will effect a complete cure. The Lord Ogul hath promised his hand to the female slave that brings him a basilisk. Thou seest that I leave them to vie with each other in meriting this honor; and never was I less desirous of finding the basilisk than since Heaven hath restored thee to my sight."

This account was succeeded by a long conversation between Astarte and Zadig, consisting of everything that their long-suppressed sentiments, their great sufferings, and their mutual love could inspire into hearts the most noble and tender; and the genii who preside over love carried their words to the sphere of Venus.

The women returned to Ogul without having found the basilisk. Zadig was introduced to this mighty lord and spoke to him in the following terms: "May immortal health descend from heaven to bless all thy days! I am a physician; at the first report of thy indisposition I flew to thy castle and have now brought thee a basilisk stewed in rose water. Not that I pretend to marry thee. All I ask is the liberty of a Babylonian slave, who hath been in thy possession for a few days; and, if I should not be so happy as to cure thee, magnificent Lord Ogul, I consent to remain a slave in her place."

The proposal was accepted. Astarte set out for Babylon with Zadig's servant, promising, immediately upon her arrival, to send a courier to inform him of all that had happened. Their parting was as tender as their meeting. The moment of meeting and that of parting are the two greatest epochs of life, as sayeth the great book of Zend. Zadig loved the queen with as much ardor as he professed; and the queen more than she thought proper to acknowledge.

Meanwhile Zadig spoke thus to Ogul: "My lord, my basilisk is not to be eaten; all its virtues must enter through thy pores. I have inclosed it in a little ball, blown up and covered with a fine skin. Thou must strike this ball with all thy might and I must strike it back for a considerable time; and by observing this regimen for a few days thou wilt see the effects of my art." The first day Ogul was out of breath and thought he should have died with fatigue. The second he was less fatigued, slept better. In eight days he recovered all the strength, all the health, all the agility and cheerfulness of his most agreeable years.

"Thou hast played at ball, and thou hast been temperate," said Zadig; "know that there is no such thing in nature as a basilisk; that temperance and exercise are the two great preservatives of health; and that the art of reconciling intemperance and health is as chimerical as the philosopher's stone, judicial astrology, or the theology of the magi."

Ogul's first physician, observing how dangerous this man might prove to the medical art, formed a design, in conjunction with the apothecary, to send Zadig to search for a basilisk in the other world. Thus, having suffered such a long train of calamities on account of his good actions, he was now upon the point of losing his life for curing a gluttonous lord. He was invited to an excellent dinner and was to have been poisoned in the second course, but, during the first, he happily received a courier from the fair Astarte. "When one is beloved by a beautiful woman," says the great Zoroaster, "he hath always the good fortune to extricate himself out of every kind of difficulty and danger."

16. THE COMBATS

The queen was received at Babylon with all those transports of joy which are ever felt on the return of a beautiful princess who hath been involved in calamities. Babylon was now in greater tranquillity. The Prince of Hircania had been killed in battle. The victorious Babylonians declared that the queen should marry the man whom they should choose for their sovereign. They were resolved that the first place in the world, that of being husband to Astarte and King of Babylon, should not depend on cabals and intrigues. They swore to acknowledge for king the man who, upon trial, should be found to be possessed of the greatest valor and the greatest wisdom. Accordingly, at the distance of a few leagues from the city, a spacious place was marked out for the list, surrounded with magnificent amphitheaters. Thither the combatants were to repair in complete armor. Each of them had a separate apartment behind the amphitheaters, where they were neither to be seen nor known by anyone. Each was to encounter four knights, and those that were so happy as to conquer four were then to engage with one another; so that he who remained the last master of the field would be proclaimed conqueror at the games.

Four days after he was to return with the same arms and to explain the enigmas proposed by the magi. If he did not explain the enigmas he was not king; and the running at the lances was to be begun afresh till a man would be found who was conqueror in both these combats; for they were absolutely determined to have a king possessed of the greatest wisdom and the most invincible courage. The queen was all the while to be strictly guarded: she was only allowed to be present at the games, and even there she was to be covered with a veil; but was not permitted to speak to any of the competitors, that so they might neither receive favor, nor suffer injustice.

These particulars Astarte communicated to her lover, hoping that in order to obtain her he would show himself possessed of greater courage and wisdom than any other person. Zadig set out on his journey, beseeching Venus to fortify his courage and enlighten his understanding. He arrived on the banks of the Euphrates on the eve of this great day. He caused his device to be inscribed among those of the combatants, concealing his face and his name, as the law ordained; and then went to repose himself in the apartment that fell to him by lot. His friend Cador, who, after the fruitless search he had made for him in Egypt, was now returned to Babylon, sent to his tent a complete suit of armor, which was a present from the queen; as also, from himself, one of the finest horses in Persia. Zadig presently perceived that these presents were sent by Astarte; and from thence his courage derived fresh strength, and his love the most animating hopes.

Next day, the queen being seated under a canopy of jewels, and the amphitheaters filled with all the gentlemen and ladies of rank in Babylon, the combatants appeared in the circus. Each of them came and laid his device at the feet of the grand magi. They drew their devices by lot; and that of Zadig was the last. The first who advanced was a certain lord, named Itobad, very rich and very vain, but possessed of little courage, of less address, and hardly of any judgment at all. His servants had persuaded him that such a man as he ought to be king; he had said in reply, "Such a man as I ought to reign"; and thus they had armed him for a cap-a-pie. He wore an armor of gold enameled with green, a plume of green feathers, and a lance adorned with green ribbons. It was instantly perceived by the manner in which Itobad managed his horse, that it was not for such a man as he that Heaven reserved the scepter of Babylon. The first knight that ran against him threw him out of his saddle; the second laid him flat on his horse's buttocks, with his legs in the air, and his arms extended. Itobad recovered himself, but with so bad a grace that the whole amphitheater burst out a-laughing. The third knight disdained to make use of his lance; but, making a pass at him, took him by the right leg and, wheeling him half round, laid him prostrate on the sand. The squires of the game ran to him laughing, and replaced him in his saddle. The fourth combatant took him by the left leg, and tumbled him down on the other side. He was conducted back with scornful shouts to his tent, where, according to the law, he was to pass the night; and as he limped along with great difficulty he said, "What an adventure for such a man as I!"

The other knights acquitted themselves with greater ability and success. Some of them conquered two combatants; a few of them vanquished three; but none but Prince Otamus conquered four. At last Zadig fought him in his turn. He successively threw four knights off their saddles with all the grace imaginable. It then remained to be seen who should be conqueror, Otamus or Zadig. The arms of the first were gold and blue, with a plume of the same color; those of the last were white. The wishes of all the spectators were divided between the knight in blue and the knight in white. The queen, whose heart was in a violent palpitation, offered prayers to Heaven for the success of the white color.

The two champions made their passes and vaults with so much agility, they mutually gave and received such dexterous blows with their lances, and sat so firmly in their saddles, that everybody but the queen wished there might be two kings in Babylon. At length, their horses being tired and their lances broken, Zadig had recourse to this stratagem: He passes behind the blue prince; springs upon the buttocks of his horse; seizes him by the middle; throws him on the earth; places himself in the saddle; and wheels around Otamus as he lay extended on the ground. All the amphitheater cried out, "Victory to the white knight!"

Otamus rises in a violent passion, and draws his sword; Zadig leaps from his horse with his saber in his hand. Both of them are now on the ground, engaged in a new combat, where strength and agility triumph by turns. The plumes of their helmets, the studs of their bracelets, the rings of their armor, are driven to a great distance by the violence of a thousand furious blows. They strike with the point and the edge; to the right, to the left, on the head, on the breast; they retreat; they advance; they measure swords; they close; they seize each other; they bend like serpents; they attack like lions; and the fire every moment flashes from their blows.

At last Zadig, having recovered his spirits, stops; makes a feint; leaps upon Otamus; throws him on the ground and disarms him; and Otamus cries out, "It is thou alone, O white knight, that oughtest to reign over Babylon!" The queen was now at the height of her joy. The knight in blue armor and the knight in white were conducted each to his own apartment, as well as all the others, according to the intention of the law. Mutes came to wait upon them and to serve them at table. It may be easily supposed that the queen's little mute waited upon Zadig. They were then left to themselves to enjoy the sweets of repose till next morning, at which time the conqueror was to bring his device to the grand magi, to compare it with that which he had left, and make himself known.

Zadig, though deeply in love, was so much fatigued that he could not help sleeping. Itobad, who lay near him, never closed his eyes. He arose in the night, entered his apartment, took the white arms and the device of Zadig, and put his green armor in their place. At break of day he went boldly to the grand magi to declare that so great a man as he was conqueror. This was little expected; however, he was proclaimed while Zadig was still asleep. Astarte, surprised and filled with despair, returned to Babylon. The amphitheater was almost empty when Zadig awoke; he sought for his arms, but could find none but the green armor. With this he was obliged to cover himself, having nothing else near him. Astonished and enraged, he put it on in a furious passion, and advanced in this equipage.

The people that still remained in the amphitheater and the circus received him with hoots and hisses. They surrounded him and insulted him to his face. Never did man suffer such cruel mortifications. He lost his patience; with his saber he dispersed such of the populace as dared to affront him; but he knew not what course to take. He could not see the queen; he could not claim the white armor she had sent him without exposing her; and thus, while she was plunged in grief, he was filled with fury and distraction. He walked on the banks of the Euphrates, fully persuaded that his star had destined him to inevitable misery, and resolving in his own mind all his misfortunes, from the adventure of the woman who hated one-eyed men to that of his armor. "This," said he, "is the consequence of my having slept too long. Had I slept less, I should now have been King of Babylon and in possession of Astarte. Knowledge, virtue, and courage have hitherto served only to make me miserable." He then let fall some secret murmurings against Providence, and was tempted to believe that the world was governed by a cruel destiny, which oppressed the good and prospered knights in green armor. One of his greatest mortifications was his being obliged to wear that green armor which had exposed him to such contumelious treatment. A merchant happening to pass by, he sold it to him for a trifle and bought a gown and a long bonnet. In this garb he proceeded along the banks of the Euphrates, filled with despair, and secretly accusing Providence, which thus continued to persecute him with unremitting severity.

17. THE HERMIT

While he was thus sauntering he met a hermit, whose white and venerable beard hung down to his girdle. He held a book in his hand, which he read with great attention. Zadig stopped, and made him a profound obeisance. The hermit returned the compliment with such a noble and engaging air, that Zadig had the curiosity to enter into conversation with him. He asked him what book it was that he had been reading? "It is the Book of Destinies," said the hermit; "wouldst thou choose to look into it?" He put the book into the hands of Zadig, who, thoroughly versed as he was in several languages, could not decipher a single character of it. This only redoubled his curiosity.

"Thou seemest," said this good father, "to be in great distress."

"Alas," replied Zadig, "I have but too much reason."

"If thou wilt permit me to accompany thee," resumed the old man, "perhaps I may be of some service to thee. I have often poured the balm of consolation into the bleeding heart of the unhappy."

Zadig felt himself inspired with respect for the air, the beard, and the book of the hermit. He found, in the course of the conversation, that he was possessed of superior degrees of knowledge. The hermit talked of fate, of justice, of morals, of the chief good, of human weakness, and of virtue and vice, with such a spirited and moving eloquence, that Zadig felt himself drawn toward him by an irresistible charm. He earnestly entreated the favor of his company till their return to Babylon.

"I ask the same favor of thee," said the old man; "swear to me by Oromazes, that whatever I do, thou wilt not leave me for some days." Zadig swore, and they set out together.

In the evening the two travelers arrived in a superb castle. The hermit entreated a hospitable reception for himself and the young man who accompanied him. The porter, whom one might have easily mistaken for a great lord, introduced them with a kind of disdainful civility. He presented them to a principal domestic, who showed them his master's magnificent apartments. They were admitted to the lower end of the table, without being honored with the least mark of regard by the lord of the castle; but they were served, like the rest, with delicacy and profusion. They were then presented with water to wash their hands, in a golden basin adorned with emeralds and rubies. At last they were conducted to bed in a beautiful apartment; and in the morning a domestic brought each of them a piece of gold, after which they took their leave and departed.

"The master of the house," said Zadig, as they were proceeding on the journey, "appears to be a generous man, though somewhat too proud; he nobly performs the duties of hospitality." At that instant he observed that a kind of large pocket, which the hermit had, was filled and distended; and upon looking more narrowly he found that it contained the golden basin adorned with precious stones, which the hermit had stolen. He durst not take any notice of it, but he was filled with a strange surprise.

About noon, the hermit came to the door of a paltry house inhabited by a rich miser, and begged the favor of an hospitable reception for a few hours. An old servant, in a tattered garb, received them with a blunt and rude air, and led them into the stable, where he gave them some rotten olives, moldy bread, and sour beer. The hermit ate and drank with as much seeming satisfaction as he had done the evening before; and then addressing himself to the old servant, who watched them both, to prevent their stealing anything, and rudely pressed them to depart, he gave him the two pieces of gold he had received in the morning, and thanked him for his great civility.

"Pray," added he, "allow me to speak to thy master." The servant, filled with astonishment, introduced the two travelers. "Magnificent lord," said the hermit, "I cannot but return thee my most humble thanks for the noble manner in which thou hast entertained us. Be pleased to accept this golden basin as a small mark of my gratitude." The miser started, and was ready to fall backward; but the hermit, without giving him time to recover from his surprise, instantly departed with his young fellow traveler.

"Father," said Zadig, "what is the meaning of all this? Thou seemest to me to be entirely different from other men; thou stealest a golden basin adorned with precious stones from a lord who received thee magnificently, and givest it to a miser who treats thee with indignity."

"Son," replied the old man, "this magnificent lord, who receives strangers only from vanity and ostentation, will hereby be rendered more wise; and the miser will learn to practice the duties of hospitality. Be surprised at nothing, but follow me."

Zadig knew not as yet whether he was in company with the most foolish or the most prudent of mankind; but the hermit spoke with such an ascendancy, that Zadig, who was moreover bound by his oath, could not refuse to follow him.

In the evening they arrived at a house built with equal elegance and simplicity, where nothing favored either of prodigality or avarice. The master of it was a philosopher, who had retired from the world, and who cultivated in peace the study of virtue and wisdom, without any of that rigid and morose severity so commonly to be found in men of his character. He had chosen to build this country house, in which he received strangers with a generosity free from ostentation. He went himself to meet the two travelers, whom he led into a commodious apartment, where he desired them to repose themselves a little. Soon after he came and invited them to a decent and well-ordered repast during which he spoke with great judgment of the last revolutions in Babylon. He seemed to be strongly attached to the queen, and wished that Zadig had appeared in the lists to dispute the crown. "But the people," added he, "do not deserve to have such a king as Zadig."

Zadig blushed, and felt his griefs redoubled. They agreed, in the course of the conversation, that the things of this world did not always answer the wishes of the wise. The hermit still maintained that the ways of Providence were inscrutable; and that men were in the wrong to judge of a whole, of which they understood but the smallest part.

They talked of passions. "Ah," said Zadig, "how fatal are their effects!"

"They are in the winds," replied the hermit, "that swell the sails of the ship; it is true, they sometimes sink her, but without them she could not sail at all. The bile makes us sick and choleric; but without bile we could not live. Everything in this world is dangerous, and yet everything is necessary."

The conversation turned on pleasure; and the hermit proved that it was a present bestowed by the deity. "For," said he, "man cannot give himself either sensations or ideas; he receives all; and pain and pleasure proceed from a foreign cause as well as his being."

Zadig was surprised to see a man, who had been guilty of such extravagant actions, capable of reasoning with so much judgment and propriety. At last, after a conversation equally entertaining and instructive, the host led back his two guests to their apartment, blessing Heaven for having sent him two men possessed of so much wisdom and virtue. He offered them money with such an easy and noble air as could not possibly give any offense. The hermit refused it, and said that he must now take his leave of him, as he set out for Babylon before it was light.

Their parting was tender; Zadig especially felt himself filled with esteem and affection for a man of such an amiable character.

When he and the hermit were alone in their apartment, they spent a long time in praising their host. At break of day the old man awakened his companion. "We must now depart," said he, "but while all the family are still asleep, I will leave this man a mark of my esteem and affection." So saying, he took a candle and set fire to the house.

Zadig, struck with horror, cried aloud, and endeavored to hinder him from committing such a barbarous action; but the hermit drew him away by a superior force, and the house was soon in flames. The hermit, who, with his companion, was already at a considerable distance, looked back to the conflagration with great tranquillity.

"Thanks be to God," said he, "the house of my dear host is entirely destroyed! Happy man!"

At these words Zadig was at once tempted to burst out a-laughing, to reproach the reverend father, to beat him, and to run away. But he did none of all of these, for still subdued by the powerful ascendancy of the hermit, he followed him, in spite of himself, to the next stage.

This was at the house of a charitable and virtuous widow, who had a nephew fourteen years of age, a handsome and promising youth, and her only hope. She performed the honors of her house as well as she could. Next day, she ordered her nephew to accompany the strangers to a bridge, which being lately broken down, was become extremely dangerous in passing. The young man walked before them with great alacrity. As they were crossing the bridge, "Come," said the hermit to the youth, "I must show my gratitude to thy aunt." He then took him by the hair and plunged him into the river. The boy sunk, appeared again on the surface of the water, and was swallowed up by the current.

"O monster! O thou most wicked of mankind!" cried Zadig.

"Thou promisedst to behave with greater patience," said the hermit, interrupting him. "Know that under the ruins of that house which Providence hath set on fire the master hath found an immense treasure. Know that this young man, whose life Providence hath shortened, would have assassinated his aunt in the space of a year, and thee in that of two."

"Who told thee so, barbarian?" cried Zadig; "and though thou hadst read this event in thy Book of Destinies, art thou permitted to drown a youth who never did thee any harm?"

While the Babylonian was thus exclaiming, he observed that the old man had no longer a beard, and that his countenance assumed the features and complexion of youth. The hermit's habit disappeared, and four beautiful wings covered a majestic body resplendent with light.

"O sent of heaven! O divine angel!" cried Zadig, humbly prostrating himself on the ground," hast thou then descended from the Empyrean to teach a weak mortal to submit to the eternal decrees of Providence?"

"Men," said the angel Jesrad, "judge of all without knowing anything; and, of all men, thou best deservest to be enlightened."

Zadig begged to be permitted to speak. "I distrust myself," said he, "but may I presume to ask the favor of thee to clear up one doubt that still remains in my mind? Would it not have been better to have corrected this youth, and made him virtuous, than to have drowned him?"

"Had he been virtuous," replied Jesrad, "and enjoyed a longer life, it would have been his fate to be assassinated himself, together with the wife he would have married, and the child he would have had by her."

"But why," said Zadig, "is it necessary that there should be crimes and misfortunes, and that these misfortunes should fall on the good?"

"The wicked," replied Jesrad, "are always unhappy; they serve to prove and try the small number of the just that are scattered through the earth; and there is no evil that is not productive of some good."

"But," said Zadig, "suppose there were nothing but good and no evil at all."

"Then," replied Jesrad, "this earth would be another earth. The chain of events would be ranged in another order and directed by wisdom; but this other order, which would be perfect, can exist only in the eternal abode of the Supreme Being, to which no evil can approach. The Deity hath created millions of worlds, among which there is not one that resembles another. This immense variety is the effect of His immense power. There are not two leaves among the trees of the earth, nor two globes in the unlimited expanse of heaven that are exactly similar; and all that thou seest on the little atom in which thou art born, ought to be in its proper time and place, according to the immutable decree of Him who comprehends all. Men think that this child who hath just perished is fallen into the water by chance; and that it is by the same chance that this house is burned; but there is no such thing as chance; all is either a trial, or a punishment, or a reward, or a foresight. Remember the fisherman who thought himself the most wretched of mankind. Oromazes sent thee to change his fate. Cease, then, frail mortal, to dispute against what thou oughtest to adore."

"But," said Zadig — as he pronounced the word "But," the angel took his flight toward the tenth sphere. Zadig on his knees adored Providence, and submitted. The angel cried to him from on high, "Direct thy course toward Babylon."

18. THE ENIGMAS

Zadig, entranced, as it were, and like a man about whose head the thunder had burst, walked at random. He entered Babylon on the very day when those who had fought at the tournaments were assembled in the grand vestibule of the palace to explain the enigmas and to answer the questions of the grand magi. All the knights were already arrived, except the knight in green armor. As soon as Zadig appeared in the city the people crowded round him; every eye was fixed on him; every mouth blessed him, and every heart wished him the empire. The envious man saw him pass; he frowned and turned aside. The people conducted him to the place where the assembly was held. The queen, who was informed of his arrival, became a prey to the most violent agitations of hope and fear. She was filled with anxiety and apprehension. She could not comprehend why Zadig was without arms, nor why Itobad wore the white armor. A confused murmur arose at the sight of Zadig. They were equally surprised and charmed to see him; but none but the knights who had fought were permitted to appear in the assembly.

"I have fought as well as the other knights," said Zadig, "but another here wears my arms; and while I wait for the honor of proving the truth of my assertion, I demand the liberty of presenting myself to explain the enigmas." The question was put to the vote, and his reputation for probity was still so deeply impressed in their minds, that they admitted him without scruple.

The first question proposed by the grand magi was: "What, of all things in the world, is the longest and the shortest, the swiftest and the slowest, the most divisible and the most extended, the most neglected and the most regretted, without which nothing can be done, which devours all that is little, and enlivens all that is great?"

Itobad was to speak. He replied that so great a man as he did not understand enigmas, and that it was sufficient for him to have conquered by his strength and valor. Some said that the meaning of the enigmas was Fortune; some, the Earth; and others the Light. Zadig said that it was Time. "Nothing," added he, "is longer, since it is the measure of eternity; nothing is shorter, since it is insufficient for the accomplishment of our projects; nothing more slow to him that expects, nothing more rapid to him that enjoys; in greatness, it extends to infinity; in smallness, it is infinitely divisible; all men neglect it; all regret the loss of it; nothing can be done without it; it consigns to oblivion whatever is unworthy of being transmitted to posterity, and it immortalizes such actions as are truly great." The assembly acknowledged that Zadig was in the right.

The next question was: "What is the thing which we receive without thanks, which we enjoy without knowing how, which we give to others when we know not where we are, and which we lose without perceiving it?"

Everyone gave his own explanation. Zadig alone guessed that it was Life, and explained all the other enigmas with the same facility. Itobad always said that nothing was more easy, and that he could have answered them with the same readiness had he chosen to have given himself the trouble. Questions were then proposed on justice, on the sovereign good, and on the art of government. Zadig's answers were judged to be the most solid. "What a pity is it," said they, "that such a great genius should be so bad a knight!"

"Illustrious lords," said Zadig, "I have had the honor of conquering in the tournaments. It is to me that the white armor belongs. Lord Itobad took possession of it during my sleep. He probably thought that it would fit him better than the green. I am now ready to prove in your presence, with my gown and sword, against all that beautiful white armor which he took from me, that it is I who have had the honor of conquering the brave Otamus."

Itobad accepted the challenge with the greatest confidence. He never doubted but what, armed as he was, with a helmet, a cuirass, and brassarts, he would obtain an easy victory over a champion in a cap and nightgown. Zadig drew his sword, saluting the queen, who looked at him with a mixture of fear and joy. Itobad drew his without saluting anyone. He rushed upon Zadig, like a man who had nothing to fear; he was ready to cleave him in two. Zadig knew how to ward off his blows, by opposing the strongest part of his sword to the weakest of that of his adversary, in such a manner that Itobad's sword was broken. Upon which Zadig, seizing his enemy by the waist, threw him on the ground; and fixing the point of his sword at the breastplate, "Suffer thyself to be disarmed," said he, "or thou art a dead man."

Itobad, always surprised at the disgraces that happened to such a man as he, was obliged to yield to Zadig, who took from him with great composure his magnificent helmet, his superb cuirass, his fine brassarts, his shining cuishes; clothed himself with them, and in this dress ran to throw himself at the feet of Astarte. Cador easily proved that the armor belonged to Zadig. He was acknowledged king by the unanimous consent of the whole nation, and especially by that of Astarte, who, after so many calamities, now tasted the exquisite pleasure of seeing her lover worthy, in the eyes of all the world, to be her husband. Itobad went home to be called lord in his own house. Zadig was king, and was happy. The queen and Zadig adored Providence. He sent in search of the robber Arbogad, to whom he gave an honorable post in his army, promising to advance him to the first dignities if he behaved like a true warrior, and threatening to hang him if he followed the profession of a robber.

Setoc, with the fair Almona, was called from the heart of Arabia and placed at the head of the commerce of Babylon. Cador was preferred and distinguished according to his great services. He was the friend of the king; and the king was then the only monarch on earth that had a friend. The little mute was not forgotten.

But neither could the beautiful Semira be comforted for having believed that Zadig would be blind of an eye; nor did Azora cease to lament her having attempted to cut off his nose. Their griefs, however, he softened by his presents. The envious man died of rage and shame. The empire enjoyed peace, glory, and plenty. This was the happiest age of the earth; it was governed by love and justice. The people blessed Zadig, and Zadig blessed Heaven.

PEDRO DE ALARÇON

The Nail

I

The thing which is most ardently desired by a man who steps into a stagecoach, bent upon a long journey, is that his companions may be agreeable, that they may have the same tastes, possibly the same vices, be well educated and know enough not to be too familiar.

When I opened the door of the coach I felt fearful of encountering an old woman suffering with the asthma, an ugly one who could not bear the smell of tobacco smoke, one who gets seasick every time she rides in a carriage, and little angels who are continually yelling and screaming for God knows what.

Sometimes you may have hoped to have a beautiful woman for a traveling companion; for instance, a widow of twenty or thirty years of age (let us say, thirty-six), whose delightful conversation will help you pass away the time. But if you ever had this idea, as a reasonable man you would quickly dismiss it, for you know that such good fortune does not fall to the lot of the ordinary mortal. These thoughts were in my mind when I opened the door of the stagecoach at exactly eleven o'clock on a stormy night of the Autumn of 1844. I had ticket No. 2, and I was wondering who No. 1 might be. The ticket agent had assured me that No. 3 had not been sold.

It was pitch dark within. When I entered I said, "Good evening," but no answer came. "The devil!" I said to myself. "Is my traveling companion deaf, dumb, or asleep?" Then I said in a louder tone: "Good evening," but no answer came.

All this time the stagecoach was whirling along, drawn by ten horses.

I was puzzled. Who was my companion? Was it a man? Was it a woman? Who was the silent No. 1, and, whoever it might be, why did he or she not reply to my courteous salutation? It would have been well to have lit a match, but I was not smoking then and had none with me. What should I do? I concluded to rely upon my sense of feeling, and stretched out my hand to the place where No. 1 should have been, wondering whether I would touch a silk dress or an overcoat, but there was nothing there. At that moment a flash of lightning, herald of a quickly approaching storm, lit up the night, and I perceived that there was no one in the coach excepting myself. I burst out into a roar of laughter, and yet a moment later I could not help wondering what had become of No. 1.

A half hour later we arrived at the first stop, and I was just about to ask the guard who flashed his lantern into the compartment why there was no No. 1, when she entered. In the yellow rays I thought it was a vision: a pale, graceful, beautiful woman, dressed in deep mourning.

Here was the fulfillment of my dream, the widow I had hoped for.

I extended my hand to the unknown to assist her into the coach, and she sat down beside me, murmuring: "Thank you, sir. Good evening," but in a tone that was so sad that it went to my very heart.

"How unfortunate," I thought. "There are only fifty miles between here and Malaga. I wish to heaven this coach were going to Kamschatka." The guard slammed the door, and we were in darkness. I wished that the storm would continue and that we might have a few more flashes of lightning. But the storm didn't. It fled away, leaving only a few pallid stars, whose light practically amounted to nothing. I made a brave effort to start a conversation.

"Do you feel well?"

"Are you going to Malaga?"

"Did you like the Alhambra?"

"You come from Granada?"

"Isn't the night damp?"

To which questions she respectively responded:

"Thanks, very well."

"Yes."

"No, sir."

"Yes!"

"Awful!"

It was quite certain that my traveling companion was not inclined to conversation. I tried to think up something original to say to her, but nothing occurred to me, so I lost myself for the moment in meditation. Why had this woman gotten on the stage at the first stop instead of at Granada? Why was she alone? Was she married? Was she really a widow? Why was she so sad? I certainly had no right to ask her any of these questions, and yet she interested me. How I wished the sun would rise. In the daytime one may talk freely, but in the pitch darkness one feels a certain oppression, it seems like taking an unfair advantage.

My unknown did not sleep a moment during the night. I could tell this by her breathing and by her sighing. It is probably unnecessary to add that I did not sleep either. Once I asked her: "Do you feel ill?" and she replied: "No, sir, thank you. I beg pardon if I have disturbed your sleep."

"Sleep!" I exclaimed disdainfully. "I do not care to sleep. I feared you were suffering."

"Oh, no," she exclaimed, in a voice that contradicted her words, "I am not suffering."

At last the sun rose. How beautiful she was! I mean the woman, not the sun. What deep suffering had lined her face and lurked in the depths of her beautiful eyes!

She was elegantly dressed and evidently belonged to a good family. Every gesture bore the imprint of distinction. She was the kind of a woman you expect to see in the principal box at the opera, resplendent with jewels, surrounded by admirers.

We breakfasted at Colmenar. After that my companion became more confidential, and I said to myself when we again entered the coach: "Philip, you have met your fate. It's now or never."

II

I regretted the very first word I mentioned to her regarding my feelings. She became a block of ice, and I lost at once all that I might have gained in her good graces. Still she answered me very kindly: "It is not because it is you, sir, who speak to me of love, but love itself is something which I hold in horror."

"But why, dear lady?" I inquired.

"Because my heart is dead. Because I have loved to the point of delirium, and I have been deceived."

I felt that I should talk to her in a philosophic way and there were a lot of platitudes on the tip of my tongue, but I refrained. I knew that she meant what she said. When we arrived at Malaga, she said to me in a tone I shall never forget as long as I live: "I thank you a thousand times for your kind attention during the trip, and hope you will forgive me if I do not tell you my name and address."

"Do you mean then that we shall not meet again?"

"Never! And you, especially, should not regret it." And then with a smile that was utterly without joy she extended her exquisite hand to me and said: "Pray to God for me."

I pressed her hand and made a low bow. She entered a handsome victoria which was awaiting her, and as it moved away she bowed to me again.

*****

Two months later I met her again.

At two o'clock in the afternoon I was jogging along in an old cart on the road that leads to Cordoba. The object of my journey was to examine some land which I owned in that neighborhood and pass three or four weeks with one of the judges of the Supreme Court, who was an intimate friend of mine and had been my schoolmate at the University of Granada.

He received me with open arms. As I entered his handsome house I could but note the perfect taste and elegance of the furniture and decorations.

"Ah, Zarco," I said, "you have married, and you have never told me about it. Surely this was not the way to treat a man who loved you as much as I do!"

"I am not married, and what is more I never will marry," answered the judge sadly.

"I believe that you are not married, dear boy, since you say so, but I cannot understand the declaration that you never will. You must be joking."

"I swear that I am telling you the truth," he replied.

"But what a metamorphosis!" I exclaimed. "You were always a partisan of marriage, and for the past two years you have been writing to me and advising me to take a life partner. Whence this wonderful change, dear friend? Something must have happened to you, something unfortunate, I fear?"

"To me?" answered the judge somewhat embarrassed.

"Yes, to you. Something has happened, and you are going to tell me all about it. You live here alone, have practically buried yourself in this great house. Come, tell me everything."

The judge pressed my hand. "Yes, yes, you shall know all. There is no man more unfortunate than I am. But listen, this is the day upon which all the inhabitants go to the cemetery, and I must be there, if only for form's sake. Come with me. It is a pleasant afternoon and the walk will do you good, after riding so long in that old cart. The location of the cemetery is a beautiful one, and I am quite sure you will enjoy the walk. On our way, I will tell you the incident that ruined my life, and you shall judge yourself whether I am justified in my hatred of women."

251

As together we walked along the flower-bordered road, my friend told me the following story:

Two years ago when I was Assistant District Attorney in — — , I obtained permission from my chief to spend a month in Sevilla. In the hotel where I lodged there was a beautiful young woman who passed for a widow but whose origin, as well as her reasons for staying in that town, were a mystery to all. Her installation, her wealth, her total lack of friends or acquaintances and the sadness of her expression, together with her incomparable beauty, gave rise to a thousand conjectures.

Her rooms were directly opposite mine, and I frequently met her in the hall or on the stairway, only too glad to have the chance of bowing to her. She was unapproachable, however, and it was impossible for me to secure an introduction. Two weeks later, fate was to afford me the opportunity of entering her apartment. I had been to the theater that night, and when I returned to my room I thoughtlessly opened the door of her apartment instead of that of my own. The beautiful woman was reading by the light of the lamp and started when she saw me. I was so embarrassed by my mistake that for a moment I could only stammer unintelligible words. My confusion was so evident that she could not doubt for a moment that I had made a mistake. I turned to the door, intent upon relieving her of my presence as quickly as possible, when she said with the most exquisite courtesy: "In order to show you that I do not doubt your good faith and that I'm not at all offended, I beg that you will call upon me again, *intentionally*."

Three days passed before I got up sufficient courage to accept her invitation. Yes, I was madly in love with her; accustomed as I am to analyze my own sensations, I knew that my passion could only end in the greatest happiness or the deepest suffering. However, at the end of the three days I went to her apartment and spent the evening there. She told me that her name was Blanca, that she was born in Madrid, and that she was a widow. She played and sang for me and asked me a thousand questions about myself, my profession, my family, and every word she said increased my love for her. From that night my soul was the slave of her soul; yes, and it *will be forever*.

I called on her again the following night, and thereafter every afternoon and evening I was with her. We loved each other, but not a word of love had ever been spoken between us.

One evening she said to me: "I married a man without loving him. Shortly after marriage I hated him. Now he is dead. Only God knows what I suffered. Now I understand what love means; it is either heaven or it is hell. For me, up to the present time, it has been hell."

I could not sleep that night. I lay awake thinking over these last words of Blanca's. Somehow this woman frightened me. Would I be her heaven and she my hell?

My leave of absence expired. I could have asked for an extension, pretending illness, but the question was, should I do it? I consulted Blanca.

"Why do you ask me?" she said, taking my hand.

"Because I love you. Am I doing wrong in loving you?"

"No," she said, becoming very pale, and then she put both arms about my neck and her beautiful lips touched mine.

Well, I asked for another month and, thanks to you, dear friend, it was granted. Never would they have given it to me without your influence.

My relations with Blanca were more than love; they were delirium, madness, fanaticism, call it what you will. Every day my passion for her increased, and the morrow seemed to open up vistas of new happiness. And yet I could not avoid feeling at times a mysterious, indefinable fear. And this I knew she felt as well as I did. We both feared to lose one another. One day I said to Blanca:

"We must marry, as quickly as possible."

She gave me a strange look. "You wish to marry me?"

"Yes, Blanca," I said, "I am proud of you. I want to show you to the whole world. I love you and I want you, pure, noble, and saintly as you are."

"I cannot marry you," answered this incomprehensible woman. She would never give a reason.

Finally my leave of absence expired, and I told her that on the following day we must separate.

"Separate? It is impossible!" she exclaimed. "I love you too much for that."

"But you know, Blanca, that I worship you."

"Then give up your profession. I am rich. We will live our lives out together," she said, putting her soft hand over my mouth to prevent my answer.

I kissed the hand and then, gently removing it, I answered: "I would accept this offer from my wife, although it would be a sacrifice for me to give up my career; but I will not accept it from a woman who refuses to marry me."

Blanca remained thoughtful for several minutes; then, raising her head, she looked at me and said very quietly, but with a determination which could not be misunderstood: "I will be your wife, and I do not ask you to give up your profession. Go back to your office. How long will it take you to arrange your business matters and secure from the government another leave of absence to return to Sevilla?"

"A month."

"A month? Well, here I will await you. Return within a month, and I will be your wife. To-day is the fifteenth of April. You will be here on the fifteenth of May?"

"You may rest assured of that."

"You swear it?"

"I swear it."

"You love me?"

"More than my life."

"Go, then, and return. Farewell."

I left on the same day. The moment I arrived home I began to arrange my house to receive my bride. As you know I solicited another leave of absence, and so quickly did I arrange my business affairs that at the end of two weeks I was ready to return to Sevilla.

I must tell you that during this fortnight I did not receive a single letter from Blanca, though I wrote her six. I started at once for Sevilla, arriving in that city on the thirtieth of April, and went at once to the hotel where we had first met.

I learned that Blanca had left there two days after my departure without telling anyone her destination.

Imagine my indignation, my disappointment, my suffering. She went away without even leaving a line for me, without telling me whither she was going. It never occurred to me to remain in Sevilla until the fifteenth of May to ascertain whether she would return on that date. Three days later I took up my court work and strove to forget her.

*****

A few moments after my friend Zarco finished the story, we arrived at the cemetery.

This is only a small plot of ground covered with a veritable forest of crosses and surrounded by a low stone wall. As often happens in Spain, when the cemeteries are very small, it is necessary to dig up one coffin in order to lower another. Those thus disinterred are thrown in a heap in a corner of the cemetery, where skulls and bones are piled up like a haystack. As we were passing, Zarco and I looked at the skulls, wondering to whom they could have belonged, to rich or poor, noble or plebeian.

Suddenly the judge bent down, and picking up a skull, exclaimed in astonishment:

"Look here, my friend, what is this? It is surely a nail!"

Yes, a long nail had been driven in the top of the skull which he held in his hand. The nail had been driven into the head, and the point had penetrated what had been the roof of the mouth.

What could this mean? He began to conjecture, and soon both of us felt filled with horror.

"I recognize the hand of Providence!" exclaimed the judge. "A terrible crime has evidently been committed, and would never have come to light had it not been for this accident. I shall do my duty, and will not rest until I have brought the assassin to the scaffold."

III

My friend Zarco was one of the keenest criminal judges in Spain. Within a very few days he discovered that the corpse to which this skull belonged had been buried in a rough wooden coffin which the grave digger had taken home with him, intending to use it for firewood. Fortunately, the man had not yet burned it up, and on the lid the judge managed to decipher the initials: "A.G.R." together with the date of interment. He had at once searched the parochial books of every church in the neighborhood, and a week later found the following entry:

"In the parochial church of San Sebastian of the village of — — , on the 4th of May, 1843, the funeral rites as prescribed by our holy religion were performed over the body of Don Alfonzo Gutierrez Romeral, and he was buried in the cemetery. He was a native of this village and did not receive the holy sacrament, nor did he confess, for he died suddenly of apoplexy at the age of thirty-one. He was married to Doña Gabriela Zahara del Valle, a native of Madrid, and left no issue him surviving."

The judge handed me the above certificate, duly certified to by the parish priest, and exclaimed: "Now everything is as clear as day, and I am positive that within a week the assassin will be arrested. The apoplexy in this case happens to be an iron nail driven into the man's head, which brought quick and sudden death to A.G.R. I have the nail, and I shall soon find the hammer."

According to the testimony of the neighbors, Señor Romeral was a young and rich landowner who originally came from Madrid, where he had married a beautiful wife; four months before the death of the husband, his wife had gone to Madrid to pass a few months with her family; the young woman returned home about the last day of April, that is, about three months and a half after she had left her husband's residence to go to Madrid; the death of Señor Romeral occurred about a week after her return. The shock caused to the widow by the sudden death of her husband was so great that she became ill and informed her friends that she could not continue to live in the same place where everything recalled to her the man she had lost, and just before the middle of May she had left for Madrid, ten or twelve days after the death of her husband.

The servants of the deceased had testified that the couple did not live amicably together and had frequent quarrels; that the absence of three months and a half which preceded the last eight days the couple had lived together was practically an understanding that they were to be ultimately separated on account of mysterious disagreements which had existed between them from the date of their marriage; that on the date of the death of the deceased, both husband and wife were together in the former's bedroom; that at midnight the bell was rung violently and they heard the cries of the wife; that they rushed to the room and were met at the door by the wife, who was very pale and greatly perturbed, and she cried out: "An apoplexy! Run for a doctor! My poor husband is dying!" That when they entered the room they found their master lying upon a couch, and he was dead. The doctor who was called certified that Señor Romeral had died of cerebral congestion.

Three medical experts testified that death brought about as this one had been could not be distinguished from apoplexy. The physician who had been called in had not thought to look for the head of the nail, which was concealed by the hair of the victim, nor was he in any sense to blame for this oversight.

The judge immediately issued a warrant for the arrest of Doña Gabriela Zahara del Valle, widow of Señor Romeral.

"Tell me," I asked the judge one day, "do you think you will ever capture this woman?"

"I'm positive of it."

"Why?"

"Because in the midst of all these routine criminal affairs there occurs now and then what may be termed a dramatic fatality which never fails. To put it in another way: when the bones come out of the tomb to testify, there is very little left for the judge to do."

In spite of the hopes of my friend, Gabriela was not found, and three months later she was, according to the laws of Spain, tried, found guilty, and condemned to death in her absence.

I returned home, not without promising to be with Zarco the following year.

IV

That winter I passed in Granada. One evening I had been invited to a great ball given by a prominent Spanish lady. As I was mounting the stairs of the magnificent residence, I was startled by the sight of a face which was easily distinguishable even in this crowd of southern beauties. It was she, my unknown, the mysterious woman of the stagecoach, in fact, No. 1, of whom I spoke at the beginning of this narrative.

I made my way toward her, extending my hand in greeting. She recognized me at once.

"Señora," I said, "I have kept my promise not to search for you. I did not know I would meet you here. Had I suspected it I would have refrained from coming, for fear of annoying you. Now that I am here, tell me whether I may recognize you and talk to you."

"I see that you are vindictive," she answered graciously, putting her little hand in mine. "But I forgive you. How are you?"

"In truth, I don't know. My health — that is, the health of my soul, for you would not ask me about anything else in a ballroom — depends upon the health of yours. What I mean is that I could only be happy if you are happy. May I ask if that wound of the heart which you told me about when I met you in the stagecoach has healed?"

"You know as well as I do that there are wounds which never heal."

With a graceful bow she turned away to speak to an acquaintance, and I asked a friend of mine who was passing: "Can you tell me who that woman is?"

"A South American whose name is Mercedes de Meridanueva."

On the following day I paid a visit to the lady, who was residing at that time at the Hotel of the Seven Planets. The charming Mercedes received me as if I were an intimate friend, and invited me to walk with her through the wonderful Alhambra and subsequently to dine with her. During the six hours we were together she spoke of many things, and as we always returned to the subject of disappointed love, I felt impelled to tell her the experience of my friend, Judge Zarco.

She listened to me very attentively and when I concluded she laughed and said: "Let this be a lesson to you not to fall in love with women whom you do not know."

"Do not think for a moment," I answered, "that I've invented this story."

"Oh, I don't doubt the truth of it. Perhaps there may be a mysterious woman in the Hotel of the Seven Planets of Granada, and perhaps she doesn't resemble the one your friend fell in love with in Sevilla. So far as I am concerned, there is no risk of my falling in love with anyone, for I never speak three times to the same man."

"Señora! That is equivalent to telling me that you refuse to see me again!"

"No, I only wish to inform you that I leave Granada to-morrow, and it is probable that we will never meet again."

"Never? You told me that during our memorable ride in the stagecoach, and you see that you are not a good prophet."

I noticed that she had become very pale. She rose from the table abruptly, saying: "Well, let us leave that to Fate. For my part I repeat that I am bidding you an eternal farewell."

She said these last words very solemnly, and then with a graceful bow, turned and ascended the stairway which led to the upper story of the hotel.

I confess that I was somewhat annoyed at the disdainful way in which she seemed to have terminated our acquaintance, yet this feeling was lost in the pity I felt for her when I noted her expression of suffering.

We had met for the last time. Would to God that it had been for the last time! Man proposes, but God disposes.

V

A few days later business affairs brought me to the town wherein resided my friend Judge Zarco. I found him as lonely and as sad as at the time of my last visit. He had been able to find out nothing about Blanca, but he could not forget her for a moment. Unquestionably this woman was his fate; his heaven or his hell, as the unfortunate man was accustomed to saying.

We were soon to learn that his judicial superstition was to be fully justified.

The evening of the day of my arrival we were seated in his office, reading the last reports of the police, who had been vainly attempting to trace Gabriela, when an officer entered and handed the judge a note which read as follows:

"In the Hotel of the Lion there is a lady who wishes to speak to Judge Zarco."

"Who brought this?" asked the judge.

"A servant."

"Who sent him?"

"He gave no name."

The judge looked thoughtfully at the smoke of his cigar for a few moments, and then said: "A woman! To see me? I don't know why, but this thing frightens me. What do you think of it, Philip?"

"That it is your duty as a judge to answer the call, of course. Perhaps she may be able to give you some information in regard to Gabriela."

"You are right," answered Zarco, rising. He put a revolver in his pocket, threw his cloak over his shoulders and went out.

Two hours later he returned.

I saw at once by his face that some great happiness must have come to him. He put his arms about me and embraced me convulsively, exclaiming: "Oh, dear friend, if you only knew, if you only knew!"

"But I don't know anything," I answered. "What on earth has happened to you?"

"I'm simply the happiest man in the world!"

"But what is it?"

"The note that called me to the hotel was from *her*."

"But from whom? From Gabriela Zahara?"

"Oh, stop such nonsense! Who is thinking of those things now? It was she, I tell you, the other one!"

"In the name of heaven, be calm and tell me whom you are talking about."

"Who could it be but Blanca, my love, my life?"

"Blanca?" I answered with astonishment. "But the woman deceived you."

"Oh, no; that was all a foolish mistake on my part."

"Explain yourself."

"Listen: Blanca adores me!"

"Oh, you think she does? Well, go on."

"When Blanca and I separated on the fifteenth of April, it was understood that we were to meet again on the fifteenth of May. Shortly after I left she received a letter calling her to Madrid on urgent family business, and she did not expect me back until the fifteenth of May, so she remained in Madrid until the first. But, as you know, I, in my impatience could not wait, and returned fifteen days before I had agreed, and not finding her at the hotel I jumped to the conclusion that she had deceived me, and I did not wait. I have gone through two years of torment and suffering, all due to my own stupidity."

"But she could have written you a letter."

"She said that she had forgotten the address."

"Ah, my poor friend," I exclaimed, "I see that you are striving to convince yourself. Well, so much the better. Now, when does the marriage take place? I suppose that after so long and dark a night the sun of matrimony will rise radiant."

"Don't laugh," exclaimed Zarco; "you shall be my best man."

"With much pleasure."

*****

Man proposes, but God disposes. We were still seated in the library, chatting together, when there came a knock at the door. It was about two o'clock in the morning. The judge and I were both startled, but we could not have told why. The servant opened the door, and a moment later a man dashed into the library so breathless from hard running that he could scarcely speak.

"Good news, judge, grand news!" he said when he recovered breath. "We have won!"

The man was the prosecuting attorney.

"Explain yourself, my dear friend," said the judge, motioning him to a chair. "What remarkable occurrence could have brought you hither in such haste and at this hour of the morning?"

"We have arrested Gabriela Zahara."

"Arrested her?" exclaimed the judge joyfully.

"Yes, sir, we have her. One of our detectives has been following her for a month. He has caught her, and she is now locked up in a cell of the prison."

"Then let us go there at once!" exclaimed the judge. "We will interrogate her to-night. Do me the favor to notify my secretary. Owing to the gravity of the case, you yourself must be present. Also notify the guard who has charge of the head of Señor Romeral. It has been my opinion from the beginning that this criminal woman would not dare deny the horrible murder when she was confronted with the evidence of her crime. So far as you are concerned," said the judge, turning to me, "I will appoint you assistant secretary, so that you can be present without violating the law."

I did not answer. A horrible suspicion had been growing within me, a suspicion which, like some infernal animal, was tearing at my heart with claws of steel. Could Gabriela and Blanca be one and the same? I turned to the assistant district attorney.

"By the way," I asked, "where was Gabriela when she was arrested?"

"In the Hotel of the Lion."

My suffering was frightful, but I could say nothing, do nothing without compromising the judge; besides, I was not sure. Even if I were positive that Gabriela and Blanca were the same person, what could my unfortunate friend do? Feign a sudden illness? Flee the country? My only way was to keep silent and let God work it out in His own way. The orders of the judge had already been communicated to the chief of police and the warden of the prison. Even at this hour the news had spread throughout the city and idlers were gathering to see the rich and beautiful woman who would ascend the scaffold. I still clung to the slender hope that Gabriela and Blanca were not the same person. But when I went toward the prison I staggered like a drunken man and was compelled to lean upon the shoulder of one of the officials, who asked me anxiously if I were ill.

VI

We arrived at the prison at four o'clock in the morning. The large reception room was brilliantly lighted. The guard, holding a black box in which was the skull of Señor Romeral, was awaiting us.

The judge took his seat at the head of the long table; the prosecuting attorney sat on his right, and the chief of police stood by with his arms folded. I and the secretary sat on the left of the judge. A number of police officers and detectives were standing near the door.

The judge touched his bell and said to the warden:

"Bring in Doña Gabriela Zahara!"

I felt as if I were dying, and instead of looking at the door, I looked at the judge to see if I could read in his face the solution of this frightful problem.

I saw him turn livid and clutch his throat with both hands, as if to stop a cry of agony, and then he turned to me with a look of infinite supplication.

"Keep quiet!" I whispered, putting my finger on my lips, and then I added: "I knew it."

The unfortunate man arose from his chair.

"Judge!" I exclaimed, and in that one word I conveyed to him the full sense of his duty and of the dangers which surrounded him. He controlled himself and resumed his seat, but were it not for the light in his eyes, he might have been taken for a dead man. Yes, the man was dead; only the judge lived.

When I had convinced myself of this, I turned and looked at the accused. Good God! Gabriela Zahara was not only Blanca, the woman my friend so deeply loved, but she was also the woman I had met in the stagecoach and subsequently at Granada, the beautiful South American, Mercedes!

All these fantastic women had now merged into one, the real one who stood before us, accused of the murder of her husband and who had been condemned to die.

There was still a chance to prove herself innocent. Could she do it? This was my one supreme hope, as it was that of my poor friend.

Gabriela (we will call her now by her real name) was deathly pale, but apparently calm. Was she trusting to her innocence or to the weakness of the judge? Our doubts were soon solved. Up to that moment the accused had looked at no one but the judge. I did not know whether she desired to encourage him or menace him, or to tell him that his Blanca could not be an assassin. But noting the impassibility of the magistrate and that his face was as expressionless as that of a corpse, she turned to the others, as if seeking help from them. Then her eyes fell upon me, and she blushed slightly.

The judge now seemed to awaken from his stupor and asked in a harsh voice:

"What is your name?"

"Gabriela Zahara, widow of Romeral," answered the accused in a soft voice.

Zarco trembled. He had just learned that his Blanca had never existed; she told him so herself — she who only three hours before had consented to become his wife!

Fortunately, no one was looking at the judge, all eyes being fixed upon Gabriela, whose marvelous beauty and quiet demeanor carried to all an almost irresistible conviction of her innocence.

The judge recovered himself, and then, like a man who is staking more than life upon the cast of a die, he ordered the guard to open the black box.

"Madame!" said the judge sternly, his eyes seeming to dart flames, "approach and tell me whether you recognize this head?"

At a signal from the judge the guard opened the black box and lifted out the skull.

A cry of mortal agony rang through that room; one could not tell whether it was of fear or of madness. The woman shrank back, her eyes dilating with terror, and screamed: "Alfonzo, Alfonzo!"

Then she seemed to fall into a stupor. All turned to the judge, murmuring: "She is guilty beyond a doubt."

"Do you recognize the nail which deprived your husband of life?" said the judge, arising from his chair, looking like a corpse rising from the grave.

"Yes, sir," answered Gabriela mechanically.

"That is to say, you admit that you assassinated your husband?" asked the judge, in a voice that trembled with his great suffering.

"Sir," answered the accused, "I do not care to live any more, but before I die I would like to make a statement."

The judge fell back in his chair and then asked me by a look: "What is she going to say?"

I, myself, was almost stupefied by fear.

Gabriela stood before them, her hands clasped and a far-away look in her large, dark eyes.

"I am going to confess," she said, "and my confession will be my defense, although it will not be sufficient to save me from the scaffold. Listen to me, all of you! Why deny that which is self-evident? I was alone with my husband when he died. The servants and the doctor have testified to this. Hence, only I could have killed him. Yes, I committed the crime, but another man forced me to do it."

The judge trembled when he heard these words, but, dominating his emotion, he asked courageously:

"The name of that man, madame? Tell us at once the name of the scoundrel!"

Gabriela looked at the judge with an expression of infinite love, as a mother would look at the child she worshiped, and answered: "By a single word I could drag this man into the depths with me. But I will not. No one shall ever know his name, for he has loved me and I love him. Yes, I love him, although I know he will do nothing to save me!"

The judge half rose from his chair and extended his hands beseechingly, but she looked at him as if to say: "Be careful! You will betray yourself, and it will do no good."

He sank back into his chair, and Gabriela continued her story in a quiet, firm voice:

"I was forced to marry a man I hated. I hated him more after I married him than I did before. I lived three years in martyrdom. One day there came into my life a man whom I loved. He demanded that I should marry him, he asked me to fly with him to a heaven of happiness and love. He was a man of exceptional character, high and noble, whose only fault was that he loved me too much. Had I told him: 'I have deceived you, I am not a widow; my husband is living,' he would have left me at once. I invented a thousand excuses, but he always answered: 'Be my wife!' What could I do? I was bound to a man of the vilest character and habits, whom I loathed. Well, I killed this man, believing that I was committing an act of justice, and God punished me, for my lover abandoned me. And now I am very, very tired of life, and all I ask of you is that death may come as quickly as possible."

Gabriela stopped speaking. The judge had buried his face in his hands, as if he were thinking, but I could see he was shaking like an epileptic.

"Your honor," repeated Gabriela, "grant my request that I may die soon."

The judge made a sign to the guards to remove the prisoner.

Before she followed them, she gave me a terrible look in which there was more of pride than of repentance.

*****

I do not wish to enter into details of the condition of the judge during the following day. In the great emotional struggle which took place, the officer of the law conquered the man, and he confirmed the sentence of death.

On the following day the papers were sent to the Court of Appeals, and then Zarco came to me and said: "Wait here until I return. Take care of this unfortunate woman, but do not visit her, for your presence would humiliate instead of consoling her. Do not ask me whither I am going, and do not think that I am going to commit the very foolish act of taking my own life. Farewell, and forgive me all the worry I have caused you."

Twenty days later the Court of Appeals confirmed the sentence, and Gabriela Zahara was placed in the death cell.

*****

The morning of the day fixed for the execution came, and still the judge had not returned. The scaffold had been erected in the center of the square, and an enormous crowd had gathered. I stood by the door of the prison, for, while I had obeyed the wish of my friend that I should not call on Gabriela in her prison, I believed it my duty to represent him in that supreme moment and accompany the woman he had loved to the foot of the scaffold.

When she appeared, surrounded by her guards, I hardly recognized her. She had grown very thin and seemed hardly to have the strength to lift to her lips the small crucifix she carried in her hand.

"I am here, señora. Can I be of service to you?" I asked her as she passed by me.

She raised her deep, sunken eyes to mine, and, when she recognized me, she exclaimed:

"Oh, thanks, thanks! This is a great consolation for me, in my last hour of life. Father," she added, turning to the priest who stood beside her, "may I speak a few words to this generous friend?"

"Yes, my daughter," answered the venerable minister.

Then Gabriela asked me: "Where is he?"

"He is absent — "

"May God bless him and make him happy! When you see him, ask him to forgive me even as I believe God has already forgiven me. Tell him I love him yet, although this love is the cause of my death."

We had arrived at the foot of the scaffold stairway, where I was compelled to leave her. A tear, perhaps the last one there was in that suffering heart, rolled down her cheek. Once more she said: "Tell him that I died blessing him."

Suddenly there came a roar like that of thunder. The mass of people swayed, shouted, danced, laughed like maniacs, and above all this tumult one word rang out clearly:

"Pardoned! Pardoned!"

At the entrance to the square appeared a man on horseback, galloping madly toward the scaffold. In his hand he waved a white handkerchief, and his voice rang high above the clamor of the crowd: "Pardoned! Pardoned!"

It was the judge. Reining up his foaming horse at the foot of the scaffold, he extended a paper to the chief of police.

Gabriela, who had already mounted some of the steps, turned and gave the judge a look of infinite love and gratitude.

"God bless you!" she exclaimed, and then fell senseless.

As soon as the signatures and seals upon the document had been verified by the authorities, the priest and the judge rushed to the accused to undo the cords which bound her hands and arms and to revive her.

All their efforts were useless, however. Gabriela Zahara was dead.

LUIGI CAPUANA

The Deposition

"I know nothing at all about it, your honor!"

"Nothing at all? How can that be? It all happened within fifty yards of your shop."

"'Nothing at all,' I said, ... in an off-hand way; but really, next to nothing. I am a barber, your honor, and Heaven be praised! I have custom enough to keep me busy from morning till night. There are three of us in the shop, and what with shaving and combing and hair-cutting, not one of the three has the time to stop and scratch his head, and I least of all. Many of my customers are so kind as to prefer my services to those of my two young men; perhaps because I amuse them with my little jokes. And, what with lathering and shaving this face and that, and combing the hair on so many heads — how does your honor expect me to pay attention to other people's affairs? And the morning that I read about it in the paper, why, I stood there with my mouth wide open, and I said, 'Well, that was the way it was bound to end!'"

"Why did you say, 'That was the way it was bound to end'?"

"Why — because it had ended that way! You see — on the instant, I called to mind the ugly face of the husband. Every time I saw him pass up or down the street — one of those impressions that no one can account for — I used to think, 'That fellow has the face of a convict!' But of course that proves nothing. There are plenty who have the bad luck to be uglier than mortal sin, but very worthy people all the same. But in this case I didn't think that I was mistaken."

"But you were friends. He used to come very often and sit down at the entrance to your barber shop."

"Very often? Only once in a while, your honor! 'By your leave, neighbor,' he would say. He always called me 'neighbor'; that was his name for everyone. And I would say, 'Why, certainly.' The chair stood there, empty. Your honor understands that I could hardly be so uncivil as to say to him, 'No, you can't sit down.' A barber shop is a public place, like a café or a beer saloon. At all events, one may sit down without paying for it, and no need to have a shave or hair-cut, either! 'By your leave, neighbor,' and there he would sit, in silence, smoking and scowling, with his eyes half shut. He would loaf there for half an hour, an hour, sometimes longer. He annoyed me, I don't deny it, from the very start. There was a good deal of talk."

"What sort of talk?"

"A good deal of talk. Your honor knows, better than I, how evil-minded people are. I make it a practice not to believe a syllable of what I am told about anyone, good or evil; that is the way to keep out of trouble."

"Come, come, what sort of talk? Keep to the point."

"What sort of talk? Why, one day they would say this, and the next day they would say that, and by harping on it long enough, they made themselves believe that the wife — Well, your honor knows that a pretty wife is a chastisement of God. And after all, there are some things that you can't help seeing unless you won't see!"

"Then it was he, the husband — "

"I know nothing about it, your honor, nothing at all! But it is quite true that every time he came and sat down by my doorway or inside the shop, I used to say to myself, 'If that man can't see, he certainly must be blind! and if he won't see, he certainly must be — Your honor knows what I mean. There was certainly no getting out of that — out of that — Perhaps your honor can help me to the right word?"

"Dilemma?"

"Dilemma, yes, your honor. And Biasi, the notary, who comes to me to be shaved, uses another word that just fits the case, begging your honor's pardon."

"Then, according to you, this Don Nicasio — "

"Oh, I won't put my finger in the pie! Let him answer for himself. Everyone has a conscience of his own; and Jesus Christ has said, 'Judge not, lest ye be judged.' Well, one morning — or was it in the evening? I don't exactly remember — yes, now it comes back to me that it was in the morning — I saw him pass by, scowling and with his head bent down; I was in my doorway, sharpening a razor. Out of curiosity I gave him a passing word as well as a nod, adding a gesture that was as good as a question. He came up to me, looked me straight in the face, and answered: 'Haven't I told you that, sooner or later, I should do something crazy? And I shall, neighbor, yes, I shall! They are dragging me by the hair!' 'Let me cut it off, then!' I answered jokingly, to make him forget himself."

"So, he had told you before, had he? How did he happen to tell you before?"

"Oh, your honor knows how words slip out of the mouth at certain moments. Who pays attention to them? For my part, I have too many other things in my head — "

"Come, come — what had he been talking about, when he told you before?"

"Great heavens, give me time to think, your honor! What had he been talking about? Why, about his wife, of course. Who knows? Some one must have put a flea in his ear. It needs only half a word to ruin a poor devil's peace of mind. And that is how a man lets such words slip out of his mouth as 'Sooner or later I shall do something crazy!' That is all. I know nothing else about it, your honor!"

"And the only answer you made him was a joke?"

"I could not say to him, 'Go ahead and do it,' could I? As it was he went off, shaking his head. And what idea he kept brooding over, after that, who knows? One can't see inside of another man's brain. But sometimes, when I heard him freeing his mind — "

"Then he used to free his mind to you?"

"Why, yes, to me, and maybe to others besides. You see, one bears things and bears things and bears things; and at last, rather than burst with them, one frees one's mind to the first man who comes along."

"But you were not the first man who came along. You used to call at his house — "

"Only as a barber, your honor! Only when Don Nicasio used to send for me. And very often I would get there too late, though I tried my best."

"And very likely you sometimes went there when you knew that he was not at home?"

"On purpose, your honor? No, never!"

"And when you found his wife alone, you allowed yourself — "

"Calumnies, your honor! Who dares say such a thing? Does she say so? It may be that once or twice a few words escaped me in jest. You know how it is — when I found myself face to face with a pretty woman — you know how it is — if only not to cut a foolish figure!"

"But it was very far from a joke! You ended by threatening her!"

"What calumnies! Threaten her? What for? A woman of her stamp doesn't need to be threatened! I would never have stooped so low! I am no schoolboy!"

"Passion leads men into all sorts of folly."

"That woman is capable of anything! She would slander our Lord himself to His face! Passion? I? At my age? I am well on in the forties, your honor, and many a gray hair besides. Many a folly I committed in my youth, like everyone else. But now — Besides, with a woman like that! I was no blind man, even if Don Nicasio was. I knew that that young fellow — poor fool, he paid dearly for her — I knew that he had turned her head. That's the way with some women — they go their own gait, they're off with one and on with another, and then they end by becoming the slave of some scalawag who robs and abuses them! He used to beat her, your honor, many and many a time, your honor! And I, for the sake of the poor husband, whom I pitied — Yes, that is why she says that I threatened her. She says so, because I was foolish enough to go and give her a talking to, the day that Don Nicasio said to me, 'I shall do something crazy!' She knew what I meant, at least she pretended that she did."

"No; this was what you said — "

"Yes, your honor, I remember now exactly what I said. 'I'll spoil your sport,' I told her, 'if it sends me to the galleys!' but I was speaking in the name of the husband. In the heat of the moment one falls into a part — "

"The husband knew nothing of all this."

"Was I to boast to him of what I had done? A friend either gives his services or else he doesn't. That is how I understand it."

"Why were you so much concerned about it? ".

"I ought not to have been, your honor. I have too soft a heart."

"Your threats became troublesome. And not threats alone, but promise after promise! And gifts besides, a ring and a pair of earrings — "

"That is true. I won't deny it. I found them in my pocket, quite by chance. They belonged to my wife. It was an extravagance, but I did it, to keep poor Don Nicasio from doing something crazy. If I could only win my point, I told myself, if I could only get that young fellow out of the way, then it would be time enough to say to Don Nicasio, 'My friend, give me back my ring and my earrings!' He would not have needed to be told twice. He is an honorable man, Don Nicasio!"

"But when she answered you, 'Keep them yourself, I don't want them!' you began to beg her, almost in tears — "

"Ah, your honor! since you must be told — I don't know how I managed to control myself — I had so completely put myself in the place of the husband! I could have strangled her with my own hands! I could have done that very same crazy thing that Don Nicasio thought of doing!"

"Yet you were very prudent, that is evident. You said to yourself: 'If not for me, then not for him!' The lover, I mean, not Don Nicasio. And you began to work upon the husband, who, up to that time, had let things slide, either because he did not believe, or else because he preferred to bear the lesser evil — "

"It may be that some chance word escaped me. There are times when a man of honor loses his head — but beyond that, nothing, your honor. Don Nicasio himself will bear me witness."

"But Don Nicasio says — "

"He, too? Has he failed me? Has he turned against me? A fine way to show his gratitude!"

"He has nothing to be grateful for. Don't excite yourself! Sit down again. You began by protesting that you knew nothing at all about it. And yet you knew so many things. You must know quite a number more. Don't excite yourself."

"You want to drag me over a precipice, your honor! I begin to understand!"

"Men who are blinded by passion walk over precipices on their own feet."

"But — then your honor imagines that I, myself — "

"I imagine nothing. It is evident that you were the instigator, and something more than the instigator, too."

"Calumny, calumny, your honor!"

"That same evening you were seen talking with the husband until quite late."

"I was trying to persuade him not to. I said to him, 'Let things alone! Since it is your misfortune to have it so, what differ-

276

ence does it make whether he is the one, or somebody else?' And he kept repeating, 'Somebody else, yes, but not that rotten beast!' His very words, your honor."

"You stood at the corner of the adjoining street, lying in wait."

"Who saw me there? Who saw us, your honor?"

"You were seen. Come, make up your mind to tell all you know. It will be better for you. The woman testifies, 'There were two of them,' but in the dark she could not recognize the other one."

"Just because I wanted to do a kind act! This is what I have brought on myself by trying to do a kind act!"

"You stood at the street corner — "

"It was like this, your honor. I had gone with him as far as that. But when I saw that it was no use to try to stop him — it was striking eleven — the streets were deserted — I started to leave him indignantly, without a parting word — "

"Well, what next? Do I need tongs to drag the words out of your mouth?"

"What next? Why, your honor knows how it is at night, under the lamplight. You see and then you don't see — that's the way it is. I turned around — Don Nicasio had plunged through the doorway of his home — just by the entrance to the little lane. A cry! — then nothing more!"

"You ran forward? That was quite natural."

"I hesitated on the threshold — the hallway was so dark."

"You couldn't have done that. The woman would have recognized you by the light of the street lamp."

"The lamp is some distance off."

"You went in one after the other. Which of you shut the door? Because the door was shut immediately."

"In the confusion of the moment — two men struggling to-gether — I could hear them gasping — I wanted to call for help — then a fall! And then I felt myself seized by the arm: 'Run, neighbor, run! This is no business of yours!' It didn't sound like the voice of a human being. And that was how — that was how I happened to be there, a helpless witness. I think that Don Nicasio meant to kill his wife, too; but the wretched woman escaped. She ran and shut herself up in her room. That is — I read so after-wards, in the papers. The husband would have been wiser to have killed her first. Evil weeds had better be torn up by the roots. What are you having that man write, your honor?"

"Nothing at all, as you call it. Just your deposition. The clerk will read it to you now, and you will sign it."

"Can any harm come to me from it? I am innocent! I have only said what you wanted to make me say. You have tangled me up in a fine net, like a little fresh-water fish!"

"Wait a moment. And this is the most important thing of all. How did it happen that the mortal wounds on the dead man's body were made with a razor?"

"Oh, the treachery of Don Nicasio! My God! My God! Yes, your honor. Two days before — no one can think of everything, no one can foresee everything — he came to the shop and said to me, 'Neighbor, lend me a razor; I have a corn that is troubling me.' He was so matter-of-fact about it that I did not hesitate for an instant. I even warned him, 'Be careful! you can't joke with corns! A little blood, and you may start a cancer!' 'Don't borrow trouble, neighbor,' he answered."

"But the razor could not be found. You must have brought it away."

"I? Who would remember a little thing like that? I was more dead than alive, your honor. Where are you trying to lead me, with your questions? I tell you, I am innocent!"

"Do not deny so obstinately. A frank confession will help you far more than to protest your innocence. The facts speak clearly enough. It is well known how passion maddens the heart and the brain. A man in that state is no longer himself."

"That is the truth, your honor! That wretched woman bewitched me! She is sending me to the galleys! The more she said 'No, no, no!' the more I felt myself going mad, from head to foot, as if she were pouring fire over me, with her 'No, no, no!' But now — I do not want another man to suffer in my place. Yes, I was the one, I was the one who killed him! I was bewitched, your honor! I am willing to go to the galleys. But I am coming back here, if I have the good luck to live through my term. Oh, the justice of this world! To think that she goes scot free, the real and only cause of all the harm! But I will see that she gets justice, that I solemnly swear — with these two hands of mine, your honor! In prison I shall think of nothing else. And if I come back and find her alive — grown old and ugly, it makes no difference — she will have to pay for it, she will have to make good! Ah, 'no, no, no!' But I will say, 'Yes, yes, yes!' And I will drain her last drop of blood, if I have to end my days in the galleys. And the sooner, the better!"

LUCIUS APULEIUS

The Adventure of the Three Robbers

The great satire of Lucius Apuleius, the work through which his name lives after the lapse of nearly eighteen centuries, is "The Golden Ass," a romance from which the following passage has been selected and translated for these Mystery Stories. Lucius, the personage who tells the story, is regarded in some quarters as a portrayal of the author himself. The purpose of "The Golden Ass" was to satirize false priests and other contemporary frauds. But interspersed are many episodes of adventure and strange situations, one of which is here given.

As Telephron reached the point of his story, his fellow revelers, befuddled with their wine, renewed the boisterous uproar. And while the old topers were clamoring for the customary libation to laughter, Byrrhæna explained to me that the morrow was a day religiously observed by her city from its cradle up; a day on which they alone among mortals propitiated that most sacred god, Laughter, with hilarious and joyful rites. "The fact that you are here," she added, "will make it all the merrier. And I do wish that you would contribute something amusing out of your own cleverness, in honor of the god, to help us duly worship such an important divinity."

"Surely," said I, "what you ask shall be done. And, by Jove! I hope I shall hit upon something good enough to make this mighty god of yours reveal his presence."

Hereupon, my slave reminding me what hour of night it was, I speedily got upon my feet, although none too steadily after my potations, and, having duly taken leave of Byrrhæna, guided my zigzag steps upon the homeward way. But at the very first corner we turned, a sudden gust of wind blew out the solitary torch on which we depended, and left us, plunged in the unforeseen blackness of night, to stumble wearily and painfully to our abode, bruising our feet on every stone in the road.

But when at last, holding each other up, we drew near our goal, there ahead of us were three others, of big and brawny build, expending the full energy of their strength upon our doorposts. And far from being in the least dismayed by our arrival, they seemed only fired to a greater zeal and made assault more fiercely. Quite naturally, it seemed clear to us both, and especially to me, that they were robbers, and of the most dangerous sort. So I forthwith drew the blade which I carry hidden under my cloak for such emergencies, and threw myself, undismayed, into the midst of these highwaymen. One after another, as they successively tried to withstand me, I ran them through, until finally all three lay stretched at my feet, riddled with many a gaping wound, through which they yielded up their breath. By this time Fotis, the maid, had been aroused by the din of battle, and still panting and perspiring freely I slipped in through the opening door, and, as weary as though I had fought with the three-formed Geryon instead of those pugnacious thieves, I yielded myself at one and the same moment to bed and to slumber.

Soon rosy-fingered Dawn, shaking the purple reins, was guiding her steeds across the path of heaven; and, snatched from my untroubled rest, night gave me back to day. Dismay seized my soul at the recollection of my deeds of the past evening. I sat there, crouching on my bed, with my interlaced fingers hugging my knees, and freely gave way to my distress; I already saw in fancy the court, the jury, the verdict, the executioner. How could I hope to find any judge so mild, so benevolent as to pronounce me innocent, soiled as I was with a triple murder, stained with the blood of so many citizens? Was this the glorious climax of my travels that the Chaldean, Diophanes, had so confidently predicted for me? Again and again I went over the whole matter bewailing my hard lot.

Hereupon there came a pounding at our doors and a steadily growing clamor on the threshold. No sooner was admission given than, with an impetuous rush, the whole house was filled with magistrates, police, and the motley crowd that followed. Two officers, by order of the magistrates, promptly laid hands upon me, and started to drag me off, though resistance was the last thing I should have thought of. By the time we had reached the first cross street the entire city was already trailing at our heels in an astonishingly dense mass. And I marched gloomily along with my head hanging down to the very earth — I might even say to the lower regions below the earth.

At length after having made the circuit of every city square, in exactly the way that the victims are led around before a sacrifice meant to ward off evil omens, I was brought into the forum and made to confront the tribunal of justice. The magistrates had taken their seats upon the raised platform, the court crier had commanded silence, when suddenly everyone present, as if with one voice, protested that in so vast a gathering there was danger from the dense crowding, and demanded that a case of such importance should be tried instead in the public theater. No sooner said than the entire populace streamed onward, helter-skelter, and in a marvelously short time had packed the whole auditorium till every aisle and gallery was one solid mass. Many swarmed up the columns, others dangled from the statues, while a few there were that perched, half out of sight, on window ledges and cornices; but all in their amazing eagerness seemed quite careless how far they risked their lives. After the manner of a sacrifice I was led by the public officials down the middle of the stage, and was left standing in the midst of the orchestra. Once more the voice of the court crier boomed forth, calling for the prosecutor, whereupon a certain old man arose, and having first taken a small vase, the bottom of which ended in a narrow funnel, and having filled it with water, which escaping drop by drop should mark the length of his speech, addressed the populace as follows:

"This is no trivial case, most honored citizens, but one which directly concerns the peace of our entire city, and one which will be handed down as a weighty precedent. Wherefore, your individual and common interests equally demand that you should sustain the dignity of the State, and not permit this brutal murderer to escape the penalty of the wholesale butchery that resulted from his bloody deeds. And do not think that I am influenced by any private motives, or giving vent to personal animosity. For I am in command of the night watch, and up to this time I think there is no one who will question my watchful diligence. Accordingly I will state the case and faithfully set forth the events of last night.

"It was about the hour of the third watch, and I was making my round of the entire city, going from door to door with scrupulous vigilance, when suddenly I beheld this bloodthirsty young man, sword in hand, spreading carnage around him; already, no less than three victims of his savagery lay writhing at his feet, gasping forth their breath in a pool of blood. Stricken, as well he might be, with the guilt of so great a crime, the fellow fled, and, slipping into one of the houses under cover of the darkness, lay hidden the rest of the night. But, thanks to the gods who permit no sinner to go unpunished, I forestalled him at daybreak, before he could make his escape by secret ways, and have brought him here for trial before your sacred tribunal of justice. The prisoner at the bar is a threefold murderer; he was taken in the very act; and, furthermore, he is a foreigner. Accordingly, it is your plain duty to return a verdict of guilty against this man from a strange land for a crime which you would severely punish even in the case of one of your own citizens."

Having thus spoken, the remorseless prosecutor suspended his vindictive utterance, and the court crier straightway ordered me to begin my defense, if I had any to make. At first I could not sufficiently control my voice to speak, although less overcome, alas, by the harshness of the accusation than by my own guilty conscience. But at last, miraculously inspired with courage, I made answer as follows:

"I realize how hard it is for a man accused of murder, and confronted with the bodies of three of your citizens, to persuade so large a multitude of his innocence, even though he tells the exact truth and voluntarily admits the facts. But if in mercy you will give me an attentive hearing, I shall easily make clear to you that far from deserving to be put on trial for my life, I have wrongfully incurred the heavy stigma of such a crime as the chance result of justifiable indignation.

"I was making my way home from a dinner party at a rather late hour, after drinking pretty freely, I won't attempt to deny — for that was the head and front of my offense — when, lo and behold! before the very doors of my abode, before the home of the good Milo, your fellow-citizen, I beheld a number of villainous thieves trying to effect an entrance and already prying the doors off from the twisted hinges. All the locks and bolts, so carefully closed for the night, had been wrenched away, and the thieves were planning the slaughter of the inmates. Finally, one of them, bigger and more active than the rest, urged them to action with these words:

"'Come on, boys! Show the stuff you are made of, and strike for all you are worth while they are asleep! No quarter now, no faint-hearted weakening! Let death go through the house with drawn sword! If you find any in bed, slit their throats before they wake; if any try to resist, cut them down. Our only chance of getting away safe and sound is to leave no one else safe and sound in the whole house.'

"I confess, citizens, that I was badly frightened, both on account of my hosts and myself; and believing that I was doing the duty of a good citizen, I drew the sword which always accompanies me in readiness for such dangers, and started in to drive away or lay low those desperate robbers. But the barbarous and inhuman villains, far from being frightened away, had the audacity to stand against me, although they saw that I was armed. Their serried ranks opposed me. Next, the leader and standard-bearer of the band, assailing me with brawny strength, seized me with both hands by the hair, and bending me backward, prepared to beat out my brains with a paving stone; but while he was still shouting for one, with an unerring stroke I luckily ran him through and stretched him at my feet. Before long a second stroke, aimed between the shoulders, finished off another of them, as he clung tooth and nail to my legs; while the third one, as he rashly advanced, I stabbed full in the chest.

"Since I had fought on the side of law and order, in defense of public safety and my host's home, I felt myself not only without blame but deserving of public praise. I have never before been charged with even the slightest infringement of the law; I enjoy a high reputation among my own people, and all my life have valued a clear conscience above all material possessions. Nor can I understand why I should suffer this prosecution for having taken a just vengeance upon those worthless thieves, since no one can show that there had ever before been any enmity between us, or for that matter that I had ever had any previous acquaintance with the thieves. You have not even established any motive for which I may be supposed to have committed so great a crime."

At this point my emotion again overcame me, and with my hands extended in entreaty, I turned from one to another, beseeching them to spare me in the name of common humanity, for the sake of all that they held dear. I thought by this time they must be moved to pity, thrilled with sympathy for my wretchedness; accordingly I called to witness the Eye of Justice and the Light of Day, and intrusted my case to the providence of God, when lifting up my eyes I discovered that the whole assembly was convulsed with laughter, not excepting my own kind host and relative, Milo, who was shaking with merriment. "So much for friendship!" I thought to myself, "so much for gratitude! In protecting my host, I have become a murderer, on trial for my life; while he, far from raising a finger to help me, makes a mock of my misery."

At this moment a woman clad in black rushed down the center of the stage, weeping and wailing and clasping a small child to her breast. An older woman, covered with rags and similarly shaken with sobs, followed her, both of them waving olive branches as they passed around the bier on which lay the covered bodies of the slain, and lifted up their voices in mournful outcry: "For the sake of common humanity," they wailed, "by all the universal laws of justice, be moved to pity by the undeserved death of these young men! Give to a lonely wife and mother the comfort of vengeance! Come to the aid of this unhappy child left fatherless in his tender years, and offer up the blood of the assassin at the shrine of law and order."

Hereupon the presiding magistrate arose and addressed the people:

"The crime for which the prisoner will later pay the full penalty, not even he attempts to deny. But still another duty remains to be performed, and that is to find out who were his accomplices in this wicked deed; since it does not seem likely that one man alone could have overcome three others so young and strong as these. We must apply torture to extract the truth; and since the slave who accompanied him has made his escape, there is no other alternative left us than to wring the names of his companions from the prisoner himself, in order that we may effectually relieve the public of all apprehension of danger from this desperate gang."

Immediately, in accordance with the Greek usage, fire and the wheel were brought forth, together with all the other instruments of torture. Now indeed my distress was not only increased but multiplied when I saw that I was fated to perish piecemeal. But at this point the old woman, whose noisy lamentations had become a nuisance, broke out with this demand:

"Honored citizens, before you proceed to torture the prisoner, on account of the dear ones whom he has taken from me, will you not permit the bodies of the deceased to be uncovered in order that the sight of their youth and beauty may fire you with a righteous anger and a severity proportioned to the crime?"

These words were received with applause, and straightway the magistrate commanded that I myself should with my own hand draw off the covering from the bodies lying on the bier. In spite of my struggles and desperate determination not to look again upon the consequences of my last night's deed, the court attendants promptly dragged me forward, in obedience to the judge's order, and bending my arm by main force from its place at my side stretched it out above the three corpses. Conquered in the struggle, I yielded to necessity, and much against my will drew down the covering and exposed the bodies.

Great heavens, what a sight! What a miracle! What a transformation in my whole destiny! I had already begun to look upon myself as a vassal of Proserpine, a bondsman of Hades, and now I could only gasp in impotent amazement at the suddenness of the change; words fail me to express fittingly the astounding metamorphosis. For the bodies of my butchered victims were nothing more nor less than three inflated bladders, whose sides still bore the scars of numerous punctures, which, as I recalled my battle of the previous night, were situated at the very points where I had inflicted gaping wounds upon my adversaries. Hereupon the hilarity, which up to this point had been fairly held in check, swept through the crowd like a conflagration. Some gave themselves up helplessly to an unrestrained extravagance of merriment; others did their best to control themselves, holding their aching sides with both hands. And having all laughed until they could laugh no more, they passed out of the theater, their backward glances still centered upon me.

From the moment that I had drawn down that funeral pall I stood fixed as if frozen into stone, as powerless to move as anyone of the theater's statues or columns. Nor did I come out of my stupor until Milo, my host, himself approached and clapping me on the shoulder, drew me away with gentle violence, my tears now flowing freely and sobs choking my voice. He led me back to the house by a roundabout way through the least frequented streets, doing his best meanwhile to soothe my nerves and heal my wounded feelings. But nothing he could say availed to lessen my bitter indignation at having been made so undeservedly ridiculous. But all at once the magistrates themselves, still wearing their insignia of office, arrived at the house and made personal amends in the following words:

"We are well aware, Master Lucius, both of your own high merit and that of your family, for the renown of your name extends throughout the land. Accordingly, you must understand that the treatment which you so keenly resent was in no sense intended as an insult. Therefore, banish your present gloomy mood and dismiss all anger from your mind. For the festival, which we solemnly celebrate with each returning year in honor of the God of Laughter, must always depend upon novelty for its success. And so our god, who owes you so great a debt to-day, decrees that his favoring presence shall follow you wherever you go, and that your cheerful countenance shall everywhere be a signal for hilarity. The whole city, out of gratitude, bestows upon you exceptional honors, enrolling your name as one of its patrons, and decreeing that your likeness in bronze shall be erected as a perpetual memorial of to-day."

PLINY, THE YOUNGER

Letter to Sura

Our leisure furnishes me with the opportunity of learning from you, and you with that of instructing me. Accordingly, I particularly wish to know whether you think there exist such things as phantoms, possessing an appearance peculiar to themselves, and a certain supernatural power, or that mere empty delusions receive a shape from our fears. For my part, I am led to believe in their existence, especially by what I hear happened to Curtius Rufus. While still in humble circumstances and obscure, he was a hanger-on in the suite of the Governor of Africa. While pacing the colonnade one afternoon, there appeared to him a female form of superhuman size and beauty. She informed the terrified man that she was "Africa," and had come to foretell future events; for that he would go to Rome, would fill offices of state there, and would even return to that same province with the highest powers, and die in it. All which things were fulfilled. Moreover, as he touched at Carthage, and was disembarking from his ship, the same form is said to have presented itself to him on the shore. It is certain that, being seized with illness, and auguring the future from the past and misfortune from his previous prosperity, he himself abandoned all hope of life, though none of those about him despaired.

Is not the following story again still more appalling and not less marvelous? I will relate it as it was received by me:

There was at Athens a mansion, spacious and commodious, but of evil repute and dangerous to health. In the dead of night there was a noise as of iron, and, if you listened more closely, a clanking of chains was heard, first of all from a distance, and afterwards hard by. Presently a specter used to appear, an ancient man sinking with emaciation and squalor, with a long beard and bristly hair, wearing shackles on his legs and fetters on his hands, and shaking them. Hence the inmates, by reason of their fears, passed miserable and horrible nights in sleeplessness. This want of sleep was followed by disease, and, their terrors increasing, by death. For in the daytime as well, though the apparition had departed, yet a reminiscence of it flitted before their eyes, and their dread outlived its cause. The mansion was accordingly deserted, and, condemned to solitude, was entirely abandoned to the dreadful ghost. However, it was advertised, on the chance of some one, ignorant of the fearful curse attached to it, being willing to buy or to rent it. Athenodorus, the philosopher, came to Athens and read the advertisement. When he had been informed of the terms, which were so low as to appear suspicious, he made inquiries, and learned the whole of the particulars. Yet none the less on that account, nay, all the more readily, did he rent the house. As evening began to draw on, he ordered a sofa to be set for himself in the front part of the house, and called for his notebooks, writing implements, and a light. The whole of his servants he dismissed to the interior apartments, and for himself applied his soul, eyes, and hand to composition, that his mind might not, from want of occupation, picture to itself the phantoms of which he had heard, or any empty terrors. At the commencement there was the universal silence of night. Soon the shaking of irons and the clanking of chains was heard, yet he never raised his eyes nor slackened his pen, but hardened his soul and deadened his ears by its help. The noise grew and approached: now it seemed to be heard at the door, and next inside the door. He looked round, beheld and recognized the figure he had been told of. It was standing and signaling to him with its finger, as though inviting him. He, in reply, made a sign with his hand that it should wait a moment, and applied himself afresh to his tablets and pen. Upon this the figure kept rattling its chains over his head as he wrote. On looking round again, he saw it making the same signal as before, and without delay took up a light and followed it. It moved with a slow step, as though oppressed by its chains, and, after turning into the courtyard of the house, vanished suddenly and left his company. On being thus left to himself, he marked the spot with some grass and leaves which he plucked. Next day he applied to the magistrates, and urged them to have the spot in question dug up. There were found there some bones attached to and intermingled with fetters; the body to which they had belonged, rotted away by time and the soil, had abandoned them thus naked and corroded to the chains. They were collected and interred at the public expense, and the house was ever afterwards free from the spirit, which had obtained due sepulture.

The above story I believe on the strength of those who affirm it. What follows I am myself in a position to affirm to others. I have a freedman, who is not without some knowledge of letters. A younger brother of his was sleeping with him in the same bed. The latter dreamed he saw some one sitting on the couch, who approached a pair of scissors to his head, and even cut the hair from the crown of it. When day dawned he was found to be cropped round the crown, and his locks were discovered lying about. A very short time afterwards a fresh occurrence of the same kind confirmed the truth of the former one. A lad of mine was sleeping, in company with several others, in the pages' apartment. There came through the windows (so he tells the story) two figures in white tunics, who cut his hair as he lay, and departed the way they came. In his case, too, daylight exhibited him shorn, and his locks scattered around. Nothing remarkable followed, except, perhaps, this, that I was not brought under accusation, as I should have been, if Domitian (in whose reign these events happened) had lived longer. For in his desk was found an information against me which had been presented by Carus; from which circumstance it may be conjectured — inasmuch as it is the custom of accused persons to let their hair grow — that the cutting off of my slaves' hair was a sign of the danger which threatened me being averted.

I beg, then, that you will apply your great learning to this subject. The matter is one which deserves long and deep consideration on your part; nor am I, for my part, undeserving of having the fruits of your wisdom imparted to me. You may even argue on both sides (as your way is), provided you argue more forcibly on one side than the other, so as not to dismiss me in suspense and anxiety, when the very cause of my consulting you has been to have my doubts put an end to.

Footnotes

[1] Arise!

[2] Frog-island.

[3] A collection of prescriptions indorsed by the Faculty of Paris.
— *Trans.*

[4] For the narrative "Melmoth the Wanderer," and a description of Balzac's debt to its author, see Volume III, page 161. — EDITOR.

[5] Protested.

[6] Referring to John Melmoth — see note at head of this story. — EDITOR.